The Girl from Menekaunee

The Girl from Menekaunee

Nancy J. Kaufman

This novel is a work of fiction, inspired by actual events in my mother's life. It's based on real characters, but their names have been changed to ensure their privacy.

Menekaunee (MIN ee KAW knee) is part of an Algonquin language name for a small Native American village on the Wisconsin side of the mouth of the Menominee River in northeast Wisconsin. Eventually incorporated into the city of Marinette, it was for decades the home of the fishing fleet worked by residents of Marinette and its twin city, Menominee, Michigan. Area residents in the 40s, 50s, and 60s remember Menekaunee's short main street for its shoulder-to-shoulder taverns.

In memory of my mother,
Jean Katherine Setunsky Kaufman.

"In the family, the task is the transmission of life. In doing this we transmit both the gifts and wounds."
—John Greenfelder Sullivan, *To Come to Life More Fully*

CONTENTS

Chapter 1. Eighteen Candles (1937)

Catherine had tried to sleep in on this Saturday morning, but eventually she was drawn toward the kitchen by the delicious aroma of sugar and vanilla. She was pretty sure those smells meant her mother had made her a birthday cake, so she rose and dressed for the day. Sure enough, there it sat in the middle of the well-worn table in the tiny dark kitchen. She squeezed past the cast iron cook stove, still ticking as it cooled, to get a closer look. A beautiful layered cake covered with her favorite fluffy white icing had been set in the center of the table. Only her mother could make a cake like that. It was adorned with eighteen candles. Martha stood stooped over the sink with her head down, washing the baking dishes.

Catherine scowled at her mother's back, clenched her right fist, then slammed it into the center of the cake. She raised her fist, now covered with frosting and cake crumbs and ran out the back door. Her mother's voice followed her— "Catherine. Have you lost your mind?" Pepper, her Boston Bull terrier, barked furiously as Catherine jumped down the rickety steps and ran to her old rusted-out 1923 Model T.

It wasn't a single incident that caused her violent anger that morning. It had been building for years. It had come to a head in the past twenty-four hours. All she really wanted right now was to get out of her parent's house and—as soon as she could—out of town.

It's been almost two years since I graduated from high school and started working a real job, she thought. *My goal then was to have a place of my own, but I'm still living in the same disgusting situation—with my crazy and unpredictable parents.* Very little had changed in those two years. The one big change was breaking up with her long-term boyfriend Henry a couple of weeks earlier. She had thought she was in love with him, but all he wanted to talk about was getting married. That was wrong for her in so many ways. Among other reasons, she needed to keep her job to support her goddamn family. She knew if she were married, she'd have to quit her job. Married women didn't work. They stayed home to take care of their husbands and children, but she wasn't ready for that. Henry didn't understand, but she knew it was time for her to have some fun.

She had a date with Jibo tonight to go dancing at the Silver Dome, where a new big swing band, the Continentals, was playing. Catherine and Jibo hadn't known each other well in high school. Not only had he been two years ahead of her, but they hung out with different crowds. She was a cheerleader and he was on the staff of the student newspaper—sort of an intellectual, she thought. But she never forgot the thrilling dance they once had together at a Marinette High School sock hop just before Jibo graduated and went off to college. Catherine had stayed in Marinette, working to help support her family for the past two years. She wondered why he called her. *Had he moved back to Marinette? Did he know it was her birthday? Did he know she had broken up with Henry? Did he remember their wonderful dance?* Jibo was a swell swing dancer and she could follow his every move. Even if they had nothing to talk about, they had connected on the dance floor. She loved to dance. Henry had no rhythm. Catherine told him he danced like he had his pants full.

She drove with her clean hand on the steering wheel, the other coating the shift lever with sticky frosting. *I'm not in the mood for my goddamned eighteenth birthday*, she thought. She drove aimlessly for a while and then turned and headed back toward the Menekaunee shoreline near her home. She pulled up close to the water. Not a soul to be seen on this chilly May afternoon. The sun shone, but the wind blowing off Green Bay was unyielding. A scattering of seagulls, scouting for a catch, flew near the water, while a few more left footprints in the sand. The strong steady wind from the northeast built big whitecaps, which crashed on a sandbar not far from shore. She spotted a sad-looking fishing boat pounding through the waves, trying to get back to shore. Her father might be on that boat. Whose boat was he working on today, she wondered? He took what jobs he could find. Just looking out of the car window made her shiver. Lighting a Lucky and looking out over the water she wondered what to do next. She needed to get the frosting off her hand and clean up her car, but she didn't want to go home.

Not after what happened again last night.

She finished her cigarette and struggled with her clean hand to open the door against the powerful wind. Dropping the butt on the beach, she fought against the blowing sand and mist from the bay. Her dark curly hair covered her face. Trying to stay warm, she tightened her jacket around her as she walked toward the water to wash her sticky hand. As she reached down to wash it, a wave splashed up her arm and into her face.

"Shit," she said aloud, as the ice-cold water ran up her arm. At that moment, she also realized she had not brought anything to wipe off the shift lever.

Catherine plopped herself down on the damp sand surrendering to the weather. What did she think it would be like in early May? Confusion wracked her brain. She hated her life! She'd been working nearly two years already and what did she have to show for it? She needed her job to keep herself and her parents afloat. Unemployment was still high in Marinette in 1937 and she knew she was lucky to have a job—and one she liked at that. She needed to pay Stella back for the car, and then there was the light bill, in addition to the grocery bill at Stepniak's Market. She wanted a place of her own, but that was impossible. She had graduated from Marinette High school when she was sixteen and had been working ever since. She longed for a different life.

She was tired of living with her messed-up parents, but what choice did she have?

Last night Catherine was abruptly awakened when her drunken father came storming into the bedroom, where she shared a bed with her mother. He reached over Catherine who slept protectively on the outside of the bed, and he grabbed her mother by the arm to pull her out of bed. Her mother struggled against him. Catherine grabbed a high-heeled shoe she kept at the ready for times like this. She hit her father with the sharp heel, banging it over and over against his arm, but he was not to be deterred. He was a big, strong man who swatted his daughter away like a mosquito. He dragged his wife into his adjacent bedroom. Catherine tried to cover her ears from her mother's cries. "*Ga af mig, din gris!*—Get off me you pig! *Jeg hader dig!*— I hate you!" Sounds of struggle, and then, "Get your filthy hands off me." She could picture her mother's fists pounding against him as he raped her. Catherine knew when Martha fell back on Danish she was speaking from raw emotion with no filter—from her heart and soul.

Finally, his heavy breathing stopped. *I hate him! I hate him! I hate him!* Catherine screamed in her thoughts as she pounded her pillow. Her hate for her father at these moments was overwhelming. She was furious at her mother, too, for letting this go on time after goddamned time. Why didn't she kick the bastard out? She had to confess she had affection for her father, but she knew, even as a young kid, that his behavior toward her mother breached real boundaries. As much as she cared about her father, she could not abide his behavior toward Martha. If need be, Catherine could support herself and her mother in a smaller place, although that thought made her quiver. She longed for a place of her own.

Then there was Henry. In the moment's immediate wash of anger and frustration, she still had to think about Henry. She had thought he was the man for her, but now she wasn't sure.

Everybody liked this friendly, quiet young guy who had been a star on the Marinette Marines football team and was as handsome as Clark Gabel—his hair, dark as a moonless sky, and his eyes green with little specs of brown.

Henry, maybe, but Henry's mother was another matter. Louise with her smothering sense of self-importance was what Catherine's mother would have called a "piece of work." Louise had graduated from County Normal Teacher's College, and she was helping her husband with what she derisively termed his "floundering" coal and beer businesses. As the men in the Korn Krib might say with heavy irony, "Louise is one of those folks who thinks she knows a thing or two."

Catherine was aware that Louise considered her a notch

below her son. Reviewing the way she felt today, Catherine thought that, just perhaps, Louise might be right.

Shortly after noon, Catherine, wet and cold, walked back to her car and went straight to the Korn Krib, a favorite hangout of Menekaunee fishermen. The smells of sour beer and cigarette smoke hit Catherine as she walked into the half-lit tavern. Cigarette butts, dirt and assorted discarded wrappers were mixed with peanut shells beneath the stools along the bar. She took the first stool closest to the door and waited for Bud, the bartender, to get her order. At the far end she spotted three of her father's drinking buddies leaning on their elbows— Franky, John and Corny, all fishermen like her father—and she waved a brief hello. Two men she didn't know completed the drinking party. Each one had a bottle of Kingsbury in front of him and sported the familiar knit cap known locally as a *chook*.

The bar was dim except for a streak of light from a small high window behind her. On a shelf behind the bar was a big glass jar filled with pickled eggs, an open crock of pickles, and five bottles of what Prohibition drinkers would have called rotgut. No top-shelf booze for the discriminating drinker at the Korn Krib.

As Bud ambled toward her end of the bar, Catherine called out, "It's my goddamn eighteenth birthday today. How about buying me an old fashioned?"

He was back in no time with a shot and a beer. "Is that old fashioned enough for you? It's on me." He paused, studied her face. "You don't look very happy to be eighteen," he said.

She slammed the shot followed by the beer chaser. "Make that two and I might start smiling," she quipped.

Bud was a little like family. Too many times she had come here at her mother's behest to drag Mike home. On other occasions her father would bring her along when he came to the bar to sit around and drink. Even though she wasn't old enough to drink legally, Bud would serve her. Today, the beer was legal. The side shot was over the line, but, as everyone in Menekaunee believed, what went on in the Korn Krib stayed in the Korn Krib. Today she knew he would listen patiently to her frustration over her father's behavior.

"Where's the old man today?" Bud asked.

"Who knows?" She shrugged her shoulders. "I hope he's on one of the boats. We need the money. I don't want to talk about him today. It's too depressing."

"Yeah, he's quite a handful," he paused, recalling past scenes, and smiled. "Yeah, but he can be the funniest son of a—"

She cut him off. "Don't go there, Bud, unless you want to piss me off on my birthday."

"That's quite a mouth on you for an eighteen-year-old young woman." he patted her hand, then grimaced. "What the hell is all over your hand?"

"It's cake and frosting. My mother made me a birthday cake and I punched my fist into it."

Bud stared at her for a moment, poised to hear details, but then thought, *Yeah, another Sabinsky family event. I won't even ask.* "Jesus Christ, that's a funny way to celebrate." He said, looking at her.

"Hey, Bud, just throw me a bar rag, so I can clean up my hand and my shift lever."

He threw a wet towel on the bar and walked back over to the far end to get another round for the fishermen.

Catherine cleaned up her shift lever, came back in, and dropped the rag on the bar. She left the Korn Krib, a small buzz taking a little off the edge she had been feeling. She parked her car in the alley, happy her father's Model T pickup was gone. *Thank god he's not back home,* she thought. One of them at a time is all she could handle. Her two brothers and two sisters had moved on. Catherine, the youngest of five, was left at home to deal with Martha and Mike. There were no buffers left.

As she walked up the steps to the back door, she tripped over the broken board in the middle step. *Damn it,* she thought. *Papa still hasn't fixed this. What a dump.*

Catherine longed for Stella this afternoon. Her oldest sister had moved out at sixteen, well before she finished high school, had landed in Chicago and then changed her last name from Sabinsky to Sabin. She wanted to be gone, long gone, from Marinette, which she always called "a lousy little hick town." She had a sense of style, Catherine knew, and she had ambition. She landed a job at Carson Pirie Scott in the lingerie department. Martha received a letter every week addressed to Mrs. M. Sabin. Once in a while she'd find a five-spot tucked in. That helped a little. The family hadn't seen Stella for several years.

Catherine knew that if Stella were here, she would make her feel better. She'd help her find just the right outfit to wear to go dancing with Jibo tonight, not that she had much of anything for an evening of dancing. Stella would put a little pink on her cheeks and style her hair. God knows her mother would surely be no help. *She's probably in the kitchen right now wringing her hands over where I've been,* Catherine thought. *When she finds out her daughter had a few drinks, she'll feel sorry for herself for having such a rebel.* Her mother played the victim role like a star. *How could Stella have left me in this mess?* she mourned. *I don't care that I ruined the damn cake and I don't feel like apologizing. I'm not in the mood.* She acknowledged to herself that "old fashioned" wisdom was taking over.

When Catherine walked in the door Martha was sitting at her usual place at the table, and she was sitting in what had become her usual pose—her head in her hands. Catherine walked behind her, put her hands on her mother's shoulders and said, "I'm sorry about the cake . . ., " and then it all spilled out. "If you and Dad can't get it together, I'm moving out, and that's *it!* I'm eighteen now. I can do whatever I want. Living in this house with a drunk for a father, a nervous wreck of a mother and trying to make goddamn ends meet every day is *not* what I *want!*"

Martha's chest heaved and she reached back for her daughter's hand. Her voice was a suppressed sob, almost inaudible. "You can't leave me. Please, please don't leave me. You're all I have left in the world." Catherine shook off her mother's hand, turned, and went to her room. Pepper scampered behind on his short little legs.

She closed the door, sat on her bed, kicked off her damp shoes. "I'm scared, Pepper. I can't stand the thought of being the last thing left in my mother's world. I know what's coming. All the rest of them are gone and I'm left with my mother, and, oh, my father!" She slapped her hand against her forehead. "What am I going to do with them? Am I going to have to take care of them for the rest of their sorry lives? What if I want to get married or even live by myself some day?"

Pepper licked her bare foot.

Still wearing her wet sandy jacket, Catherine threw herself down on the bed. Pepper was close behind. She wasn't in the mood to get dressed up to go out with Jibo. She was lonesome for Henry. He hadn't even sent her a birthday card. She didn't get a present from her mother or father, but she wasn't expecting one. They could seldom afford birthday presents. When the fish were running her father might make quite a haul in one day. Sometimes he'd come home with a whole roll of money. If there weren't any fish in the nets, the pickings were lean. Often, he came home penniless after he'd spent his day's wages at the Korn Krib or Jimmy's. Lately, it seemed he was having more trouble getting jobs on the fishing boats.

Catherine assessed her family resources. Stella was living the high life in Chicago. Another sister, Clara, was still in town, but with her husband Nels she kept popping out babies every year, so Catherine expected no help from her. Brother Charlie had been on the Great Lakes ore boats for over a year already. He had been the man around Menekaunee, handsome, muscular, and mysterious. Charlie wasn't interested in settling down, and he could have had a different date every night if he'd wanted one. He probably didn't even realize there were problems with his parents. Or maybe he didn't want to know. Charlie had only been interested in girls and beer. He was a young stud who wanted to live a carefree life. Steve, the middle sibling, had moved out not long after Stella. He'd graduated from Marinette High school and moved to Madison, where he got a job as a loan officer at a bank. He was about to marry Helen, who was said to be one hot mama, a real looker. Steve wasn't about to move back and take care of his mother and father.

Catherine forced herself to get ready for her date. She discovered at the back of her closet a flared, flowered skirt and a sheer pink blouse that showed off her well-toned arms and shoulders. Her mother offered up a strand of pearls and matching earrings that had been a gift to her mother from Stella for Christmas last year. Stella had given Catherine a bottle of "Tabac Blond" perfume. According to Stella it was all the rage and would make her feel elegant.

Catherine didn't think she would ever use it, but as she

finished dressing she remembered the exquisite bottle of pale-yellow liquid at the back of her underwear drawer. Stella had told her to put a dab behind each ear and on each inner wrist. The scent of musk and vanilla made her swoon.

When Jibo knocked at the door at 7:30 sharp she was ready. She opened the door and there he stood, dressed in a stylish gray jacket with shoulders almost as wide as the door frame. Checked tapered pants and an ivy cap completed the ensemble. He had a tall, thin dancer's body.

"You look like a million bucks, Jibo!" Catherine exclaimed, waving him inside.

"You don't look so bad yourself," he said, as close as he might come to a real compliment, but she was pleased that she had taken the time to prepare. With a grin he handed her a single red rose that he had hidden behind his back. "Happy Birthday!"

Catherine's face lit up with a broad smile. He knew! Somehow, he knew it was her birthday. She wondered how he found out.

Catherine and her friends were casual athletic types who wore trousers and blouses and smelled like soap. She couldn't remember when she felt this elegant. As they walked to the car, she wondered, *How do I act on a date like this?* Skating, sledding, picnics—those were the kind of dates she was used to. Driving to the Dome, Catherine was feeling a little out of her league. Jibo pulled a flask out of his breast pocket after he the parked the car and they each had a couple of nips. That soothed her anxiety. He put his arm around her and tried to kiss her, but she twisted away. She wanted to dance, not kiss. He could save the kissing for later.

"You smell like a dream, Catherine," he said. They walked through the dark parking lot into the Dome with Jibo's arm around her shoulders and headed toward the bar, where soft music was playing. Sitting down on the only two vacant stools left in the dimly lit room, Jibo gestured to the bartender.

"Hi. I'm Tommy. What can I get for you two lovebirds?"

"Tommy," Jibo replied, "Please get the birthday girl a glass of your best champagne. Make that two. Today is this beautiful woman's birthday. She deserves to be treated like a queen." Catherine was impressed by his courtly demeanor. He had been careful not to say it was her eighteenth birthday.

Treated like a queen! Catherine couldn't believe her ears. Wow! She had never been treated like a queen before. Tommy delivered two glasses of champagne. One had a blue umbrella stuck into a cherry, and this the bartender placed in front of Catherine.

"I have never had champagne before," she said looking up at Jibo. She took a small sip, grinned. "I feel like I'm in another world. I could get used to drinking this."

When the band started playing "I'll Never Smile Again," Jibo placed his hand in the middle of her back and walked her into the dance hall. He took her hand and gracefully guided her across the floor, and she followed like a pro. They moved exquisitely—stepping, twirling, twisting, and dipping as if they were on air. When the Continentals played "It Don't Mean a Thing if You Ain't Got That Swing," they tried some savvy new swing and jitterbug steps. Jibo pulled her through his legs and twirled her under his arms. He lifted her off the floor and swung her from one side to the other. She felt weightless in his arms. The band played all Catherine's favorites, "A Nightingale Sang in Berkeley Square," "Frensie," "Night and Day," and more. The couple danced the night away.

There were only a few more songs. Catherine poured

her soul into her moves but tripped over Jibo's left foot. She felt the heel crack off her shoe and her ankle twist. Pain shot up her leg as she fell into Jibo's arms. He took the opportunity to hold her tight and she succumbed to his embrace for an instant, then realized the evening was almost over.

"This is the last dance," she exclaimed to Jibo. "Come on! We have to dance! We can't stop now."

He held her back. "You can't dance with your broken shoe and sore ankle. It might be sprained or even broken."

"It's fine. I'm fine. The dance is more important than my ankle. I want to dance the last dance. I can do it in my stocking feet. Let's get out there before it's over."

Jibo took her into his arms for the last dance. "Somewhere Over the Rainbow" was the perfect song to end the evening. He was impressed by her tenacity. He held her tightly and glided her gently around the floor. She rested her head on his shoulder. He dipped her on her good side. She limped back to their table with Jibo's solid support. "You are aces, Jibo, the keenest dancer ever!"

He helped Catherine out to the car and tried to hug her before they got in, but she gently moved away. They rode home in friendly silence. "My birthday is ending on a good note, much better than the way it started," she told Jibo. "I had a great time dancing with you, even if you tried to break my ankle," she joked. He squeezed her hand.

As the car pulled up in front of her house, she thought she spotted Henry's Ford pickup truck parked on the street a couple houses up. *No, it can't be. It's over between us.* She could feel her heart pounding. Jibo helped her out of the car and up the stairs to a small stoop. As they were walking toward the porch, the truck pulled away. *Why did I break up with him?* Distracted by these thoughts she and Jibo said their goodbyes in an unromantic, but friendly way.

Catherine stayed on the porch until Jibo drove away. She didn't feel like going in yet. Even though her teeth were chattering from the chilly May air, she sat on the top step curled up in her coat like a snail in its shell, and she lit a Lucky. The moon was bright in an inky sky. She needed someone to talk to, but who was there besides Pepper? Her best friend Alta was busy with her boyfriend. Catherine and Henry had double dated with them. Catherine knew Alta wouldn't like to hear about her swell dance with Jibo.

Thinking about the evening, and dancing with Jibo like they were Astaire and Rogers was exciting and fun. Jibo was flashy, confident, and a flawless dancer. Henry would never be able to dance like that even if he practiced for the rest of his life. Worse, he wouldn't consider trying to learn. He was a football kind of guy. Did she want a flashy guy like Jibo or an unpretentious, prudent guy like Henry? They'd been dating for more than two years, but was there something more exciting out there for her? Maybe Jibo needed more consideration. *He knows how to treat a girl,* she thought.

Taking a long drag of her cigarette, she thought about being eighteen. To the world, she was now a grown-up. What would she do with her life? She had a good job, friends, a car—even though she owed Stella for most of it. What options were there? Stella had mentioned that she had room for Catherine in her apartment in Chicago. Steve would probably help her get started in Madison, but they both knew their mother likely would be a part of the package. Martha could not live alone. She wasn't emotionally stable enough and certainly couldn't stay alone with their father. He might kill her.

Stella had quit school and moved to Chicago. She had gotten out of the house and out of Marinette. *Could I do that?*

Catherine wondered. Would Henry ever leave Marinette? He was helping his father, V.R., with his struggling coal and beer businesses, but she knew he wanted to get a job at Scott Paper Mill. Maybe he'd have a chance to get into the mill, but he probably wouldn't. If he did, they could get married and she could stay home with the kids. Is that what she wanted to do with her life? What might Jibo do with his life? He was a college graduate. *That's a little rich for my blood.*

Charlie, too, had quit school to work on the fishing boats in Menekaunee, and then he, too, had left town. Clara had quit school to get married to Nels. Catherine and Steve were the only ones who had finished high school. If she got married, what would she do with her mother? Did she even want to get married? She was the only one in the in the family at home making a decent wage. She made nine dollars and fifty cents a week. Charlie sent a little money home, but he wasn't making much. Though the Depression was supposed to be over, it was still hard times for many families. How would her mother and dad live without her?

The thought that she had actually seen Henry's truck up the street made Catherine's heart leap. She admitted to herself that she missed him a lot. He was on her mind constantly. Had she made a terrible mistake breaking up with him? She was eighteen now. It was time for her to get on with her life. She just didn't know where to start.

Chapter 2. One Smart Cookie (1935)

Life really had been no easier to figure out two years earlier, when Catherine was sixteen. It had just seemed easier, because others were making her big decisions, especially about her last days of high school. Catherine's graduation from Marinette High was held in the football stadium where she in her purple MHS cheerleading outfit had cheered the Marines to victory. It was a cold June day, and a chilly breeze blew as the sun was setting over the field. Families and friends of graduates nearly filled the concrete stadium. Some of the proud parents were wrapped in blankets, others were dressed in heavy jackets and hats. This weather wasn't unusual in June in northern Wisconsin. Locals knew how to brave the elements.

When the Marinette High School Band broke into "Pomp and Circumstance" graduates rolled across the field to the beat of the music like a wave of purple and white. The band stopped playing when the new alumni had all found seats in the bleachers that had been placed on the side of the field facing the crowd. A few guests were still straggling in as Principal Allen Harbort walked to the podium to welcome the crowd. With butterflies in her stomach, Catherine looked up at the nearly-filled stands. It was a lot easier to be leading a cheer for the home team than to give the graduation speech, she thought.

"How can I ever stand up in front of all these people and give a speech?" Catherine whispered to her friend Alta who was sitting next to her. "This isn't any honor. It feels more like a punishment."

"Yeah, and it doesn't help to be freezing to death," said Alta, her teeth chattering.

"I'm so cold I'm shaking. I should have worn a sweater or something else under my robe," Catherine said, blowing into and rubbing her hands trying to warm them up. When Catherine spotted a large man in a red-and-black checked wool jacket and a hat with turned-up ear flaps limping toward the bleachers, she couldn't believe her eyes.

He hates events like this, she thought. *He's usually drunk by this time of night at home or still at the bars. Mom told me she would try to get here, but never in my wildest dreams did I expect to see Papa at my graduation.* She wondered if she were dreaming. Her father's pronounced limp, an old knee injury from an accident with a too-heavy net of whitefish, and the bright pink birthmark covering the left side of his face, set him apart. Catherine spotted her mother following closely behind her big burly husband, a marked contrast with her small frame and rounded shoulders. Martha was dressed in her "good" gray coat and straw hat with spring flowers, a matching purse, shoes and gloves. Catherine blinked back tears. Her mom and dad looked so vulnerable in the crowd. She sensed how out of place they must feel. This crowd—any crowd—was "society," and Catherine knew that this was beyond her parents' sense of their place in the world.

Alta elbowed her out of her daze. "Hey!" she whispered. "It's your turn."

Oh, dear God, she thought, as she heard Principal

Harbort introducing her. He stood on a raised platform at the fifty-yard line and spoke into a gleaming microphone that sent his voice echoing across the field, all the way to the school building back behind him. Catherine had missed his opening comments, but she very clearly heard his next words.

"Family and friends! Teachers and classmates! It is my great honor to introduce our valedictorian of the class of 1935, Catherine Sabinsky!"

Polite applause. Catherine's nervously fought to control each step as she rose to climb down the bleachers. It was really happening . . .

Harbort continued. "Not only does she have outstanding grades, but she has never missed a day of school in junior high or high school! She is the only, *the only* student of all the graduates with these two remarkable achievements!"

This brought a loud cheer from the crowd. She crossed the field and stepped up to the podium. The principle gave her a bright smile, a bigger smile than he had ever given her before, shook her hand, and stepped back.

She laid her speech on the dais, tried to smooth out the pages she had curled from clutching them so tightly. She looked up at the crowd. Her heart was pounding in her chest, her mouth was dry, and her top lip stuck to her teeth as she started to speak. *I'm sure I'll look like a fool,* she thought. *He told them I did swell in school, but all that these people are going to remember is how I botched this speech and wrecked graduation.*

Nothing in her schooling had hinted to Catherine this moment would come, but it was here, like it or not. This all began that spring day when she was called out of Mr. Bromund's algebra class to go see the principal. *What did I do?* she thought. *Nobody gets called to see the principal unless they did something . . . *Or maybe her parents were sick, her dad hurt again on the boats . . .

Harbort's manner didn't help. He wasn't her cheering section then, not like tonight.

When she pulled open the heavy office door, he was standing right there, facing the door with his thick arms across his chest. That look! *I'm a goner,* she thought. He invited her in, called her Miss Sabinsky, directed her to a chair facing his desk, and took his seat.

"Catherine, you are probably wondering why I have you here.*"*

Yes, I am . . .

"I have some news for you that you might not know," he said. She was almost shaking, couldn't control her leg bouncing up and down, but then he added, "You have the highest overall academic record in your class even though you skipped a grade. What this means, Miss Sabinksy, is that you have earned the distinction of being the valedictorian of the senior class of 1935. And to top this off you are the only senior who has never missed a day of high school. This is a remarkable record."

Catherine nodded, wondered, *Is it really so remarkable to have not missed a day of school?* She started to rise and say thank you and go back to class, but the principal waved her back down and began to smile.

Catherine looked at him quizzically. She had never heard the word "valedictorian" before.

"Congratulations, Miss Sabinsky!" He rose, reached across the desk, shook her hand. "You look surprised but have faith in yourself. You will realize your full potential one day."

Fat chance, she thought, but she smiled, thanked him, still pondering what valedictorian really meant for her.

Heading back to algebra, she was scared, thrilled, confused, but it secretly pleased her that the first teacher who would find out was Mr. Bromund. After Catherine had earned the highest grade on his first algebra test in her freshman year he made it clear to the whole class that it would never happen again, because boys were much better in algebra and smarter than girls. She almost believed it, when her final grade that year in algebra would be her one and only C.

Valedictorian. She only learned later that it meant having to make the commencement speech and here she was.

She began reading. "Welcome, family and friends. Thank you for helping us get to where we are today. It's been four years since we started high school. We came here as kids and now we're adults—well, almost . . . "

Catherine giggled nervously. It was true for most of her classmates, but she was younger. The crowd seemed to laugh a bit with her, letting her forge ahead and speak with a little greater strength and conviction. Classwork had seemed so easy, but writing this speech was the hardest thing she had ever done. She had tried out a few jokes on Alta and they seemed okay.

"Tonight, I stand before you filled with a great sense of accomplishment. My classmates and I have worked hard—we have earned the right to be here. It wasn't easy, and there were times when I thought I might not make it to the end. But our struggles only make this moment sweeter for all of us."

It was time to name names. "We survived diagramming sentence after sentence with Miss Newell and we solved equations with Mr. Bromund. He didn't think girls could do math." She paused, and a sense that she was getting even with him gave her more strength. She said emphatically, "But he sure found out we could!

"Some of us typed under the stern eye of Miss Frothingham and others did woodshop with Mr. Bates. Mr.

Blackman and Miss Green didn't smile much, but at least now we know what happened to the Greeks and the Romans and we can speak fluent Latin . . . "

Catherine hadn't been sure about the next line, but she used it. "And we'll never tell who put the ink in Mr. Forber's plant." She heard her classmates laughing—that was a relief. That line hadn't been in the speech when she went over her first draft with Miss Newell.

"But those teachers all taught us well. Sometimes it was even fun! I'll never forget the time one of us—again, we'll never tell—put a tack on Miss Brook's chair. I had never seen her move that fast!" Laughter from both students and parents." *All was going well. She was going to make it through.*

"She was a good sport about it. Believe it or not, after she caught her breath, she laughed with us! We are grateful to all of you, our teachers, for your dedication and support. How many times have we sat where you are all sitting this evening, cheering for the Marines until we lost our voices?" Some applause, and Catherine clapped, too. "I loved the sock hops in the gym. We danced the shimmy and the foxtrot until we dropped. Fires on the beach were my favorites—but what we did there we won't share."

Her classmates laughed and hooted. Preparing her speech, she had decided she wanted to end on a serious note. She felt that she should sound like she was speaking for her class, although she had trouble accepting that. She had been just a cheerleader, not one those she thought of as the "smart kids," the ones who worked on the class paper or the yearbook. She read on.

"The thought of leaving high school and going out on my own scares me, even though I have been well-prepared by my teachers, coaches, and many others along the way. We are leaving the familiarity and comfort of our own Marinette High and going out into a new kind of life where we will be responsible for ourselves and the decisions we make. Some of us will be going on to college, joining the military, getting real jobs. Others of us might get married. Our education and experiences have readied us to face the future. Many of our families have experienced economic hardships during our high school years, but the future is looking brighter every day. We've been given the great gift of education and now it's time for us to give back.

"So, again, thank you all . . . our dedicated teachers, supportive families and great friends who have made this moment possible. We couldn't have done it without you."

She scanned the stadium, found her parents, spotted her father's checked jacket only a few rows up and near the entrance end. Energized and looking their way, Catherine raised her fist, and her voice boomed out of the speakers at each end of the stadium. "Let's get out there and help change the world! Three cheers for the graduates of the class of 1935!"

Clapping and cheering followed her back to her seat in the bleachers. When she turned around to face the audience, she saw with a thrill that some people were actually standing and clapping. Alta gave her a big hug. "Great job, Cat!"

"Alta, I was so nervous, I almost peed my pants!"

"Oh, that would have been cute. The valedictorian peeing her pants in front of everyone in Marinette County."

She ought to have felt great pride, but what Catherine experienced was incredible relief that the speech was over. Now it was just line up, get called by name in alphabetical order, get up and get the diploma. It was going to be a cold wait for "S" to be called.

The morning after graduation Catherine was awakened

by a smell coming from the kitchen of something sweet. She dressed quickly in her everyday trousers and blouse to get to the kitchen and snare whatever smelled so good. The fire in the cook stove and the morning sun coming through the small window over the sink warmed the kitchen but her mother's frown added no warmth.

"Catherine, your trousers are getting too short on you." She shook her head. "And that blouse! You can't wear that anymore. Look, look, the buttons are pulling across your front. You've grown like a weed this year. I guess I ought to make you some new clothes or let out some seams." She shook her head. *More work,* Martha thought. *It never ends.*

Martha stood up from the table. "Here . . . Let's go back-to-back." She reached behind and put her finger on the back of Catherine's head where her own head stopped. She spun around in surprise.

"*Ah, Gud!* Look at that! You're two inches taller than me. That would put you at about five-eight."

"Yup. You're the shrimp in the family now, Mom," Catherine teased, reaching for her coffee cup, hanging on a hook near the stove. Soon, steam from the strong coffee was rising from both cups as the women sat together. The sun coming in the east window over the sink highlighted the four fresh muffins on a chipped yellow plate in the center of the table. Catherine grabbed one, and slathered it with homemade strawberry jam, while her mother still tried to deal with these changes in her daughter.

Martha studied Catherine. "You're tall. You're a grown woman, for God's sake! Your hair . . . that could use a little trim. Sure wish I had natural curls like you. You take after your father—dark hair, hazel eyes and fair skin." She inhaled a great sigh. "Put that all together and I'd have to admit you're a beauty. The men are going to be after you—watch out, my dear." She wagged her index finger at her daughter as a warning. "I know how men are."

Catherine, ignoring her mother's warning, was more fixed on her breakfast treat. "Wow, these are delicious!" she said, shoving the last bite of the first muffin into her mouth and reaching for another.

Martha was secretly pleased, but she could only say, "You're going to get fat if you eat many more muffins."

It was another chilly day. Catherine wrapped her hands around her coffee cup. She suddenly had an image of the night before, and shook her head, "I can't believe Papa came to the graduation last night. It was swell to see both of you walk into the stadium. I thought you might get a ride from someone, but not Papa. I have to admit though that I was disappointed when I saw him leave even before I got my diploma."

"*Ja*, he said he was leaving, and did I want a ride. I wanted to stay to the end, but you know how he is. I am so proud of you, Catherine. You never told—"

"Wait. Stop," Catherine said. "How in the heck did you get home?"

"I walked."

"You walked all that way in the cold?" Catherine closed her eyes, raised her eyebrows, and shook her head. "You didn't even have practical shoes on. What were you thinking?" Catherine felt anger rise in her throat. *Beer and whiskey are more important to him than me,* she thought. *I'm not surprised he left, but it breaks my heart.* And leaving her mother there to find her own way home? *What a selfish bastard!*

"Well, I can tell you my feet are sore this morning, and I even have blisters on my bunion and heel." *Okay,* Catherine thought, *here comes the sad whine, my poor mother who takes all this crap and then complains to me.* "And I froze all the way home. You know how your father is. I can't ever count on him. I've raised you kids by myself. I'm used to this. You just don't know how tough it's been." Martha said.

"Yeah, Mom, sure. I've heard this sad story a million times now." Catherine fixed her gaze on her mother, who looked away.

"But what could I do?" Martha continued. "Don't think I'm not mad. He always pulls this stuff on me." Martha hung her head. It had all been said before.

"Mom, get your chin off your chest and look at me." Martha didn't move. "Look at me, dammit!"

Martha raised her head slowly with her eyes cast down. Catherine went on. "I'll tell you the choice you have. Being mad, as usual, isn't enough, is it? It hasn't worked for thirty years. How's this any different? You can leave that SOB. He treats you like shit and you let him. He's going keep it up if you don't stand up to him."

Martha's chin was quivering, and the tears blossomed in the corners of her eyes. "What am I supposed to do? If I try to stand up to him, he beats me down. I don't have anywhere to go, Catherine. You know that."

Catherine had no response. She knew in her heart Martha couldn't stand up to her mean, alcoholic husband. And anyway where *would* she go? The truth was, she was stuck. "Listen, I'm at the end of my rope with this mess. I'm sick of it. It goes on and on and on. I want out," Catherine said.

She took a deep breath and a swig of coffee. *If I don't get out of this shit hole, I'm going to lose what little is left of my mind* she thought. She looked at her mother who was starting to cry. *Oh, my good god, here we go again for the hundredth time. I know she is in a horrible situation. She has nowhere to go. She has no money of her own. If*

I leave, she'll die. If I don't leave, I might die. The three of us are stuck here until one of us dies. Oh . . .my . . .God . . .

She pushed her chair away from the table, stood up and put her hand on her mother's shoulder. She sighed in resignation. "Mom, try to control yourself. I know how scared you get when I say I want to leave—but I want to leave. That's the truth. I hate how we live here. Papa's a drunk, he's mean to you, we don't have enough money to pay our bills. If it weren't for the few fish he brings home once in a while, we might starve. As much as I'd like to move out right now, I won't leave you here alone with him. I promise you that."

Martha wiped her eyes and looked up at her angry daughter. "You're a good girl, Catherine. I don't blame you. I'm sorry to be so helpless." The tears started up again.

"I'd like to cry, too, but it won't do a damn bit of good. I need to find a job. That's all there is to it. It won't solve all the problems, but at least we might be able to pay some of the bills. Dry your eyes, Mom." *I need to keep my cool,* she thought. *Yelling at my poor pathetic mother isn't going to help anything.*

"I have to return my cap and gown to school. I'll stop at Stepniak's on the way home and see if he has any work for me. I could stock shelves or work the cash register. I'll find something."

Through her sobs Martha looked up at Catherine and said, "I'm so proud of you, Honey. I didn't know you were getting an award. You never told me."

"You know, Mom, you never asked. You never talked to me about school. You had to worry about how to get through a day at a time. I guess you never had time to think about it." She wanted to say, *You were too busy feeling sorry for yourself,* but that wouldn't help the pathetic situation they were in.

Chapter 3. Change Comes Hard (1935)

There was a loud knock on the front door. "Come in," Catherine yelled from the kitchen table. A couple of muffins were left, but the conversation about graduation was pretty much done.

Martha jumped up, pulled her robe tighter. "Who in the heck could that be this early in the morning?" Her eyes swept the kitchen. "*Min Gud. Se pa mig!* Look at me. I'm still in this dirty robe. I'm not fit for company, that's for sure."

"Hi! Nels here!" Martha's son-in-law ambled into the kitchen, carrying a big blanket rolled up in his arms.

"Hey, Nels," Catherine greeted her brother-in-law. "Whaddaya doing here? I was just on my way to school to take my cap and gown back. Aren't you supposed to be working?"

"*Ah, Gud*, Nels!" Martha rose from the table, eyeing her escape to the bedroom. "I haven't even put my lipstick on, let alone get dressed."

"Aww, Martha, sit down. I don't give a darn what you have on as long as you're covered up," he said. He looked proud of himself for being so clever.

"That's a man for you," she mumbled under her breath. "Nels, you're terrible," she said, smiling, not wanting to hurt his feelings.

The husband of Catherine's sister Clara, Nels was a short, stocky man with a perpetual smile. He was known in the family as the guy who never said no but who didn't always follow through on his pledges. It was often hard to tell what he might be thinking behind that persona.

Today, that smile in place, Nels looked at Catherine. "Is this the home of a high school graduate and valedictorian of her class?"

Catherine ignored the compliment and instead craned her neck to see what Nels was carrying. "Hey, what's wrapped up in that blanket?" she asked.

"Clara asked me to deliver this graduation present to you," he said, holding the bundle back. "It was her idea, but getting all our kids dressed and loaded into the car was more than we wanted to tackle, so she sent me. We are both so proud of you," he said, handing her a squirming bundle. "A lot of girls don't graduate these days. Clara never did . . . ah, maybe you'd better sit back down before you open that."

Catherine opened the blanket slowly. She peeked in and saw a tiny black puppy's wrinkled-up face and barely-opened eyes. She heard a tiny whimper, and the puppy emerged.

"Blow my wig!" Catherine squealed. "Is this really mine?" She gingerly picked up the puppy and held him next to her face, pressing her nose into the shiny black fur. "You are as black as pepper," she whispered, "and you are going to be Pepper. Pepper, I have fallen in love with you already!"

She jumped up and gave her brother-in-law a hug. "Nels, you'll never know how much I need this right now! Thanks a million!" She paused, then remembered whose idea this had been. "And please thank Clara for me! I didn't even know Polly had a new litter of puppies."

"Yeah, she had a litter a few weeks ago." He looked

from the puppy to Catherine's smiling face. "You're going to have to wean and house-break him now. That's a big job, y'know. Think you can do it?"

"Oh, I can, I can! I'll treat him like a prince, and I promise I'll come over to see Pepper's brothers and sisters."

"Yeah, okay then," Nels said, turning toward the door. "I have to get out and collect some insurance premiums, so I can feed all those little hungry mouths at home."

"He's a good guy, that Nels," Catherine said as the door closed behind him. "It's so nice of them to give me a puppy." She hugged the little black bundle. "Clara could have sold you and made some money, but I'm sure glad she didn't!"

"What do you think Papa's going to say?" Catherine asked, as her mother came over for a closer look at the tiny Boston Bull.

"Hard to know what your father is going to say about anything," she sighed. "We'll just have to wait and see. It was nice of Clara to think of you." She leaned over and petted Pepper's head. "But I don't know about that Nels. Clara worries about him when he's collecting money from the pretty women who are home alone. She's a jealous one, that Clara."

Catherine stared at her mother in disbelief. "Do you think he cheats on her?" The idea had never occurred to her.

Martha turned away, shaking her head, muttering. "You can never tell about those men. I don't trust a one of 'em."

Catherine was quick to change the topic away from her mother's obsessive disgust with men. "Do you think you can take care of Pepper while I return my cap and gown and stop at Stepniak's Market? I have to have everything back at school by 4 p.m." She couldn't keep her eyes off her new best friend. *Oh, Pepper, you don't know how much I need you.*

Martha's reply was typical—downbeat, ambiguous. "I

guess it's not a bad idea, though, to ask Mr. Stepniak about a job. But who knows if anybody's hiring yet? Jobs are still pretty scarce I've heard, but it wouldn't hurt to try, I guess. Don't be surprised if you don't find one."

"Well, let me ask at Stepniak's," Catherine replied. "I was best at typing and shorthand, but I know I'd never get a job in an office." Her thoughts ran afoul of the sudden joy of having Pepper. *I know I'm too young and inexperienced. Besides that, I wouldn't have the slightest idea of how to act in an office. I don't want to work with a bunch of snobby people who think they're better than everyone else anyway.* She looked at her mother, sitting silently. *I guess I have to resign myself to staying in this shit hole for the rest of my sorry life,* she thought. *It's true . . . I'll be in Menekaunee forever.*

Stop! she told herself silently. *Just do something. Get out of here for a couple of hours.* "Will you take good care of Pepper while I'm gone? I just hate to leave him." She collected her cap and gown from the front hall closet.

"Just go, Catherine. I've raised a lot of puppies in my life."

Catherine walked to Marinette High School with her head down, her graduation gown wrapped around her shoulders. In the bright sunlight she watched her shadow lead her down the sidewalk. *How can I be so mournful on such a nice day? I should feel so good about graduating and having a puppy all my own.* She decided today was not the day to look for a job. After she dropped off her cap and gown, it would be a good day to go home and play with Pepper.

Miss Libal, the principal's secretary, greeted Catherine from her desk, where she guarded the door to the principal's office.

"Well, look who's here! Our own valedictorian! Congratulations, Catherine."

"Yeah, thanks, Miss Libal."

"Catherine, what's going on? You look like you lost your last friend. You should be so proud! You're a special young woman."

Special. Uh-huh. But she put on a brave face as she handed over her cap and gown. "Actually, I just got a new friend, a new puppy!"

"That's a great bit of news," Miss Libal said. "And my bit of news is that Miss Frothingham wants to see you before you leave. She said she'd wait for you in her classroom."

"Why?" Catherine exclaimed. "I'm done here. I turned in all my assignments to her."

"Don't ask me." Miss Libal shook her head. "I'm just the messenger."

When Catherine tentatively peeked in through the crack in the classroom door, she saw her teacher sitting at her desk engrossed in what she assumed was her work. Miss Frothingham looked up when she heard the tentative knock.

"Oh, Catherine. It's you. Please come in and sit down for a moment." she said as she pointed to the chair next to her desk. She was almost smiling.

This is new, Catherine thought. *I don't remember her ever smiling before.* She had told her mother that Miss Frothingham was her favorite teacher. Even though this teacher was stern and exacting, she was always fair—and there was an air of mystery about her. She remembered when she told her mother that Miss Frothingham and Miss Austin, the music teacher, lived together. Her mother asked if they were related. No one knew for sure if they were just old maids living together or as her Menekaunee neighbors might call them, "fairies." Catherine hoped the latter was true. She chuckled to herself thinking how drawn she was to people who were different. She knew her mother would never understand—she'd be downright dismayed.

"You have been a good student, Catherine," Miss Frothingham said. "You've always turned your work in on time, your typing and stenography skills are strong, and your attendance has been perfect."

Catherine gulped. She thought she must be dreaming. Miss Frothingham had never praised her during all their time together. If she got an A it was because she did well. If she got a B, she knew she had to work harder.

Miss Frothingham looked up at Catherine. "Judge Sullivan called me yesterday and asked if I could refer a couple of good students to him. He's looking for a new secretary, and he needs one right now. Mrs. Miller has been working for him ever since he became a judge, but now she's getting married and can't work any longer."

She paused. Catherine wondered why in the world Miss Frothingham was telling her about the marriage of some woman she never heard. She'd never even heard of the judge. She squirmed in her chair.

"I am going to refer you and two other girls in your class to the judge."

Catherine's eyes opened wide. "What? I don't think I heard what—"

Miss Frothingham cut her off. "Yes, you heard me right. I hope that is to your liking."

"No, it isn't," Catherine replied hurriedly. She began wringing her hands but caught herself. *Heaven help me, I'm my mother!* she thought.

"Why on earth not?" Miss Frothingham looked shocked, signaling clearly she'd expect anyone to jump at this opportunity.

Catherine was tongue-tied and struggled to keep her hands in check, but finally, after a long pause, looked up at her former teacher. "Miss Frothingham! Are you kidding? Why would a judge or anyone else want me? I don't have a chance. I'm only sixteen with no work experience except for selling under-sized whitefish in my wagon around my neighborhood when I was a kid."

The teacher grasped the impact of her surprise announcement and the surprising reluctance of her prized student. "Tell you what. I'll give your name to the judge and you can decide later if you want to make an appointment."

She doesn't understand. She doesn't know I know nothing! Catherine's right leg bounced up and down. Tears welled up in the corners of her eyes. Through her sniffles she confessed. "I don't know how to make an appointment, I don't know his address, I don't know what to say, I don't have a typewriter . . . and I'm sorry for acting like this."

There was another long silence. Catherine couldn't have been more humiliated. How would she ever face Miss Frothingham again? Then she thought of Stella's advice and pulled herself together. Mustering all her courage, she asked her teacher if she would help her write a letter to the judge asking for an appointment to talk to him about the job.

Catherine walked home with the letter—typed, addressed and stamped—held tightly in her hand. She walked in the door, picked up Pepper, went into the bedroom she shared with her mother and closed the door.

"Hey, Little Guy." She lay down on her side of the bed and put Pepper on her belly. "I wish you could tell me what to do. I'm so scared about this goldang interview. I don't know how to dress or talk or act with educated people. A judge? Really? I fit right in with the guys in the taverns. I can hold my own with them." Catherine pulled her hand away from Pepper's belly. He stuck his nose into Catherine's hand to remind her that he needed her full attention. "Sorry, Buddy," she said resuming her scratching.

"I like Papa's friends at the bars," she confided to her silent friend, who would never reveal her secrets. Freddy always has a Gold Brick candy bar waiting for me. Jimmy's smells like stale beer, cigarette smoke, and fish guts, but who cares, right? I'll bet the judge has never been in Jimmy's. He probably thinks he's too good for that place. The guys hanging out there are just as poor as we are. Everyone is just trying to drown their sorrows and talk about finding steady work. Everybody hoping that FDR can finally make things better."

Suddenly a big smile covered her face. "Pepper, you wouldn't believe how funny Papa is sometimes. I love to hear his stories when I'm with him. He tells such funny stories. No matter how bad things are, he cheers everybody up. He's the life of the party—until he gets too drunk to talk."

Catherine stood up, put her head back, closed her eyes and ran her fingers through her hair. She picked up Pepper and set him on the piece of training paper that had been wrapped around the half pound of ground beef she'd picked up. "Maybe the smell of meat will make you pee on the paper. Just smell the beef, little Pepper, not all the bread they added. House-breaking you is going to be quite a job." Catherine's mouth watered as she thought about a real hamburger with no day-old-bread added to stretch it out.

Catherine stood in front of her wardrobe, looking at her meager collection of sad options. "What the heck am I going to wear to an interview with an important person like a judge, Pepper? Look at this stuff, would ya? I don't own a single decent skirt, let alone a pair of shoes suitable for the judge. I'll need nylons and a garter belt. Where will I get those? How will I pay for them? My best dress that I wear on Sundays is too small for me now. I know this much—I can't wear a cotton dress with puffed sleeves, and a Peter-Pan collar with a ruffle around the bottom."

Catherine saw that her confidant had fallen asleep on the newspaper. She picked up Pepper, cradled him, and threw herself back the bed. "I can't go to that interview, Pepper," she whispered "I'm going to have Miss F. cancel it. I don't have a nickel to buy a suit, a dress, or shoes."

She felt the softness of her hand-quilted comforter as she lay there with her new puppy. She sank her face into the blanket and cried as her body, limp beneath what seemed the weight of her world.

As Catherine lay in bed the next morning deciding whether to ever get up again, she had a moment of clarity. Maybe Stella would give her some advice. Her mother would probably discourage her from even applying, but she'd write to Stella.

"Pepper, just so you know," Catherine said confidentially, "Stella's the only one in this pitiful family with any class or ambition."

Dear Stella,

Please help me. I need a job. My typing teacher told me I should apply for the stenographer's position that's open in a judge's office in the Court House in Marinette. My teacher helped me write a letter to the Judge asking for an interview. We have set it for two weeks from now and I'm scared to death. I'm thinking of cancelling the appointment. I have nothing to wear. I have nothing to say. I feel so stupid. No judge or anyone with any brains would hire me. I'll make a fool of myself. I have nothing to offer.

I'm desperate. Should I cancel the appointment? I need your advice. Maybe I should ask the judge if we could meet at the Korn Krib. I feel right at home there. Ha Ha!
Love and Kisses, Catherine

A letter from Stella finally came five days later. She ripped the envelope open:

Dear Catherine
      At least you haven't lost your sense of humor. You're tough, Kiddo. Don't let some highfalutin judge get you down! You can do this. If your teacher recommended you apply for the job, you must be pretty good. If I can make it in Chicago, you can make it in Marinette. Quit feeling sorry for yourself. Buck up little sister!
Love, Stella

Well, it wasn't much, but it gave her something to think about. *How did Stella have the guts to go to Chicago on her own when she was about my age?* she wondered. She couldn't imagine doing that herself. Having an interview even in a housedress seemed easy compared to that.

Her thoughts ran on. *I know I'm a good typist. Maybe I could scour through some clothes at the Salvation Army to find a skirt at least. On the other hand, I'm only sixteen and I sure wish I could have a little fun before I settle down to a serious job. But I know if I don't work our family would be just as poor as ever. Papa's not much help paying the bills these days. Graduating early isn't all it's cracked up to be.*

Her hands were knotted into fists, her mind awhirl. *If I were still in school, I wouldn't have to think about a serious job, but now I have to think about a serious job interview. If I worked at Stepniak's I wouldn't have to worry about what to wear. I probably wouldn't even have to work full time. Why do I have to figure this out myself?*

She assessed herself in the mirror, hoping the image she saw might take a form that made sense, give her a sense of direction, but to no avail. "Pepper, it's a stinkin' mess."

The days were getting a little warmer in early June. She rode her bike down to the beach and walked along the water. The sand felt uneven under her feet. Just as she was trying to stay away from the water to keep her shoes from getting wet, a wave splashed on top of her feet. Her shoes, socks and pants were soaked up to her knees. What else could go wrong?

Nothing. It was all a mess.

The sky was bright and nearly cloudless, and she gazed out over the water.

Maybe one of those fishing boats out in the water is making a good catch and Papa's on it, she thought. "Oh, murder! I'm sick and tired of hoping Papa will make a decent living," she shouted out to no one. *I will not stand in another bread line. I'm going to interview for this job and make something of myself. If Stella can do it, I can do it.* She was determined.

Caught up in her thoughts, she was surprised to find herself at the Menekaunee docks. The "Elly May" and the "Betty" had just come in with their catches. Fishermen in their boats cleaned the whitefish, herring and perch. Still wearing their chooks, rubber boots, and slickers, they scaled fish with their razor-sharp knives. The scales flying in the air looked like snowflakes on a warm sunny day. Fish guts were thrown back into the harbor and the cleaned silvery fish were flung into buckets to be delivered to Pederson's Fish House, where they were sold to the public or delivered to local restaurants and bars.

Dozens of seagulls circled the boats, squawking, screaming, plunging for fish innards and heads. The pungent smell of the warm entrails made her stomach queasy.

She walked through Menekaunee back to the beach to get her bike. She had known—her parents always made clear—that Menekaunee was on the "wrong side of the tracks." The main drag, Hosmer, was two blocks long and nine taverns wide. These joints were mainly a hangout for fishermen and an occasional lumberman at the end of long days and nights. The gravel road running between the taverns was potholed and occasionally covered in horse dung. It called for careful walking and bike riding. There were a few old trucks and wagons parked on both sides of the street.

Marinette had a handful of well-to-do residents who lived on the river on the other side of town, but most of the city's residents were middle-class laborers or just plain poor folks. The Depression had hit them hard. Even in 1935 when some of the country was starting to recover, the residents of Marinette weren't feeling it. Unemployment was still at a peak and wages were low for those people who were lucky enough to have jobs. Lumbering, the major industry in Marinette County, was one of the hardest hit industries throughout the country. It hadn't recovered, might not ever recover.

She cycled down Main Street past a couple more taverns and Stepniak's Grocery. *I hope to heck Mr. Stepniak doesn't see me. We owe him so much money. I feel so guilty.* She turned her head toward the street, so she didn't have to look into the store.

I'm not going in there to look for a job. I'm determined to meet the judge. What do I have to lose? I've been humiliated all my life and lived through it. As she pedaled home, she smiled to herself. *I know how to deal with tough men. I've had to cope with my father and two older brothers all my life. Maybe I can take on the judge, too.*

When she rode into the alley, she saw the old rusted out, dented Model-T parked near the fence. She closed her eyes and steeled herself for what she might encounter. As she walked into the dark kitchen, she found her mother and father sitting at the table facing each other. That didn't happen often. Mike, still wearing his fishing pants with thick suspenders over his long gray underwear top, sat jiggling his bad leg. The birthmark on his face was redder than usual. *I don't think he's drunk but he's not fishing either,* Catherine thought. Martha, in an old house dress with a hairnet, wrung her hands. Neither was talking.

"Hi, you guys. What's going on? Papa, you're home early."

"Oh, Catherine you're not going to believe this." Martha was near tears. "Mike, tell her what's going on. It's just terrible."

Mike sat up straight and wagged his finger at nothing in particular. "Yeah. Jesus Christ, things kin change in a goddamn hurry. We're tryin' to figure out how Charlie's gonna git to Chicago."

"What? Charlie's going to Chicago?" Catherine looked shocked and puzzled.

"Yeah, I guess so. He told me this morning he was gonna try to get a job on the Great Lakes ore boats. He had a good tip from some hard-boiled guy he met at Jimmy's last night. He has to go to Chicago to get hired. I think it might be a good job, but how the Christ is he gonna git there?" He slammed his fist on the table.

"*Ah, Gud,*" Martha said. "We'll probably never see him again. He's such a good boy." She sunk her face in her hands.

"Oh, for chrissake, Martha." Mike said. "Catherine, get me a beer." He pointed to an open case in the corner. "He's twenty-six years old. He ain't no goddamn boy. It's about time he does somethin' with his life. He ain't gonna make any dough here—that's for damn sure. I'll miss him on the fish boats, though. He's a good worker. But, he kin do better than this."

"I sure as heck don't want him to leave, and neither does every girl in Marinette and Menominee," Catherine said, as she reached for a bottle. "There will be many tears. He's got quite the reputation."

"How the hell is he gonna git there, that's the question," Mike said. "He doesn't have a dime to his fuckin' name. He spends his money faster than he can make it."

"He told me his buddy said a bus ticket to Chicago costs twenty-three dollars. That's a fortune," Martha said.

Charlie walked in the back door, saw the family huddle, and guessed he was the topic of discussion.

"Don't worry none about me," he said in his usual low and slow way. "I'm gonna hitch- hike to Chicago. I'll be leavin' in a couple days. Billy from the Korn Krib loaned me a sawbuck to get me started. He said he knew I'd be good for it if I ever get back to Marinette. I've dropped a fiver at his bar many a time."

Underneath the bravado, Catherine thought he must be overwhelmed. He'd never been away from home.

"Charlie, aren't you scared to go to the big city of Chicago all on your own? That takes a lot of crust." Catherine said.

"Hell, Cat. If Stella can do it, I can too." He enunciated every syllable. "I might even look her up if I get a chance. If I go bust, I can always come back," Charlie said.

"Yeah, with your tail between your legs." Mike laughed as he hit his knee. "That'd be the day."

The next two days Catherine and Martha helped Charlie get ready to leave. Martha was a nervous wreck and let everyone know it.

"What if Charlie gets lost? What if he got picked up by a crazy person on the road? How could he find the boat office in such a big city?" Martha went on and on.

"Shaddup, for chrissake, Martha. Leave him alone," Mike yelled. "Don't gum up the works with yer goin' on and on and on. Ya ain't helpin' Charlie and yer drivin' me nuts!"

Catherine and Martha washed Charlie's clothes and Catherine hung them on the line in the back yard. The chickens scratched at the barren soil, looking for bugs and worms, and they ran around her feet clucking as if she were taking up prime real estate. They annoyed her, and she wished they would go to their nests and lay some eggs and leave her alone. When the clothes were almost dry, she picked them off the line and ironed every piece. The wrinkles came right out if the clothes were damp.

Charlie had been a big help around the house. With biceps as big as grapefruits, he was ready for any physical task. Catherine wondered who would fix the doors when they came off the hinges or wash the windows and change the screens and storms every spring and fall.

"I'll probably have to kill the chickens now myself and haul around the big bags of chicken feed. And who's going to go out and drag you home, Papa, when you stay out and drink too much. How're we supposed to get along without you, Charlie?" Catherine asked.

At least getting Charlie ready to go was keeping her from thinking about meeting with the judge. She still didn't know what she'd do about that situation. One minute it seemed feasible and the next minute her heart would be pounding, and she'd gasp for air. She told herself to put it out of her mind, if that was possible, until they got Charlie out the door.

On Thursday morning Charlie's friend "Ears" showed

up to drive him out to U.S-41 as it left Marinette heading south. With a good set of rides, this highway would take Charlie right along the Chicago waterfront and all the way to Gary, Indiana, if that's where he might need to go.

Martha and Catherine had packed his clean clothes in an old duffle bag and filled another bag with fresh baked bread, sugar cookies, boiled eggs and a good-sized piece of Velveeta cheese left from the last box of commodities.

"Don't go making a fuss over me. I'm gonna be fine," he said slowly. "And don't get all teared up, neither."

His father was out on the water already to avoid having to say goodbye to his oldest son. They were close, but they fought a lot, sometimes even with their fists. Charlie gave Catherine and his mother each a big hug.

"I gotta make tracks. 'Ears' is here," he said as he quickly walked down the stairs. Ears was Charlie's dear friend Roger, but most people only knew him by his nickname, earned in childhood because of the great wings on either side of his skull.

"If I can't get on a Laker, I'll most likely be back," Charlie called over his shoulder as he got into the rolling wreck of a Model T that Ears managed to keep running. "I'll write when I get a chance," he said and slammed the vehicle door.

They knew he wouldn't write. The car rattled away down the bumpy dirt street.

Catherine and Martha stood on the porch, holding one another, watching until the car turned the corner at the end of the block.

Chapter 4. Martha's Travail (1935)

"Oh, my dear girl—" Martha started to cry and then to cough. She struggled to catch her breath.

Catherine leaped to her mother's side. "Mom! Are you okay?"

"Do I look okay?" Martha snapped. "Pretty soon I'm going to be here alone with your drunken father. You'll all be gone. What in the world will I do then?"

"What do you mean?" Catherine asked, as she ran to the kitchen to get her mother a glass of water. "What's going on?" She asked as she held out the water. "Tell me . . ."

Her mother's whole body was heaving, her face was wet with mucus and tears. Catherine sat beside her on the couch, rubbing her back, repeating over and over that it would all be okay. Finally, Martha's pain seemed to be easing.

"Y'know what? That sounds pretty, but it won't be okay. Face the facts, my dear girl. Charlie just left—he won't be back. You're done with school—you won't be around much longer." She took a drink of water and sighed deeply. "Do you have any idea how afraid I am of living alone with your father? He could kill me!" Distraught, she looked up, as though Mike might walk in the door at that moment.

Catherine didn't know what to say. She knew her mother was right. The fear on Martha's face broke her daughter's heart.

"I don't know how you've stayed with him this long . . ."

"Believe me, it hasn't been easy. Oh, how I wish I had never met that man!" She broke down again. Catherine sat down on the davenport beside her in silence with her arm around her mother's shoulders trying to sooth her.

"Hey, how about a cup of coffee? How does that sound?"

Martha nodded, "Maybe."

Catherine came back to the front room with the coffee. As she handed it to her mother she asked, "Why did you marry Papa?"

"Catherine, I have never told anyone why I married that man. I can't face it. I'm not about to tell you either. It's the biggest mistake I made in my whole life." Her chin quivered as she covered her eyes with her hands. "I can't stand this anymore," she cried.

Catherine could see the pain in the gray pallor and puffiness of her mother's face, her bloodshot eyes and her trembling body. Catherine rubbed Martha's arm and shoulder and gently reached for her hand. They sat that way as Martha slowly calmed down.

"Mom," Catherine started, "maybe it's time to talk about what you've kept inside for all these years. I promise not to tell a soul, and it might help to get it off your chest." She leaned her head closer to Martha's. "How old were you when you met Papa?"

"Sixteen."

"That's how old I am now!"

"I know. I was just a young girl. We were both working on a farm, a big one north on M-35."

"I didn't know you worked on a farm. What did you do? Like, plant corn?"

"No, for God's sake, I didn't work in the fields." She looked at Catherine, the internal struggle over whether to share her story apparent on her face. "All I can tell you is to stay away from men. They're all good for nothing! I thank God that you don't have a boyfriend."

Catherine gulped. She hadn't told her mother that she and Henry just started going steady, and she was not about to, not right now. "What about your dad? Your own sons, Charlie and Steve? All good for nothing?"

"Well, my father was a different story—may he rest in peace—he was a gentleman. But those brothers of yours! They had a piss-poor example in your father. I don't know how they'll turn out, for pity's sake. There's so much you never know . . ."

"Mom, you are so bitter about something," Catherine said, inviting Martha to open up.

"Yes, and I have a right to be. You just wait . . ." Martha wagged her finger at Catherine.

Catherine would not be put off. "How'd you meet Papa?"

"I already *told* you that. We worked at the same farm."

"What did you do there?" Catherine smiled, tried a lighter tone. "If you weren't out in the cornfield, I mean . . ."

"I worked in the house taking care of the kids and helping Mrs. Ingerson with a few odds and ends, basically, whatever she needed me to do." Martha's face began to soften, and she went on. "The Ingersons treated me like I was one of the family. We got along swell."

"How many kids?"

"Three, all girls. They were such nice kids. I taught them how to read and do their numbers." Catherine heard pride in her mother's voice. "It was a good place to work, but it wasn't what I wanted to do. I saved every penny I made so someday I could go to school and be a librarian. I loved books. We had so many at my house. I read all the time, but I never went to high school. I wanted to go so badly."

"What? I didn't know that! Why not?"

When she finished 8th grade, Martha said, her family had come on hard times.

"My father was a proud, dignified man who owned a good fishing business in Hirshals, Denmark, but he set his sights higher. He sold everything to come to America."

"He must have been a brave man, my grandpa," Catherine said.

"*Ja*, and he was a good man. I don't think he had a mean bone in his body. But his business didn't do so well and over time he lost almost everything. He had to sell off most of his land to live."

"Do you remember Denmark?"

"Oh, no, my dear girl. I was born in America. My mother was in a family way when they landed on these shores in 1889. I was born here. I was the only real American in the family."

Over the years Catherine had heard only hints of her grandparents' story. She hoped this was the moment to learn much more.

"You know, Catherine, I don't ever remember my father when he wasn't wearing a dark blue suit with a chain across his belly and a watch fob. Even when his suits were threadbare he still wore them with a white shirt." She had a faint smile that lightened her face for a moment.

"I've never seen Papa in a suit. Does he have one?"

Martha shook her head "He probably had one sometime, but I don't remember it."

"Did he wear one at your wedding? He must have."

"No, uh-uh, not then . . ."

"Did you wear a fancy wedding dress?"

"You're asking an awful lot of questions, my dear girl."

Catherine realized it was time to back off. Her mother might not say anymore if she kept pushing. She dropped the wedding talk.

"Did you guys have enough to eat?"

"We always had enough to eat, but I was the only one left at home. My folks were getting older and by the time I finished eighth grade money was really hard to come by, so they got me a job. My mother cried when they realized I couldn't go to high school. But, you know, they did the best they could. The Ingersons went to the same church we did. When my dad heard the Ingersons needed help with their three girls, he offered me up."

"What? What does that mean?" Catherine was surprised, shocked. "Offered you up? For what?"

"To take care of the girls and help Mrs. Ingerson with her stuff. She had meetings with the women at church and meetings in town. I don't remember. A long time ago that was."

"So you moved in with a strange family? You lived with them? That must have been hard. You really lived with a strange family when you were fourteen?" Catherine couldn't believe it. "I would have hated that when I was fourteen."

"*Ja*, I guess, but I saw my family every Sunday at church and I really liked those little girls and they liked me. They were so cute. They liked to learn. And, Catherine, you wouldn't believe how pretty their farm was. There was a creek, lots of woods behind the fields, beautiful gardens with so many pretty flowers. They had vegetables and fruits trees, blueberries and raspberries that I could pick right off the bushes and eat until my heart was content. I loved to walk around the grounds." She closed her eyes for a minute. "I can see it like it was yesterday."

"Did the girls go with you on your walks?"

"Uh-huh. They couldn't wait for our walks. I taught them the names of the flowers and birds." Martha, relaxed now in reverie, closed her eyes and lay back on the couch. "We'd visit the pigs and horses and throw feed for the chickens. One fall we collected the colorful leaves and pressed them in books. They were quite the kids."

She was silent for a moment and looked lost in thought. Catherine saw a smile on her mother's face.

"But my favorite times were before the girls woke up and after they went to bed when I'd go for walks on my own. I loved the peace and quiet of the farm at night and early in the morning before the others came to work. I can still hear the sound of the water flowing gently over the rocks in the stream."

Then, she stopped dead. Catherine saw the expression on Martha's face change from peaceful to hard-edged. She waited for Martha to resume her tale, but sat as still as a rock.

"Mom, what's wrong. You look like you saw a ghost." Martha didn't answer.

"I want to hear more about the farm. I—"

"Stop!" Martha said. "I'm *done* with this conversation." She got up from the couch and walked to the kitchen.

Catherine was close behind. "I'll warm up the coffee,"

she said.

Martha sat down at the kitchen table, bowed her head and brought her hands up to her face. "This hurts too much. Leave me alone," she mumbled through her hands.

Catherine set the coffee on the table in front of her mother. "I'm sorry. I really am. Something terrible must have happened to you. I wish you'd tell me about it."

"Stop! Leave me alone!" She waved Catherine away.

"I'm going to make us a little lunch," Catherine said. She inspected the icebox contents and selected leftover egg salad and liver sausage. She cut two slices of bread from a freshly-baked loaf, spread the toppings, and precisely cut each slice in four pieces to make eight open-faced little triangles, just the way her mother liked them.

"Here. Have a little sandwich. I'm hungry." While Catherine ate, Martha continued to sit with her head in her hands. Catherine eased the plate with the remaining wedges of sandwich right under her mother's face and decided to try again.

"How long did you stay with the Ingersons?"

"Until I was eighteen. I watched those little girls grow up."

Catherine, pleased to have gotten a response, pressed on. "They couldn't have all grown up in four years. Why'd you leave then?"

Martha got up, ignored the sandwiches, shuffled to her bedroom, and muttered as she walked away, "You ask way too many questions, my dear girl. You've tired me out." She closed the bedroom door.

Some hours later Catherine woke with a start as she heard the back door open and close.

She had fallen asleep, her brain constantly shifting from

the new story she was hearing to her mother's reluctance to say more. Her mind was foggy with sleep. The house was dark. Her stomach was empty and growling. She stood up slowly to turn on a light when she heard her father's voice booming from the kitchen.

"What the Christ is goin' here? It's seven a clock and it's pitch dark. I shoulda' stayed at Jimmy's, where at least there are some live bodies around."

She clicked the light on. "Hi, Papa! I'm in here."

"Well, get your ass out here and make me some supper."

She walked into the kitchen, shaking her head to try to clear it.

Mike stood at the table looking around, still trying to figure out why it was dark and empty of family and food. "Where's yer mother?"

"I think she's in the bedroom. I fell asleep on the couch."

"Well, I won a little cash playin' smear down at Jimmy's." He threw down a couple of bills and change. "Here, buy yerself a treat on me."

"You're in a jolly mood tonight," she said, smiling.

"Well, hell! Who wouldn't be? The guys were pissin' and moanin' when I left with me bein' so far ahead." He slapped his knee in glee.

"I'll throw a little food together while you clean up." As she slipped past him she noted that, as usual, the odor of fish on his clothing was overlain with the smell of stale beer and cigarette smoke.

Catherine gathered leftover mashed potatoes and fish from the night before, put two plates on the table, added two cups of coffee, and had a cold supper ready when her father came in from his wash-up behind the house.

"Why ain't your mother eatin' with us? Havin' another spell?"

"She's sad that Charlie left."

"Well, hell, he'll make himself some big money if he lands a job on the boats. I wish I'da done that when I was young. Shit. I'm stuck here tryin' to make a livin' catchin' fish and broke mosta the time. This'll be good for him."

"I agree, but Mom's worried all her kids will leave her and she'll be alone."

"Well, hell! She got me! She ain't got bein' alone to worry about."

Catherine wondered if her dad had any idea that Martha didn't want to live with him.

"It was so weird. We were talking about how you met each other at the farm. Then she just clammed up. She went into our room and shut the door and I haven't seen her since."

"Christ, I don' know. That farm was a damn good place to work. Did she tell ya about the bonfires we used to make? We'd sit around on hay bales—one a' the guys had a guitar or a banjo or some damn thing he played. The fire would be roarin', the guys would be singin', passin' around a little hooch. Those were the days . . ." His voice trailed off in remembrance.

"Did Mom come to the fires?"

"Yeah, a couple times. There weren't too many gals workin' on the farm, but if another gal came along, she'd probably be there. Yer mother was a pretty little thing in those days."

"Did she sing?"

"You betcha. I'd try to sit next to her just t' listen to her pretty voice. She was a looker, that woman. Hey, grab me a beer!"

Catherine knew well enough not to argue with her father when he wanted a beer, even though she knew he'd had enough already. She set the beer on the table, sat down and continued to probe. She had never heard her parents talk about this part of their lives before. She wanted to hear more.

"So, did you hold her hand when you sat by her?"

"Naw. She was kinda proper. I knew she wouldn't go for that." He took a long draw on his beer that he held by the neck with his first and second fingers, smiled and went on. "She was workin' at the farm before I got there, a couple a' years, I think. She knew the ropes. I was just learnin'."

"How did you get to know her?"

"Well, ya know, that's a damn good question." He finished his beer in a second swig and wiped his mouth on his shirtsleeve. "I gotta take a piss. Get me another brew and I'll tell ya a little more about that. Be right back." He limped out to relieve himself off the back porch.

Catherine sat the beer bottle on the table and got herself a glass of water. She was eager to find out what her mother wouldn't tell her.

"Phew—that's better." Mike said as he sat back down. "Ya know, funniest thing, it turned out we both liked ta walk. I'd get to the farm early so I could take a walk around before the other hands got there. Once work started there wasn't much time for anything else. Nice place to walk. There was a stream runnin' right through the farm. There was even some fish in it, though I never fished any there."

Mike was silent for half a minute, sifting through memories, shook his head, and went on. "I was just thinkin' of the time I was walkin' toward the creek when the sun was risin' when I heard a small voice callin' for help. I ran over to where the voice was comin' from and there was your mother layin' on the ground under a big old oak, layin' in the roots and dirt. She looked like a helpless little thing. There was blood comin' from her knee and her head. She musta tripped and fell hard. I pulled out the clean rag I had in my pocket. I wiped off some a' the blood and asked her if she wanted ta try to get up. She didn't say nothin', but she lifted up her arm t'me. I helped her git to her feet. She told me it hurt to step on her leg, so she hung on to my arm to keep some a' the weight off. I got her to the house and Mrs. Ingersol took over. Your mother thanked me plenty for helpin' her. The missus did, too."

"I'll bet she was glad you were around that morning," Catherine said.

"Yeah. She sure seemed like it."

"So, then what?" Catherine asked. "Were you friends after that?"

"I guess ya could say that. I'd see her some at a bonfire or walkin' around the farm. We got a little chummy after that."

"When did you decide to marry her?"

"I can't keep track a' the time no more. I dunno, maybe a year, maybe a little longer. I was sweet on her before she was sweet on me, but after while she came around and we tied the knot."

"Did you have a wedding? Did you get all gussied up?"

"Naw. We didn't want no fuss. We lived on the farm with the Ingersons for a while and kept workin', the both of us 'til we had enough saved up so we could make it on our own."

He raised his arms in a stretch, and Catherine knew she would hear no more stories tonight. "Enough of this talkin' for me. I gotta get up for work in the mornin'. We're goin' up to Stephenson to set nets. The perch are runnin' good, I heard."

Catherine sat for a long time after her dad went to bed. She didn't know what to think. Her father said they were "sweet on" each other. Her mother said she didn't want to marry him, and she wouldn't talk about it. Catherine knew there was more to this story. Based on the way they got along now, she couldn't imagine them ever having been happy together.

She didn't sleep much that night. Tossing, turning, nightmares about her upcoming job interview. Pepper's consistent breathing was the only stability she had. When Catherine flopped over in bed, he would wake up and lick her face. What would she do without Pepper?

When Catherine walked into the kitchen the next morning, her mother was thrusting wood into the cook stove like she wanted to demolish it. She accidently knocked her hand on the edge of the cast iron opening and yelled "son-of-a-bitch," bringing her hand to her mouth to suck on the injury. She grabbed the plate lifter for the stove cover and banged it against the stove. She was in a rage.

"Mom! What the heck?"

No answer from Martha.

"Mom, you're not going to win a battle with an iron stove," Catherine said, forcing calm into her voice. "Put the handle down before you hurt one of us. Let's sit down at the table. I'll make us some coffee."

Martha thrust the plate lifter into the wood box and spun around to face her daughter. "Don't let's-sit-down me! I'm making a fire and I'm making my coffee! Don't think I'm going to sit there while you make the coffee, Catherine. I can take care of myself, and don't you forget it!"

"Okay, okay, I'm going to get dressed." Catherine turned toward the bedroom but called back to her mother, "Try not to burn the house down."

"Don't get snotty with me! I heard every word you and

your father said last night!" Catherine stopped but did not turn around. "He's a lying son-of-a-bitch and you, Little Miss Gullible, believed every word he said! He ruined my life, and don't you forget it!"

Catherine continued to the bedroom, listening as Martha's rant slid down to a hard-edged mumble. She was hearing stronger language than her mother normally used.

"Hey, Pepper, how do you think we should handle this one," but the Boston Bull just wagged his tail and licked her leg. She dressed hurriedly, aware of her own inability to deal with a new crisis. "Where's Charlie? Where's Henry? Where's anybody? I need to be thinking about a job interview and a million other things! And now I think my mother might lose her mind or kill my father!" She scooped up her pet. "Pepper, you're the only one I have right now."

Martha had made the fire, and the tea kettle was on the stove. Catherine put Pepper down and watched her mother spoon coffee into the pot, break an egg on top of the grounds, and pour water over the mixture. Martha was clearly still angry, but to Catherine's relief her mother wasn't slamming the coffee utensils. *That's some progress, I guess*, Catherine thought. Martha poured cream from the top of a bottle of milk into a pitcher, set it on the table and returned with two steaming cups of coffee. The coffee smelled wonderful, but Catherine knew this was not going to be a relaxing interlude.

Catherine was the first to speak. "What the heck's going on?" she asked.

Martha did not look at her daughter. "I wasn't going to tell you about your good-for- nothing father, but he lied." The words came out of her mouth like hot coals. "But I am going to tell you, so you know the truth. And don't ask me any questions! I want to get this over with.

"I did fall, and he did pick me up. At least that much was true!" Martha shaped her words through clenched teeth. "At the time I thought that was nice, but it wasn't long before I realized that bastard had been following me!" Catherine was again surprised by her mother's language. "At first I had thought, hey, what a nice guy, telling funny stories around the bonfires, making everybody laugh. He was a little crass sometime, but he sure was the life of the party."

Martha smiled bitterly, but continued. "Anyway, I knew he liked me. He'd sit next to me sometimes when we were singing or chatting. A couple of times I'd run into him during my morning and evening walks. I didn't think much of it then. But one time, I was sitting by the stream at my favorite spot, listening to the water flowing over the rocks, just sitting there minding my own business."

She took a deep breath and a swallow of coffee and closed her eyes. Catherine wondered if she would go on. It took everything she could muster to remain silent. She waited quietly.

Please, Mom she thought. *Please go on.*

Martha pushed her chair away from the table. Catherine was beside herself, but she didn't move. Her mother refilled her coffee cup, came back to the table and plunked herself into the chair. Catherine started to breathe again.

"I don't want to remember . . ." She turned and stared at Catherine. "Just so you know, girl, this is killing me to tell you. I never told anyone, not even my sisters!" She brought the coffee to her lips, took a long sip, put the cup down and settled back in her chair, closing her eyes.

"Where was I?"

"You were sitting by the stream . . ."

"Oh, *ja*. There were fish in the stream. I was off in

another world, savoring the moment, when I heard the brush break behind me. I looked back, and there was your father. He sat himself down next to me. At first, when he took my hand, I was uncomfortable, but it was nice at the same time. I never had much to do with boys," she confessed, almost wistfully, but a brittle edge returned to her voice.

"Before I knew it, he was kissing me! I was scared. *No, I* tried to say. I didn't want to kiss him. I tried to push him away, but he was big and strong. I pounded on his chest and arm! I kicked! I tried to yell!"

Martha started to cough, and tears sprouted. "For the love of God, I don't want to tell you this!" She rose suddenly from her chair and leaned on the edge of the table for support. She pressed her face close to her daughter, her words flung with flecks of spittle.

"That dirty bastard forced himself on me! Are you hearing what I'm saying!" Almost a scream. "*Are you?*

"I pushed and kicked! I bit! I scratched and screamed! I could not move under his weight! That filthy pig! It hurt every part of my body. I thought I was going to tear open . . ." She fell back into her chair, laid her head on the table. Pounding her fists, she sobbed. "I *hate* him. I hate . . ." Her voice trailed off, her body went limp.

Catherine rushed for a glass of water, placed it in front of her mother, and kneaded her shoulders until her mother's hoarse breathing sagged toward normal. A sudden idea came to Catherine.

"Don't leave me," Martha begged, as Catherine released her hold and strode away.

"I'm not leaving you," Catherine called back. She walked into her father's room, found his booze stash, and came back with a bottle of bathtub gin. She poured a generous shot into Martha's coffee, stirred in thick cream and two heaping spoons of sugar, and put it in front of Martha on the table. She resumed the massage of her mother's back and head, until Martha finally lifted her head. Catherine was shocked—her mother looked as though she had aged twenty years. Her face was pallid, deeply lined. Her eyes were red, vacant, and her white hair stood in clumps. The front of her grey, worn housedress was damp with tears.

Catherine gestured toward the spiked coffee. "I have just the thing for you, Mom."

Martha eyed the full cup suspiciously, raised it and took a tentative sip. She screwed up her face and spit the drink out across the table. She slammed the cup down, spilling its contents. "Are you trying to kill me?" She pushed it away.

"Mom, please. Think of it as medicine right now. You'll feel better."

Martha picked up the cup and gulped the remains, followed by the glass of water. She had no fight left in her. Finally, the story was told. Finally, someone else knew . . .

"Now, you, and only you, know the ice cold, shameful truth about your mother." Her eyes were filled with pain. "I wouldn't blame you if you never talked to me again. I did a terrible thing." Martha shifted to the place where she always found comfort, holding her face in her hands.

Catherine saw only that her mother was a victim, attacked, hurt. She couldn't grasp the meaning of any sense of guilt her mother might feel. What terrible thing did she do? She did nothing! It was done to her!

"Jeeze, Mom. What'd you think you did? I don't get it!"

"Oh, my good God, girl. Men can't control themselves—the pigs. Sex is a dirty, filthy habit. Men are good for nothing. I know that now, but I didn't then. I should never have been walking out alone. I was an ignorant young girl. My stupid walks ruined my life."

Martha's voice sounded stronger. *Maybe the gin is hitting,* Catherine thought.

Martha shook her head and waved a warning finger at her daughter. "You know, now, and you best learn from a bad example."

"But he forced himself on you! You tried to push him away!"

"I should have never been out there in the first place! Don't you see? I *knew* it was my fault. I couldn't tell anyone. I'm so ashamed. I deserve everything that happened to me. I wanted to die." She hit the table a strong blow, rattling the empty cup and glass. "I will never, ever to my dying day forgive him or myself!"

Catherine knew there was more, wanted more, waited for more . . . "Oh, Mom. You poor thing. What did you do?"

"I felt like a fallen woman! A tramp! I felt dirty. I was so ashamed. Just thinking of it all these years later makes me want to puke. You will never know, dear girl, how terrible, terrible, terrible it was."

"But you married him anyway?"

"I was trapped. Three months later I realized I was pregnant. I was a disgraced woman. Now you know why I married your father. You can't begin to imagine how desperate I felt." She offered her hands to Catherine, extended upward, empty, revealing that no other reasonable option was available. "So I slashed my wrists, hoping to die, but Mrs. Ingerson saved me."

"Oh, my God, Mom. I'm so glad she saved you! I wouldn't have been born if she hadn't saved you!"

"I would have saved myself a world of pain, Catherine."

"What did your parents say?"

"What do you think they said, dear girl? You have made us proud?" The old pain, the old anger, twisted her face. "They disowned me. What do you think they would do? Remember, my father was a proud dignified man. Mrs. Ingerson saved me again. She told them the circumstances and offered Mike and me a place to live until Stella was born. We went to a different county to get married by a judge. We didn't move back to Marinette until Stella was six months old. We told everybody we eloped. Nobody asked any questions as far as I know. Mike got the job fishing on Mr. Seidl's boat, and that's where he's been ever since. I never loved him—in fact, I hated him, but I've tried to make a life with him. What else have I got? I had no respect for him or myself after that. We never had a pot to pee in, but we raised five kids. None of you turned out too bad."

Catherine wondered if she and her siblings were all born of rape. She had experienced first-hand how her father sometimes came home drunk, dragged her mother out of the bed Catherine shared with her, and forced himself on her. Some of the pieces of the puzzle of her family were beginning to fit together. She felt sick to her stomach thinking of what her mother had gone through all her life. Catherine knew at that moment that her mother would need help for the rest of her life, and that help would most likely come from her last daughter at home.

Catherine's heart was in her throat.

Chapter 5. Ironing Is My Specialty (1935)

When Catherine, still in her nightgown, walked into the kitchen, Martha was sitting at the kitchen table having her morning coffee and a slice of freshly-made bread with her homemade raspberry jam. It seemed so normal, but nothing was really normal this morning. She was seeing her mother in a whole new light, seeing her as a woman who had built a life, raised her children, on a foundation of sand and sawdust.

"There's coffee on the stove, dear girl," Martha said. She handed Catherine the jam jar. "It's the last one until the raspberries bloom again, so let's enjoy it."

Catherine spread the preserves on a thick slice of bread and studied her mother, believing that praise and thanks were the medicine of the moment. "I want to learn to make jam, just like yours."

"That would be nice. There'll be plenty of raspberries to practice on in a couple months. I could use a little help once in a while. I've made it oh-so-alone my whole life."

As she rose to pour her coffee, Catherine heard her mother's poor-me message, one that she had heard in some way almost every day, but this morning it had new meaning. She sat back down, took her first sip.

"Ouch!" she cried, spitting the boiling hot coffee down the front of her nightgown. "Shit! I burned my tongue!"

"How you talk, Catherine!"

"It's not like I've never heard anybody say 'shit' in this house. Get over it." She smiled, winked. In fact, despite the burn, she relished her mother's coffee, made with a raw egg in the tradition of Martha's Danish parents.

No mention so far of yesterday. That was good. "I have only eight days before my interview with the judge. I've decided I'm going through with it. What do I have to lose? Right? I mean I might as well." Catherine feigned a casual voice, but her fingers drummed lightly on the table and her crossed leg rocked up and down.

"Well, you have more starch in you than I do, that's for sure."

Catherine got up and poured herself and her mother another cup of coffee.

"I don't know what the heck I'm supposed to wear to this la-di-da interview." Catherine hunched her shoulders, made a dismissive flip with her hand.

"I sure can't help you with that. I don't have any idea. I don't run in those circles." Martha shook her head. "Nothing fits you anyway," she added.

Catherine recalled her survey of her closet and finding nothing she thought would be appropriate. "Not my circles either, Mom. All my clothes are too short or too tight, but even if they did fit, I couldn't very well wear a pair of short slacks and a blouse with ruffles to an interview with a judge. I don't think they dress like that in the courthouse." Sighing, "Stella would know . . ."

"Yes, my dear girl, Stella would know, but she's not much help right now."

Catherine knew that if she was going to do this, she had to just charge ahead. She rose to get dressed. "I'm going to take a powder to downtown and do a little sniffing around. Maybe I'll go to the Bell Store to see what's there, or maybe I'll go to the bank to check out the tellers." She crouched down and touched her puppy.

"Keep an eye on Pepper, would ya? I have to get this figured out."

"Quit your worrying about that darn dog! Do you think I was born yesterday?" Catherine caught a hint of the prior morning's anger.

"Don't call Pepper a 'darn dog,' Mom," she said, scooping him up and nestling the puppy under her chin. "It hurts his feelings."

Catherine felt exhausted after her two-mile walk across town from Menekaunee to the Bell Store. Although she knew she'd feel better if she had slept better, the reality of the length of her trek hit home. *If I were by some chance to get this job, this is most of my walk to work.*

The last thing she wanted to do was go into the store. She'd been there a few times with her mother, but because Martha sewed most of her clothes Catherine had had no reason to go shopping.

A fish out of water. That's how she felt. Maybe it took someone from Menekaunee to think of fish in a clothing store. Where were the dresses? Her eyes were drawn to the sight and sound of a basket with the drooping arm of a sweater scooting on a wire above her head to a balcony at the far end of the store. Women in wondrous hats, crisp new dresses, and pumps walked past her with shopping bags in their hands, confident in knowing exactly where they were going. Clerks in their fashionable dresses helped equally fashionable customers.

Catherine looked down at her too-short slacks and faded blouse, buttons pulling the fabric tight over her rapidly growing breasts and was mortified. *Fish out of water. I can't stay in this place another minute. I must look like a fool.* Before anyone could ask her if she needed help, she bolted out the door.

Standing on the corner of Main Street and Pierce Avenue, she didn't know which way to turn. This was the hardest thing she'd ever done in her life. She wanted to go home to cuddle with her puppy. *Who do I think I am, trying to get a job with a judge?* she thought. *I must be nuts.*

The next step, as she had pledged to her mother, was to visit the Stephenson National Bank to sneak a peek at what the women employees were wearing. She carefully crossed Hall Avenue, dodging a mixture of fast automobiles and assorted piles of horse dung. Inside the bank she saw the tellers were men, not women. Way in back Catherine spotted a middle-aged woman busy at a typewriter. She was wearing a dark green dress with huge shoulders and a big notched collar. The woman pulled a piece of paper out of the typewriter, got up and walked quickly into an office behind her. The typist's shoes were black with low heels and her skirt was about calf length. The way the material hung made it look heavy, maybe wool.

Catherine knew there was no way for her to come up with that kind of work ensemble. Hands in her slack's pockets and chin on her chest, she turned and left, grateful that no one had noticed her and asked if they could help her. Her day's adventure was done, unsuccessful.

Rounding the corner from Hall Avenue onto Main Street, Catherine passed a storefront with two stylish dresses on faceless models in the window. The sign above the door in large sweeping letters said The Smartshop. With no forethought Catherine put her nose to the glass door and wrapped her hands around her eyes to peer inside. She was startled to find a woman on the other side of the door, looking right back at her. The woman—"dressed to the nines," as Martha would say—opened the door.

"What can I help you with, young lady?" Catherine was caught. The ice in the shopkeeper's tone froze Catherine in place. The woman continued to stare, waiting. Catherine broke her gaze, lowered her head, and turned to flee.

"Wait a minute, young lady! Could you please tell me what you want?"

Catherine was ready to bolt, but something lingered from her mother's revelations, something that said, *No, I'm not going to be submissive. I'm going to be different.* She would tough this out. She turned toward the woman, who seemed to tower over her, though they were close to the same height. She hoped the woman couldn't see her heart pounding through her blouse. Looking more closely, Catherine did not see anger. It was more like the stern look of a teacher, waiting for an answer.

"My name is Mrs. Johnson. I own this shop." Catherine heard no warmth in the woman's words, but, again, no anger. "What's your name?"

Catherine's voice came unstuck. "I'm Catherine," she said, looking away from the woman's piercing gaze.

"And what can I help you with, Catherine?" With a professional's eye the shopkeeper instantly saw that this young woman could not afford anything in her store.

There were no customers that Catherine could see in the dress shop. She had the woman's full attention and she felt trapped. Why did she think this trip across town was a good idea? She finally stuttered, "I j-just stopped to l-look."

The woman who stood before her, hands casually crossed, seemed relentless in her questioning. "May I ask you what you're looking for?"

Just say it, Catherine's inner voice argued. "Well," she said nervously, "I need a dress to go to a job interview."

The shopkeeper studied the young girl before her, dressed so typically in hand-me-downs and home-stitched clothing. Her response was frank and skeptical.

"Really, my dear, I think you are much too young to be going to a job interview in a professional dress. Why are you here, really?"

Catherine realized instantly that her personal story would not be obvious to anyone outside her friends and family. Again, the inner voice said, *tell.*

"I guess I look young, missus, but I graduated from high school two weeks ago, a year early. My typing teacher recommended me and two other girls for a job as secretary to Judge Sullivan."

"With Judge Sullivan, really? I know the judge and his wife well." Disbelief in her voice. "Why did you graduate early?"

"Well," she said, almost in a whisper, looking at her feet. "I guess they thought I was, y'know . . . *smart."* Catherine would not be convinced they were right.

Mrs. Johnson studied the young girl. *She doesn't look smart. She looks like a child with clothes she has outgrown, clean and ironed but matching no conventional style.* She saw that the girl's shoes were worn, likely hand-me-downs.

"So, you say you're looking here for something to wear to this job interview?" The woman clearly had zero confidence that this young woman, almost a ragamuffin, would get any kind of good job, let alone a job with a local judge.

Something inside Catherine broke, and words came rolling out of her mouth like pennies out of a slot machine. She raised her head, looked imploringly at the woman, pleaded, "I don't even know what secretaries wear! I don't know how to talk to a judge. I don't know how to talk to you!"

And more. "I don't have any shoes or nylons or a garter belt or money! My mother and father don't have any money! I need a dress. How will I take care of my parents if I don't have a job!"

Oh murder! I'm spinning out of control, she thought. *Thank God I didn't tell her my father rapes my mother!*

The shopkeeper was struck by the girl's confession. She knew so many families that had been devastated by the Depression, but here was a young woman with a genuine chance to build a future. *What do I say to this girl?* She wondered if she should simply thank Catherine for sharing her story and wish her luck, or if there were some way she could actually help her.

"Catherine, please come inside." Door closed, racks of colorful and fashionable clothing on all sides, the shopkeeper asked, "Catherine, what is your biggest problem right now?"

The answer was simple. "I need something to wear to the interview and I don't know how to make that happen."

Mrs. Johnson hesitated. She wasn't sure she knew how to make that happen, either. *The shop's not doing great right now.* She was sure Catherine probably couldn't pay a penny toward a dress. *I can't simply give her something off the rack.*

"I think I'd like to help you," Mrs. Johnson said tentatively, "but I need some time. Can you come back tomorrow so we can discuss this further?

Catherine felt only embarrassment. She could barely look at Mrs. Johnson as she muttered, "Thank you, and I'm sorry." As she left, she passed a woman coming in who gave her same look Mrs. Johnson had given her in their face-off at the door. *I'm not good enough to be in this shop. The Smartshop? That's not me . . ."*

As Catherine got ready to head back across town on the two-mile walk to The Smartshop the next afternoon, she hoped she was picking something better to wear—a school skirt and blouse but still accented with her old, soiled, cracked, brown and once-white saddle shoes, hand-me-downs from Clara. She added an old fishing slicker on this chilly, drizzling day. When she arrived, dreary and unsure, her clothes were damp and sticking to her body. The dark sky did not lighten her mood. The humidity caused Catherine's hair to be even curlier than usual and it stuck to her head. She could hear her mother telling her she looked like a drowned rat.

Mrs. Johnson looked at her with compassion and new eyes, seeing her now as a determined young woman who showed up despite the weather and the odds. She was surprised to see her and didn't have much faith in Catherine's chance to get the job, but she was struck by the young woman's sense of determination. *I think she deserves a break,* the shopkeeper thought.

"Good morning, Catherine," Mrs. Johnson said.

"Hi," Catherine responded, again feeling out of her element and avoiding the woman's gaze.

"Sit down here." The shopkeeper led her to a desk in the back of the shop near a pair of dressing rooms. Just as Catherine sat, a soft bell rang, announcing a customer. Mrs. Johnson excused herself.

"Well, hello. Edith!" Mrs. Johnson warmly greeted the woman.

Catherine glimpsed the customer through a clothing rack. Thin, a beige stylish suit with pumps, brown hair curling out from under a flat-brimmed hat. Shoulders held back, head high, Catherine spotted bright red lipstick, red nails, and a flash of gold at the woman's ears and on her wrist.

The shopkeeper stepped back, appraised. "Edith, that suit you bought last month looks wonderful on you. What brings you in today?"

"Oh, I just had to get out of the house, Brownie," she said tipping her head, leaning to the side with her arm bent at the elbow up and her hand bent backward at the wrist. "I just couldn't stay inside any longer. The children are out of school now so it's raucous at home these days. Thank God for Margaret."

Brownie? Catherine smiled to herself by the playful name for this proper woman.

"And who may I ask is Margaret?"

"Oh, she's my summer nanny. Trying to take care of four little ones by myself is too much for me to do alone. I told her I had some errands to run. So, here I am! You're my errand!"

She laughed a tight little laugh. *This woman seems to think she's clever, but my mother would think she's uppity*, Catherine thought.

"And how's Ed?"

"He's fine. He works all the time to support us in the way we've become accustomed." Another giggle, her arm up again. The customer spotted Catherine sitting at the desk in back. "So, who's your visitor? I don't think I've seen her around before?"

The shopkeeper, uncertain yet of her own role in dealing with this young girl, was caught off guard. She came up with a quick cover.

"Ah, well, she just stopped by to see if the shop would contribute to a fund to raise money for the high school library."

"What a fine cause!" This was just the kind of community cause that Edith believed life called on her to support. "Young lady, how much money are you expected to raise?"

Catherine was trying to engage her brain to follow what was unfolding, but Mrs. Johnson immediately jumped in, "She's trying to raise ten dollars."

"That's quite a bit," Edith said. As much as she appeared to Catherine to be indifferent to expense, the woman clearly knew the value of money in 1935. She walked back to where Catherine was sitting. Mrs. Johnson followed. "How much money have you raised so far?" she asked.

Think fast! She had lied plenty of times in her life. "None yet. Mrs. Johnson is my first stop," she answered with feigned confidence. "This is the first time I've ever tried to raise money. It's really hard."

"You look happy. You must enjoy fundraising."

"I've never done it before, but my mother told me to keep a smile on my face when I was asking for money." Catherine's smile wasn't forced. She was smiling because she thought of what her mother might say about Edith. *Ach, she's one of those people who think their own shit doesn't stink!*

"Your mother must be very wise. That's lovely advice."

"Yes, she's a wise woman." *Wiser than you think!* "I'm so lucky to have a mother like her."

"Does she work?"

Catherine was stung and felt a surge of anger. The only way her married mother would be working would be as a domestic, maybe like one of the helpers this nosy woman might need just to get herself dressed in the morning. She held her anger in check and said only, "Yes, she works very hard taking care of all five of us by herself. She's a great cook. She runs the house while my father works."

Catherine suddenly wanted to take that back, fearing that the next question would be about her father's on-and-off work in the Menekaunee fishing fleet. She didn't quite know how to answer that. She abruptly stood up and looked at Mrs. Johnson. "I need to get to my next stop. I'll come back, Mrs. Johnson, when you're not so busy.

"Just a minute," Edith said, opening her purse. "I'd like to make a small contribution to the school library. My children will benefit. It's important that they have fine literature." She handed Catherine a fifty-cent piece. "Good luck. I hope you can meet your goal."

Catherine gulped again. *Now what?* she thought. She took a deep breath. "Thank you very much, Mrs . . . uhm . . . Edith. That's one heck of a lot of money!" And out the door she flew.

She was flabbergasted to have earned fifty cents by telling a lie. What if Mrs. Edith found out? Would she have Catherine arrested? *I could end up on the wrong side of the judge's bench.* She guessed that there was something very funny in that mental picture.

It was still damp and misty outside, and she wasn't sure where to go. After wandering around Dunlap Square for some minutes she found herself in Lauerman's Department Store. She decided to kill some time there before going back to The Smartshop. When she reached the second floor, she noticed a rack of dresses. Warily, before she went to the rack, she scouted for clerks—she wanted to avoid having to explain again the reason for her search for a dress. She spotted a single clerk already busy with a customer.

She made space in the collection and slid dresses past her eyes, and her thoughts seemed to jumble themselves again.

Where should she even start? All she wanted was a simple job at the grocery store near her home. This was all too much. A job with a judge was over her head. Her teacher's recommendation was all wrong! She turned on her heel and ran down the stairs as quickly as she could move her feet.

When Catherine got out onto Main Street, she saw Mrs. Johnson's customer leaving The Smartshop, a box under her arm. Catherine had promised to return. *Might as well do this*, she thought.

Mrs. Johnson's greeting seemed friendlier than earlier. The first thing Catherine did was pull the fifty-cent piece out of the pocket of her slacks and offer it to Mrs. Johnson, who told her to put it on the desk and sit down.

"It's been a very interesting afternoon hasn't it, Catherine?" The corners of the woman's mouth crept up.

Catherine nodded, answered sincerely, "That's for sure! I think I got myself into some real trouble." Catherine felt more comfortable now, looked directly into the woman's face, said, "I got a lot of money for lying . . ."

Mrs. Johnson interrupted, raised her hand to say stop. "First of all, Catherine, I'm the one who started that little deception. I didn't think my friend Edith needed to know your circumstances."

Catherine nodded appreciatively. The shopkeeper continued, "Next, I was quite impressed how you held your ground and how you so quickly gave the answers that didn't make me look foolish. I tossed you a hot potato, and you performed well," Mrs. Johnson said. "So, now, let's talk about the reason you came here in the first place."

Catherine breathed a sigh of relief. She crossed her fingers on her left hand away from Mrs. Johnson, hoping no one else would come in until they finished and praying that

Mrs. Johnson might actually help her.

"I've been doing a lot of thinking about you since yesterday," the woman began. "I have an idea, and I want you to listen until I finish." She raised her hand, her fingers ticking off the points she wanted to make.

"First, I'm impressed with your tenacity. You came back, just as you said you would, and you walked a long way to get here in the drizzle.

"Next, you handled yourself very well with Edith today. That showed poise beyond what I might expect from a young lady your age."

Catherine sat a little straighter in her chair.

"Finally, Catherine, I have to respect the wisdom of your teacher, who clearly believes that you have the personal and social skills to work at the courthouse. I don't think that not having the right dress should be an obstacle in the way of that opportunity.'

The woman dropped her hand, sat back. "I have a proposal for you, Catherine."

Catherine crossed her fingers more tightly but was ready. She was beginning to see that this woman, rather than being cold and aloof, was careful in her words and professional in her dealings. *That must be what it takes to run a business*, Catherine thought.

Waving vaguely at a corner of the store, Mrs. Johnson said, "I have a dress on the rack that I think might do nicely for your interview, but I won't give it to you. If you like the dress I have in mind, you can work for it."

Catherine smiled. "I know how to work, that's for sure!" Then, eagerly, "What would I be doing?"

"Tell me," the shopkeeper asked, almost confidentially, leaning forward. "Do you know how to iron?"

"Do I know how to iron! I sure do, Mrs. Johnson!" *This could be my lucky day,* she thought. "I've been helping my mother iron for years! We iron everything in our house, including sheets, pillowcases, tee shirts, underwear—everything! Ironing is my specialty!" She was proud of her skill.

"Okay, Catherine, first of all, you can call me Brownie. All my customers know me by that name. And here's how you can help. My shipments of new clothes come in big boxes and every piece must be ironed before it can be hung out here on a rack. It's hard work to open boxes, sort the clothes, and get them ironed."

"I think I can do that, Mrs. Johnson . . . I mean . . . Brownie." Was it really going to be this easy?

"Well, then, young lady, let's make a plan. You show me that you can iron, and I'll show you the dress I have in mind for your interview." Catherine could not believe what she was hearing. She practically jumped out of the chair to follow her potential new boss to a rack of dresses. She told herself to calm down, stay alert. This deal wasn't done yet.

"Take a look at this dress, Catherine." She pulled off the rack a dark green rayon dress with enormous shoulders. She held up it and glanced at Catherine and back at the dress. "This would make a good dress for an interview."

This is one big deal, and that's a swell dress, Catherine thought. Her mother always sewed her clothes. She realized she wouldn't have known how to pick an appropriate dress off a rack. It occurred to her suddenly that, working here, she might learn how to do that.

"Let's see what size you might be, dear." Catherine was asked to slowly turn around, and she felt this inspection was much friendlier than the way she had been sized up the day before.

Brownie took two dark green dresses off the rack and led Catherine to the dressing room.

She pulled the curtain back, hung the dresses on the hook and stepped aside as Catherine squeezed herself into the small space.

"Try the smaller one in front first. When you get the dress on, walk out so we can both look at it."

Catherine stepped out of her shoes, slacks and blouse and pulled the dress over her head. It went on easily. She bent to put on her worn shoes and realized how foolish she would look in this fancy dress and so, barefoot, she quickly walked out to show the dress to the woman who called had just called her "dear." Brownie again told her to turn around slowly and looked her up and down again.

"Stand still for a moment, Catherine. I have to zip and button you up."

"Sorry. I forgot to do that."

Brownie led her to the mirror. Catherine stood straight, shoulders back, admiring herself. *I want to jump up and down and shout yes! I want to run over and hug Brownie. She's looking at me and not smiling or saying a word. I don't even care! I love the dress!* She smiled at herself in the mirror and spun around once.

"What do you think, Catherine?"

"I love this dress! I have never seen a nicer dress in my whole life!"

Still studying her, nodding at inner thoughts, the shopkeeper gave a hint of smile. "It fits you quite well . . . but it's a little too long . . ." With a flash of fear, Catherine thought the choice was being rejected, but Brownie continued, ". . . but I do alterations, so I can take up an inch and a half for you."

Catherine wouldn't lose this wonderful dress. "Could you really?" she asked, looking for confirmation.

"I really could," Brownie said, "but we'll have to come to an agreement before I do any alterations. Please sit down, and you can leave the dress on for now."

Catherine smoothed the skirt across her lap and crossed her legs in the most lady-like way she could. "I feel like a million bucks!"

That brought an actual smile to the shopkeeper's face. "Well, the dress is expensive, but not that expensive. It costs $3.99, but it will last forever. I can pay you 10 cents an hour, so you would have to work for 40 hours to pay your bill."

"It's a deal," Catherine said without a second thought. "That will be just fine, Brownie. I can start right now!"

As instructed, Catherine stood erect in front of the mirror without moving while the new hemline was pinned into place. She was admiring herself in her beautiful dress as she waited impatiently to start working. She was thinking that Brownie took way too long to make decisions about small stuff. She wanted to run out into the street to show everyone her dress.

"Before we go any further, I need to inspect your ironing, so get back into your own clothes. Hang the dress carefully—leave it in the fitting room and come into the back room with me so I can show you the procedure."

Brownie lifted a large box onto a worktable and showed Catherine how to open the box and put all the wrinkled items on hangers.

"Before you begin, plug in the iron and set it to medium high for cotton."

"I'm so happy you have an electric iron. We got one just lately—it's so much easier than heating the iron on the cook stove," Catherine said.

"Oh, my dear, you are so right about that!"

She remembered the wait while an iron warmed on the cook stove. She and her mother were thrilled when Stella sent them an electric iron for Christmas last year. They always picked clothes off the line when they were still a little damp. They'd roll them up to keep them damp and would not have to sprinkle them when ironing time came.

Catherine took the first dress off the hanger and put it on the ironing board. Brownie was about to give instructions but held back, opting to watch the girl's technique first. The young woman promptly ironed the dress, flipping it to match seams and pleats, received a warm nod of approval, and hung it on the workroom rack.

"You have passed the test with flying colors," Brownie said. "I am impressed with your work. When will you be able to start?"

"When, you say?" She had a big smile on her face. "How about right now?" Catherine was practically jumping out of her skin.

By the end of the afternoon Catherine had emptied three boxes and had hung a collection of dresses and blouses on a rack in the back room. Brownie was very particular about how the dresses should be hung and how the packing paper should be folded in the boxes. Catherine had no trouble with ironing but had to do a lot of folding before she got the hang of it. She worked until it was time to close the store.

"It's nice to hear you sing while you work," Brownie said, as Catherine passed her to leave.

"I love to sing," Catherine said.

This was the happiest she had been in a long time. She walked home in the drizzle with a bounce in her step.

Chapter 6. Here Comes the Judge (1935)

Martha was at her usual place at the table when Catherine came home. She sat down beside her mother and told her the whole story, including the fifty cents she got from the pretentious woman. Martha actually laughed.

"Mom, you won't believe the dress! It blows my wig! I've never seen anything so nice."

"I'm impressed with your get-up-and-go," her mother said. "I know where you'll be spending your spare time for a while. It'll be good for you, but . . . " Martha hesitated. She hated to dampen her daughter's enthusiasm, but she saw the future unfolding. " . . . but you won't be around here much to help me, I guess."

That's my mother and her fears talking, Catherine thought. She chose to not reply, refusing to let her mother dampen a day she wanted to celebrate. She counted the days left before the interview. The shop was closed on Sunday and today was Wednesday. She had four days to work to pay for her dress. That would be pushing it, she realized, but she was sure she could figure it out.

The next morning Catherine was waiting at the front door of The Smartshop when Brownie came into the shop from the back alley. As she let Catherine in, she said, "Why, you're here bright and early, Catherine."

"Yup, I'm ready to iron."

Brownie tilted her head, took a teacher-like tone. "Let me say, Catherine, if you're going to work for the judge, you're not going to be using the word 'yup,' and for that matter, 'nope.' It will be just yes and no while you're working here. Good practice."

"I'll try my hardest, Brownie." The nickname already came so naturally. This woman Catherine had at first so feared was in her own quiet way very warm.

It was another day of learning the ins-and-outs of a small clothing store. As they closed for lunch on the second day of ironing, Brownie asked Catherine if she would like to step across the street with her to look at shoes at O.A. Haase's shoe store.

Catherine turned away, looked down. "I can't afford shoes," she said.

"Do you have any other shoes you can wear?" Brownie asked but was pretty sure of the answer. Catherine shook her head.

"That won't do. Here's the fifty-cent piece from Edith. We'll start with that."

"Oh, no! I can't take that from her or you."

"After you get your job, you can pay her back. If you don't, we'll figure out something else. Catherine, please, we need to focus on one thing at a time, and you need shoes."

The store manager welcomed Brownie like they were old friends, and she in turn introduced Catherine, who for the first time could see the wide selection on display inside the store.

"Wow! I can't believe how many shoes there are in here! This blows my wig! I hope I don't have to decide which shoes to buy." She looked at Brownie, confided, "I'm a little nervous."

Brownie turned to the salesman, businesslike. "Bill, can you help me find an inexpensive pair of black pumps for Miss Sabinsky? They just need to service her for a job interview and, perhaps a couple of months of work."

"Sure thing," Bill said. "Please sit down right here." He waved her over to a bench, reached behind him and grabbed a strange metal device from a shelf. "I need to measure your feet."

"Measure my feet? What the heck does that mean?" she asked, looking at both her attendants. There was no answer. The salesman knelt down to take off her shoes, and a new thought struck. *What if I have holes in my socks? Oh murder!*

She looked down at her foot as Bill took off the old, soiled saddle shoe. "Oh, I do have a hole in my sock. I'm so embarrassed!" Her face turned bright red and she covered her face with her hands. *I just want to die.*

Brownie saved her again. "Oh, Bill, Catherine didn't know we were going shoe shopping today. She walks everywhere. I can see why she might have a hole in her sock."

"Don't worry about it. You're not the first person who has had a hole in her sock," he said with a grin, as he measured Catherine's foot.

"You're a perfect seven and a half." He walked into the back room to fetch a pair of shoes. The black pumps slipped easily onto both feet.

"Stand up and take a few steps to see how they feel," Bill said.

"I feel like Cinderella, but I sure wouldn't want to lose one!" She was grinning from ear to ear.

Brownie and Bill smiled at Catherine's excitement.

Catherine turned to her new employer. "How many hours will I have to work to pay you back for the shoes?"

"The shoes cost $1.39," Bill told them.

"That means thirteen more hours of ironing," Brownie said.

After the second full day of ironing, Brownie asked Catherine to sit down for a moment. "Your meeting with the judge . . . I think it's coming up soon?"

"Yeah, real soon. On Tuesday at 2."

"Yes," Brownie quickly corrected. "Well, then, let's talk about some things you might want to tell him. For example, what would you say if he asks you what your strengths are?"

Catherine thought for quite a while. With a twinkle in her eye she said, "Well, I could tell him how well I can iron."

Brownie shook her head, looked at Catherine sternly. "Let's try that again. What do you want him to know about you?"

This is a real lesson, Catherine thought, and she offered a serious answer. "I want him to know that I can type 64 words a minute and I'm good at shorthand."

Brownie told her that was a good start, but it was not enough.

"What about your attendance at school? Did you get to school on time? Did you always get your homework done? Have you had any other jobs? The judge is going to want to know all about you. He might ask you about your family or your friends or what you do when you're not in school. I want you to think about how you would answer those questions."

Catherine's mind raced as she walked home from The Smartshop. What if the judge knew about her family already? What if he knew her father had been in jail? She conceded to herself that she had to go through with this interview now. It was too late to back off. She tried to sooth herself, saying that the worst the interview could do was to leave her humiliated and unemployed. So, what was new? *Ah, but I'll still have a beautiful fancy dress and a nice pair of shoes that I can wear when Papa takes me to Jimmy's.* Should she laugh or cry about that? The thought came that she might never have another place to wear that new dress.

On Monday, her fourth day of ironing and the day before the interview, Brownie wanted another sit-down conversation. She had come to feel a personal investment in the success of this 16-year-old's interview.

"Catherine, do you realize what you're doing?"

"Oh, like winding this string around my finger?"

"Yes! That silly string! You know you can't be doing that when you're talking to the judge. You have some childish habits you have to break. And look at your legs—they're shaking so much it looks like you have you have ants in your pants."

Catherine looked at her own legs. "Wow, I didn't even know I was doing that."

"Please look at how I'm sitting," Brownie said sternly.

Catherine thought Brownie looked like she had a rod going down her back—no ants in that woman's pants! Her legs were crossed at her ankles, her knees tight together and hands cupped in her lap over a carefully smoothed skirt.

"I don't think I could ever sit like that. Are you comfortable?" Catherine asked.

"This is not about comfort. It's about propriety." She pulled her shoulders back even more.

"Boy, Brownie, I'm really going to have to practice that. I don't think I'd want to sit like that for even a minute," although she did straighten up a bit and pull her legs together an inch or two as she talked. She thought Brownie looked like a statue. Catherine realized she had a growing list of things she shouldn't do or say—no slouching, no knees apart, no "yup" or "nope."

"I sure as heck hope I can remember all of this."

"And no 'heck' either." Even the boss smiled at that.

On her walk home the sun had started to go down on a beautiful late-spring day. Summer would officially begin soon. Catherine's shadow was long and dark against the gray cement sidewalk. She had so many things to do tonight. She wanted to make a list of all the things she thought the judge should know about her, but all she could think of were the things she didn't want him to know. Could she pretend she lives in a normal family with good manners, that doesn't swear or fight or get drunk? She knew she was not good at pretending. She liked to tell it as she saw it, thought it. She didn't want to appear to be, as she would say, "putting on the dog." Her own mother looked stupid, Catherine thought, when she tried to do that.

The next day Catherine arrived at the shop precisely at noon to dress for her interview and, under Brownie's thoughtful gaze, in a twinkling she was transformed into a young professional woman. There was no money left in her budget and no time to do more ironing, so she would not be wearing nylons or a garter belt. Bare legs would have to do. Over Catherine's protests Brownie drew a thin brown line from the back of her thigh to her heel to mimic the seam in a pair of real silk stockings, saying this was not unusual. Catherine was more than satisfied when she checked the result in full-length mirror.

"If I have to say so myself, Brownie, I look pretty darn good for a girl from the wrong side of the tracks." She twirled around a couple times and smiled into the mirror. She was ready to meet the judge.

She counted the steps as she walked up to the judge's office—exactly twelve. On the second floor she found a huge door with a frosted glass window and the name "Judge William Sullivan" printed in bold capital letters in a semi-circle on the top half of the glass. "Circuit No. 1" was in smaller letters underneath. Her hand shook as she turned the knob and pushed the heavy door open. The waiting room overwhelmed Catherine. Dark wood wainscoting covered the lower third of the pale gray walls that rose to a ceiling a mile away. Large armchairs with soft beige fabric flanked the desk. The room smelled of lemon furniture polish and a hint of cigar smoke.

There was no one sitting at the desk in the center of the room and nothing on the desktop. The door behind it was closed. She didn't know what she should do. Knock on the closed door? Stand and wait for someone to come in? Sit and wait in one of the plush chairs, or maybe one of the wooden chairs? Was she in the right place? Was she here at the right time? She chewed on her fingernails while she paced back and forth on the thick gray carpet.

Huge pictures in ornate frames hung on the walls, formal aging photographs of old men with white beards, curled mustaches, and squinty eyes. Catherine felt as though they were staring at her. It gave her the creeps. She plopped down on a plush chair to catch her breath and tried to remember how she looked in the mirror at The Smartshop. If she could only feel the same confidence she had learned to feel with Brownie. She wished her mentor were here, coaching her through this moment.

After a wait of about twenty minutes—a wait that seemed like hours to Catherine—the outside door opened and in walked a middle-aged man with thinning brown hair, wearing a gray double-breasted suit with huge lapels and shoulders, and shiny brown wingtips, polished so brightly they looked like patent leather.

Catherine leaped up. Her first thought was that this man wasn't much taller than she was. "You must be . . . you must be . . ." He rubbed a thumb and forefinger together, as though asking for an answer.

"Catherine Sabinsky." Not a good start, she thought. *He didn't even remember my name.*

"Oh, that's right." He nodded. That clicked with what he had been told. "You're the second girl I've met with today . . . Catherine." He gestured back toward the chair from which she had leapt. "Please sit here in reception. I have a few things to do in my office. I'll let you know when I'm ready to see you."

He opened the door behind the empty desk and walked into his office, firmly closing the door behind him, and Catherine already felt rejected. She hadn't known what to expect in a judge, but it was not someone who was unfriendly, didn't remember her name and didn't even apologize for making her wait.

She waited for him for another ten minutes. He finally opened his door and beckoned her in. By that time, she had some fire in her belly. She walked in with her head held high without looking at him. He told her to take a seat in front of his desk as he sat down in his huge leather chair behind the desk, leaned back, and propped his feet on his desktop. Catherine noticed that, despite the sheen on his shoes, one sole was almost worn through.

"What do you think of this office?" he asked gesturing with his palm up across the room.

"It's quite an office," she said, her lips a thin line.

"Tell me about yourself, Catherine."

She looked straight into his eyes. "Okay. Let's get this out of the way first. My father has been in court twice and in jail twice. He may have been in your courtroom. If that disqualifies me, I'll leave now. There's no sense in going through an interview if I don't have a chance."

The judged raised his eyebrows, brought his feet to the floor, put his palms on the desk top, and leaned forward. Catherine clearly had his attention.

"So, what was he charged with?"

"Fights in bars," Catherine replied.

"Hmm . . ." The judge looked down for a moment. Catherine couldn't guess what impact her outburst might have had, and she was not about to stop and think about it. All she knew for sure was that she was not going to be treated indifferently. She had worked hard to be in this chair. Maybe she had already put the nail in the coffin for this job, but she was not going to be like her mother, accepting of any slight.

Judge Sullivan's contemplation was brief. He looked up, saying, "Okay, let's move on," continuing as if nothing had been said about Catherine's father.

"Here's how we'll proceed with the interview." He handed her a steno pad. "I'm going to tell you the requirements for this job. I want you to take down everything I say. Then type the notes and give them back to me. I will be looking at your speed and accuracy."

Judge Sullivan told her at some length what he expected from his secretary, tasks that included making his coffee, keeping his files in order, taking dictation, typing, and accompanying him to court, along with other details, such as logging calls and visitors, when he could be interrupted, and other minutiae of maintaining a busy office.

Catherine's brain and fingers went into overdrive. These were the skills that won her the interview. Completing her notes, she banged away at a typewriter in the outer office and pulled the last page out with a flourish. She knew she had done her best. She knocked on his door.

When he opened it, she handed him four sheets of typed paper. "That was pretty quick," he said. "How'd it go?"

Catherine didn't feel anxious now. What he had asked for was what she knew. "I did the best I could," she said.

Judge Sullivan waved her back down into the chair, and she sat quietly while he read over the typed pages. She had her legs crossed at the ankles and her hands in her lap like Brownie had taught her. When he was finished, he put the papers down.

"How old did you say you were?"

"I didn't say, but I'm 16."

"Did you finish high school?"

Catherine nodded "Yes."

He looked her over. "How'd you finish so young?"

"I skipped a grade," she said.

"Well, it looks to me like you did a pretty good job on your assignment. I didn't see any errors, but I read it quickly. There might be some there," he said, waving his hand dismissively over the pages.

"There might be, but I'm usually pretty accurate," Catherine said. The longer they talked, the better she felt. She wasn't going to let any highfalutin judge get her down. She remembered that Stella had told her she could do this, and how important it was for her mother that Catherine get this job. She kept working on sitting up straight with her ankles crossed, knees together and hands folded in her lap.

"My secretary is getting married and won't be staying on. I need someone as soon as possible. If you get the job, when could you start?"

"I could start tomorrow or whenever you need me. I'm working for Brownie at The Smartshop now, but she knows I'm applying for this job, so that shouldn't be—"

He interrupted. "Well, your teacher said you and two others were good students. I still have one more girl to interview. I'll give Brownie a call, too. My wife buys her clothes there and we know Brownie well. We'll see what she thinks of you."

"Yeah, sure." Hearing Brownie's name, she remembered the "yes" rule." She quickly said, "I mean, yes."

"About your father . . ." *Oh, no, here we go.* "When was he in jail?"

"I don't know. My mother just told me a few days ago. I didn't know he had ever been in jail. I'm pretty embarrassed about that." She squirmed in her chair and her head went down.

"Catherine." When her head came up, she saw he was looking directly into her eyes. "Why did you tell me?"

She thought for a moment, choosing her words.

"Because I thought you'd find out anyway. I didn't want to have to worry about it. I didn't want you to find out later. I didn't want it hanging over my head."

"Do you have any other skeletons in your closet that we should talk about."

Her heart started to pound. What if? She really didn't know. Based on what she was learning from her mother, she wouldn't be surprised if there were more. "Not that I know of," she said honestly.

When Judge Sullivan stood up, Catherine knew the interview was over. He told her he would let her know in a few days. He said he hoped to hire someone as soon as possible.

She walked slowly and properly out of the room. When the door shut, she practically ran down the hall and took two steps at a time out of the building. Her thoughts were still reeling from the interview. There were so many things she wished she had said and other things she probably shouldn't have said. She second-guessed herself all the way to The Smartshop. She wanted to tell Brownie about the whole experience.

Brownie was with a customer. Catherine ran into the back room, took off her beautiful dress and shoes, and put on her everyday clothes. She took a dress out of the box and started ironing immediately. She still had lots of hours to put in. When Brownie came into the back room, she sat watching Catherine iron a skirt. When she finished the skirt, Brownie gestured her to sit down.

"How did it go?"

Catherine told her the whole story, hardly stopping to breathe—how rude she felt the judge was when she first got there, how impatient she felt while waiting, what the assignment required of her, and how she felt better about the assignment than the interview.

"Judge Sullivan said he'd let me know in a few days. He still has another girl to interview. I think I'd rather work for you than the judge." Brownie's formal language and her stern manner sometimes still scared her a little, but Catherine trusted her. Brownie did what she promised to do.

"Actually, as you get to know Judge Sullivan better, you will learn that he is a nice man. I don't have steady work for you, but you have done a fine job unpacking and getting the clothes ready for the shop. I might be able to give you some part-time work ..."

"I have to get back to my ironing. I still have nine and a

half hours left." She figured she could get in two hours yet today.

By Thursday, she had finished her work at The Smartshop. Getting a peek at how the "other half" lived turned out to be an unexpected treat. Her mother might have learned some of the social niceties from the Ingersons and maybe even her own family, but this was Catherine's first experience. She sure didn't learn any of this how-to-hold-a-teacup stuff when she was growing up. By the time Catherine was born her mother had probably given up on any social niceties she might have had.

It was an education, watching and listening to Brownie with her customers—their lives, their problems that were so much different than hers or her family's. These people faced challenges such as what to wear to a cocktail party and how to please a husband. One needed a new cleaning lady. Another asked for a recommendation for a painter to paint her living room and kitchen. Catherine kept her ears open to learn to make small talk. How are your children? What grades are they in now? How does your husband like his new job? It was enjoyable to be with you at Riverside for dinner last week. She took it all in. She was proud to be able to pay for her dress and shoes, too.

On Friday Catherine helped her mother with spring cleaning. The rugs were hung over the clothesline in the back yard, and Catherine beat them with a wire paddle until they were free of dust and dirt. The chickens jumped around, squawked, flapped their wings and ran away. The work was hard, but it relieved her impatience. The winter clothes were hung on the line to be aired out before being packed away until fall. On their hands and knees, Catherine and Martha scrubbed the wooden floors with a stiff bristled brush and a bar of Fels-

Naptha soap. By the time they were finished, the little house smelled clean and fresh.

She had hoped to have heard from Judge Sullivan by now. Her feelings about the job were mixed. It would be a relief to have a steady income, but she didn't know if she wanted to work for Judge Sullivan. He seemed a little uppity. Her family thought that people with money and professional jobs were pretentious. The Sabinskys were only comfortable with people who had as little as they had—or less. Catherine's feelings came to her honestly.

Chapter 7. The Visit (1935)

Martha and Catherine were exhausted after a day of spring cleaning. They sat in the front room marveling at the result of their labors. The house was spotless—the windows washed, the curtains ironed, the floors scrubbed. They heard a car coming down the alley. A door slammed, then another. It didn't sound like Mike's truck. The back door opened, and Stella walked in.

"Stella!" Catherine screamed. "Is that really you?" She ran to her sister, jumped into her arms, and threw her legs around Stella's waist. The felt feathers on Stella's wool bowler hat went flying, and the suitcase and shopping bags she was carrying hit the floor. It had been almost three years since they had seen each other. Stella and Catherine hugged each so hard that both could barely breathe. Martha wormed her way in between her daughters. They all were crying, laughing and hugging. When they finally untangled themselves, Catherine noticed there was someone else in the room. A dark-haired handsome man in gray pleated trousers and a white shirt, a blue blazer on his arm, watched the carryings-on.

"Who the heck is that?" Catherine whispered as she looked at the stranger. Martha, engrossed in Stella, didn't notice him.

Stella saw Catherine looking at Anthony. She pulled

herself away from Martha and announced, "Mom and Catherine, this is my husband, Anthony."

"A husband!" The news was far beyond anything Catherine had ever imagined about her older sister. "You didn't ask us if you could have a husband!"

"We wanted to surprise you. Guess we did!" She proudly flashed a big diamond and a wedding band on her left hand.

Catherine gasped, staring at Stella's ring. "Anthony, you must be some kind of rich guy to buy my sister a rock like that!"

"Catherine, mind your manners," Martha scolded, but she, too, was in awe.

With a big smile on his face he reached his hand out to Martha. "I'm so happy to finally meet you, Mrs. Sabin. I've heard so much about you and your family. Please call me Anthony."

Martha stuttered out a "Hel-hello, umm, Anthony." She was uncomfortable with this sophisticated man from Chicago. Stella's husband. How could this be? It was surprise enough to see Stella, but with a husband?

Catherine did not move to greet this strange man. "Hi, Anthony. I hope you're nice to my sister."

Stella leaped to his defense, took his arm, looked at him warmly. "He's a kind and wonderful man," she said.

We'll see, Catherine thought. Even at sixteen, she'd thought she'd seen enough to know there were bad men out there. Anthony gave Catherine a warm smile and held out his hand to her. Catherine looked him in the eye as she said hello, then backed away. She was not ready to share her big sister with anyone.

Stella sensed her sister's coolness to Anthony and

strove to keep things upbeat. She retrieved her hat and grabbed a kitchen chair. "Hey, let's sit down! We all need a drink! Anthony, get out the bottle! It's been a long drive!"

Catherine looked at her sister lounging back on the old chair, draped in a long, soft, flower-print dress that could have come off the rack at The Smartshop. Anthony undid the snaps on a wide brown suitcase and pulled out a pint of Twelve Plus Rectified Whiskey and a bottle of 7 Up. "Seven and sevens for the group!" he announced.

"Mom, can Catherine have a drink? A short one?" Stella asked.

Catherine pleaded her case. "C'mon, Mom. It's a party and I am a high school graduate. I'm old enough to drink."

Martha didn't want to be a stick-in-the-mud. She admitted to herself it was a celebration, and against her better judgment, she gave in. She said she herself would have only 7 Up.

"Catherine," Anthony asked, "could you please get me some ice?"

"Nope," said Catherine. "Joe hasn't brought ice for a while. We owe him money and he won't give us ice until we pay up. I mean, no ice."

Martha gave Catherine a dirty look. This fancy man from Chicago didn't need to know about the Sabinskys' finances. It shamed her.

Stella caught her mother's glance, worked again to keep things light. "Then we'll have warm drinks," she said. "Better than no drinks at all!"

Drink in hand, Stella settled back for a family update. "So, Catherine, when's the big meeting with that judge coming up?" she asked.

"Oh, I had it already, on Tuesday, but I haven't heard if

I made the cut."

"You're kidding, Kiddo! I brought you the perfect interviewing outfit. Why didn't you tell me you had the interview scheduled?"

"Oh, Stella, I haven't even had time to pee! Getting ready for this damn thing has been a nightmare. I probably won't get the job anyway . . ."

"Cut out that kind of talk! I'll bet you a buck you'll make it."

"I'm really tired of putting on the dog. Mrs. Johnson gives me at least ten new things a day that I'm supposed to do and not supposed to do—how to sit, how to walk, how to talk. I hate it! I'd like to tell the judge where to put it!"

"Catherine, mind your mouth!" Martha said sternly, but Stella just laughed.

"I don't think your friend Mrs. Johnson, whoever that is, would approve of what you just said," Stella reminded her.

Catherine told Stella and Anthony her story, beginning with the job prospect when she brought back her cap and gown, her willingness to abandon the offer when she found herself unable to shop for proper clothes, the accidental meeting of The Smartshop owner and the ironing job that enabled her to pay for a dress and shoes. She laughed when she recounted the incident with Edith and the phony school library book fundraiser, and she spoke with some embarrassment about her small explosion in the judge's office. She carefully gave no hint of what she had learned about her mother's past. She wondered how much Stella actually knew herself.

"I'm impressed with your courage, baby sister, and the way you have gotten things done. You're one tough cookie—and smart!"

Martha couldn't wait to round out the story. "Did you

know your baby sister got some kind of big award at graduation? She even gave a speech to the whole darn bunch of people that practically filled the football stadium! I don't know how she ever did that." Martha shook her head. "I couldn't do that if you put a gun to my head."

"What's this about an award, Catherine?" Anthony asked.

"Mom," Catherine pleaded. "Don't— "

Anthony pressed ahead. "Awards are wonderful, something to be proud of," he said.

"I'd tell you," Martha opened her palms, helpless to explain more, "but I can't remember the name of it. I never heard of such a thing before."

"Okay, little sis. Spit it out," Anthony said, smiling, sipping his drink.

"Oh, Jeeze," she said, covering her face, mumbling into her hands. "Okay, I was the class valedictorian. There, now I don't want to talk about it."

"Didn't you skip a grade, too, when you went into high school?" Stella asked, taking a big swig of her Seven and Seven. "And what is a *valley-dick-whatever?*"

"Wow!" Anthony stood up and bowed to Catherine. "The valedictorian! That's serious stuff! Do you know what that means, Stella?" Anthony asked.

"Obviously not, Anthony," Stella said, just a bit tartly. "As I told you when we first met, I never even graduated from high school."

Anthony kept looking at Catherine with astonishment. "Really, this is incredible! It means she had the highest grades of all the students in her class." Anthony raised his glass. "For all four years!"

Martha added that Catherine had never missed a day of

school when she was in junior or senior high.

"Well, if that isn't something to celebrate! Anthony, that calls for another drink!" Handing him her glass, Stella turned back to her sister. "Cat, the last I heard, you were too scared to have the interview. I was coming to dress you up and drag you to the judge's office. Now that I know you're a genius, I'm confident you'll get the job. Good for you, Cat!

"Come on, you guys. Can't we talk about something else?" Catherine begged.

"Okay, so, what's the schedule with the judge?" Stella asked.

"I thought maybe I'd know today, but no such luck. I'm sick of the whole thing. That judge is a snob!" Anthony and Stella laughed at that one.

"*Min Gud!* People like that should have a good kick in the rear!" Martha said. She always considered a well-placed kick as an answer to any sign of the arrogance of power and privilege.

"I suppose you want to know why we're here," Stella said.

"Well, yeah. I think this is the biggest surprise of my life. I'm too old for a shock to my system like this," Martha said.

"I know, Mom, but we weren't sure if we could get here and I didn't want to build you up and then let you down."

Catherine pulled her chair as close to Stella as she could. "I don't ever want you to leave," she said as she put her head on Stella's shoulder.

"Anthony and I got married by the justice of the peace on Tuesday."

Catherine sat up straight and exclaimed, "That's the same day I had my interview! What time did you get married?"

"It was after lunch, probably about two."

Catherine jumped up from her chair, "That's when I had my interview!" She reconsidered. "No, actually, that's when I was sitting waiting for the judge. Maybe it's a good omen."

Then Anthony took the floor. "I am madly in love with your daughter," he said to Martha. "She's one swell gal. We didn't tell you we were coming because we didn't want you to bother getting ready for us."

"You sure picked a good day to come. Mom and I just finished spring cleaning. We worked our butts off. You're lucky you weren't around, or we'd have put you to work, too," Catherine said. "Just look at the floor. Mom had me on my hands and knees with a scrub brush and Fels-Naptha. My hands may never recover. See how red they are." She held them out for all to see.

"We don't have a blame thing for you to eat," Martha moaned. "I could have made you a nice supper if I had known."

"Don't you worry about it, Mom," Anthony said.

Mom? Martha was taken aback. *Don't try to get too familiar that way, Chicago boy!* Tailored clothes, a scent of money. Martha wasn't sure she was going to like her new son-in-law.

But Anthony continued. "We took care of food already. We stopped at Stepniak's Market and picked up a few things." He reached into a paper bag ad pulled out a big fat steak, then another. Soon, five steaks hand-trimmed by Stepniak's butcher lay in white paper on the table.

"Steak," Catherine bleated. "I haven't had steak since . . . since . . . since I can't remember! I'm drooling already."

She gave Stella a big hug and a bigger smile. A couple of trips to the car yielded potatoes, eggs, bread, butter, carrots, celery, bacon, cookies. Catherine's eyes got a little wider with every bag that was opened. They also brought another bottle of whiskey—a whole fifth—along with a case of beer, six bottles of Coca Cola, Hershey bars and popcorn. Both Catherine and Martha were dumbfounded. Martha started to cry again. She wasn't sure if it was gratitude or shame that she couldn't provide the food. Maybe both.

"I guess the only trip we have to make now is to get some ice to store this food," Stella said. "I wonder if we can get ice at Stepniak's . . ."

"I hope Mr. Stepniak doesn't know who you are. We owe him a pretty penny," Catherine blurted out. "I don't want go ever go there again." Martha glowered at Catherine and put her index finger up to her lips to silence her.

"You're all paid up," Anthony said.

"No, no, Anthony!" Martha cried. "We can't let you . . . " She was humiliated, embarrassed.

"Please, Mom!" Stella reached out to her mother. "We want to do this for the family. It's over. It's done. That subject is off the table, and I have something more important to tell you."

Martha wanted to protest more, but Stella had her attention. *I already have the news she is married. What else could be coming?*

"Okay, here's the story. Anthony got a promotion at General Electric. It's a swell job. He couldn't turn it down." She looked with pride at her new husband.

"Gee, that's pretty keen," Catherine said.

"What it means is that we'll be moving to Connecticut once we leave here."

Not so keen, Catherine thought.

"What's Connecticut," Martha asked.

"It's one of the forty-eight states, Mom," Catherine said. "It's on the East Coast, Atlantic Ocean, all that stuff, a long way away." A hole was opening in her life.

Stella moved her chair closer to her mother. "It's a lot farther than Chicago," she said. "It will take us three days to drive there."

"Oh, my God!" Martha felt tears coming again and buried her face in her hands. "I'll never see you again."

"Yeah, I know, Mom, it'll be harder to get back here, but we'll try. It's tough for me, too, but the truth is I haven't seen much of you in the last twelve years."

Catherine's heart was racing. Was it the drink she just had or was it the thought of maybe never seeing her sister again? Even though she didn't see Stella often, she knew she could get to Chicago in a lot less than three days. Charlie hitch-hiked there last week, or at least she hoped he got there. But Connecticut?

She had to know how much time she had with her big sister. "How long are you staying, Stel?"

"Anthony has to start work a week from Monday, so we thought we could stay until early Wednesday morning. We don't have a place in Manchester, so we'll stay in a hotel or a boarding house until we find an apartment. We'll be fine. Anthony knows how to take care of things, so I don't have to worry."

Martha fought for control. "This news is a lot for me to handle, Stella."

"I know, Mom. It's a lot for me, too. It's hard to get used to." She needed to soften the blow. "Anthony is a wonderful man. Hey, maybe someday you'll visit us. You could even live with us. That would make me so happy."

Martha shook her head. "Don't hold your breath on

that, my dear girl. I haven't been more than an hour away from Marinette my whole life and I don't plan to change that now." She didn't want to talk about this anymore, didn't really want to talk about anything. "Let's stop talking foolishness," she said, rising, turning away from the table. "You and Anthony probably need a rest after your long drive. You can stay in Catherine's room."

As Stella and Anthony headed to the bedroom, Catherine whispered in her mother's ear. "Oh, my God, Mom. Are you going to sleep with Papa?"

"Leave it alone! I mean it," Martha hissed. Catherine knew then that she was the only child who knew the truth of her parents' history.

Anthony asked Stella to begin unpacking and he would go for ice. As she grabbed stray hangers and searched for some drawer space, she reflected on her situation. She had a lot on her mind. This marriage was so new, this visit so emotionally charged for reasons she did not completely understand. She prayed she had done the right thing, was doing the right thing. She knew in her heart that Anthony was crazy in love with her. She had felt his eyes on her as they sat around the table, and she was sure that in his eyes she was the cream of the crop. He would do anything for her.

Stella was sad that she did not feel the same passion for her new husband, but she liked him and took pride in his success. She knew he would take good care of her, would provide security, would ease that anxiety about her future that had led her to leave home so young. She had sought to leave behind a prospect of continued poverty and likely settling for some local dolt who worked at the paper mill. She was 28 and almost past the marrying age. Anthony made good money and would support her in style in Manchester, Connecticut.

Anthony would never know that the man she loved so intensely was still in Chicago. Her most important goal was to get as far away from him as possible. He was a crumb, and she knew it. Nothing good came from being with him. When Anthony revealed his promotion and move, she knew it was marrying time. She would get out of Chicago and build a life with Anthony.

In the kitchen, Martha and Catherine got things ready for the feast. They peeled the potatoes and carrots and put them on to boil, salted and peppered the steaks, cut some slices of Martha's homemade bread, and set the table for five. Salt, pepper, ketchup, and butter sat in the center of the table.

"I hope Papa comes home for supper," Catherine said. "I'm so excited Stella and Anthony are here. Oh, how I miss my brothers and sisters."

Anthony returned after a successful search for a block of ice. "Guy down the street, a bar called the Korn Krib—good Wisconsin name!—said he'd sell some ice. I probably paid twice what it is worth, but I got it."

Stella and Anthony made themselves a highball and opened a coke for Catherine. Martha wanted only a little coffee. The threesome at the table chatted while Martha mashed the potatoes, fried the steak, made gravy from the drippings, buttered the carrots, and put the food on the table.

"I remember that you always made the most delicious gravy in town, and now I can tell you it may be the best between here and Chicago, Mom," Stella said. The complement raised Martha's spirits a bit. She was proud of her cooking. A leaf was added to the table, and the mouthwatering feast was set in the center.

"Watch out! The cookstove is still hot," Martha cautioned, as they jockeyed for a place to sit. "Don't burn yourselves. We haven't had a meal like this in a long time."

As knives and forks clattered onto empty plates, Anthony got up from the table to top off his and Stella's cocktail. "I don't think I have ever had a meal as delicious in my whole life," he said as he mixed the drinks. "Mom, your gravy is out of this world. You should open a restaurant."

"You haven't tasted anything yet," Stella said. "Wait 'til you have her apple pie!"

"Yeah," Catherine agreed. "Mom, you have to make a Danish puff for breakfast." She looked at Anthony. "You'll want to move in after that."

Martha was beaming. The luxury of the meal and the praise heaped on her cooking brightened Martha's mood. "You tell me what you're hungry for, Anthony, and I'll make it."

Catherine was stunned to see her mother apparently genuinely happy. "This is like a dream," Catherine bubbled. "Everyone at this table is happy. I wonder if this is what heaven is like."

At that moment Mike walked in the door. It was clear he had stopped at one of his favorite Menekaunee haunts, most likely Jimmy's. *Papa's got a bun on*, Catherine told herself. *We'll see how long this happy feeling lasts.*

Mike almost fell over when he saw Stella sitting at the table. "Well, I'll be goddamned! What the hell are you doing here?" He gave Stella a huge smile and a hug. "Who's the stranger?"

They all started to tell him at once, but Mike's focus shifted to filling his plate. He really didn't care about an answer. He just wanted to eat.

"Where'd this fancy grub come from?" He didn't care about that either, but that didn't stop all but Anthony from trying to provide the answer. Anthony instead got up from the table and pulled down another glass.

"I'll bet you could stand a little cocktail with your supper, Mike," as he mixed the drink. He immediately became Mike's best friend. Martha's face changed from happy to downcast. She knew what was coming.

Stella got up to get the cookies they brought for dessert. She put them on a plate on the table, and everyone grabbed one except Martha, who frowned at the platter. "How can you stand to eat those store-bought cookies? They taste like cardboard. I'll bake some decent ones tomorrow."

"Yeah, and Mom doesn't like to share her recipes either. In fact, she doesn't even need recipes. A pinch of this and a handful of that turns into something delicious," Catherine boasted.

By the time Mike finished his meal, Mike and Anthony had imbibed several more cocktails and Stella wasn't far behind. Drinking disgusted Martha. She didn't hide her feelings. She went into Mike's bedroom and crawled into the bed. She knew he would be too drunk by the time he came to bed to know she was even there. Catherine cleaned up the kitchen, washed and dried all the dishes, put them away and went to join the others in the crowded but spotless living room.

Martha lay in bed too angry to sleep. She hated it when they all partied and got drunk. She wasn't happy with Anthony for bringing the whiskey and feeding it to Mike.

Martha got up to a cold and gray morning but was pleased to see how well Catherine had cleaned the kitchen. Thankfully, Catherine had not only washed the dishes but had also put them away. A nice start for the day. Martha pulled some dry kindling out of the wood box to start a fire in the cookstove. She stacked the dry kindling on top of crumbled Sears Roebuck catalog pages and the paper wrappings from the grocery store, layered small dry logs with enough space between them to give the fire room to breathe. As soon as the match hit the paper, the fire caught and crackled, warming the kitchen. Martha busied herself making coffee the Danish way with a raw egg to absorb the grounds. While the coffee boiled, she threw together a Danish puff. Even if other food items in the home might run short, she always made sure there was enough flour and sugar to do a little baking.

While waiting for the crew to crawl out of bed, she sat at the table with her coffee thinking about last night. It was great to be with Stella again. She had missed her so much. What a blessing that she had come home, but what distressing news she had brought. Suddenly married to this stranger, and just as suddenly vanishing to some far away city. She wasn't sure about Anthony. He drank too much. Alcohol had always been the bane of her existence. Mike could be an ugly drunk, especially to her. He was the life of the party until he became obnoxious. He ordered and pushed her around, was mean to the kids when they were small, and spent most of the money he made on beer and whiskey.

Some days after a good catch, he'd come home with a roll of money and give it to Martha. But then he'd need a drink and bully her into giving it back. Whenever she had a chance, she'd pull off a bill or two to hide in her underwear drawer. She knew there'd be hell to pay if he found out. That's how she made payments on their bills, but there was never enough to keep up. Now, she was worried there would be a party every night while Stella and Anthony were here.

And what about Stella? Martha was unhappy to see the way her daughter kept up with Anthony. When the aroma of the Danish puff filled the house, the family crawled out of their beds, one by one. Mike had gotten up early to go out on the boat. He always got up in the morning, no matter how much he drank the night before. *How can he do that?* Martha often wondered.

As they sat around the table drinking coffee with heavy cream and eating the delicious pastry, Stella made plans for her few days in Marinette. She wanted to go to Clara's as soon as they finished breakfast. She hadn't seen her aunts, Mildred and Ivy, for years and she'd like to visit them, too. Who knew when she'd be back?

With full bellies the breakfast crowd—Stella, Anthony, Catherine, and Martha, too—hopped into Anthony's roadster and made their way to Clara's. Clara opened the door and saw Stella and Anthony standing there.

"Stella? Is that really you? You're all gussied up! Who's the guy with you?" Clara was elated. She cried with joy and grabbed Stella's hands. "What's going on? I can't believe my eyes. Am I dreaming? I must be dreaming!"

Stella wrapped her arms around her sister, almost lifting her off the ground. "It's not a dream, Clare! It's really me!" she squealed as the two sisters embraced. Still embracing Clara, Stella leaned back, nodded her head toward Anthony. "And, here, I want you to meet my husband."

"Your what? You have a husband?" She looked at Anthony and then back at Stella. "He sure is handsome." They all laughed.

Clara suddenly backed away from Stella and looked down at a dirty apron tied on top of a nightgown. "Oh, I have to go change my clothes. I look like a washer woman."

"You're beautiful, Clara. I don't look as good as you do when I'm dressed up ready to go out steppin'."

All agreed that Clara was the beauty of the family. She had light brown hair with a little wave, round pink cheeks, small bowed lips and bright hazel eyes that were now wet with tears. Dressed for an evening out, something that seldom happened now, she could be a stunner.

Little towheads now popped out on either side of their mother. She took their hands and led her visitors through the living room and dining room, cautioning them to avoid stepping on toys or children. The living room hazards included dolls, trucks, a bassinette, a baby swing. In the dining room a playpen filled with blankets and more toys stood next to the table. It was a home centered on the raising of four small children.

Clara left the group in the kitchen, calling back over her shoulder, "I'll be right back. I have to get out of my robe." She returned wearing a clean housedress, one she quickly grabbed that didn't look too wrinkled or faded, and a clean apron. She still wore her bedroom slippers.

Everyone was gathered around the yellow enameled kitchen table and matching yellow chairs, all showing much use. The big table was pushed against two chairs and the wall to make an everyday working walkway into the back bedroom and bathroom.

"We hardly fit in this kitchen anymore. Pull the table out from the wall. The kids can squeeze behind. We've outgrown this house."

Tommy, the baby of the family, wiggled around on Stella's lap. Glenny and Sandy stood behind the table waiting for a lap, a treat, or both. They knew Aunt Catherine had candy somewhere. And there it was—four pieces of brightly colored hard candy in the palm of their aunt's hand. In no time, the kids had candy juice drooling down their chins.

"Hey, you little darlings!" Martha called out. "Get over here so I can wipe your messy chins, and I need a hug from every one of you!"

"Mo' canny, mo' canny," Sandy begged.

"Come to Mamie, little one." Martha held out a finger covered with sugar toward the toddler. "Look what I have for you."

Sandy sucked the sugar off her grandmother's finger with joy.

"Ouch, Sandy. You can't bite Mamie's finger. That hurts. You sure do have pretty curls in your hair." Martha was in her glory. She was happy to have her finger bitten by that adorable child. The kids were satisfied for the moment.

"Okay, that's enough," Clara said. "Shoo! Go build a nice fort to show Aunt Stella." She brushed them away gently with her hands.

Clara served coffee from the pot on the stove that she always had at the ready. She put a small bottle of cream, a bowl of sugar, and a plate of banana bread in the middle of the table.

"This is delicious, Clare," Stella said. "I think I've gained five pounds and I haven't been here twenty-four hours."

They spent the next hour or so catching up. Stella told Clara about the big move to Connecticut she and Anthony were making and how that influenced their getting married. Anthony added a few details, including how much he loved Stella and how well he would take care of her.

"What about your job, Stel?" Clara asked. "In the last letter, you wrote how happy you were about your promotion to manager of the lingerie department."

"I loved my job," Stella answered. "It's hard to give it up. When I landed that job at Carson Pirie Scott twelve years ago, I knew I had found a great place to work. I made a lot of good friends working there, and I'll miss the heck out of them. And I had quite a few regular customers who liked me and kept coming back."

She reached and took her new husband's hand. "But Anthony can make more money than I can, so off we go. He says he wants to take care of me. I'll try being a good housewife. I've been on my own taking care of myself for a long time now. It might be good to be pampered for a while."

"You won't be pampered for long if you have a house full of kids!" Clara answered, and without pausing she swept up Tommy, who had wandered into the kitchen, and she snuggled her face into his soft fuzzy head. "What would I do without these kids?"

"What about Nels?" Martha wondered. "How's he doing?"

"What about Nels, Mom? He's gone day and night selling insurance. Who knows what he's doing when he stops to collect from all those pretty little housewives?" She laughed, but there was an edge in her voice.

"Well, it looks like he's not gone all the time," Anthony said, indicating the brood.

Everybody, including Clara, laughed at the innuendo.

"What about you, Catherine?" Clara asked. "What have you been doing since you graduated? You'd think we lived miles apart for all that I see you. I'm proud of you, by the way."

"Thanks, Clare, and thanks for Pepper! I love him so much! What a great graduation present!" Catherine paused. "I guess you don't know about the judge, do ya? Oh, I mean, do you. I've been told many times I need to speak well if I'm going to work in a judge's office."

"Tell me about this job . . ."

"I guess the judge asked my stenography teacher for recommendations to fill a secretarial position in his office. Miss Frothingham gave him my name along with a couple of other girls."

"What?" Clara exclaimed. "You got recommended? Did you get the job?"

"I don't know yet. He was kind of a pill when he interviewed me. He kept me waiting for what seemed like hours in a big, fancy office with no one else there except the big spooky pictures of old men staring down at me. Then he gave me a test. I'm not crazy about him."

"How did you do on the test?" Stella asked.

"I don't know," Catherine answered off handedly. "I don't even know if I want that stupid job, and I'm not getting my hopes up."

"Why wouldn't you want the job?" Anthony inquired.

"Because I want someone to take care of me," Catherine said mockingly. She looked to see if she had stung Stella but saw no reaction.

Anthony jumped in. "Well, then, come and live with Stella and me. I'll take care of both of you."

"Thanks for the offer, Anthony, but I need to be on my own."

That caught Martha's attention. "What?" she exclaimed. "I need someone to take care of me! I've been taking care of everyone all my life. It's about time somebody thought about me." She looked at each of her daughters. "All I do is cook and clean and wash dishes and laundry. I've taken care of the rest of you—well, except you, Anthony—and what do I have to show for it?"

Martha looked scared, victimized and mad, all at the same time. "Who's gonna take care of me? And what about Mike?"

Silence reigned, broken finally by little Sandy's wail.

"Mama, Gweny pulled my hair and took my dowy." All

eyes turned to Sandy and Glenny. Clara put Tommy down, picked up Sandy and plopped the child in her lap.

Anthony finally spoke, offering to go to a nearby market and get some food for lunch.

"Are you kidding me?" Stella put her hand on her belly. "I'm still stuffed from Danish puff and banana bread."

"I have a hunch this won't be a quick conversation," Anthony said, rising, "and I want to look around the town anyway. We'll all be hungry by the time you're done."

"Malmstadt's is almost right around the corner and we have an account there." Clara handed him a list. As he was leaving, he invited Catherine to accompany him.

Catherine's eyes widened as she climbed into the front seat. "Snazzy car you have here, Anthony. This is the sweetest car I've ever been in. And it's red!" Catherine felt the soft seats, pressed every button on the dashboard and rolled the window open. "This must have cost you a few bucks."

"Close that window before I freeze. It might be June, but it's still chilly," Anthony said with a smile on his face.

Catherine couldn't stop poking and prodding. She opened the glove compartment, closed it, checked out the shift lever.

"Where's Malmstadt's?" Anthony asked.

Catherine directed him to the market, but when they stopped in front. Anthon made no move to get out of the car. "What's this about wanting to be on your own? You're only sixteen. You might not be old enough to be on your own."

"Anthony, honestly, I can't stand to be in that house anymore. Papa's seldom home and when he is, he's usually drunk. Mom, when she's not busy making meals and taking care of the house, sits at the kitchen table, wrings her hands and worries and complains about everything." Okay, Catherine conceded to herself, maybe there *was* a lot to worry about. "But I just can't stand it!"

"What does she worry about?" Anthony asked.

"Oh, I dunno. Everything. I know she's afraid now that I've graduated that I'll move out and leave her alone with Papa."

"Would that be bad?"

"Well, yeah. Papa comes home drunk and is mean to her. He drinks up most of the money he earns. We have bills everywhere." With what she now knew, Catherine had to be careful what she said.

"I had no idea. Poor thing. She looks a little fragile."

"Sometimes she doesn't leave her bedroom for days at a time. She talks about having a nervous breakdown. I don't know what that means. Anthony, it scares me." Catherine aimlessly twisted a knob on the dashboard. "I feel so helpless not being able to do anything to make her feel better. Now that Charlie's gone, I'm all alone with her. She's scared I'm going to leave her. You heard her today. It's so blue at home."

"That's a lot for a 16-year-old to have to navigate. What about this potential job?"

"It would sure help in the money department. Papa's not earning enough fishing to pay all the bills. It would get me out of the house every day. That would be sweet." It was nice to have someone listen to her, pay attention to her, treat her like an adult. "I don't think I'll get the job because I have too many things going against me. I'm young, inexperienced, live on the wrong side of the tracks—just to name a few. Mrs. Johnson is helping me with my grammar and proper office behavior. I appreciate that. She's teaching me all kinds of things and giving me a lot of support."

"She sounds like a nice woman."

"Yeah, Anthony, but I feel trapped." She wrapped her arms around herself. "I know I can't leave now. I have nowhere to go and no money to get there. But what about the future? Am I always going to have to take care of my parents? They can't take care of themselves, that's for sure and my sisters and brothers are all gone."

"Catherine, my dear, I think you are on the right track. You have the possibility of getting an excellent job for a 16-year-old. If you get the job, hang tight for a while, do the very best you can do, learn all you can and see what happens." Anthony put his hand on the door lever, made ready to exit the vehicle, but offered a few more words of advice.

"Focus on yourself and how you can have a good life now despite living in a difficult situation. If you don't get this job, you seem to be well qualified to find another. Don't give up. Never give up. Use the next couple of years to better yourself. You have a lot of potential."

He waved toward the storefront. "Now, let's get into the grocery store before Clara comes after us. And remember—you'll always have a home with us."

Chapter 8. The Job (1935)

On Monday morning a special delivery letter arrived at the Sabinsky house. It was addressed to Catherine and it carried Judge William Sullivan's name and seal on the back. Catherine ripped it open with hope and trepidation.

"Oh murder! The judge! He wants me to come for another interview!" She stood there speechless for all of ten seconds. Then she gasped.

"I . . . I wasn't prepared for this." Holding the letter in front of her, she took a few steps over to Stella and put it up to her face. "I didn't think I'd ever hear from him again."

"Shows how much you know, little Sis." Stella smiled as she patted Catherine's shoulder. "The judge must be pretty interested in you if he asked you to come for another interview."

"Do you really think so? That's hard to believe."

"Well, get over it." Stella was firm. "If he didn't want you, he'd have sent you an 'I'm sorry' letter. Come on, Kiddo. Buck up. We have to get you ready. I didn't bring those outfits for nothing, after all."

Stella beckoned Anthony. "Honey, would you please get the huge suitcase we left in the front hall?"

"That one's a back-breaker. I could hardly haul it in here. You're hard on me, Stel." The look on his face suggested she could ask him to do anything.

"I can't tell you how thrilled I am to be here on this momentous occasion," Stella sang out to no one in particular. "Off we go into the boudoir, my little one."

Catherine bristled. "First off, you and mom can stop calling me 'little one.' How am I supposed to have any confidence to interview if I feel like a little one?"

"Well, you are my littlest sister . . ."

"Stella! Stop it!"

Stella didn't pursue the point. What mattered now was the suitcase full of clothes, shoes, belts and purses that Stella wouldn't be wearing as a housewife in Connecticut. It was a fact of life that Catherine had junk for clothes. Martha had herself made most of them. It was another apparent fact that Catherine had no sense of style. She'd need help getting ready for her second meeting with the judge.

"What did you wear at your first interview?"

"Oh, Stella! You have to meet Mrs. Johnson!"

Anthony had put the suitcase on the end of the bed, and Stella began sorting through the contents. "Who the heck is she?"

"It's a long story. I'll tell you all about it later. She owns a dress shop and she saved my life! Her nickname is Brownie—I think she's much too fancy a lady for that nickname—but you absolutely have to meet her while you're here!"

"Okay. Enough about Brownie. Let's get to work." Stella tried to get Catherine out of the clouds and out of her dowdy clothes and focused on the task at hand.

The Sabinsky sisters spent the entire afternoon in the bedroom as Catherine tried on skirts, blouses, belts and shoes.

Martha heard their laughter, their oohs, their ahs, their squeaks, and giggles. She ventured in and out occasionally, checking on their progress, but she knew full well they didn't give a hoot about her opinions. Clothes and accessories covered the bed, dresser and floor. There was a pile for "keepers," a pile for "needs altering"—that would be Martha's job—and a pile of rejects. Shoes, hats and purses littered an accessory pile.

While his wife and sister-in-law were focused on fashion, Anthony thought this was a good time to try to win over Martha. A business professional, he was well versed in breaking down barriers, and he knew from dinner comments that Martha's cooking and Martha's canning offered an opening.

"Mom, I was looking around in the basement and I saw shelf after shelf of jars of food! Do you put up all that food?"

"Anthony, if I didn't can all those vegetables and all that fruit, I don't know how we'd get by. Mike brings home some fish sometimes and I may have to kill a chicken, but that's what we live on."

Martha rose, put down her coffee cup, waved him toward the back door. "There isn't much growing yet, but come on, I'll give you a tour of the back yard. It'll take about five minutes." Martha's housedress was pressed, her hair was nicely coiffed. She looked happier than she had in a long time. Anthony followed her out the back door, sure that he had sounded the right note.

When Anthony and Stella had first arrived, he had seen the sprawling collection of garden vegetables, an orange and rust-covered hand pump, an outhouse. A chicken coop rested against a neighbor's red barn, which had long-since sagged its way toward eventual collapse. The area around the coop was enclosed with chicken wire nailed to a ragged collection of posts. A rooster strutted proudly just inside the fence.

Across the alley, a fishing boat sat in its cradle, both boat and cradle showing signs of rot. It was clear the *Annabelle* would never see a launch ramp again.

Martha pointed to the coop. "*Ja*, Charlie put that up. It keeps the chickens from running into the alley and out on the street. But we usually let them run in the yard." She looked at Anthony, not sure how much bigger Chicago might be than Marinette. "You never did meet up with Charlie in Chicago, did you?" She didn't wait for an answer. "Those chickens give us our eggs, you know, and when the hens get too old to lay, I make chicken stew with dumplings."

"I wish one of those hens would stop laying while I'm still here." Another chance to praise Martha's cooking. "My mouth is watering just thinking about the gravy."

Anthony pointed at the outhouse. "Hey, that privy over there . . . do you use it anymore?" "I don't," Martha said. "Mike still does, but it's darn cold on winter mornings. Thank God our landlord has a heart. He's good to us." She waved toward the pump. "Mike uses that, too, when he comes home covered with fish scales."

Anthony was impressed with the garden layout. Martha had set a stake in front of every row with the name of each vegetable written on a tag. The yard was a market of beets, carrots, chard, lettuce, onion sets, peas, seed potatoes, and radishes, and beyond Anthony's roadster stood tall vines of tomatoes, stalks of sweet corn and raspberry bushes.

"This is quite an operation you have back here, Mom. I've never seen anything like this before. I grew up in Chicago in an apartment building, so I know nothing about gardens or back yards."

There he goes with that "Mom" stuff again, Martha thought, but she heard warmth in his voice and thought it might be okay.

All this work! Anthony thought. "When do you do your planting?"

"I start getting the dirt ready once the frost is out of the ground. Working the chicken manure in is a back breaker. Charlie used to help me with that. I don't know what I'll do with him gone. I guess Catherine will have to take over. Mike helps sometimes on a good day."

Anthony studied the expanse of garden. "I don't claim to know anything, but are some of those plants getting a little dry?"

Martha wheeled around. "You leave the gardening to me, Anthony! I've been doing this since you were a snot-nosed kid!"

Anthony saw his mistake, laughed. He was appreciating his mother-in-law's spunkiness.

"Speaking of Charlie, what's up with him? Have you heard anything from him yet?"

"Oh, Anthony, don't even get me started. He hitchhiked to Chicago last week to find work on the ore boats. He got a tip from a friend who said they were hiring. I was hoping he could get in touch with Stella, but now she's leaving the city. I haven't heard a word from him. He's not so good at keeping in touch, but he's such a good boy. I miss him every day. My kids are all leaving me, Anthony."

"What about Catherine and Mike and your sisters."

"Catherine doesn't want to stay around here, maybe for a couple more years, and Mike . . ." she searched for the right way to explain this to Anthony, ". . . is not dependable." *He's worse than having no one*, Martha thought but did not say. She shook her head, shaking the thought away, continued the garden tour toward an empty strip. "I have bulbs planted over here, tulips and my special favorite, daffodils. Look! Look over here. You can see a few green shoots popping through."

Just then Stella called out through the kitchen window, "Get in here, Mom! You, too, Anthony! Quick, quick! I think we've found the perfect outfit for Catherine to wear tomorrow!"

The reviewing panel assembled in the kitchen, and Catherine strutted out of the bedroom. "Look at that girl! She looks like a million bucks, doesn't she?" Stella was pumped up. "The judge will hire her on her looks alone!"

Catherine was wearing a red long-sleeved frock with a high black-belted waist, broad shoulders, slim cut with a slight flair at the mid-calf hemline and a black scarf draped around her neck. A black narrow-brimmed hat with a hawk feather sat rakishly on her head. Her feet sported a contrasting-colored reptile-skin pair of laced-up heels with intricate designs along the sides. Stella had transformed a 16-year-old girl into a 20-year-old professional working woman.

"Wow! Who is this dashing young woman? She's one classy dame!" Anthony said, saluting Catherine with a wolf-whistle.

"You sure look ritzy, Catherine . . . too rich for my blood," Martha said, looking her daughter up and down. *Oh, how I wish I had had a chance like this when I was her age.*

"Wait 'til Brownie sees this outfit," Catherine said gleefully. "I'm going to stop in and show her my get-up before my interview. She always gives me good advice, helping me from the beginning. I need all the help I can get." A sudden thought. "Hey, you should come with me, Stel. I'd be so proud to show her my sophisticated sister."

Catherine waved back toward the bedroom at a pile of clothes at the foot of the bed. "And, Mom, Stella brought more clothes for me. Some need to be altered and I told her you would do that for me."

Ja, I get the work while everyone else gets the credit, Martha thought.

Catherine paced the kitchen and living room, sporting her new clothes and trying to get used to the strange shoes. Stella had told her they were all the rage, and Catherine was confident that Stella was in the know.

On the day of the interview, Anthony dropped Catherine and Stella at the front door of The Smartshop with plans to pick them up in thirty minutes and deliver Catherine to the courthouse.

"Catherine, I hardly recognized you. You look like a sophisticated young woman! What a lovely outfit." Brownie Johnson's admiration was sincere. "And your shoes! My goodness, Catherine! I've only seen shoes like that in pictures!"

Catherine was bursting with pride in her sister, whose clothing appeared to really impress Brownie. She grabbed her sister's arm. "This is my sister Stella! Everything I am wearing was hers! Her pick!"

Catherine went on to explain that Stella and her new husband Anthony had made a surprise visit and that Stella had brought a trunk of clothing for her. "They're leaving tomorrow, and I wanted her to meet you. I told Stella how you saved me!"

"Why, thank you, Catherine, but I think we helped each other out." She waved them into the back room to a small table. "Come, sit down for a few minutes so Stella and I can get acquainted. I know your appointment with Judge Sullivan is at ten, so we don't have much time."

"Hey, Stel! This is where I did my ironing to pay for my dress and shoes." Catherine was nearly jumping up and down with excitement.

"Thank you, Mrs. Johnson, for all you have done for my sister. You were here to help her when I couldn't be. I frankly don't know how she could have done it without you."

"Stella, please call me Brownie. Don't you think for a minute that Catherine couldn't have gotten the initial interview without us. She's quite resourceful on her own. Ask her sometime to tell you how she got an outfit to wear to her initial interview. She's a very impressive and determined young woman, although she doesn't look young today. Are you responsible for that?"

"I'll have to take the blame," Stella said as she looked at her sister with love. "I brought her a few of my working clothes I won't be needing in Connecticut. I'm thrilled Catherine will be able to make use of them."

"I'm feeling nervous this morning." Catherine said. "Yeah, I'm jittery all over. What should I do, you guys? Oh, yeah—I mean yes—and by the way, Mrs. Johnson, how did you know I was having another interview and that it was at ten? I didn't know until yesterday."

"Watch using the word 'guys,' too. I don't really think you need advice, Catherine. You're doing just fine by yourself. If you remember to use proper English, not slang, you'll be fine. I can tell you're working on that. And, to answer your question, the judge called me to get a reference for you. He had a great many questions. Then he told me he was going to see you again today."

"What did he say about me?"

"Let me say that he wouldn't be interviewing you for a second time if he weren't interested in you. Be yourself and you'll do fine."

Brownie asked Stella about her move to Connecticut with Anthony and her previous job at Carson Pirie Scott. They traded stories about fashion and selling women's clothing and lingerie, and they were not even close to being finished with their conversation when Catherine reminded them it was time to leave.

She knew exactly what to expect when she opened the door to the judge's reception room. The door to the judge's office was closed, but this time instead of sitting and waiting—and with a mix of trepidation and confidence—she went right to his door and knocked. It had helped to talk to Mrs. Johnson. Having Stella and Anthony here gave her a big boost as well. Judge Sullivan opened the door quickly and thanked her for letting him know she was here. When he sat at his desk, his feet were on the floor this time. He seemed more interested in her than he was at their first interview.

"Catherine, why are you interested in this job?"

"To tell you the truth, Judge Sullivan, working here would never have occurred to me if it weren't for Miss Frothingham. I was thinking about looking for a job as a waitress at the Gateway or a clerk in Stepniak's Market. I know that I'm a good typist and stenographer, but I'm young and inexperienced. I didn't think in my wildest dreams I would be working in an office. At least not yet."

"What appeals to you about working for a judge?"

"It would be nice to have a steady income. I don't know for sure that working for a judge does appeal to me. I've have never done anything like this in my life, but I'm all in to giving it a try if you hire me. I like to learn new things. I'd be proud to say I'm the judge's secretary."

"It seems like we're on the same page, Catherine. I'm concerned about your age and your total unfamiliarity with office work, let alone what an officer of the court does. There will be a steep learning curve. You have much to learn. I'm not sure you're up to this job, but you do have promise. I admire you for being honest about your family. I know you're smart, and your recommendations from Mrs. Johnson and Miss Frothingham were positive."

He paused. Catherine started to fidget in her chair, then remembered Mrs. Johnson's advice. She sat patiently waiting for the judge to continue. "Here's what I would like to offer you—"

Oh, my God, she thought. *He's making an offer.* She bit the side of her cheek hard to keep from jumping up and down.

"—a six-week trial to see if you like this kind of work and if you can get the job done to my satisfaction. I'll pay you nine dollars a week to start. If we both agree after six weeks that we're a good match, the job will be yours for the taking with a twenty-five cent a week raise. Can you start tomorrow?"

"I can, and I will! What time do I start?"

"You understand this will not be easy, Catherine. It's a demanding job. Be here at 8:30 on the dot. You'll have the coffee ready when I arrive at nine. I will make sure that Betty, who works for the sheriff, is here to get you started. Get a good night's sleep. You'll need it!"

Before she even got in the car she was jumping up and down, flailing her arms, shouting, "I got a trial! I got a trial!"

Anthony and Stella both laughed at Catherine's physical display. Anthony asked Catherine whether having a trial meant she had to go before the judge instead of working for him. But the couple agreed that this suddenly stylish young woman jumping around like a kid was a sight to see.

"Thanks, you guys, for waiting for me," she said, climbing into the back seat of the roadster and trying to catch her breath. "I have a blister on my foot already from wearing these spiffy shoes, and I have to be at work at eight-thirty tomorrow." Everything seemed to be happening very quickly.

Back at the house, Catherine unlaced and took off her shoes as she told Martha, Anthony and Stella the details of the judge's offer. She was thrilled with the plan he had suggested. She liked him better this time, particularly because he didn't keep her waiting and he remembered her name.

"We'll celebrate tonight," Stella said with a big smile. "This is our last night here. Catherine has a job at least for six weeks, Anthony has a promotion, and I am going to be a kept woman." She smiled at her new husband. "Here's the plan. Anthony and I will go shopping. Mom, you'll have to cook because you're the only one here who knows how."

Catherine feigned indignation. "Wait a darn minute, my dear sister! I'm almost as good as mom."

Anthony sought to soften any insult. "No offence, Miss Stenographer, but I want some of your mother's blue-ribbon gravy. You and Stella can plan your outfit for tomorrow while your mother cooks. I've never eaten such food. A gift of the gods!"

Martha tried to hide her pride, but it showed on her face. Anthony would be her favorite for the rest of her life. "Well, it will be chicken stew with Danish dumplings and mashed potatoes. Would you pick up some sugar, too? I want to make a decent dessert."

Stella rose. "Okay, the menu is planned. Let's go, Anthony."

It was a night when Mike made it home for dinner, and the meal had barely begun before Anthony again praised Martha's cooking, and asked her to move to Connecticut to cook and care for them. "Catherine could come, too, although I don't know that I could get her a job with a judge."

"Wha'ja just say, Anthony? Catherine has a job with a

judge?" Mike was confused. "When the hell did that happen? How did that happen? Catherine, what's goin' on?"

"Well, Papa, I was just going to tell you. My teacher told Judge Sullivan that I was good at typing and taking shorthand, so he hired me today, or at least for six weeks."

"Well, how the hell did my daughter get a job with a judge? That's one for the books. I can't tell my pals at Jimmy's or the Korn Krib. They might think I'm a squealer." Mike could not hide his pride and could not wait for the chance to brag about his daughter. "That's it. I won't be able to show my face around Menekaunee."

"Papa, I'll be making nine dollars a week for six weeks and I'll get a raise if he wants to keep me."

"That's a hell of a lot of money. That's a good break, Kiddo. I knew you were smart, but not that smart. Hey, Anthony, that calls for a drink! I'll have a shot a' that top-shelf whiskey ya brought."

Anthony, Mike, and Stella had cocktails before and after the delicate maple cream pie Martha had made for dessert. The dinner and dessert got rave reviews.

"That old lady a' mine sure kin cook," Mike said to no one in particular.

While Martha and Catherine were cleaning up and washing the dishes, Stella, Anthony, and Mike got out the cards to play a game of smear. Martha knew what was coming next. They'd play cards, drink, and act foolish all night. With a clenched jaw she told Catherine she was going to sit in the living room and darn some socks.

"Judge Sullivan told me that I should get a good night's sleep, so I better get to bed, though I'd like to stay up and watch them play. It's so much fun. Mom if you're up before me wake me up. I have to leave here by eight to get to the courthouse by eight-thirty."

When Catherine arose, everyone but Mike was having breakfast. Stella and Anthony were ready to leave for their new life in Connecticut, but Stella wanted to help Catherine get ready for her first day on the job. They would give her a ride to the courthouse on their way out of town. Leaving was hard for all of them. Martha and Stella held on to each other for a long time. They didn't know when they'd see each other again. Martha had taken a liking to Anthony and would miss him, too. She told him she was happy he married Stella and she knew he would take good care of her.

Sitting alone in her kitchen, Martha felt desolate. Her oldest two children were out of her reach. Nothing could be done about it. She felt there was nothing she could do about anything. She walked into her bedroom and closed the door.

At the courthouse Catherine, Stella and Anthony said their goodbyes with hugs and tears and promises to write often. Catherine didn't know which made her more anxious—starting a new job or saying good-bye to Stella and Anthony.

Betty, who had been working at the courthouse for eighteen years for the sheriff, saw a sophisticated young woman coming up the stairs. She was dressed in an over-the-top stylish outfit like nothing Betty had seen before

"Could I help you, Miss?" Betty asked.

"I hope so. I'm new here and I'm looking for Betty."

"You're not Catherine Sabinsky, are you? No, you couldn't be!"

"Yes, I'm Catherine Sabinsky. I am starting a job with Judge Sullivan today and he told me Betty would get me started. I must have coffee ready when the judge gets to his desk. I want to make a good first impression. Where can I find Betty, please?"

"I'm Betty and I'm surprised you're Catherine. I expected to see a green young kid stumbling around and looking scared. You look like you're a seasoned professional."

"I might look like that, but it's not how I'm feeling. I'm a nervous wreck. I don't want to make any mistakes. I have no idea what I'll be doing or how to do it. My sister was visiting, and she brought me these clothes. She did my hair and makeup this morning. I may never look like this again, because she's on her way to Connecticut right now."

Betty rose, beckoned Catherine to follow. "Of course, you're a nervous wreck. I was, too, when I started. I know how it feels. Let's get going on the coffee."

Betty was kind and efficient. She spent most of the time showing, not talking. Catherine watched every move, never having used an electric coffee pot before. Betty scooped coffee from a storage tin into the basket of the percolator, filled the pot with water, and plugged in the pot at exactly 8:45.

"When the bin is low, buy more coffee at Lauerman's, and just tell the clerk to grind it for the judge. They know the grind and the billing . . ."

Betty filled a pitcher with water, put it on a tray with a clean glass and cup. At the moment they heard Judge Sullivan unlock his office door, Betty filled the cup with coffee and showed Catherine the amount of cream and sugar the judge liked. Then she handed Catherine the tray. "Put it in the center of Judge Sullivan's desk."

The door to his office was open, the judge was studying the top sheet of a stack of papers when Catherine set the tray down.

"Good morning, Catherine" he said without looking up. He sipped the coffee. "Well done. It tastes exactly right. Have a seat."

"Good morning, Judge Sullivan."

The judge did a double take as Catherine sat. *Who is this girl-woman I hired? Sixteen years old and she looks like a twenty-one-year-old fashion model that stepped out of a magazine.* Her father was in jail? She comes from Menekaunee? He couldn't quite put it all together.

"Well, Miss Sabinsky! You're looking fine today. Are you ready for work?" *Well, for starters, she looks the part,* he thought.

"Thank you, Judge. I am anxious to get to work." Her legs were shaking, and she was thankful the desk hid them. She knew Brownie would not approve. She quieted them and smiled.

"Well, here's our docket for the week, I mean day." He was still a little disconcerted. "We will be in court at ten this morning. You'll take notes of everything anyone says in the courtroom and then type them up while I prepare for my next trial, which is at 1:30.

"In the meantime, you can begin to familiarize yourself with the files in my office and the cloakroom. Lunch starts when the noon whistle blows and ends at 1 p.m. sharp. The day ends at 5:30 or when everything is finished. Please have your steno pad and pencil with you at all times. Your notes and transcriptions must be accurate. There is no room for failure when human freedom, human fortunes or human lives may be involved. Do you understand?"

"Yes, I understand." *Whether I can do it or not is another question,* she thought. "It sounds daunting, but I'll do my best."

"I have arranged for Betty to take you on a tour of the courthouse today, depending on how long the trials take. She will also give you some material about the judiciary in Marinette County and the State of Wisconsin for you to read at home."

When Catherine got back to her desk, she felt like she was caught in a tornado. What to do first? She typed a list of the day's events and what the judge expected from her, so she wouldn't slip up. Her steno pad and pencil were center stage on her desk. She felt like putting a string on the tablet so she could wear it around her neck, leaving her hands free for the many other tasks. She smiled as she thought of the judge's reaction to that.

She examined every nook and cranny of her desk and its contents, and then got herself a cup of coffee and tried to pull herself together. Six weeks was a long time to be miserable. She wanted to go home and snuggle on the couch with Pepper. She wanted to put her head down and cry. Just as she was considering running out of the office, Judge Sullivan's door opened.

"Time for court, Catherine. Grab your steno pad. Let's go."

She jumped up quickly and tripped on the leg of her chair. Judge Sullivan was several steps ahead of her and either didn't notice or didn't care. Her feet hurt already from Stella's shoes. When they arrived in the judge's chambers Betty was there waiting. She explained the chamber was a private office for the judge behind the courtroom where he might have conferences during a trial or perhaps an-off-the-record meeting with a lawyer or a plea bargain negotiation.

"I have no idea what any of that means, Betty."

"You don't need to right now. All you need to know is where you sit in the courtroom and to have your steno pad and pencil ready to go. Today Judge Sullivan is having a non-jury proceeding. The plaintiff and the defendant—"

"Stop! What do you mean plaintiff and defendant? I don't know those words. And what is a non-jury proceeding?"

"You do have a lot to learn, my dear Catherine. I know you must be confused. You'll learn all this in time. Don't worry about it today. All you need to know is how to take dictation. I don't know much about this case except a certain Mr. Johnson, the plaintiff, is suing his neighbor, a certain Mr. Engler, the defendant, for damages to his corn crop when Johnson's cows broke through the fence and ate the seedlings of Engler's corn. They each have a lawyer but there is no jury at this trial. The judge will decide who has the winning argument or the best case. All you have to do is write down everything that everybody says."

"Oh, that sounds easy," Catherine said, mocking her own inexperience.

Betty led Catherine into the stately courtroom. The doors were still closed to the public. "Holy cow, Betty. I'm supposed to be part of *this*? I want to go home. Really."

Betty brought Catherine over to her small desk with a reading lamp, and a wooden chair.

She suggested that Catherine sit down so she could get a feel for her place in this enormous room. The judge's bench was on a podium next to hers, so she could always clearly see and hear him. The large area behind the rail was for spectators.

"Will all those chairs be filled today? There must fifty out there."

"Maybe. We never know how many visitors we'll have. The two tables inside the rail are for the plaintiffs and defendants and their lawyers. No one can approach the judge's bench without his permission. The chair on the other side of the bench is the witness stand. You must be able to see and hear the witnesses clearly, too. Position yourself to have the best possible view."

At that moment the door of the courtroom opened,

and people started streaming in.

Catherine barely had a chance to breath before she heard the bailiff's cry. "All rise! Hear ye, hear ye! The First Circuit Court of Marinette County is now is session, Judge William Sullivan presiding. Everyone remains standing until the judge enters and is seated!"

Catherine started writing at a feverish pace and didn't take her pencil off the paper until Judge Sullivan declared, "Not guilty!" and gaveled the hearing closed around noon. She walked to her desk and collapsed in her chair. Never had she taken dictation at that pace or for that long.

And so many legal terms she hadn't heard before. It was her earnest hope she could understand at least some of what she had on her steno pad. Realizing she only had a little more than an hour before the next trial, it was clear that lunch was but a fleeting thought. The fingers on her Remington clicking along sounded like a Fred Astaire tap dance. She needed to get her notes transcribed in a hurry.

Another session, another focus on getting her scrawl to capture the words of attorneys and witnesses, and at 5:20 p.m. she handed Judge Sullivan the transcripts of both trials.

"How'd the first day go, Catherine? It looked like you were really pushing your shorthand skills."

"I'm afraid I didn't do very well, Judge Sullivan. I'm not used to your pace. It was pretty fast for me. To tell you the truth, I have never taken dictation for this long at one time. My hand aches and so does my brain."

"You got quite a hazing today. It won't be this busy every day. But at times it's even busier. Don't be alarmed about not getting every word. I had Betty doing stenography as a backup. I knew it would be challenging today. She'll help for a couple of days until you get the hang of it. I'll bet you didn't have time for lunch today."

"No, and I'm starving! I hope my mom has a good supper waiting for me. I didn't get my courthouse tour, either."

The judge smiled. "There will be time for that," he said and left the office.

By the time Catherine walked home her energy was depleted. She was ready to flop on the couch. Pepper met her at the door. She scooped him up and went into the kitchen. Her mother was nowhere to be seen. There was no sign of supper. Catherine guessed what was going on. She opened the door to her bedroom and found her mother in the rocking chair with that vacant look in her eyes. Martha didn't acknowledge Catherine's greeting. She knew her mother wouldn't respond to a question, so instead of asking she began telling her about her first day at the courthouse. Her mother just kept rocking.

"Pepper, it's going to be you and me tonight. Let's see if we can scrounge up something to eat. Maybe Papa will come home for supper, although that isn't likely. Should we cook or cuddle on the couch? Let's cuddle until I get my bearings. It's been quite a day."

Catherine woke up when she heard the clanking of her father's truck coming up the alley.

She jumped up with the puppy in her arms and met Mike coming in the kitchen door. He smelled like fish and looked like he'd come in from a snowstorm with his rubber parka covered with shiny scales. He stood in the doorway.

"Hey, Catherine. Where's your mother? What's for supper?"

"Mom's in the bedroom in her rocking chair. It looks like she's been there all day. She's still in her nightgown."-

"So, another one of those goddamn spells, it sounds

like. Jeeesus Christ! I wonder how long she'll stay in the bedroom this time. Last time she didn't snap out of it for a couple weeks. Here we go again. I can't figure that woman out. I'm goin' out to the pump to clean up."

In the meantime, Catherine pulled some leftovers from last night's dinner out of the icebox. The ice Anthony had purchased was almost gone, but it was the only place to keep leftovers. They'd have to eat them tonight before they spoiled. After heating the chicken, potatoes and gravy on the hot plate and opening a jar of her mother's canned beans from last year's garden, she fixed three plates and left her mother's on the bedside table. Martha would pick at her food. Sometimes she wouldn't eat anything.

Mike came in still smelling like fish, but he had cleaned himself up at the pump. At least the fish scales were gone, and he had changed out of his fishing clothes. As they were eating Mike reached into his pocket, pulled out eleven one-dollar bills and some change. He pushed the money toward Catherine.

"We had a good run today. The gill nets were filled. Use this money to pay off Joe so we can have some goddamn ice in this house. And use the rest to pay any other bills we have, Stepniak's, the light bill . . ."

"Thanks, Papa. I'll take care of those tomorrow."

She didn't tell him that Anthony and Stella had paid the bill at Stepniak's. There were plenty of other places that money could go.

"It looks like we won't be seein' Stella around here for a while. I think she got a swell guy there in that Anthony. Too bad they have to move so far away. Hard to get there. My truck sure couldn't make it."

"I had my first day at my new job today, Papa. I took dictation at two trials and typed my notes for the judge. I'm exhausted. I still have some reading to do about the judicial system in Wisconsin and Marinette County."

"It sounds like that judge is workin' you pretty hard. You can do it if you put your mind to it. You know how to work hard and yer smart. So, let's use some of your brains to figure how we can keep your ma out of the loony bin. Whaddaya think?"

"Well, we can't get Stella or Charlie back, not right now anyway. I'll make sure she eats something, so she doesn't get too run down, but I can't stuff food down her throat. If she's still in her rocker in a couple days, we'll have to see if we can get Dr. Koepp to come and take a look at her. These nervous breakdowns sure get the best of her."

Catherine wasn't ready to accept sole responsibility of her mother in her dark moments. "Maybe Clara could get Nels to drive her and the kids over. She loves those kids. Holding Pepper might be a comfort to her. Who knows, Papa? It's scary. It probably didn't help that I went to work today. She was all so alone." She thought but did not say aloud . . . *and what you do only makes things worse!*

Catherine fell asleep with "The History of the Marinette County Judiciary" on her chest and her mother lying beside her, curled in a fetal position with her eyes wide open.

Chapter 9. Summer (1935)

When Catherine woke up on her second day of work, Martha was in the exact position she had been in when Catherine slipped into bed beside her last night—curled up like a baby with her vacant eyes wide open. It looked like she hadn't moved an inch. Catherine was familiar with this scene. There was nothing to do that made a difference. Martha's deep depressions were happening more often. Catherine sometimes wondered if these bouts of not moving and not eating meant they would have to take Martha to the hospital to keep her from starving to death. *Is that where things are going?* she asked herself.

Now, should she leave her mother in bed or get her into the rocking chair before leaving for work? She opted to leave her mother in bed. As she walked the two miles to work, she was feeling blue. She didn't notice the beautiful lavender lilacs that were in full bloom or the yellow daffodils that had already opened as she walked down Main Street.

The incomplete dictation from yesterday's court activity was foremost in her mind, interrupted by the occasional vision of her catatonic mother. Whom could she lean on? Her father was unavailable most of the time. Stella and Anthony were gone, Charlie was gone. Her good friend Alta was busy with a boyfriend. Catherine been dating Henry off and on for a while, but he didn't understand her feelings very well. If she told him she was feeling glum, he'd probably say, "Yup, it's tough all over." He was right about that, but it didn't make Catherine feel any better. Anyway, she didn't want to tell Henry all her family secrets. She still wanted to impress him.

Betty was in the coffee room when Catherine arrived. "Hi, Betty. Hey, I can do the judge's coffee today. At least I remember that much."

"I'm sure you did fine, Catherine. It was your first day. Did you walk?"

"Yup—I mean, yes."

"A beautiful day at last, the yards, the fields blazing with color. And by the way, you can say 'yup' to me. Don't worry about it."

Catherine carefully followed Betty's step-by-step instructions to make coffee in the electric pot. "To tell you the truth, I didn't notice much. I fretted all the way today thinking about how I messed up the dictation yesterday."

Betty was warm and reassuring. "Catherine, don't worry about your dictation. How could you get all of it? It's your first day and I'm sure you aren't familiar with all the legal language either. I'll bet your teacher never went that fast."

"You're right on all accounts, Betty. I really struggled. And I didn't get my reading done either. I didn't understand half of it anyway."

"Let's go over the dictation later. Just focus now on the judge's coffee. Always remember that he likes it fifteen minutes before he starts his meetings at nine. Today he has a pretrial hearing at ten. He'll want you there. Let's talk after that, maybe over lunch. You'll catch on soon enough."

Catherine placed the coffee and water on the tray on

Judge Sullivan's desk, right in the middle where he wanted it.

"Thanks, Catherine. Sit down for a minute," he said as he motioned to the chair on the other side of the desk. She sat down just the way Brownie had taught her.

"How do you feel after your first day?"

"I feel I have volumes to learn."

"Yes, you do, but we both knew that before you started. Let's wait a while before we make any snap judgments. I read over your transcription from yesterday. You missed some things, but not as much as I had anticipated. Go over your notes with Betty so you can fill in what you missed. That will help you learn the legal language. Starting a new job is never easy, especially when you've had no prior experience in an office or with the law. I'll see you at ten in my chambers."

It had been an interesting day, she thought, as she walked home along Water Street to Menekaunee. Even though the sidewalks weren't all finished, she needed the calm of a quieter street. Horses and cars fought for space on Main Street. It would be a mess at this time of the day. A canopy of budding weeping willows and oaks hung over the street. Catherine's shoes were soaking wet and covered with mud. She was glad she carried her good shoes in a bag.

The wild white trillium, bloodroot, and trout lily nearly took her breath away. Catherine used to accompany her mother for walks in the woods and fields along the shore, looking for these spring ephemerals. *Those were some of my favorite times with my mother,* she thought now. Finding a yellow lady's slipper was always a thrill, but they were few and far between. The robins and meadowlarks sang a harmonious melody. The piercing squawk of a redwing blackbird protecting her eggs was an irritating contrast, but Catherine didn't mind. It felt good to be walking.

As she neared home, her thoughts shifted from her day at the courthouse to her mother. What would she find? She was sorry for her mother, but she was resentful, too. No matter how hard she tried, there was really nothing Catherine could do when Martha was, as she herself would say, "down in the dumps."

Pepper was happy to see her when she walked in, but Martha was nowhere to be seen.

Catherine scooped up the puppy and opened the door to the bedroom she shared with her mother. Martha was still in bed. The oatmeal that Catherine had made her for breakfast was partially eaten, and she had turned over in bed. These were hopeful signs.

"Hi, Mom." Catherine sat on the edge of the bed, lightly touched her mother's shoulder. "I'll bet you would really like a sponge bath, right?" Martha didn't respond. "I'm going to heat some water. Is there anything you want?"

"Water," Martha whispered. A response! Catherine was relieved.

After bringing her mother a glass of water, Catherine heated a kettle of water on the hot plate. When it was boiling, she poured it into a basin and added cold water to make it just the right temperature. After tucking a bar of soap into her pocket and throwing a washcloth into the basin she brought her accoutrements into the bedroom and set them on the wash stool.

Martha complained with a few sighs and ouches as Catherine slid the nightgown over her mother's head, but she sat up on the edge of the bed without being held. While Catherine washed her mother from head to toe, she talked about her second day of work.

"The pudgy judge wasn't too bad today."

Her mother half smiled at that. "Is he really pudgy?"

"No, but I thought that was funny. He was actually decent about the mistakes I made on my transcriptions yesterday. He seems to understand it might take me a while to catch on."

Martha seemed to be listening.

"You'll get a hoot out of this one, Mom, but you can't tell anyone about what I tell you about my job or I'll get fired."

Martha didn't acknowledge, but Catherine continued her story.

"So, this middle-aged couple comes strutting into the judge's chambers dressed to the nines. Here's what they looked like. The crease in the guy's gray wool pleated pants was sharp enough to slice your liver sausage."

Martha made a half-grin, and Catherine, reassured, continued. "His wife was wearing a shiny black Persian lamb stole and a hat with a feather as long as Hall Avenue. They looked snooty with their noses up in the air, trying to impress the judge. Tell me what you'd say about them . . ."

Martha whispered, "You know what I'd say. They think their shit doesn't stink."

Catherine put her ear near Martha's mouth. "Your voice is so quiet I didn't hear what you said, but I think I know." Martha said it louder and almost laughed. Catherine laughed out loud, both at her mother's oft-said put-down of pretention and in the joy that Martha might be coming out of her latest episode.

"I know, Mom. I couldn't keep the big grin off my face when they were walking in and I thought of you saying that."

Catherine continued her tale. "Their lawyers, looking just as proper as the couple, were close behind. The judge walked in, sat down in his chair and said, 'I will now hear the case of Cumberland v. Cumberland.' Everyone in the judge's chambers sat up straighter. The lawyers each had long, long lists of items belonging to the couple. They had previously decided who would get what, but there were still several things on which they could not agree.

"I figured they must be well-heeled to have that much stuff. The wife sat at one table with her attorney and the husband at the other with his. They went through the remaining items on the list—furniture, jewelry, photographs. It took forever but they managed, not without a lot of bickering, to agree on everything until they got stuck on the last two items, described in the list as 'a cowboy hat with a red-tailed hawk feather and a yellow-spotted, hand-carved wooden pig.' I think that's what they called them." Catherine laughed at the memory of a fancy-dressed lawyer, speaking with the serious voice of a Sunday preacher, reading out the descriptions of the last two items.

"So, Mom, they both wanted the pig and the hat. Neither of them would budge and a bitter argument ensued. Their lawyers tried to calm them down, and Judge Sullivan listened patiently, but I could tell he was getting tired of these shenanigans.

"Finally, he stood up, dug in his pocket and pulled out a coin. Looking straight into Mrs. Cumberland's eyes, he said, 'Heads or tails?' They looked at him in disbelief. 'It's either a coin flip or a trial. What would you prefer? Your differences over a pig and a hat on the front page of the *Marinette Eagle Star,* or the matter resolved quietly in my chambers?'"

"In her own hoity-toity snotty voice, Mrs. Cumberland said, 'Heads!' The judge flipped the coin, caught it, slapped in on the back of his left hand and said, 'Mr. Cumberland, you won the toss. Is it the pig or the hat?'

"You wouldn't believe the look on their faces, Mom. They had no idea the judge could settle a case with the toss of a coin. Neither did I."

"Of course, the man got to choose first!" Martha said loudly, bitterly. "Isn't that the way it always is?"

Catherine was astonished that her mother spoke with such force, but Martha wanted a bit more. "What did the mister choose?"

"Take a guess, Mom."

"The pig."

"You're right! He chose the pig. I can't figure out why the hat and the pig were so important."

Catherine whistled a tune as she helped Martha into her housedress and her slippers. "Come on, Mom. Enough stories. Let's go into the kitchen so I can find something for us to eat for supper."

Martha didn't object. Catherine was overjoyed. It would be a miracle if this bout only lasted a few days. But they weren't home yet. Cream of Wheat for supper would have to do. It had been a long day and Catherine was too tired to cook. As they were eating, Mike walked in the door with a big whitefish fresh from the waters of Green Bay.

"What the hell are you eating? Yer havin' breakfast for dinner? Here, Catherine, do somethin' with this fish, would ya? Good to see ya in the kitchen, Ma."

Nobody could fry fish like Martha, and Catherine didn't want to mess up this beautiful fish. With her mother and father's advice it was perfectly cooked. Martha ate a little of the Cream of Wheat that Catherine had prepared, stood up, walked slowly to the bedroom, and closed the door. Catherine threw a pinch of salt over her shoulder while she was cleaning up the kitchen. Maybe that would keep the devil away from her mother.

Catherine joined Mike in the front room after she finished the dishes.

"What are we gonna do about your ma? She's havin' too many of them damn spells lately. I never know what I'll find when I walk in the door."

"Hey, Papa, wait a minute. We never know when you're coming home or what shape you'll be in. Maybe the two of you could come to a truce. You come home when you're done working and before you start drinking, and she'll have your supper ready. You don't have to go to Jimmy's every night after work. We'd like to see you sometimes. It's nice to have you home tonight."

"I don't go Jimmy's every night. I go to the Korn Krib sometimes."

Catherine didn't appreciate her father's joke. "Don't be a smartass, Papa. You know what I mean. You spend too much time and money at your hangouts. Why can't we have a normal life? I started working yesterday and I'm bushed. It's hard work learning a new job. I need your help."

"What's so damn hard about yer work? You sit on your ass all day in a fancy office and type a little. You don't know a goddamn thing about hard work!"

In her attempt to bring peace to her home, Catherine had tapped into a well of bitterness. Mike waved his bottle of beer and railed at his daughter. "I'm awake before the sun is up! I'm on a goddamn boat everyday rain or shine, settin' nets, haulin' 'em in! Them sons-a-bitches are heavy! At least we hope they're heavy. If they ain't, we don't eat. If they are, I have to scale and gut every one of them goddamn fish! Then I come home to a woman who won't have anything to do with me! It's a damn-sight friendlier with my buddies at the bars. At least we have some good laughs. Did ya' ever think I might need yer help, or yer mother's, for that matter?"

As Catherine listened to her father's side of the story, she thought how complicated life was. Her mother and father came from different worlds. Martha came from a family that had valued education and the finer things of life. Mike's brother was said to have killed a man in a bar fight. Mike was from somewhere in Michigan's Upper Peninsula, and she hadn't met anyone on his side of the family except for Big Louie, Mike's oldest brother. Papa didn't talk much about his early years, except for a few funny stories, and Catherine loved them.

Maybe this was a moment to settle her father down, get him to sit back and tell one of those tales. Her foolish attempt to make peace between her parents was a stupid thing to do. She had a favorite tale, and even though she had heard it many times, she always enjoyed it, probably because Mike made a few changes with every retelling. She pleaded with him to tell it one more time.

"Please, Papa. It's been so long."

"Well, okay. I guess I could do that for my girl who just got a big job. Go, get me another beer first."

"Oh, thanks, Papa. That would make me so happy!" She handed him the beer, pulled her chair next to his, and leaned against him.

Mike took a swig of his beer and began. "Me, Charlie—he was only fourteen, but he was strong—and Big Louie set out with Jiggs, Big Louie's pony, to haul in the net we had set in the ice the day before. We had to chop and saw a hole big enough to set a net in eight inches of that goddamn ice. Do you know how damn hard that was? Just imagine it. And it was colder than a well-digger's ass. It took us damn near four hours, but we got 'er done."

Catherine felt her father relax. His anger of only

minutes ago seemed to seep away with his telling of the familiar tale.

"When we set out to lift the net the next day it was seven degrees 'below the hole.' The wind was about eighteen miles per hour, blowin' hard from the northwest. We thought we was gonna freeze our nuts off. We were wearin' all the gear we had, long underwear, heavy mackinaws, snow pants—Christ, them goddamn things are hard to get on—heavy rubber boots, hats with earflaps pulled way down. Big Louie even had a scarf around his face. Christ, it was cold."

Catherine knew what a late January day on the ice of Green Bay was like. She and her friends had skated so many days on the offshore ice, but some days were just too bitter even for those winter pleasures.

Mike continued. "We hiked for quite a while with our heads down against the wind. Even the damn pony was shiverin'. All we could see for miles was white ice covered with snow that the wind was blowin' around. Weaker men than us woulda stayed home that day, but the time was right fer a big catch. We woulda been a helluva lot smarter if we'd a'stayed home. Big Louie and Jiggs led the charge to the orange flag that marked the net. Yer not gonna believe this, but the goddamned ice filled the hole again. More choppin' and sawin'."

Another swig of beer. Catherine was enjoying the familiar tale, and Mike put his arm around his daughter's shoulders.

"We was all set to haul in the net with the pony's help. Everything seemed to be in order. Big Louie got on his knees and stuck his head in the hole fer one last look. That's when Jiggs saw the movin' target—Big Louie's fat ass!"

Even after many tellings Mike laughed, his punchline coming . . .

"The pony sauntered slowly over to that big bull's eye and butted him headfirst into the goddamn drink. All that stuck out of that hole were Big Louie's big feet! Charlie and I started laughin' so hard we almost pissed our pants. We ran right over to pull Big Louie out, Charlie on one leg and me on the other, and when we got him out all he could say was, 'Son of a bitch! Son of a fucking bitch!' His beard and his hair was turned to ice."

"Oh, my God, it makes me shiver just to think about it," Catherine said.

"Well, that ain't all of it," Mike said. "Big Louie walked over and faced Jiggs head-on. He pulled back with his right arm and punched the pony right between the eyes. The poor thing swayed a couple times before his front legs collapsed under him. He was out like a light." Mike laughed until he started coughing.

"Dad, are you okay?" Catherine asked as she was slapping him on the back. Catherine had never paid much attention to how the story ended, because by the time Papa got to that part everyone, including Papa, were laughing so hard that she never learned how they kept her uncle from freezing to death. Now she had a chance to ask him.

"Did you ever haul your nets out of the hole?" Catherine asked.

"Hell, yes! We got enough fish out of that catch fer a few rounds a'beer and some left over fer your mother."

"How did Uncle Louie survive after coming out of that freezing water into the cold, brutal wind?"

"Oh, Christ! I can't remember. We prob'ly took off his gloves and wrapped him in a canvas or somethin'. We was tough back then."

Catherine still loved the rocking horse Big Louie had

made for her when she was a toddler, but she was too young to remember him. After she heard the story for the first time, she named the rocker Jiggs and put it in a prominent place in her bedroom.

"Thanks, Papa. This is a swell way to end the day. I have to get to bed. I have some stuff to read for work and get ready for tomorrow. We need a few groceries. If I gave you a list, do you think you could stop at Stepniak's and pick them up?" She knew in her heart it would never happen.

The next few weeks went by quickly. The more Catherine learned, the more enthusiastic she became about her work. Judge Sullivan had been patient and helpful. Betty was kind and supportive. After five weeks the judge told her the job was hers. He offered a twenty-five-cent-a- week raise, and he said he hoped she would accept his offer. Catherine was thrilled to hear the judge compliment her on so many skills. The most important were her accuracy, speed and the courage to be truthful. He also offered some advice.

"You need to start building some confidence in yourself. You've done a good job so far. You still have a lot to learn, but you have come a long, long way in just five weeks. You don't need to be so nervous."

Catherine jumped out of her chair, leaned over his desk and shook his hand. "You've got yourself a deal, Judge Sullivan!"

Catherine ran almost all the way home. She ran up the steps into the kitchen. Martha was baking bread when Catherine grabbed her mother around the waist, lifted her up and swung her around in a circle.

"What in the world . . .? What's come over you?" Martha was still on shaky ground. Her journey back to what looked like a normal life had been long and hard. She was still sleeping a lot but was at least able to get herself up in the morning, put on a housedress and an apron and make a simple meal. Catherine was relieved to no longer have to come home from work and cook.

"Sit down, Mom. I have something to tell you. Hurry up, sit down!"

Martha didn't hurry. She kept on kneading the bread dough until Catherine took her by the arm and sat her in a chair.

"You're not going to believe this. I hardly do. Judge Sullivan hired me after just five weeks for the permanent job with a twenty-five cent a week raise! I'm so excited! We'll be able to buy groceries and even have a little extra to pay Joe for the ice and catch up on the bills! We can count on nine dollars and twenty-five cents every week."

When Catherine got her first paycheck she gave Brownie fifty cents to pay Edith back for the contribution the woman had made to the bogus High School Library Fund. Brownie would make the excuse for the refund. Catherine also began building a little private fund for an occasional new dress at The Smartshop. The great classy hand-me-downs from Stella would only last so long, particularly if Catherine kept adding an inch or two here and there.

The summer of 1935 went by quickly. When Catherine wasn't at work she hung out with Henry and their friends. Henry lived on the other side of Marinette on a small farm with an apple orchard, a cow for milking, a horse for riding and work, along with some chickens, pigs and a goat. They had a garden three times the size of Martha's. Sometimes Henry rode his bike to Catherine's after she got home from work. The couple would sit on the front porch and talk or play cards. They might take a walk to the bay to look at the fishing boats or sit on the docks and watch the seagulls and an occasional kingfisher. Mike loaned Henry a fishing pole so he could fish.

On the weekends they would swim at Victory Beach in Menominee with their friends. The water never warmed up much in Green Bay. They'd dive in at the end of the breakwater and swim to shore. After doing that a few times, sitting in the sun wrapped in a towel was necessary before frostbite set in. Feeling pins and needles in their extremities was a warning sign. There wasn't enough money to go to movies or eat in restaurants, but picnics on the beach were the rage. Ample driftwood lining all the shores was gathered to make enormous fires. Sometimes Henry would sneak beer from his father's fledgling business that was run out of a shed behind the family home. Sometimes one of the guys would find a way to get a hold of a pint of rotgut whiskey.

Henry's friend Babe played the banjo and the group sang at the top of their lungs. Favored tunes included "All of Me," "Brother, Can You Spare a Dime," and "Dark Town Strutters' Ball." Catherine knew the words to so many songs and usually sat next to Babe, recommending the next one he might play. Henry might tap his foot in some approximation to the rhythm of a song, but a note never came out of his mouth.

Over the summer Henry became a frequent visitor at the Sabinskys'. He liked the freedom he had there. There were no rules. Mike enjoyed having him around, and for the most part Martha did, too. He was willing to lend a hand when it was needed, and he was easy-going. The feeling was not reciprocal. Catherine was not welcome at Henry's home. Louise was imposing. She loved her three boys with a passion and wanted only the best for them. As far as Catherine could surmise, Louise labeled Catherine as coming from the wrong side of town and not good enough for Henry. Catherine wasn't sure she was good enough for Henry either.

One night in late August after a beer delivery, Henry pulled up in front of the Sabinsky house in his dad's Ford pickup. He blew the horn and Catherine came running out, jumped into the truck and off they drove to John Henes Park. She hadn't known he was coming, but she was always happy to see him. Pulling the pickup into in a remote spot, he cut the engine. Catherine's heart was beating, and Henry didn't know what to say. He put his arm around her shoulder and pulled her close to him. When Catherine turned her head to Henry, he kissed her on the lips. It wasn't a long amorous kiss, but it was a serious kiss. Catherine responded. He put his arms around her, and they held each other tight. This was her first real kiss. Their bodies were filled with passion. They didn't say a word but their hunger for each other was palpable.

Catherine softly pushed Henry away. They didn't look at each other for a while. Finally, Henry said, "Catherine, will you go steady with me? You're a swell girl and I want you to wear my ring."

"Henry, what will your mother say? She doesn't like me or my family."

"Well, I like you and your family. She'll probably give me a lecture, but I don't care. I want you to be my girl."

"Yes," Catherine said. "I love you."

Chapter 10. The Asylum (1937)

The late afternoon sky was heavy with dark gray clouds as Catherine drove down the long empty gravel road to the asylum. Except for the ruins of an old barn on the far side of a field of frozen skeletons of corn stalks, there was no building in sight on the mile-long entrance to the facility. Snow-covered pines blocked the view of the facility itself. The long driveway seemed to be part of a goal to get "undesirables" as far away as possible from the community. She heard the wind whistle and felt the cold air blowing on her cheek from the crack in the car window. She was in unfamiliar country—in more ways than one—and she was a little scared.

The driveway had small pockets of ice where melted snow had collected and frozen. The car, with its worn tires, wanted to go straight when Catherine wanted to turn and turn when she wanted to go straight, but she was learning to handle it. There was no working heater and she had worn boots, but she would never complain. If Stella had not loaned her the money for this junker, she would not be driving to see her mother.

Catherine wondered what brought people to this god-forsaken place. Were all the patients crazy? Haunting stories filled with hopelessness and dread concerning the "nut house"

—as it was commonly called—circulated around the area. When she finally reached the parking area of a sprawling red brick building, she wanted to turn around and go back home. Did her mother really belong here? She wasn't crazy—she was sick! It had filled Catherine with pain to watch Martha close herself off from the world around her—she had stopped talking, eating, and finally giving up all movement—but she didn't run around like a lunatic, yelling or screaming. That's what crazy people did, wasn't it?

Dr. Koepp told Catherine and Mike that Martha had clinical depression, and he referred to her current condition as a nervous breakdown. Catherine didn't know much about depression, except that it had brought her mother down to a dark, dark place. This current episode was the worst she ever had. It wasn't like a broken arm or ulcers that could be diagnosed and treated and then the patient sent on her way. She had heard that it was brought on by a person's weakness of spirit. If people just tried hard enough they could get over it. Was that really true?

Catherine was bound and determined she would never let this happen to her. She wondered if her mother's depression had something to do with Papa when she got pregnant before they were married. She wanted to solve the puzzle of the cause of her mother's depression. She sure didn't want to have it. If it really was caused by weakness, she hoped she was stronger than her mother. She had to be strong. *So far, so good,* she thought, crossing her fingers.

Catherine sat in the car, trying to gin up the courage to go in and face the bitter music. She took a long drag of her Lucky. When Martha had been sent to Marinette General Hospital in early summer, she had been fed intravenously to keep her from starving, and she had been given warm baths three times a day to calm her nerves. That hospital stay had burned up every extra dollar Catherine had managed to save. Back home, the recovery took months, and trying to keep dinners made, the garden weeded, and the house in some order burned up every extra minute Catherine had. During the summer and fall, however, Martha was busy and productive. She worked feverishly in her garden, put up fruits and vegetables for the winter, cooked and kept a spotless house. Catherine returned to a cheerful mother after work each day. What a treat it was, but how long would it last?

After the canning was done Martha started spending more time sitting at the kitchen table with her head in her hands. She cooked periodically and kept the house reasonably clean. By the time Thanksgiving rolled around she was in her bedroom with the door closed twenty-four hours a day. Her eyes were milky and absent. She constantly rocked in her chair, stopped eating, then moved to her bed and stayed there. It was disconcerting to sleep night after night with a mother who seemed barely alive. When there was no sign of recovery after a week, Catherine asked Dr. Koepp to come to the house.

"Your mother is having a severe nervous breakdown. She presents right now as catatonic. Her condition is critical. She's much too sick to be treated again at Marinette General."

Catherine was terrified. "Is she going to die? She can't die! You must be able to help her. You're a doctor, for pity's sake!"

"The only choice left is treatment at the Marinette County Asylum. She'll starve to death if she stays home."

"You mean the Peshtigo nuthouse?" she cried. "She's not crazy, she's sick! Don't tell me that!"

"Catherine," he said patiently, trying to calm her. "It's an asylum for the mentally ill, not crazy people. Depression is a mental illness. The asylum offers treatments that could help your mother. We have no other choices."

After she stopped crying, she asked the doctor, "What treatments do they offer that she can't get at Marinette General?"

"One is called insulin shock therapy. It involves daily insulin injections to produce comas over several weeks. They could jolt her out of her mental illness."

"What if this treatment kills her?"

"I doubt it will kill her, but it *is* an invasive therapy. She will lose her memory during the treatments and perhaps for a while after. Usually the memory comes back. We can't guarantee anything. We need to wait to see how she responds."

That conversation had led to this moment at the asylum, and Catherine was still fighting the urge to leave. She looked at her watch—*Thanks, Stella!*—and realized she had been wasting time sitting in the car. Visiting hours were over at seven and it was already after six. She climbed out of the car and a gust of icy wind blew the door closed. It started to snow. She pulled her coat tightly around her as she walked across the slippery, uneven gravel driveway toward the building. The wind made her face ache. In front of her loomed a wide dark entrance and a huge, heavy wooden door she could barely open.

Catherine, nearly paralyzed with fear of what she might encounter, forced herself to go in. *Oh, dear God, this is much worse than any of my expectations,* she thought. Before she had taken a step inside she was hit by the overpowering smell of urine. A wide hall with a concrete floor painted a shiny gray barely covered the cracks and gouges. Her steps echoed from the empty walls and ceilings that seemed to reach to the sky. As she made her way down the long hall to the nurses' station, she noticed patients in wheelchairs or straight wooden chairs on both sides of the hall. Men and women, young and old, sat in silence with their chins on their chests or heads leaning to either side. Some were drooling, others had their tongues hanging out of their mouths, and many had their eyes closed. No one looked up or seemed to notice Catherine as she passed. Ashen faces, beige gowns and dark gray walls were ubiquitous. One loud scream from somewhere down the hall punctuated that eerie silence. She felt like she was walking through a hallway of ghosts. She was terrified. In her red dress she felt like a single flower in hell.

With the help of an attendant she found her mother lying lifeless in a fetal position on a cot in a large room painted the same shiny gray as the hallway. No pictures hung on the walls, no curtains accented the single small window. Fifteen cots furnished the room, which was lit with a single bulb hanging on a wire. Martha lay on a cot covered with a dingy white blanket, and fourteen other women filled the remaining cots. An indistinct moan, groaning pleas for relief, seemed to fill the room.

Catherine looked around at the ward. First, she stared at Martha, who had two IV drips in her gray, boney arm—the loose hanging skin a sad reminder of an arm once so husky. The bed next to her mother held a woman in restraints, who whispered incessantly for the nurse to get the black poisonous spiders off her body. Directly across from Martha, a woman pleaded hoarsely with Catherine to get her out of "this goddamn hell hole."

The moaning and gentle cries in the room seemed as though they had gone on forever, but Martha apparently heard none of it. Was her mother dead? Would anyone here notice or care? Holding her hand in front of Martha's nose, she felt a slight breath. The acrid smell in the room and her mother's ashen immobile face made her stomach queasy. She sat down on the cot, putting her head between her knees to keep from fainting. Her mother's hand felt clammy when Catherine held it in hers. As a rule, she didn't pray, but there was nothing else to do.

On her way out, she stopped at the nurse's station to ask about her mother's condition. The nurse, without looking up from her paperwork, said, "You expect me to know who your mother is? I've got too many other things to do than keep track how every patient in this looney bin is doing. I got all this paperwork and pills to keep track of. What do you think your doctor's for?"

As Catherine staggered along the corridor back between the rows of the silent statues of gravely ill patients, she was overcome with nausea. As soon as the heavy door closed behind her, she heaved and retched until there was nothing left in her. She knelt in the newly-fallen snow and wept. When she arose, she found that a fine powder of snow had already blanketed the car.

As a new driver in a north Wisconsin winter, it was a long drive home. The snow-covered roads and the lack of a heater made the drive a terrible finale to the asylum visit. When she finally pulled into the alley behind her house, she was relieved to see her father's beat-up truck in the alley. *So great!* she thought. *He came right from his boat today and didn't hit the bars.* She was shivering and crying when she walked in the door. Her father was sitting in the living room, listening to the radio. She threw herself on the couch next to him.

"Come here, Kiddo," her father said, putting his arm around her and pulling her close. Neither of them spoke, but they felt the other's sadness and fear. Catherine, warming now from the stove in the corner of the living room, sensed also the warmth of her father's touch. Pepper jumped up beside her on the couch and licked her face, happy to have her home.

They sat in silence for some minutes, but Catherine was still overcome by her visit to the asylum. "What are we going to do, Papa? I think Mom is dying. She's in this horrible smelly place with people who look like they're either going to die or kill someone."

She snuggled closer to her father. "She's just lying there on her side with a slack jaw, not moving a muscle. I talked to her, but I don't think she heard a word I said. I sat on her bed holding her limp hand and rubbing her bony back, listening to others in the room whispering and moaning. Someone somewhere was screaming." She shuddered at the memory. "It's the worst place I've ever been in my whole life. She'll die there, Papa. I know she will. I couldn't even find someone who would tell me what was happening to her."

The tears were falling down her cheeks, mucus from her nose was running down her upper lip, and she sobbed even harder. She wiped her nose with the back of her hand.

Mike shook his head. "I feel bad for the poor thing. She just can't hold it together, Kiddo. I still love that woman, but she won't give me the time of day. I guess I know why. I ain't been a good husband. I tried at first, but she didn't want a man like me. She wanted a proper husband like her old man."

After a long pause, Mike asked, "What did the doc say?"

"I haven't talked to him since she's been in the asylum. He said before we won't know anything until we see how she responds to the insulin shock. Maybe you could go visit her."

"I would, Kiddo, but I don't wanna make it even worse. I don't think she'd wanna see me. How 'bout we go together?

That might help you some."

"I sure don't feel like going to work tomorrow. I'm a wreck. I can't think of anything but Mom lying in that bed. We need the money, so I'll go. I'm ashamed to tell Betty or the judge that my mother's in the Peshtigo nuthouse." She paused and pushed her face further into her father's chest. "Oh, Mom! Why can't you be normal?"

Mike was soberly reflective. "There ain't that many normal people, if ya wanna know the truth of it. Everybody's got somthin'. Even the rich bastards got problems."

"Do you know any rich people, Papa?"

"Well, think about my goddamn boss. Hell, he's got a pile a'money, but I know he ain't happy."

"Papa, you don't think Mr. Seidl is happy? He seems like it to me."

"Yah. He puts on a good front."

Minutes clicked by as they held each other. Catherine was thankful for each minute that her father did not get up to retrieve a beer. She knew, though, that her father would never manage this family health crisis.

"I'll call Dr. Koepp from my office tomorrow and see what he says," Catherine said. "Tomorrow night we can decide when we can go see her."

When Catherine called the doctor the next day, he told her it was way too early to tell how Martha was responding.

"I won't know for two or three weeks if the treatment is having any impact. Wait at least two weeks before you visit her again. Actually, maybe three would be better. She won't be responding to you if you visit, and we won't know much until her insulin injections are over. I'll call if there's any change one way or the other."

"What if she dies? I need to keep checking on her to

make she's still living." Three weeks seemed far too long. "Maybe it'll help her get better if I spend some time with her."

"Catherine, let me assure you, she won't know if you're there or not. I promise to let you know if she takes a turn for the worse. Give me a call in a week and I'll give you an update. It took a long time for her to get this bad and it will take just as long for her to get better."

Not being able to see her mother made Catherine even more anxious. When she wasn't at work, she worried about Martha constantly. Only the distraction of the demands at the courthouse gave her some respite. She and Betty had become friends over the last two years as they shared their hopes and dreams during their daily lunches in the coffee room.

"You haven't been yourself lately, Catherine. What's going on with you? Is it Henry?"

Catherine started to cry. It took her a moment to be able to speak. "No, it's not Henry. It's my mother. I think she's on her deathbed. I'm so scared, Betty. I don't know what to do." She covered her face with her hands.

"What are you talking about?" Betty asked in disbelief. "What is wrong with your mother? When did she get sick?"

"It's a long story and a tough one. It's hard for me to talk about. I haven't told anyone. Only my family knows."

"Is she in Marinette General?"

"No." Catherine started to cry again. She couldn't get the words out.

Betty stood up and walked over to Catherine's chair. She gently rubbed Catherine's back and shoulders. They remained quiet until she stopped crying. "Would you like to talk about it? I think you know you can trust me. But I'll understand if you don't want to tell me," Betty said.

"Betty, she's in the Marinette asylum in Peshtigo—you

know, the 'nut house.'" Catherine talked through her tears. "The doctor says my mother has nervous breakdowns. She's had them for years—now I know what they are called—but she usually gets over them by herself. The doctor says she has depression. We've always just called it a 'spell.' She had a bad one this summer and spent some time in Marinette General. It took most of the summer for her to recover, but when she did, she was ball of fire. In the fall, I started to see signs again. By Thanksgiving she was very sick. She stayed in bed and wouldn't eat. I thought she might snap out of it, but by the time the doctor saw her he said Marinette General couldn't help her. Our only option is the asylum. I went to see her earlier this week after she had been there for two days. It's a horrible, horrible place!"

"What can they do there that the hospital can't?"

"They're giving her something they don't do in the hospital, they called it 'insulin shock therapy,' or whatever. I don't understand it but the doctor said it's only for the serious cases. He said it might jolt her back to life. I think it might kill her. She's not strong."

"Jesus. Why haven't you told me this before? You must be going through hell. How can do this by yourself? What about your father?"

She took a deep breath and leaned herself back into Betty's shoulder massage. *How much to tell?* She was already trusting Betty as more than a co-worker, as a genuine adult confidant, someone outside her own collections of friends and families to whom she could tell very private things. "My father isn't much help. He doesn't know what to do either. He just drinks a lot."

The floodgates of revelation opened. "The whole thing is so embarrassing. I already hate the word 'asylum.' I already hate the words 'mental illness.' Betty, they seem phony! I think, people think, that if you just worked hard enough you wouldn't have a nervous breakdown. Just pull yourself up by the bootstraps! Get a grip!" She was crying again. "My mother can't seem to do that, even though I think she tries a little."

Catherine wiped her eyes, looked at her friend. "Betty, I need a tissue and a drink of water."

A box of tissue sat on the table in the corner, available to the women as they fixed their makeup. Betty brought the box and a coffee cup of water. She sat, reached into her purse, and expertly shook a pack of Lucky Strikes so that only one protruded from the opening. "Here, have a cigarette, Cat."

Catherine looked at her with gratitude. She was so profoundly grateful to have someone with whom to share her story. "Sometimes, Betty, she seems like a broken woman, and then other times she seems normal—even peppy." All her sense of helplessness was coming to the fore. "I can't figure it out. She's a wonderful cook. She bakes the best bread and cakes. She sews, keeps a spotless house. But then I see the bad times coming again—she starts pulling away from everything and stays in bed for days at a time. Then she gets better. I always am praying that she'll stay that way, but then everything falls apart and she has another spell. This is the worst one ever."

"I know the vile things they say about those poor people in the asylum," Betty said. "I'm sorry, Cat. I'll do anything I can to help you."

"I know you will. Betty, I don't know what I'd do without you."

"Does the judge know about this?"

"No! I can't tell *him!* He already knows my father was in jail twice, and for him to find out my mother is in a loony bin might put me out of a job. I'm too embarrassed to tell him."

Betty touched Catherine's shoulder. "Do not worry about Judge Sullivan. He would never, ever let you go for these family problems. Telling him is your call. But . . . what about Henry? Have you told him?"

"He figured it out. He knew Mom could be in her bedroom with the door closed a lot of the time. He didn't know she was in the asylum until he walked past the bedroom door, saw it was open, and asked where she was. I begged him not to tell his mother. She hates me already. To her, I come from the wrong side of the tracks, y'know. If she finds out my mother is in the loony bin, she probably won't ever again let her beloved son come anywhere near me." Saying this thought out loud suddenly made it sound true, and a deep sense of loss swept through her.

"Oh, my dear Catherine, please tell me if I can help you at work. Maybe you need some time off. Some of us could fill in for you. Or you can cry on my shoulder every lunch hour."

Catherine felt some relief after talking with Betty. She was planning to stop on the way home to commiserate with Clara. She wrote Stella and Steve to update them on the latest news, but she still didn't know how to get in touch with Charlie, who was somewhere on the Great Lakes. In her letter to Stella she asked for a way to contact him. He had written that he had a good job on an ore boat, and he had begun sending money fairly regularly, but no one in the family had actually seen him since he left two years earlier. Catherine wished they had a phone. It would be so much easier to communicate with her family, but phones were too expensive. She was able to make an occasional call through the switchboard at the courthouse.

"Hey, Catherine," the judge called out as she was

leaving for the day. "Do you have time to sit down a minute?"

"Sure, Your Honor," she said, but the last thing she wanted to do right now was talk legal talk.

Judge Sullivan looked at his young aide intently. "I've been worried about you lately, Catherine. You don't have the usual energy and spark I'm used to."

"Am I messing up at the office?" Catherine asked with fear in her heart.

"No, no, this is not about your work, which you have learned to perform with speed and precision. No, I can tell there's something going on. I asked Betty this afternoon if you were okay. She said you were not okay, but she didn't have your permission to divulge your information. I'm wondering if there is anything I can do to help you? I hope it isn't about your job."

"No, Judge, it's not about my job. It's a serious family matter. The worst thing for me right now would be if it looked like it was affecting my work."

"Maybe I could help if you could tell me." He offered a smile. "You know it's in my own best interest—as well as yours—that you are satisfied and healthy. Besides, I have contacts around town that know how to get things done."

"I wish a person with influence could make a difference, but no one can. I'm not trying to be coy, Judge. I appreciate your wanting to help. My mother is seriously ill. I think she might die."

His face registered earnest surprise. "Is she in the hospital?"

Catherine rose. "Thank you, Judge, for asking and offering to help, but I really don't want to talk about it," she said stiffly, and, turning to leave, "I'll see you in the morning."

As she left the office, she didn't see the judge's look of

concern and a shake of his head in frustration.

As she walked into Clara's toy-littered living room, a small herd of children came running, jumping on her, trying to get into her lap or arms all at once, nearly knocking her over. They loved their Aunt Catherine. Holding them at bay and stepping carefully over trucks, trains, and wooden blocks, she reached deep into her coat pocket and pulled out four pieces of hard penny candy. Lickety-split, there was red, yellow and green saliva running down chins and covering hands.

"Hey, little ones, go play for a few minutes. I got to talk to your mommy. She sat herself down at the kitchen table. Clara came in and joined her sister. "Coffee?" she asked.

"Yeah, with a shot of the hard stuff!"

"Whoa!" Clara said, rising to grab a coffee cup and a decanter of brandy. "That bad, huh?"

"Even worse," Catherine said, her chin trembling.

Clara added a plate of leftover open-faced liverwurst sandwiches along with the drinks. "My neighbor came over earlier for a little coffee klatch," she explained.

Catherine grabbed a sandwich, trying to keep her sleeve away from the crumbs that littered the table. She took a sip of coffee, then took a bite of the sandwich. The flavor was a revelation and her mood brightened for a moment. "Clara, you're the best cook ever! Maybe even better than Mom! I could eat a whole loaf of your rye bread."

"You'd have to go some to beat Mom," she said. "Speaking of Mom, so, okay, tell me. Did you see her?"

There was no way to sugarcoat her feelings. "Yup, I did, and I'm afraid she's going to die."

Catherine told her about the doctor's visit, the ambulance ride to the asylum, and her trip to see their mother. When she finished the grisly details, she faced questions from

Clara that she couldn't answer. There were no answers.

"What can we do?" Clara asked.

"Nothing except hope and pray. Dr. Koepp says this method takes time and there are no guarantees . . . "

"How much time?" Clara asked.

"Don't know. We don't know anything. It's horrible not knowing and seeing her in this godforsaken place that smells like piss, looks like a torture chamber and sounds like a zoo of hungry animals."

"Oh my God, Cat—that's not where that poor thing should be."

"God, don't I know it. But what choice do we have?" Catherine said.

"How's Papa doing?" Clara asked. She understood Catherine's role as the last child home, forced to tend to both parents.

"He's worried, too, but what can he do? Reluctantly, he said he would go with me to see her, but that was before Dr. Koepp said we shouldn't visit her for two—or even better for her, he said—three weeks."

"Two or three weeks! Why?"

"The doc said she won't know we're there. Papa's worried his presence might not be helpful for Mom. He might be right about that."

"*Ah, Gud*, as Mom would say. What a heck of a mess we're in. How are you doing with all of this? Can you even concentrate at work?"

"Work is the only thing that saves me. I'm too busy to think about Mom very much, although my friend Betty and the judge asked me today if something was wrong. I told Betty everything, but I only told the judge that Mom was sick. I was too embarrassed to tell him she was in an insane asylum—it's shameful," Catherine said.

"Well, yeah, everyone makes fun of the Peshtigo nuthouse and the people in it—and now our mother's there." She put her hands on her forehead, her elbows on the table, and she, too, began to cry.

"It's so lonesome at home without her, but the last few weeks she wasn't really there anyway. I cuddle a lot with Pepper. He's good company, and I have him, thanks to you! He's the best gift I ever got!"

"Is Papa around?"

"Some. In some ways it's less tense when they're not both around at the same time. It's hard not to love that old drunk, even though he can be such a creep. When Mom's not around sometimes we play checkers. He still lets me win, just like he did when I was little."

"And now you're nearly eighteen—isn't that hard to believe! Look at these kids shooting up, too." Catherine looked over into the living room when she heard Dicky's muffled wailing.

Baby Dicky was under a pile of collapsed cushions and blankets that had been a fort. Sandy was trying to pull him out by one leg, so she could get in.

The sisters hugged each other tightly as they said their goodbyes. Clara ran over to save Dicky while yelling over her shoulder to Catherine to keep her up to date on their mother and to come over if she got lonely.

Chapter 11. Nearer to Henry, Nearer to God (1937)

When Catherine drove into the alley, she was delighted to see Henry's truck with Henry in it. She jumped out of her cold car into his slightly warmer truck. It smelled like stale beer.

First, he gave her a big warm hug and then asked about her mother.

"I just finished a couple late deliveries, so I thought I might catch you at home." She thought he looked handsome in his black wool jacket and baseball cap.

"Come on in, Henry. We'll make a fire in the stove. It'll warm up fast."

As he took off his jacket, she was impressed with the muscles in his arms and shoulders that he got from lifting heavy barrels of beer. She loved this man. They sat on the couch with their arms around each other. He knew how scared she was. He held her tighter and kissed her on the cheek. "I wish I could do something to help you, Honey."

"I know, but you can't. Nobody can. I hope you didn't tell your mother."

"I didn't, yet, but I'm going to. I really don't care what she thinks anymore. I love you. If she can't accept that, then she might lose me. It's time for her to get off her high horse."

"It would be so much nicer if she liked me."

"To tell the truth, she doesn't even know you. If she'd forget about your address and focus on you, she'd like you fine."

"I can't do much about coming from the 'wrong side of the tracks,' as I'm sure she thinks any time my name comes up."

"Your mother has always been good to me—your dad, too," Henry said. "My mother is intolerant. She doesn't like Catholics, Jews, Democrats, or anyone else who thinks differently from her. She always thinks she's right. My dad can't make any decisions, even about his business or around the house. I wish he'd stand up to her—just once."

"Papa doesn't make any decisions around our house either—but he doesn't give a hoot," Catherine said. Maybe her situation was better than Henry's. The thought surprised her.

Henry had more to say about his parents. "Listen to this one—you won't believe it! The other night when Dad was working in the basement, I went down to see what he was doing. He had made a huge cross out of old two-by-fours that he had hammered together and wrapped in old rags. When I asked what he was doing, he looked at me with a sheepish grin and said he was going to prop it up in front of St. Joe's Church, douse it with gas and set it on fire.

"I was baffled. 'What the hell, Dad? Why in the world would you do this?' He told me Mother made him to do it. She wanted the Catholics to know they weren't welcome in Marinette. Do you believe it? My own mother wanted it done and my father did it!"

"Jeeze, Henry, that's horrible! I hate to hear that! It breaks my heart!" Catherine was appalled.

"Yeah, that's what I mean. He does what she tells him, lets her be in charge. I don't know how he feels about the Catholics. He doesn't even go to church, but she's a German Methodist. She pisses me off!" Henry said through clenched teeth, adding, "He does, too, for not standing up to her!"

"My mom is ready to like almost anyone—unless she thinks they feel they're better than her." Catherine wasn't so sure about religion. "Catholics are okay, I guess, as long as I don't marry one. I don't get it, but I know a lot of people feel that way."

The room was warming, and Catherine was thrilled at the bonds of agreement being forged between them as they shared details about their families. "I'm going to get some hot chocolate—want some?"

Catherine came back from the kitchen with two steaming mugs of hot chocolate, topped with marshmallows, and handed one to Henry. Snuggled on the couch, they talked about what they would do with their kids if they were to marry someone of a different religion. Neither of them thought mixed marriage between a Catholic and a Protestant would be a good idea. Mike wouldn't care about mixed religions, but he would care a lot if one of his kids married a Republican. As Mike never failed to repeat, the guys at Jimmy's and the Korn Krib didn't like "those goddamn rich, snooty bastards." As for Martha, she didn't seem to know or care about politics, but she went to the Norwegian Lutheran Church, the only Scandinavian church in Marinette. Catherine had learned that the Norwegians and Danes didn't like the Catholics at all.

The direction of their conversation suddenly veered. "If we ever got married your mother would never accept my family," Catherine said with sadness in her voice.

Henry countered. "Your father wouldn't accept my

Republican family."

Catherine had more bad news. "I don't think that's the worst of it. If my mother lives, she'd never live alone with my father or alone in her own place. I don't think you'd be able to have me without my mother. It's pretty clear that she'll be with me until the day she dies. Put that in your pipe and smoke it," Catherine said. "I hate to bring it up, but it's true."

"Yeah. That's a lot to think about," Henry said.

"I hate to even think about my future. What man would put up living with my mother. And then there's my father . . . he couldn't live without my mother or someone else to take care of him. So, where does that leave me? I doubt that any of my sisters or brothers would be any help. Grandpa Beyer, Mom's father, lived with Clara until he died, but now that Clara's family is so big they've got every bed filled."

They were silent for a minute, then Henry gently cupped her chin, turned her face to his. "Catherine, we don't have answers to these problems yet, but I know we will." He put his face close, said in almost a whisper, "I'd sure like to marry you, Honey. I'm eighteen and you're almost eighteen. We're old enough." He sat back, relished another thought. "I can't wait to get out from under my mother's thumb."

Catherine suggested that they wait to have any talk about marriage until she got through the crisis with her mother. It was a way of putting off a decision. Even though she loved Henry, she wasn't sure she was ready for marriage yet. Catherine and Henry said their good-byes at the back door with long kisses, clinging to each other, promising to love each other forever.

When Catherine brought the judge his morning coffee, he asked her to sit down. The dark circles under her eyes, and her slumped shoulders were evidence of a sleepless night.

"I know where your mother is and why she's there."

"What?" she exclaimed. "Why would you do such a thing, Judge?" She felt spied upon, felt as though there were no secrets she could ever keep. She was indignant. "You don't need to know about my personal life! I'm sorry, you're a good boss, and I am lucky to have this job. If I do my work well, why does my private life matter to you?"

"I'll tell you why, Catherine." His tone was moderate, slightly apologetic. "First, Marinette is a small town and we all know each other's business. It's hard to keep a secret here, especially if you're well-connected. Next, you're my employee. I have spent the last year and a half training you. Your work is exceptional. You're punctual, you're pleasant, and you're funny. Everybody in this building likes you. I don't want to lose you, now that you're up and running at full speed. I know I'm not always easy to work with, but you know how to roll with the punches. Your confidence in your work has grown steadily. So, if you have something bothering you, I want to know what it is and how I can help you stay healthy and productive. It's in my self-interest, don't you see? And finally, you're a good and kind person. I don't like to see you suffer."

Catherine was both mollified and relieved.

"Well, that's a surprise. I thought for sure you'd fire me if you found out about my mother's condition. Most people think if you're in the asylum, you're damaged goods—weak, lazy, crazy, dangerous, shouldn't be out on the street."

Her anger at the injustice of it spurred her on. "You know how people think, Judge. They shun you when they find out you have family there. They think if your mother is crazy, you must be, too. So, these undesirable people are hidden out of town, in the woods, in lock-down so nobody needs to look at them or feel guilty for not helping them. It's like throwing away your rotten garbage. You don't want to smell it, taste it, look at it, and feel it, so you take it to the dump. The asylum is a human dump."

"You're right about much of that, Catherine. I can understand why you didn't want me to know where your mother was, and I appreciate your concern about the humanity of the residents there. Actually, young lady, I know more about the asylum than you might realize. Sometime I commit people to spend time there under certain circumstances."

"Really?" Catherine said. "I've never seen a case like that since I've been here."

"I don't do it very often. I have been there many times and know what a travesty it is. It's underfunded and understaffed. Many of the staff are not well trained to deal with mental illness, not even doctors. Unfortunately, it has become the human dump as you so wisely described it."

"Jeeze, Judge. I was there last night to see my mother. The people look scary, the place smells terrible. My mother doesn't belong there. She's not crazy." Catherine paused, feeling self-conscious about her outburst but still flooded with concern that her mother might soon die.

The judge remained silent, waiting for Catherine go on. "She just gets so down, Judge. She won't talk or eat or even sleep. The doctor calls it a nervous breakdown. She's had them before, but never this bad."

The judge settled back, laced his fingers. "I want to tell you about a case I had just before you started working for me. A family in town had a mongoloid child—almond shaped eyes, tongue too big for his mouth. That did not stop his parents from loving him. He went with them everywhere. They taught Marvin how to shop at the grocery store, his table manners were impeccable, and he was polite and even funny. They went to great lengths to make Marvin's life better. Neighbors and people in town got to know and accept him. He grew big and strong in his late teens."

Catherine opened her mouth to say this was a wonderful story about her community, one at odds with her own outburst about intolerance, but the judge waved her silent.

"Marvin started having irrational fears, imagining someone was after him. He barricaded himself in his room where he cried and screamed continuously. When his parents finally were able to break down the door, he attacked his mother, bludgeoning her with his fists, knocking her down and trying to strangle her. His father was not strong enough to pull him away. Fortunately, a neighbor heard the piercing screams, rushed into the house, and helped Marvin off his mother.

"Marvin's parents were determined to keep him at home, even after the heinous attack. Neighbors, however, were now afraid, and they began locking their doors and staying inside if they thought Marvin might be out. His parents held their ground, insisting there would be no repeat of his attack. It was a freak occurrence, they said. The neighbors sued, and I had to make the gut-wrenching decision to place him in the asylum. I thought it might be Marvin's demise, but the only other choice was to put him in jail. His mother would not press charges and locking him up in jail might have been worse than the asylum."

The judge paused, looked at his assistant. "You are right, Catherine. We don't know how to help people who are mentally ill, so we hide them. I'm ashamed to say, I am one of the offenders."

He leaned forward, hands on his desk, to make his point. "There really is a bright side, Catherine, if you look at it this way. Your mother is having a treatment that might save her life. It doesn't always work, but you must believe that it will. That means that your mother is not a lifetime resident of that facility. Trust that she will be back home with you and able to live a normal life."

Catherine, thin-lipped, nodded slightly, and the judge continued. "I want to be supportive in any way I can. If you need to take time off, I can have Betty or one of the other girls fill in for you. If you need money, I can advance you your pay. Don't be afraid to ask and try not to be ashamed that your mother is that terrible place. It is not your fault nor is it hers. You did not make her this way. Have faith in your doctor. You're a strong young woman. You manage to keep plugging along under these dire circumstances. Give yourself some credit."

"Judge, I have to tell you this. The first time I met you, I thought you were a jerk. You were late for my interview, you didn't remember my name, you had your feet on your desk before you started interviewing me." She realized immediately that her tongue had once again run ahead of her brain, but she saw a genuine smile spread across Judge Sullivan's face. She quickly added, "but you turned out to be a swell boss. Thanks!"

Catherine left work that day with a mixed review of her own performance. She had now been working for the judge for more than a year and a half. The judge's kind words, his expression of satisfaction with her work—plus two raises— gave some boost to her self- confidence, but she still she felt she wasn't good enough. She wondered if maybe her best skill was the ability to second-guess everything she did, from speaking to the judge to trying to mediate between her parents. She was equally torn in trying to resolve her future with Henry.

Catherine was having trouble sleeping. She felt a darkness inside, a space of restlessness, uncertainty, maybe something evil. She started berating herself for not praying or going to church enough. Her mother had fallen away from going to church as her illness progressed. Julia Mack, her previous Sunday School teacher, and Reverend Knutson, the pastor at Our Savior's Lutheran Church, would be the first to tell her that her family was being punished for turning away from the Lord. Catherine was sure she had done a few other things that would keep her out of heaven, too—drinking, smoking, dancing.

In her younger days Catherine went to Sunday school and sang in the youth choir. She even went to Luther League. Her lapse began after graduation. It wasn't as if she made a conscious decision. It happened gradually. She missed a week of church. She went back. She missed more Sundays and finally stopped going altogether. If she had lived a more pious life, maybe her mother wouldn't be suffering right now. She was praying like a zealot these days, asking for forgiveness, promising to lead a Christian life if only her mother would get better. She thought about going to church on Sunday, but she felt too guilty. She couldn't face a harsh judgment from the preacher or others in the congregation.

After two weeks, Catherine called Dr. Koepp from the switchboard at the office. He told her that Martha hadn't made any progress yet. She hadn't gotten any worse, but not any better either. He encouraged her not to visit, but to call him in another week, when he thought he might be ready to make an assessment.

She couldn't bear it any longer. Her only hope was God. Dressed in her Sunday best she walked up the wide concrete stairway leading to the sanctuary of Our Savior's Lutheran Church. As she opened the door into the nave, Mrs. Jadin, the pianist, was belting out "Nearer My God to Thee," one of her mother's favorites. Mrs. Jadin's body moved forward and backward from her hips, while her hands lifted from the keys and came back down with a flourish. The congregation stood in unison, hymnals in hands, and sang along. Catherine slid into the last pew on the right side of the nave on the far end and began singing. She didn't need a hymnal. She knew all four verses by heart. She didn't think anyone saw her come in, except maybe the choir members who sat in a balcony at the front of the church facing the pews. As she sang, every note touched her heart and reverberated through each sinew of her body. How she loved those hymns! Singing in church brought her great joy.

Pastor Knudson began his sermon with Proverbs 10:27. "The fear of the Lord prolongs life. But the years of the wicked will be shortened." There it was. Her mother was dying because they had stopped going to church and she herself had been wicked—smoking, drinking, dancing, cursing. She knew she was guilty.

Catherine tried to focus on the sermon but was distracted by all that was around her. Most of the people were still sitting in their usual pews. Her family used to sit in the second row on the left side of the nave close to the pastor's pulpit. The gigantic painting of God—standing in the clouds, holding a smoking torch high above his head, with a mop of long white hair—was still there. That God up there on the wall was clearly someone to be reckoned with. She remembered kneeling on the hard, purple velvet cushions, her hands in prayer, elbows on the white altar rail, when she took her first communion. How proud she was! Some of her old junior choir friends she noticed were in the adult choir now. She wanted to be up there with them. The stained-glass windows were a blaze of color as the sun broke from behind a cloud. It was a comfort to be in church again.

At the final "Amen" she wanted to slide out of the pew she had slid into an hour ago and sneak away before anyone could see her, but her heart sank when she realized that Pastor Knudson was going to beat her to the exit door anyway. She wasn't ready for him yet. She waited until it was her turn to leave the pew. *Oh, my God,* she thought, *I'm going to be the last one out of church and fair game for the preacher.* Could she run down the stairs on the other side and go out through Sunday school? By then it was too late. He saw her.

He held a hand out to her. He encased her hand in both of his. "Catherine, it's been a while. I've missed you, your mother and your siblings. Where have you been?"

She was trapped! She was tongue-tied! She hadn't thought up an excuse beforehand. She felt her face flush, she started to sweat.

"Please join me in the rectory for a cup of coffee. I'm sure the girls and Gladys would like to see you again."

The girls. Catherine wanted to run away. The three Knudson daughters acted like perfect angels. She knew them from school, but they didn't hang out together. They were pious girls from the right side of the tracks who went to Augsburg College, a Lutheran college in Minnesota. She always felt inadequate around them. They thought they knew everything.

Reverend Knudson led the way. As they walked into the parlor, Irma, the middle daughter, was startled by Catherine's presence. The expression on her face said *What are you doing here?* The minister invited Catherine to sit down while he went to fetch the rest of the family. As they gathered round in the parlor, he said, "Let us pray." The five women folded their hands and closed their eyes.

"Thank you, Lord, for bringing a lost sheep back into the fold. Let us pray for her forgiveness for her straying from your countenance. With your blessing we pray that Catherine will mend her wicked ways. In Romans 6:23 it is written, 'For the wages of sin is death, but the free gift of God is eternal life in Christ Jesus our Lord.'"

All Catherine heard was the ". . . the wages of sin is death." If she stopped sinning her mother would live. She felt in her heart that she had to mend her wicked ways and go back to church. Would singing in the choir help her mother get better faster? But how did he know that she had sinned? Did Pastor Knudson know she drank, smoked, danced, swore, and wore makeup, or did he only know that she hadn't been in church? She didn't ask.

When she got home, she went immediately to the back of her underwear drawer, where her half-full pack of Luckies sat next to a coin purse holding the small amount of money she had managed to salt away. It gave her comfort knowing it was there.

Henry didn't work on Sundays, but his mother still managed to get him and his one younger brother and two younger sisters to the Methodist Church. His father and older brother refused to go. Henry hadn't had the courage to revolt.

Catherine and Henry planned to go ice-skating in the afternoon. As they walked to the rink with their skates flung over their shoulders Catherine told Henry about church and Reverend Knudson's prayer with her and his whole family.

She believed she needed to stop sinning. She left her cigarettes at home and she vowed not to drink at the rink. She pledged to go to church every Sunday and she decided to join the choir. *I'm not sure I can go to work without makeup. I'll have to decide that tomorrow morning. But if I thought it would help my mother get well, I'd give that up, too.*

Henry did not grasp the depth of Catherine's new belief. "Do you really think giving up all these things you call sins will help your mother get well?"

"Reverend Knudson quoted a bible verse that said that 'the wages of sin is death.' That's in the Bible, Henry."

"I'm not as sure about that as you are. I know a lot of evil people who are not dying and good people who die. Your mother certainly isn't an evil person. I would not consider either of you a sinner. Martha is nearly a saint as far as I'm concerned." He conceded that it might be okay to give up cigarettes, although he didn't see how that would help her mother.

As soon as they got to the rink they began searching for wood to build a bonfire. Most of the wood was covered with snow, but they did have a few logs hidden behind a tree left over from the last fire. Soon after they got it burning, other friends showed up, pulling a sled filled with logs and kindling. Soon the fire was blazing.

Catherine, Henry, and their friends had made an ice rink on the bay of Green Bay over the Christmas holidays. It took them two days to push and pile enough snow to make a big enough rink.

Catherine and Henry held hands or one skated forward and the other backward like they were dancing. The train was the most fun. The person in front would crouch down; the second would lean over the first with hands on number one's knees and the rest lined up behind, all pushing forward. If one fell, so did the rest, and they would laugh uproariously. When their fingers and toes started to burn and tingle, they warmed up by the blazing fire on the snow-covered beach. The pint of bathtub gin passed through Catherine's hands into Henry's without her taking even a sip. Sitting on a log, she looked out over the endless sheet of ice and thought about her mother. She had forgotten Martha for the last couple hours, but she felt again the presence of that dark space. She forced herself back to the moment, the fire, the friends around her.

While skating she had noticed three red flags out on the Green Bay ice, indicating a net had been set. There were no sleds, fishermen or horses to be seen. She wondered if it was one of her father's nets and where her father might be.

As darkness fell, they all said their goodbyes and agreed to meet the next Sunday on Pine Hill to toboggan and sled. The smell of wood smoke lingered on Catherine's jacket for days, bringing back warm memories.

On Wednesday night she went to choir practice for the first time in more than two years. Catherine was in her glory when she was singing. Mrs. Jadin and the choir members were happy to have her back. She was by far the best alto they had. Her voice was strong and melodic as she sang from her diaphragm. Not one person told her she was a sinner. What a relief! She was surprised to find herself eager to sing in church the next Sunday.

Mike's truck was parked in the alley when she got home. Catherine noticed that he had shoveled a place for her car. It warmed her heart.

"Hi, Papa!" she said as she ran over to give him a kiss on the cheek. "I'm glad you're home. I haven't seen you since Sunday. I've been busy this week."

"Yeah, I missed ya too, Kiddo. Go on over to the stove. I fried up a few perch that I got out of the net we lifted today. Yeah, and I boiled up a few potatoes. Help yerself."

"Gee, thanks Papa. I'm starving and I didn't think we had any groceries. I forgot about the potatoes."

"Yeah, but these are the end of 'em. They still taste pretty good even if they were kind a shriveled up."

"How did you do on your lift? Was your net the one with the red flags? I noticed them when I was skating."

"Those were mine all right. We had a damn good haul today, Kiddo. One of the best we had in a while. We sold 'em all to Pederson's, except for the ones I brought home. There ain't nothin' like a fresh perch fried in lard. Be careful a' the bones."

"What a treat this is, Papa! Thanks for making supper."

He dug in his pocket and pulled out some money and put it on the table in front of Catherine. "Here's today's wages. Pay the bills and buy somethin' fer yerself. You've been workin' yer ass off lately. Don't think I didn't notice."

"Papa! Wow! What a guy you are. *Mange tak*, as Mom would say. I've been keeping most of the bills paid. We even have ice in the icebox. Maybe I'll buy us a big steak or something with the extra cash. And guess what else? I went to choir practice tonight for the first time in two years."

"Yeah? Whadja do that for?"

"Well, Pops, I've been praying a lot for Mom to get better. I don't know what else to do. But I thought maybe God could help. So, I went to church Sunday. The choir sounded like it could use an alto . . . and you know how I love to sing. It was good to be back. It lifted my feelings a little. I just finished practice."

"I know you and your ma don't like to hear me say this, but I think it's all a bunch of bullshit. That Knudson guy is nuts. All that crap about not having any fun, that don't make sense to me! If there is a God—and I ain't sure there is—he don't want people runnin' around scared to death to have a beer or two or do a little jig. Jesus H. Christ! God watchin the

Korn Krib to see how many beers are poured? Now singin' in the choir, there's nothin' wrong with that if ya like ta sing. But don't think God is gonna cure yer ma."

"That's sort of what Henry thinks, too. But don't we have to believe in something?"

"What's wrong with believin' in what we have around us? The bay, all the fish in the bay, the weather that lets us fish—the things that keep us alive!"

"But God created all of that!"

"How do we know that fer sure? Who wrote the damn Bible anyway? I don't believe it. Somebody could'a just made it up. Shit. I can make stuff up, too. I could say we have to believe in mermaids. I'd have some goddamned good stories about them half-dressed beauties. I can make guys laugh at my stories. None o' them Bible verses is funny. I have a lot more fun tellin' stories at Jimmy's than Knudson preachin' all that hell and damnation in church. He just wants to scare the shit out of everybody. That ain't no way to live."

"Papa, you could burn in hell talking like this!"

"Hey, there ya go! Burn in hell for talkin'? That's religion for ya!" Mike felt he'd scored a good point. "Hey, honey, if there's a hell, I'll be burnin' in it, but I think somebody made hell up, too. Nobody kin prove there's a hell—or a heaven, fer Christ's sake. Some poor suckers didn't have enough to do back then, so they wrote some scary stories. Why the hell did they write such sad shit?"

"You might be right, Papa. I like to have fun, too. I don't know what's wrong with dancing or going to see a picture show. But what if there really is a God? What if there really is a hell? I don't want to be in hell for all eternity."

"Here's what I believe, Kiddo. When yer dead, yer dead."

As soon as Catherine put her head on her pillow, the

dark cloud descended again. Her brain felt like a Ferris wheel gone wrong. Her thoughts were spinning so fast she lost her breath. She felt her belly tighten and bile rise in her throat. Pepper was licking her face. Catherine jumped out of bed, nearly falling. She was dizzy. Pepper jumped off the bed, too, close behind her. She pulled open her underwear drawer and grabbed her Luckys and matches. Throwing on a warm jacket over her nightgown she plunked herself down on the top step of the front porch. Her fingers were shaking as she tried to light the cigarette. Finally, she took the longest drag of her life. Nicotine never felt or tasted so good.

"Oh, Pepper, what are we going to do? I can't get my mind off Mom. I'm so scared. My heart is tearing apart. I can't sleep. When I eat, I feel like I'm going to throw up. Supper tasted good, but now it's all in my throat." She lit another cigarette. "God, Reverend Knudson. I'm sinning again. I abstained for three days but now I ruined it. I wish I had a slug of whiskey, too."

Chapter 12. We All Scream for Ice Cream (1937)

When Catherine tried to hold the receiver of the candlestick phone to her ear, her hand was shaking so hard she nearly dropped it. The call to Dr. Koepp was on its third ring, then the fourth. Oh, how she wished he would answer. He had told her last week that he might be able to make a diagnosis of Martha's condition today. She was panicked by what he might say, but she needed to hear something. The waiting had been horrible. Was her mother still alive? Following the doctor's orders, Catherine had not been to the asylum for three weeks. When she had last seen her mother the woman was comatose and barely breathing.

On the seventh ring, just as the switchboard operator was about to pull the plug, Dr. Koepp answered, breathing hard. She asked him about her mother.

"I'm glad you called, Catherine. On Wednesday they stopped giving her the insulin shock treatments. I saw her early this morning and she was awake but quite confused. She still has an IV, but the staff is introducing soft food. I still don't know how she will respond. It seems she's out of the coma, but she's not out of the woods."

A sudden sweet sense of relief swept through her. Her mother was alive! Other thoughts pressed. "Doctor Koepp, do we know if she lost her memory or has brain damage?"

"We won't know that for a while. I think it would be a good idea to visit her now. Seeing you might trigger a memory. Don't be surprised if she doesn't know who you are. That isn't unusual, and it's likely only temporary, but we won't know that for a while either. We have to be patient with her recovery. She's still very ill."

"Could I bring her something?"

"Actually, that might be a good idea. If you know of some soft food she might like that doesn't require chewing, it might be worth trying to feed her. She hasn't eaten for several weeks. All her nourishment has come from the IV. It will take some time for her to remember how to chew and swallow."

Catherine needed Clara to help her with this one. She did not want to go to the asylum alone, especially not knowing what to expect. On her way home from work she stopped to give Clara the news. As she walked in the front door, Tommy was flat on his back on the floor with Glenny's foot on his stomach, his right hand high above his head. Tommy was screaming at the top of his lungs for his mother.

"I won! I won! I beat you, Tommy! You're just a little crybaby." Sandy was sitting next to them engrossed with her rag doll paying no attention to the ruckus. Clara came running from the kitchen. "What's going on here?" she gently scolded. Catherine had seated herself on the floor next to Tommy to comfort him while trying to coax Glenny off Tommy. Catherine, as usual took four pieces of candy from her pocket.

"Glenny, come on over and sit by me." He got off Tommy when he saw the candy in her hand.

Tommy stopped screaming, too, when he realized

candy was in the offing. He quickly crawled over to Catherine.

"Sandy, what a good girl you are taking care of your baby. Come over here. You get first choice. Yellow, red, green or blue?" Sandy darted over. "'Wed', I want the 'wed' one."

"Well, then you get the red one, sweetie."

Glenny and Tommy were sitting on their knees, wide-eyed, quietly looking like perfect angels, hoping that despite the ruckus they might get a treat, too. Catherine put both her hands behind her back and asked the boys if they were ready to be nice to each other. They both nodded seriously.

"Tommy, since you were on the bottom, you get the next choice," she said as she put her closed fists in front of her. Glenny got the one in her other hand. By this time, Dicky was leaning far out of his mother's arms reaching for Catherine. "Canny, canny!" he said, laughing.

"Clara, while the troops are happy, pour me a cup of coffee, will you please? I need to talk to you about Mom. I talked to Dr. Koepp today."

After Catherine had told Clara everything the doctor told her, she asked Clara if she could get away from the kids the next day to go with her to the asylum.

"I can't do this on my own, Clare. I really need your help. I can't take Papa. She might backslide if she sees him now. At least she's living. If she sees both of us, maybe she'll perk up. Fingers crossed." She held up both hands with crossed fingers.

"I have to talk to Nels. He doesn't usually work on Saturday afternoons, so I think it'll be okay. It'll do him good to see what I have to put up with every hour of every day."

Catherine and Pepper went to bed before her father got home. She was relieved that she didn't have to go through the whole story with him. She could talk to him after the visit.

"Pepper, I'll do anything to keep our mother alive. I can take care of her if you can take care of me." Pepper licked every part of her face. She took it as a resounding yes!

What could Catherine bring her mother that she didn't have to chew and would be easy to swallow? Cream of Wheat was her mother's favorite breakfast food. Maybe she'd make some in the morning. The whole family loved the thick cream from the top of the bottle of milk. She thought about putting the cream into a jar and wrapping some sugar in a paper to put on the cereal after they got there. She tried to rest with that plan, but sleep did not come. Cold Cream of Wheat was yucky. She flopped around like a live herring in the bottom of a boat. She was racking her brain trying to think of something that would be more tempting.

"What would Mom really like?" she asked Pepper. As she lay cuddling with him she tried to think of what Martha liked most. She loved sweets, but she'd choke on cake or cookies. What was sweet that wouldn't cause her mother to choke? Ice cream! That was it! Martha loved ice cream. Catherine remembered when her mother had made it a couple of times and it was hard work. She churned the cream, sugar and eggs until her arm nearly fell off, but it was delicious.

Catherine didn't have time or the ingredients to make it. Could Clara make ice cream? Not enough time before this visit, she realized.

Suddenly a light bulb went on. She remembered the new shop on Main Street that opened recently. A huge picture in the window always caught her eye. It was an image of a giant cone topped with a huge scoop of pink ice cream. As far as she knew, it was the first time ice cream was available in a store in Marinette. Her frugality had kept her away, but now her curiosity was piqued. With the extra money from Papa, she could splurge on ice cream for her mother. She didn't know how they packaged ice cream or how much it cost, but she wanted to find out. Catherine felt uplifted by the thought and was almost positive Martha would like it. She could still bring the Cream of Wheat and trimmings just in case the ice cream plan didn't pan out.

Not wanting to get tangled up with the little ones, she blew her horn to let Clara know she had arrived. It was hard to predict what chaos was going on in that house at any given moment.

The kids were a handful and too much for Catherine today. Clara came running out of the house pulling her coat on as she carefully closed the door to be sure there were no fingers in it.

Catherine heard the screaming from inside the home even though the car windows were rolled up. Clara ran to the car and got in puffing with her hat askew, her coat unbuttoned and her gloves in one hand.

"You look frazzled, my dear sister. I could hear the commotion."

"I'm sorry Mom is so sick, but I'm so damn happy to get out of the house. I'm inside with those kids twenty-four hours a day. They sob if I'm out of their sight. Let Nels deal with them for once. He won't know where the heck to start. I know he'll keep them safe, but he'll be nuts." Clara chuckled. "He may have a lamp shade on his head by the time I get home and it will take me all night to clean up after them, but maybe he'll appreciate me a little more after this. Hah, that'll be the day! I'm thinking Mom might be right about men being good for nothing, but I still love the bastard."

"How you talk about your husband!"

"All I can say is, just wait!"

Catherine was not interested in marital advice. She had something more important she wanted to share. "Hey, Sis, I have a humdinger of an idea. Wait 'til you hear this! Do you know about the ice cream shop on Main Street?"

"Oh, yeah. Nels mentioned it. He said we'd have to take the kids in the summer. That will be a cold day in hell when that happens. But maybe I'll get lucky. Why do you think they opened an ice cream shop in the winter?"

"Don't know. Maybe they wanted to practice so they'd be ready for summer. Anyway, I've never been in it, but as I was not sleeping last night, I got to thinking of what Mom really liked to eat that was soft. I thought of Cream of Wheat. She likes that for breakfast, but it's not very exciting. So, we know she loves sweets, but I could only think of the cakes and pies she couldn't chew. Then, wham-o! Ice cream! Remember when she made it? I knew we didn't have time to make it ourselves and then I remembered the new ice cream shop. I made what the judge would call 'an executive decision' to stop and see what they have to offer that might be good for Mom. I hope you don't mind."

"Good thinking, Cat."

There was a diagonal parking place right in front of the shop. As they reached the door they encountered a huge hand-painted pink and white sign in the glass door, "I Scream! You Scream! We All Scream for Ice Cream!" The delicious smell of sugar and vanilla met them as they opened the door. The small shop was pink—counter, stools, tabletops, walls, even the curtains. Everything was pink except the small wrought iron chairs with curly backs next to the two small pink tables. A tall middle-aged man with a pink bow tie and white shirt and pants stood behind the counter. He called out, "Welcome to Mack's Ice Cream Parlor. I'm Mack and I need your business." There were no other customers in the shop.

Catherine and Clara were impressed. They had never seen anything like this before.

While Clara was peeking into every nook and cranny in the shop, Catherine spoke with Mack. "I've never seen an ice cream shop before, Mr. Mack. What's this all about?" Catherine asked.

"Just call me Mack. None of that 'mister' stuff. I'm really sticking my neck out here. Ice cream is the craze now, as you know. It's hard to make at home with all the churning and freezing it takes. Do you have a freezer in your house?" Mack asked.

"Nope, we have an ice box. Joe brings us a block of ice every week when it gets warmer. We sure don't need it now. Everything's on the back porch."

"See, that's what I mean. But you'll wish you had one in a few months. I put all my savings into this place. I sold my house, my bicycle, everything I owned to open this ice cream parlor. The bank helped me out, too. I sleep in a room in the back of the shop for now. The Depression is easing up, people are going back to work, and so I'm trying to get ahead of the game." He stepped back and turned toward his big freezer. "What do you think of this freezer I have here? Isn't she a beauty?" he asked, patting the top of the big machine.

"Is it electric?" Catherine asked.

"It sure is—and let me tell you—it cost a pretty penny! I have a brand-new electric mixer, too, so I don't have to churn the ingredients. It's quite a setup, even if I have to say so myself."

As he told Catherine about the freezer he smiled like the Cheshire cat. "You won't see another one of these parlors anywhere near here for a long time."

"Wow! You really went all the way, didn't you? That's quite an investment," Catherine said. "I hate to ask you this, Mack, but you're a guy. Why all the pink?"

"Yeah, good question. It's a little too much for me, but I let my Mom talk me into it. She said the kids and their moms would love it. What do you think?"

"I think she's right. It's a keen place."

"How would you like to sample my delicious concoctions? I have three flavors—vanilla, chocolate, and strawberry." He pointed at the containers.

"I want a sample of every one! My sister would like the same." Catherine was giggling with excitement.

"Comin' up," Mack said. He was as excited as Catherine. They stood there for a moment smiling at each other.

"Clara, get over here. Mack is getting us samples of his ice cream." After the first bite, Clara felt giddy.

"This is delicious—but it's just a tease. I need more," Clara said. "How can you make ice cream this delicious? I've never had anything that tasted this good. I'm in heaven . . ." After a little more savoring and lip-smacking, the cook in Clara came to the fore. "How can you make strawberry ice cream in the winter?"

"My dad and mom have a dairy farm out on Highway 64. Mom puts up strawberries from her garden every summer. I use her preserves to flavor the vanilla. I get cream and milk straight from our Holsteins and eggs from the chickens. My pants are a little tighter since I've been doing so much tasting," he said, smiling broadly and patting his belly.

Catherine and Clara snickered.

"Our mother is in the hospital and we would like to bring her some ice cream," Catherine said. "I'm thrilled we found this place. Not just for our mother, but for us. Do you serve ice cream to go?"

They walked out of Mack's Ice Cream Parlor holding cones piled high with strawberry ice cream and a pint of vanilla for Martha. They didn't have to worry about the ice cream melting. It was freezing outside and almost freezing in the heater-less car. They drove to the asylum bundled up in their warm winter clothes eating ice cream cones, which let them forget for some moments that they were about to visit an extremely ill mother.

"It's so nice to spend time with you alone, Clara. I miss you all at home. It gets pretty lonely when mom's having one of her non-talking spells and Papa's not around. Thank God for Pepper."

Driving toward the large sterile building on the icy driveway, they didn't speak.

Catherine was focusing on her driving to keep from sliding into a snowbank. Her balding tires skidded on the ice. She was very aware that getting stuck would be a serious problem out here in the sticks. Clara was scared, but her fear had nothing to do with the driving conditions. She was afraid of seeing her mother and had no idea what to expect.

When they finally reached the asylum Clara cried out, "This looks like a prison, for God's sake! I'm surprised it doesn't have bars on the windows. I don't want to go in, Catherine."

"You haven't seen anything yet. The inside is much worse than the outside. Hold your nose or don't breathe when you get in. It smells like piss."

"How can you bear it? I don't know how I can do this Catherine."

"You can do this. Buck up. I'm not even eighteen and I

made myself do it. Follow me and I'll show you how," Catherine said. *She's supposed to be the strong one,* Catherine thought. *I'm the youngest in the family. This doesn't make sense. Am I supposed to do everything?*

They walked down the long hall flanked on both sides with "the ghosts," as Catherine viewed the moaning, drooling, semi-comatose patients sitting in wheelchairs. Every sound they made echoed from the mile-high ceilings. Catherine walked behind her sister in case Clara fainted. She had a spirit much more tender than Catherine's. She didn't discipline her children because she didn't want to hurt their feelings.

When they reached the nurses' station at the end of the long hall, a woman in a white uniform with a dour look glanced up at them as though they were intruders. Catherine told her they were here to visit Martha Sabinsky. After looking at page after page of patients' names, she said, "We moved her. She's on the west wing now." Then she walked away.

Catherine loudly called after her, "Where is the west wing?"

"Where do you think I'm going? Follow me," the nurse said with disdain. Catherine dared to ask how her mother was doing.

"You'll see when you get there."

Clara was noticeably shaken. Catherine touched her arm to steady her. "What's in the bag?" the attendant asked.

"Food," Catherine replied, an angry edge in her voice.

"Don't be giving your mother anything that will make her sick. We have enough to do around here without the visitors making it worse. Does the doctor know you're bringing her food?"

"Yes. Actually, he suggested it," Catherine said through gritted teeth.

The ward in the west wing was not quite as crowded or depressing as the one where she had first seen her mother. It was painted white and had a window at the far end with a yellow curtain. Maybe that was a good sign. They noticed some of the patients were lying on their cots with their eyes open, while others were sleeping. They found Martha in the last bed on the left near the window. She was lying on her side with her eyes closed. Her face was gray and drawn.

Catherine touched her mother's shoulder and shook it gently. Martha's eyes opened slowly.

"Do I need to get another shot?" her mother mumbled.

"Look, Mom, it's me, Catherine, and Clara's here, too." Clara stepped into Martha's view. "We're here to visit you. You were sleeping when I was here last," Catherine said. "It's a miracle you're awake now."

The daughters sat on either side of the bed and held Martha's bony wrinkled hands. There was an IV in her left arm.

"Are you nurses? Too many nurses."

They had to strain to hear her. "We're not nurses, Mom. We're your daughters?"

Martha closed her eyes again. She seemed too tired to talk.

After rubbing her arms, head and back for a while, Catherine nudged her again. "Mom, can you wake up for a minute? We have a treat for you." Her eyes remained closed.

"We're going to prop you up on your pillows, to keep you from choking while you taste your treat." Catherine said. Clara put a dab of the ice cream on her Mother's closed lips. It melted down the sides of her mouth.

"Clara, look," Catherine said softly. "I think she might be opening her lips a tiny bit. Put some more on her lips."

Martha let more of the sweet soft ice cream into her

mouth the second time. After a few more tastes, her tongue peaked out through her lips. She wanted more. By the time she had enough, her mouth and chin were covered with the sticky remains. Hopefully, she had as much on the inside as on the outside. Martha fell asleep while Clara was washing her face.

The sisters felt better leaving than they did coming into the dreadful place. They chatted all the way home in the cold car. Seeing their mother respond to the ice cream was a step in the right direction. Clara said she would like to join Catherine if she went to the asylum again the next weekend.

"You bet, Clare. I'm happy to share the load."

Catherine drove out three nights after work the next week to visit her mother and feed her ice cream. On every visit Martha seemed to swallow a little bit more. The ice cream stayed frozen in the car until it had all been eaten. Martha still didn't recognize Catherine, but she could hardly wait to get the ice cream in her mouth. When Martha asked where she was, Catherine told her she was in the hospital.

"In the hospital?" she asked with a quizzical look on her face. "Why?"

"You stopped eating and talking. You rocked in your chair and then took to your bed. We had to bring you here, so you wouldn't starve to death."

"Do you work here?"

"No, Mom. I'm your daughter. I live with you at home."

Catherine tried not to take her mother's inquiries personally. She remembered Dr. Koepp had told her that Martha might lose her memory from the shock treatments, but it still hurt that Martha didn't recognize her.

"I'm tired now," Martha said, and she closed her eyes and went back to sleep.

It was a long road back to health. After six weeks in the asylum, Martha was transferred to Marinette General. There she stayed until she was eating three meals a day and appeared strong enough to go home. She had recovered some of her memory by then. She recognized Catherine, Mike, Clara and the grandkids, but it took a while for additional recall. There were some things she never remembered again. Fortunately, the asylum would be one of them. By late winter she was not only back to her old self, but she was on fire.

During the months of her mother's recovery Catherine had some time to breathe. Death was no longer an issue. She and Henry spent more time together. He wanted to get married, to settle down. Although she was in love with Henry, she wasn't ready to give up her life. She was looking for adventure. She wasn't quite eighteen yet. Her mother's recovery gave her the space she had yearned for. She had no interest in being tied down with a bunch of kids like Clara.

Chapter 13. Goosebumps (1937)

Everyone at work liked Catherine. She had a great sense of humor like her father, but without the raunchy edge. She was game for just about anything. Now that her mother's health was no longer a worry, she was ready to have some fun. During lunch in the staff room one snowy day, the court photographer, Donny Metzger, approached her.

"Catherine, how would you like to pose for a picture for the *Eagle-Star*?"

"Really? Do you want to put a picture of the judge's secretary taking notes at a trial? That seems pretty boring." They all laughed.

"Not exactly. But . . . well . . . actually, I'm not sure you have enough courage to do this." He knew this would hook her.

"We'll see. Spit it out," she said with a twinkle in her eye. She couldn't wait to hear his challenge.

"First of all, I need to know if you have a sexy bathing suit."

"What? This might be too much for a girl from Menekaunee and Our Savior's Lutheran! I have a bathing suit, but I don't think it's sexy."

"Okay, here's the deal," Donny explained. "I have this

great idea. Do you have skis?"

"No, I don't have skis. Where is this going?"

"Catherine, you're the only gal I know who'd be crazy enough to put on a swimming suit and boots—that's all you'd have on except for a hat and gloves—and stand on skis holding poles on the top of a hill in the snow. I'm sure the paper would publish it. I need to get my foot in the door at the *Eagle-Star* and this picture might do it for me."

"Oh, I get it. You want to be a hot-shot camera guy by freezing me to death!" Everyone laughed. "What do I get out of it besides pneumonia?"

"You might get your picture in the paper and I'll buy you a beer!"

"Go, Catherine, go! Go, Catherine, go!" Betty and the others were chanting.

"Okay, Donny, you got yourself a deal—if you make it *two* beers!"

The clerk of courts stuck his head in the door and told them to keep it down. "It's time for all of you to get back to work! What's going on here anyway? You're having way too much fun," he said with a grin.

Donny told him they were going to Pine Hill on Saturday to take Catherine's picture.

When the clerk heard the details, he said he said he wouldn't miss it for the world.

Martha was rocking in her chair in the bedroom on Saturday afternoon and saw Catherine putting on her bathing suit.

"What in the world are you doing? It's snowing and you're putting on a bathing suit? That doesn't seem right to me."

Catherine was delighted to hear her mother say three

sentences in a row that made sense. Martha knew that bathing suits and snow didn't go together. Catherine was beginning to think the shock treatments had worked. Martha was still confused but she didn't seem to be depressed. It was a miracle. Maybe Catherine's going to church or singing in the choir helped, too, even if she hadn't followed through on quitting smoking or avoiding the occasional beer.

"Oh, Mom, you're not going to believe this, but I'm going to have my picture taken in my bathing suit standing on skis in the snow."

"You're going to catch your death of cold," Martha said, but then seemed to lose interest in what her daughter was doing.

"It'll be fun, Mom. I want to have fun," she chirped. "Henry doesn't think it's a good idea either. I invited him to come, but I don't think he will. He's a stick-in-the-mud sometimes. Well, come to think of it, most of the time lately . . ."

When Betty pulled up in front of her house, Catherine was ready. She had her bathing suit under her clothes, snow pants, and heavy wool jacket. They drove to the edge of town and hiked into the woods and up Pine Hill, where Catherine had agreed to meet Donny. She was surprised to see so many of the courthouse gang waiting for her. She ran up to her friends and shouted, "I'm ready to ski! Just wait 'til you see my fancy ski clothes!" They clapped and laughed. A merry group they were.

One of guys from the sheriff's office yelled out. "You're too chicken to do this. You'll freeze that cute little ass off." Everyone laughed.

Other hecklers joined in, but Catherine was ready for them. "You don't know who you're talking to, guys! You just wait and see! Donny, you'd better get those beers opened up!"

When she got to the top of one of the toboggan runs, she saw a pair of skis with a pole stuck in the snow on either side. It was a perfect winter day, a postcard winter wonderland. The dark green limbs of the pines were weighted down with fresh snow, more than three inches deep. The toboggan runs were pristine. The contrast of black bare trunks and dark branches of the pines against the stark white blanket of snow was spectacular. As the sun burst through the clouds the snow sparkled, and scattered snowflakes danced in a light breeze.

Don asked Catherine to stand on the skis before she disrobed while he set up his Kodak box camera on a tripod. When he said he was ready, she spread her heavy coat out on the snow, took off her clothes and tossed them onto the open coat. She immediately felt the cold, but the line of pine trees on the hill was a buffer against the icy puffs of wind. The plan was for her to take off her sweater, pull on her chook, take off her pants, put on her boots and mitts, and jump on the skis. Before she grabbed the poles, Betty came over with a flask. *Bless you*, Catherine thought, as she took a swig to warm her belly. At least *that* would be warm. It took all her courage not to shiver.

She'd show them.

She grabbed the poles, bent her knees, and straightened her arms in front of her, hoping she looked like she was ready to fly down the hill. *Is this what skiers should look like?* There was a big smile on her face. Don shouted for her to keep stock-still, not to move a muscle. It was hard at this point, because she had begun to shiver, and her body was covered with goose bumps, but she kept a big grin on her face as she waved the ski poles around to show her prowess. Betty and the others cheered her on. When Donny was finished shooting, Catherine jumped off the skis and put on her clothes as Betty handed them to her piece by piece.

"I smell wood smoke. Did someone make a fire?" Catherine asked. She was in her element—a bright and jolly group of friends—and she was having a ball.

Don put his camera carefully into its case and wrapped the whole thing in a big blanket.

They walked together over to the clearing where the gang was sitting around the blazing fire.

"That was a blast," she raised her arms and shouted. "Where's the beer you promised me, Don? I'm ready. Anybody else wanna take off their clothes?" There was a resounding "Hell, no!" from the crowd.

Catherine was the hero of the day. Her friends gathered around, each raising a bottle, impressed that she had the courage to stand in a bathing suit in the icy weather. Catherine's friends liked her willingness to try just about anything. They spent the rest of the afternoon sitting around the fire talking and singing. Someone unloaded a couple of toboggans and people crowded on to fly down the hill. It had been a memorable afternoon.

When Betty dropped Catherine off at home, Henry's truck was parked on the street. He wasn't in it, so Catherine figured he must be inside.

"Hi, Mom! Hi, Henry! How are you guys doing?" Catherine was still in the bubble of the exciting day.

It had been cold on Pine Hill, but the atmosphere in the house was frigid. Neither Martha nor Henry seemed happy to have her home. They acknowledged her with a nod.

Henry spoke for the glum pair. "It's not how we're doing, Catherine. More to the point, how are you doing after being so foolish? You'll be lucky if you don't get pneumonia."

"Are you kidding, Henry?" Catherine exclaimed. "I had a ball! I was only in my bathing suit for a few minutes. Lots of my friends from the courthouse were there! They made a big fire and I warmed up in a hurry. We sat around the fire having a jolly old time. I was sorry that you didn't show up."

Henry just shook his head. "I don't know what's come over you these days, Catherine. Your mother and I were worried sick about you. You shouldn't scare your mother like this just as she's starting to come around."

"Well, I don't know what's wrong with you these days, Henry. You're such a stick-in-the-mud. You never seem to want to have fun. Sure, I like to sit around and neck, too, but I've decided this is my time to shine. I have a little money and a car. I'll be eighteen in a couple months and I plan to make the most of it."

She paused, looked first at Henry's face, then her mother's and added, "I don't think my mother was scared until you told her she should be. I didn't do anything foolish! And for your information, I know how to take care of my mother just fine."

Late Monday afternoon, Catherine was sitting at her desk, transcribing her notes from an earlier hearing, when Roger, the paperboy, placed a newspaper squarely on her desk. He usually threw it on the floor just inside the door.

"What did I do to get the paper delivered to my desk, Roger?"

The boy faced her across the desk, his dirty gray bag filled with newspapers hanging heavily on his shoulder. The courthouse was one of the first stops on his route, and the loaded bag hung almost to his knees. "D-d-don't you know, Miss C-C-Catherine?" His stutter was always stronger when he was excited about something. "L-l-look!" he said, holding the paper up. "Th-that's you, ain't it, Miss Catherine? You sure are p-p-pretty!"

"Oh, my gosh, that *is* me, Roger! Don said he'd get my picture in the paper, but I didn't believe him. And it's on the front page! Wow! Wait until Henry and my mother see that! Yikes!"

The picture on the front page above the fold of the *Marinette Eagle-Star* featured Catherine standing on the top of the hill, wearing her Lastex bathing suit and ski boots, a chook and gloves, standing on a pair of skis, and holding ski poles as though she were about to make a downhill run. Sadly, she thought, because it was a black-and-white picture, her bright red swimsuit didn't offer as striking a contrast to the dark tree trunks and white snow, but it was still a zany, freewheeling image. Fortunately, her goosebumps didn't show.

"I'm famous, Roger! It must be a slow news day." She gave him her biggest smile. "Thanks for the special delivery right to my desk. Do you by chance have an extra paper? I'd like to show my mother and dad. By the way, I like the way your knickers match your cap. You look sporty. How old are you?"

"I'm t-twelve. Gee, thanks, M-miss Catherine. It's a n-new c-c-cap. Sorry. My boss c-c-ounts out the p-p-papers I have to deliver. If-f I miss a delivery I have to p-pay for it mys-s-elf."

"Oh, no you don't Roger! How much do I owe you?"

"T-t-two cents."

Catherine reached into her purse in the desk drawer closest to her chair and pulled out three pennies. "Give two to your boss and take the other for yourself."

"You're f-f-famous and I kn-know you! I'm g-g-gonna tell my f-f-friends about you! Th-th-thanks for the penny!"

As Roger made his rounds of courthouse offices with the afternoon paper, those arriving at the judge's office included people Catherine didn't even know. People praised her courage, called her a star, laughed at the antic. Judge Sullivan, returning from a meeting, found a throng around Catherine's desk.

"What's going on here? Are we having a party? Is it five o'clock already?" He wasn't angry, just very surprised and puzzled, and then Betty held the paper's front page in front of his face. He studied it for a moment, then looked up at Catherine, standing behind her desk.

"Catherine, is that you? What in the hell were you doing?" He tried to yell over the commotion, then turned to Betty. "What was she doing?"

"What does it look like?"

"It looks like she's skiing in a bathing suit, but that doesn't make any sense at all. But, as my kids might say, it's pretty 'keen' or 'swell,' if it's true."

The judge studied the photo more closely. "It says, 'Photo by Donald Metzger.'" He called out, "Donny, are you around here?"

"Right here, Judge." He made his way through the throng.

"Please tell me you didn't use the county's camera!"

"Nope, Judge. I used my own camera. The office camera is an antique in the worst kind of way. Probably was used in the Civil War."

The judge laughed. "What a bunch of troublemakers," he said, and then he saw that Catherine was climbing onto the desk to see everyone in the room.

"Get down before you kill yourself, girl! You never cease to amaze me, but I'm happy when you're happy. That's when you do your best work." Turning to the court photographer, he said, "By the way, the picture is very clever,

Don. I can't wait to hear the whole story." Raising his voice just a bit, he addressed the office crowd. "Now, do you think we could all get back to work? Please?"

The unexpected office gathering had put Catherine a little behind schedule and she left work late. She made her regular stop at nearby Goodfellows to buy a pack of Luckys, but today was anything but regular. She had barely opened the familiar heavy wooden door with its stained-glass window when someone at the bar wolf-whistled and raised his glass.

"Hey, come over here and sit on my knee, Sweetie."

Another man, paper in hand, said to no one in particular. "That's the sexy broad who works for the judge. Look here! She's on the front page of the paper."

Catherine's job for the judge had made her known around town and particularly around Dunlap Square as "the judge's right-hand gal." Now she had a new footnote to her local fame.

When she arrived home, she threw the paper on the kitchen table, and called out to her mother, who was resting on the bed. "I brought home the paper, Mom."

Martha walked slowly to the kitchen table, sat down rubbing her eyes. Catherine noted she was fully dressed. "Why the heck did you bring me the paper? My eyes don't work so well."

Her speech was slow, soft, but the fact that she was speaking at all, and the fact that she was wearing more than a robe, was significant. She had been home from the hospital for only a couple of weeks, but she was making steady progress.

Martha slowly unrolled the paper. She moved it away from herself and then back, trying to get the big front-page picture into focus. Catherine sat alongside her mother, waiting for the moment. Then Martha swung her head, looked at her daughter. "Catherine! Is that you in this picture?"

"Yeah, Mom," Catherine said gleefully. "It's me, all right."

"It *is* you! Well, I'll be darned! You got your picture on the front page of the paper . . ." Martha stared at the photo proudly. "By gosh, this is the first time a Sabinsky ever got in the paper—for anything good, I mean. You're pretty cute. Why did Henry make a fuss about this, I wonder?"

"Mom, you're talking! You're smiling. You're dressed. I think you're cured!"

Martha looked startled. "What do you mean cured? I'm fine, just as I've always been."

Was this what Dr. Koepp meant about memory, Catherine wondered. This was much more serious than she had supposed, thinking it had only meant her mother might forget names or dates. She might not even remember she had been sick, depressed, and near death. At the moment Martha seemed even better than her past self, even had a twinkle in her eye.

How much had Martha really improved? Catherine thought she'd try her out. "Hey, Mom. Let's walk over to Stepniak's Market and buy something special for supper."

"We've got something special for supper already. I killed a chicken this morning. We're having chicken stew and dumplings. Can't you smell it? I got the second to the last jar of beans out of the fruit cellar. I made some rolls, too. I've been hungry for a big meal."

Catherine realized that she had been so focused on the revelation in the newspaper she had failed to notice the good smells, but she couldn't fail to do so now. Of course her mother was hungry! She had barely eaten before her hospitalization and was on an IV at the asylum. But this sudden appetite for a feast! And killing a chicken! And making the whole dinner! Catherine was ready to believe that the cloud of Martha's illness that had hung over the family was gone.

"Catherine, sit back down and tell me about that picture."

She gave her mother a big hug before she told her the whole story, starting with the joyful gathering on Pine Hill that Martha and Henry hadn't wanted to hear about on Saturday and continuing all the way to the gathering in the judge's office and the wolf whistling at Goodfellow's. Martha laughed joyously, proud of the friendships that Catherine was building. Just then Mike came in the back door with his earflaps down and the collar of his wool jacket buttoned up to his chin. His over-sized nose and cheeks were as almost as red as his birth mark.

"It's colder than a well-digger's ass out there," he proclaimed as he stomped the snow off his boots and wiped his runny nose with the back of his glove. "What's all the commotion about?"

"What are you doing home so early, Papa?"

"I thought I'd come back a little early and start some supper to help out some. I brought fresh perch home I thought I'd fry up."

"Mom beat you to it, Papa. She killed a chicken. There's chicken stew and fresh baked rolls for supper."

"What the hell got inta yah, Martha? I thought you was sick! Tell you what, though, I'll eat your stew over my fish any day. Catherine, put the fish in the back hall in front of the door to keep 'em cold 'til tomorrow."

Martha almost smiled at Mike, an action that Catherine found a little disquieting. From deep depression to smiling at her brutish husband? It was a small odd note in an otherwise wonderful moment.

As Mike sat down at the kitchen table, he noticed the newspaper.

"What's this rag doin' here? Since when did we start gettin' the paper?" He did a double take. "What the hell? Catherine, is that you on the front page in a bathing suit? *In the snow?* Are you nuts?"

As Catherine was telling Mike about how this picture came to be, he started to laugh. "Well I'll be goddamned. First you graduate from school with some big fancy award, then you get a job with a highfalutin' judge, and now you're on the front page of the goddamn *Eagle-Star*. What'er ya gonna do next to surprise the shit out of the old man? I don' know if this old ticker can stand much more. I need to drink to you standing half naked on the front page!" He stood up, made a circle with his index finger and thumb, brought it to the front of his dripping nose, turned it to catch the drips, and wiped his finger and thumb on his pants to dry off his hand. He pulled two cold ones out of the case in the back hall and offered one to Catherine.

She winced but knew better than to remind him to use a hanky and said, "No thanks, Papa, but thanks for the laugh. I think it's pretty funny myself. I can't wait to go to choir practice and see what the old biddies have to say. I wonder if I'll get a lecture from Sonnack."

"Don't talk to me about that holier-than-thou asshole hypocrite. Who cares what he thinks? Just because I drink a little too much don' make me a bad person. He won' even let me join the church and I don' give a shit."

Conversation about a preacher came to an abrupt halt when Martha placed in the center of the table a bowl of steaming mashed potatoes with a slab of melting butter. She followed that up with a pot of golden chicken swimming in thick, rich gravy, laced with onions and carrots.

Martha was smiling and proud as she looked over the table. They sat down to a lovely family dinner, their first in months. Catherine was going to say how happy she was, but she didn't want to jinx it.

The next evening Henry stopped by after a beer delivery. "Why didn't you tell me you were going to have your picture in the paper?" Catherine, Mike and Martha were still at the kitchen table. Henry sounded angry, as though he had been tricked.

"Can't you even say hello? We're just finishing up leftovers of a delicious dinner that Mom made yesterday. If you didn't look so crabby, I'd offer you some."

"I just want to know what was going on." He declined to sit.

"When I invited you to join us on Saturday, I just wanted to surprise you. Everyone at work thought it was aces! I wanted you to be part of the fun. And after you were such a stick-in- the-mud when I got home, I didn't want to talk about it with you anymore."

"Well, I wish you'd at least have warned me it was going to be on the front page of the paper. Christ, my mother almost fainted when she saw your picture. She said only a loose woman would pose like that. It doesn't help our situation with my mother. It's embarrassing for me. You should have heard what some of the bartenders and guys in the bars said about you."

"I'd love to hear what they said."

"I don't even want to repeat it," Henry said with marked disdain.

"Awe, come on Henry, I can take it." Catherine sneered and walked into the front room.

Henry followed. They plopped down at each end of the couch.

"How do you think it feels when someone says 'You got a hot one there. She's a looker. You better keep an eye on her. You can't tell who she might hook up with.' And even worse, my mother said, 'See what happens when you get chummy with a girl who comes from that part of town?' How am I supposed to feel about comments like that?"

"Well, aren't you just Mr. La-Di-Da!" Catherine sneered. "My own father was impressed and my mother thought it was funny as hell, and even the judge thought it was pretty cute, so put that in your puritanical pipe and smoke it! I'm really getting tired of your mother looking down on me. I was merely having fun with my friends." She felt herself moving from irritation to anger. "I didn't hurt a soul! I keep my nose to the grindstone all week! I practically run this household! And now you're all over me about having a little fun. You ain't seen nothin' yet, Henry Goodman!"

Henry knew in his heart that Catherine was right, that his mother would find any reason to criticize his choice of a girlfriend. He *had* declined to come, he *had* opened up on her when she got back from the Pine Hill. He sighed as he put his chin on his chest. Mike came limping into the living room, thinking he could patch things up.

"Don' be listenin' to these women, Henry. Yer a hell of a guy. Come on, let's go down to Jimmy's and have a quick one. That'll make ya feel better. At least it works fer me."

"Papa, you stay out of this! Fifteen minutes ago you were proud of me and now you're siding with Henry. Both of you get out of my sight!" She rose and went back into the kitchen to help her mother with the dishes. Mike and Henry drove away in Henry's truck.

"You're right, Mom. Men are *good . . . for . . . nothing!*"

Henry made himself scarce for the next few days and Catherine didn't miss him. The judge's calendar was jam-packed, meaning more work and longer hours for Catherine. To her delight, she found that when she walked in the door each night Martha had the table set for three and had supper ready. Even Papa showed up. She was living a dream. This was like a family featured in the *Saturday Evening Post!* Martha was making a remarkable recovery. The house was spotless, the smell of freshly-baked bread wafted from the oven, seed packets were spread out on the kitchen sideboard next to Martha's garden journal, the icebox had a block of ice in it, the bill at Stepniak's market had been paid in full. Life was as it should be. Except for Henry's absence, Catherine was walking on air. She was finding, though, that she sort of liked the freedom she had without him, a freedom from the claim he seemed to think he had on her.

The beer truck pulled up in front of the house late on Saturday morning. When she opened the door, Henry was standing there with a smile on his face. She didn't smile back. Her stubborn streak was showing and he knew it. She could give him the cold shoulder for days at a time and it drove him crazy.

"Can I come in?" Henry asked timidly.

"My father's not home, if that's who you're here to see."

"Come on, Catherine. You know I'm here to see you."

"It sure didn't seem like it the other night. You and my dad walked out without even saying good-bye. Did you even think of how that made me feel? I just don't get what's wrong with having a little fun."

"Come on, Honey. I came over to see if you'd go for a ride with me. Maybe we could drive to Cedar River. I heard they're having iceboat races up there. Curly Erickson has a boat in this race. He's a bartender at one of my regular stops, nice guy and full of hell. We could pack a little lunch. I have some beer in the truck and a full tank of gas. It would be fun. You said you wanted to have fun . . ."

After a little more coaxing, Catherine agreed, but she still wasn't smiling. She threw together some sandwiches of leftover chicken on Martha's homemade bread—the soft warm loaf was hard to cut—along with salted peanuts in the shell and a couple of the brownies her mother had baked that morning. They rode in the truck silently until they got to the shoreline on Green Bay at Cedar River. At least ten iceboats with furled sales were queued up just on the other side of a small ice shove. This was a local dwarf of the giant shoves, sometimes seven feet high, that would line the Green Bay shoreline as spring came.

The boats—bare beams with three metal runners and a big mast—were sitting at the starting line as Catherine and Henry arrived. Curly spotted Henry. "Waiting for a little more wind!" he yelled.

Someone gave a signal, a dozen racers began pushing their boats, swung inside the small cockpits, lay back, and the race was on.

"These guys are really moving," Catherine said excitedly. She was jumping up and down to keep warm in the ten-degree temperature and to cheer Curly on. She didn't know him, but it was keen to have someone to cheer for.

"Yeah. Curly told me with the right wind and good ice he could get up to fifty miles an hour. That's too fast for me. If you got thrown on the ice, you could bust your head open. Nope. Not my sport," Henry said.

"A few years ago, my friend Davy took me ice-boating at the Menekaunee flats. It's scary lying on the boat so close to the ice. We weren't going fifty miles an hour either. But it was a blast! There were two other boats out there, too. We almost crashed!" Catherine chirped.

"You're a daredevil, Cat."

"I like it when you call me Cat," she said, as she put her arm through his. This squabble was over.

Chapter 14. Parking Can Be Dangerous (1937)

March came in like a lion, and while the *Farmers' Almanac* said this boded well for the coming of spring, at the moment two feet of snow from the worst blizzard of the year blanketed Marinette. Most of the city would be shut down for nearly a week, but Catherine was pretty sure that "justice must still be served," and the day after the storm she bundled up and set out to walk to work. She knew the bald tires on her car wouldn't allow her to even get out of the alley, but trudging through snow drifts until she got to a plowed street was hard work. On the bright side, the wind had sculpted the snow into alluring shapes that sparkled in the bright morning sun. The only sounds Catherine could hear was that of her boots squeaking through the fresh snow. In the ghostly silence of a shut-down city she trudged to the courthouse between giant snowbanks on Main Street.

By the time she got there she was overheated in her winter slacks and heavy coat. The courthouse steps were covered with drifted snow, clear in some places and capped with huge drifts through which she battled to reach the front door, sometimes on hands and knees. She nearly cried when she reached the top step and found the front entrance blocked with a snowdrift three feet high. She felt the courthouse key in her pocket, but even if she unlocked the door she had no strength to open it against the mound of snow.

She sat in the snow catching her breath and tried to figure out what to do next. *Will I have to sit here for hours before I can get in*, she wondered. *Should I just turn around and walk back home?* It was better to just rest, still warm from the long walk and the climb up the steps. She flopped back on the soft puffy blanket right there in front of the door. The magnificent baby-blue sky—one of those wonderful post-storm skies—made her want to fly like an angel, soar in that space. She began to move her arms and legs to make an angel in the snow, just like the ones she had made as a child. She closed her eyes and imagined that she was flying freely away from all her earthly problems, from Henry begging for marriage, from this job that pulled her across town when everyone else sat nestled in the warmth of their homes, from any of her mother's future episodes, from her father's angry inebriation. Just . . . fly . . . away . . .

A pounding sound interrupted her reverie. She quickly turned her head toward the direction of the sound, feeling like she had done something wrong. She heard it again, knowing now for sure it was coming from the door. She turned over and crawled tentatively toward the noise. It was then that she saw the judge behind the big window in the door bent over in a fit of laughter. He pushed and pushed before he managed to open the door about six inches, but he could barely get the words out of his mouth. "Now I've seen it all," he said choking with laughter.

"What's so funny, Judge?" Catherine asked, as she stood up brushing the snow from her face.

"If you could see yourself, you'd know what is so funny. First of all, you're covered with snow from your boots to your chook, including your face. And second, you're a grown woman making snow angels like you're five years old—out there having the time of your life! You never cease to amaze me, Miss Sabinsky. If you could see yourself right now, you'd laugh too. You look like the snowman my children would like to build." He chuckled. "My right-hand woman, lying in the snow at the front entrance of the courthouse, making snow angels. Just wait until *that* gets around."

Catherine was greatly relieved that someone besides her was in the building. The two of them would be able to figure out how to get the door open.

"I came in the back door," Judge Sullivan said. "Someone shoveled back there to let the sheriff's deputy in and left a couple of shovels in the back hallway. I could grab one of those and slip it out to you or I can put on my jacket and bring both shovels around to the front."

"Oh, Judge, you'd have to crawl up the stairs. At least I had to."

"I think we need to shovel at least a path up the steps. City crews are out plowing and I suspect we'll have some courthouse visitors today. I'll come around with two shovels and we can share the pain."

It was work, but fortunately the snow, while deep, was not wet and heavy. Catherine and the judge cleared a working path and enough space in front of the double doors for at least one to open. Practically falling into the building, they took off their wet boots and coats in the vestibule before staggering up to the judge's office suite. They flopped down on the couch and the oversized chair in the waiting room.

"Whew! I'm beat. Did you walk here?" the judge asked Catherine.

"I did. I won't get my car out of the alley for weeks."

"You walked twice as far as I did. You must be exhausted."

"Yeah. My legs feel like noodles. I've had it!"

"Why did you come in today? You didn't have to. I'm sure everything on my calendar will be cancelled," the judge said.

"I thought that might be true, but I knew if you were going to be here you would probably need me. Besides, I need the money. Once my legs will hold me, I'll head for my desk."

"I'm just going to stay here until I stop sweating. Stay there and rest for a minute, Catherine. There's no hurry today. Tell me about your weekend."

She told the judge about the ice boat races in Cedar River and how Henry's friend, Curly, had won the race.

"Curly Erickson? How does Henry know him? I used to iceboat with Curly on the flats near your place. He's a heck of a guy and a maniac on the ice."

"I used to iceboat on the flats, too, with my old boyfriend Davy when we were in high school, but I haven't since then." It was a bit of an exaggeration, because Catherine had only gone out with Davy twice, but it was wonderful to have this small personal connection with Judge Sullivan. "It was a blast! I'd do it again in a minute."

Catherine felt a sudden rush of guilt. The empty courthouse and the shoveling effort with the judge had let her feel they were companions, equals in some way, which was so crazy. She shivered, thinking what stupid things she might have said. She jumped up. "Okay. Now I have to get to work. I'll get your coffee ready first."

"You're quite the girl, Catherine," she heard the judge mumble as she walked up the stairs.

Catherine left work that afternoon wrapped up in her warmest clothes from the morning walk, but she had only gotten a few block down Main Street, walking along the giant snowbanks left by the plows, when she took off her hat and gloves and shoved them into her pockets.

Wow, she thought. *It's practically summer.* A bright sun and a balmy 40-degree afternoon were turning the deep-piled powder into a heavy wet mass, and small streams of meltwater were trying to find a drain. This would all be treacherous ice tonight, she knew. Folks who didn't shovel their walks today would find the job twice as hard tomorrow, but she had a clear route home on the street. Traffic was at a minimum.

Sweat and wet snow turned her into a soggy mess by the time she got home. A strange vehicle was parked in front of the house. Did Henry buy a car? she wondered. She walked in the house and collapsed on the couch, still wearing her wet boots and jacket. Before she caught her breath, her mother walked into the living room followed by Catherine's old high school friend, Gary Peters.

"Gary, what in the world are *you* doing here? I haven't seen you since graduation."

"I was driving past your house, so I thought I'd stop in to see what you've been up to. I'll never forget the fun we had in Miss Newell's class."

"Jeez—we sure did! I'll never forget how to diagram a sentence. Do you think she still wears scarves, pins, and necklaces every day of her retirement? She was a hoot," Catherine said.

"Yeah. And she really got her undies in a bundle when she found us writing notes to one another," Gary recalled.

"I'll say. I remember the trouble we got into when I cracked up over your note to me about her perfume smelling like a French whorehouse——or that she smelled like a French whore. I can't remember which."

"Oh, God. I blew my wig! That's right!" They laughed

together. "Ol' Newell took us to the office so fast I thought we were done for, but Mr. Harbort only gave us detention for two weeks. We had to write Newell a letter apologizing for our dastardly behavior."

"Yeah——and remember we had to stand up in front of the class to apologize for wasting everyone's time? *We* weren't wasting time—s*he* was wasting time making us do that." It was a great memory to share. "Well, except for the brown-nosers, the whole class thought we were heroes."

Catherine savored the recollection and then saw the memory from a new angle. "Hey, Gary. Y'know, she *did* wear a lot of perfume, and was always fancied up. Never thought about it, but I wonder who she was trying to impress. Maybe Mr. Jones." The thought made her giggle—the idea of an old biddy making a play for the handsome new math teacher who had all the girls swooning.

Gary seemed to pause and give that notion some thought, then said, "Come on——let me take you for a ride. We can talk about old times."

"I'm sorry, Gary. I'd love to do that, but I'm pooped. I walked home from work in the mush. It's hard moving your feet in boots covered with slush. By the way, I figure that's your car out front. How the heck did you get it out? Mine is stuck in the alley, probably for the rest of the winter."

"Yeah, we're lucky. My dad parked in front of the house. I had to shovel the snow the plow left, plus the snow from the storm. It's so beautiful out there, though, that I thought as long as I had it out it would be a good time to drive around and see what the storm has done. I was looking for some company."

"Gary," Martha said. "Why don't you take me for a ride? I want to get out of this damn house. Okay with you, Catherine?"

"Yeah, sure, whatever... I'm going to bed. Gary, would you mind taking my Mom for a ride?"

"Let's go, Mrs. Sabinsky. Let's go see the sights!"

Catherine warned Gary about some of the shiny, slick intersections she had walked past.

Martha hurried to her dresser to put on lipstick. She never left the house without it.

Catherine, with Pepper at her feet, fell asleep almost instantly, but her last thought was about her mother and her wish to get out of the house and do something like just go for a ride. She took it as another positive sign that a genuine enthusiasm for life was animating her mother.

In the middle of the night Catherine was startled by a loud pounding on the door and Pepper barking at the noise. She put on her robe as she ran to the door. A policeman and her mother were standing on the stoop.

"Mom, are you alright? What the heck is going on?" She shook her head to clear her foggy brain.

The policeman barged in with Martha close behind.

"I'm Officer Peterson. I'll tell you what's going on, Missy." The cop looked her in the eyes and snarled. "I'm making my rounds earlier tonight through City Park—no one's out—when I saw this car pulled over with the engine running, but I couldn't tell if there was anyone in the damn car. It's pitch dark. I get out of the car to check. The windows are all steamed up—can't tell if there's anyone inside, but I was scared that if there was some fool in there, he might be dead. I shine my light in the window—and what the Christ do you think I see? Wait 'til you hear this—just wait. I see a big bare ass sticking up practically in the window—you gettin' my drift? Then I see a pair of feet on the window attached to two spread legs. Do I have to go any further?"

Catherine had no answer. She knew exactly what he meant. She looked from the officer's angry face to her mother, hair disheveled, her hands busy clutching her long coat heavily around herself.

"Your mother—this is your mother, isn't it?—was layin' on the back seat practically naked. They were so engrossed in what they were doing, they didn't even see the lights of my squad car. But when I shined my light in, *then* it was all arms and legs moving in every direction. I thought it was a couple a kids getting in trouble, but when they jumped up scramblin' for their clothes, I realized it was a young kid and a grown woman doin' a little hanky-panky. Frankly, I was disgusted. Why the hell is a young kid gettin' it on with an old broad like this one?" he asked, gesturing toward Martha.

"What the fuck is goin' on here?" Mike shouted as he came limping out of his bedroom with his long johns buttoned up to his neck. "Did I just hear that my wife was gettin' screwed by some kid in City Park? Was he raping her?"

"It didn't look like rape to me, mister. She wasn't makin' any fuss, as far as I could see."

"Holy Christ, woman! You really, really have lost your goddamn mind!" he snarled as he moved closer to her. Catherine was suddenly afraid he was going to hit her, and the officer took a step as though to get between husband and wife, but Mike's anger was focused elsewhere. "Where is that little bastard who was thowin' it into you? Wait 'til I get my hands on him! I'll break his fucking neck!" He turned toward the policeman. "Where is the motherfucker?"

"He jumped out of the car with his pants unzipped and his jacket in his hand and ran like hell. He got away from me while I was looking after your wife. I tried to get the car out, but it's stuck pretty good. That snow got pretty soft today, and they must have been parked there for a while. It'll have to be pulled out. I know who owns the car, and there's going to be hell to pay at someone's home, come morning."

The officer raised his hands, shook his head. "All adults, Mr. Sabinsky. Nobody committed a crime. No charges." He turned, ironically wished everyone a good night, and left.

There was a dead silence in the room. Mike's face was red with rage. Martha walked toward her bedroom with her head down, her face filled with dread. Catherine saw Mike reach over and grab her mother's arm. "You're comin' with me, you fuckin' slut," he whispered harshly as he dragged Martha to his bedroom. "Screwin' some young punk in City Park? I'll show you how a real man fucks a dirty whore like you!"

Catherine heard the bed springs scream as Mike threw Martha onto the bed. Her mother was howling and sobbing, and Catherine knew she was trying to push him away. Mike's curses and threats were inaudible, but Catherine knew his rage and pain were deep, and he would vent that anger brutally. It seemed to her to be only a matter of several terrible minutes before a silence, broken only by an occasional sob, descended on the household.

Catherine lay awake, a passive victim of random and disconnected thoughts. What would cause her mother to do a stupid thing like that? Had she and Gary planned this? Gary! Her friend and classmate with her mother! What would happen tomorrow? How would they all face each other? Would the judge hear about this?

She thought, too, about how her mother had changed since her time in the asylum. She'd become so cheerful lately. Was that because of Gary? She'd never stop moving all day— baking cakes, pies, and bread, cooking every meal, keeping the house spotless. Catherine could hardly keep up with her.

Martha's sister Mildred had begun stopping over for afternoon coffee klatches. Martha would prepare open-faced egg salad and liverwurst sandwiches. Perhaps most surprising, she'd even talk to Mike.

Catherine had thought all these changes were wonderful. It seemed Martha must be getting along with very little sleep. When Catherine went to bed, Martha would still be up, doing tasks like mending socks or clothing on her treadle sewing machine, and when Catherine rose at six in the morning she'd find Cream of Wheat in a double-boiler on the cook stove and muffins in the oven. Sure, Martha had had her ups and downs, but Catherine couldn't remember a time when Martha had quite this much energy. Who could believe Martha had been nearly dead a couple months before?

Did her mother's strange, unexpected episode with Gary make sense? Were there clues Catherine had missed? Had she grown up so blind?

As Catherine lay in bed, she couldn't find a place where she was comfortable or a thought that was not colored by a dark sadness. Pepper cuddled next to her, but even he couldn't console her. She knew she'd be a wreck the next day, but she'd be fooling herself if she thought sleep was coming. Finally, she got out of bed in the darkness, walked out to the couch to sit down and landed on her mother, who immediately cried, "Don't hit me!"

Catherine leapt up, turned, whispered loudly in the darkness, "Mom! I won't hit you! What are you doing here?"

Her mother didn't move. She lay on her side in a fetal position, her back to the room. She lay without a blanket, despite the winter chill. Catherine sat at end of the couch at her mother's feet. "What happened tonight?"

"I don't want to talk about it." Martha's voice was

muffled, her face pressed into the back of the couch. "Leave me alone."

With very little sleep behind her and the prospect of none ahead, Catherine was not to be denied the truth of this new family calamity.

"Mom, I am *not* going to leave until you tell me your side of the story."

"I'll never tell you." A monotone from an inert body. "All I have to say is that a woman has needs, too."

It seemed to be an impasse, but Catherine would not yield. After long uneasy silence she asked her mother, "Do you have any other surprises I don't know about? How many more secrets do you have?"

"That is none of your business."

Catherine would try a new tack. As she had tossed and turned, strange fragments of memory had begun to coalesce. "Well, because I live here and I help support this family, I think it *is* my business, and I have some questions for you."

No response from the body at the other end of the couch, and Catherine plunged ahead. "Lying in bed, trying to sleep, I thought of a couple other strange events from the past. I was just a kid, but maybe they make more sense now.

"When I was in fifth grade I remember coming home from school and the doors were locked and there were notes like, 'Dear Cat. Be a good girl and play outside until Mr. Smith leaves. Doing insurance business. Mom.' It never occurred to me until tonight that maybe you were paying the insurance man with your favors. Is that what you were doing? I was too young to know better. What about that, Mom?"

No reply.

"And what about the time Mr. Seidl, Papa's old boss, came over for supper. You cooked a feast fit for a king using our best dishes and silverware. You had everyone dressed in their Sunday clothes. The boys were even scrubbed up—ironed shirts, lectures about using proper manners. Our whole family and Mr. Seidl were scrunched around the table oohing and ahhing over the delicious food and making small talk." Even as Catherine spoke, the memory of the evening was shaking itself into fine focus.

"Mom, I remember you looked like a million bucks that day, sitting next to Papa's boss making sure he had enough to eat, enough to drink. You had your hair styled just so—the blue dress you had just finished sewing the night before was so keen. I'll never forget that night when I thought we had the perfect family, one that Papa could be proud of and impress Mr. Seidl. Maybe he'd even get a little raise. He was sitting across from you all smiles.

"After dinner was over and the table was cleared, you put your famous banana cream pie in the center of the table. We were all drooling waiting to take our first bite. Faster than we could lift our forks, Papa stood up and violently upended the table. He was raging, 'Get your filthy hands off my wife's leg, you son of a whore.' You sat there with your skirt pulled up to your underwear—Papa' boss was jerking his hand away from your leg. No one moved or said a word for a split second, until Papa started running around the table with his fists clenched. Charlie and Steve both grabbed him. He fought hard to get away, but Mr. Seidl was able to get out the door and down the steps before Papa could break their hold.

"Mom, I locked that memory away somewhere. I must have been only nine or ten when it happened, shortly before Stella left for Chicago. But, tonight as I tossed and turned, it came back to me as if it had happened yesterday. It was so strange, so unexpected, that I put it in some locked box somewhere in my brain. What does it mean, Mom? Who are you?"

Martha got up from the couch and walked into the bedroom. When Catherine dressed and was leaving work, her mother was still in bed. She let Pepper out to relieve himself, and when he came back in she hugged him and whispered, "Here we go again, Pepper."

Life in the Sabinsky household that spring was wretched. Mike was seldom home, but in those rare instances at home he was drunk and ugly. Her mother stayed in the bedroom for hours at a time. When she came out to eat or use the toilet, she would speak to no one. Mike was forcing Martha into his bed on a regular basis since she'd been discovered with Gary. At first, Martha would try to fend Mike off, but she was no match for him and finally quit fighting. She was a rag doll to his touch, but that didn't stop him.

Occasionally he asked Catherine if she'd seen the "worthless piece of shit who fucked my wife because I'd punch him a new asshole." Catherine was afraid to communicate with either of her parents for fear of starting another row. She stayed out of the house whenever possible. The only good thing at home was Pepper.

Work was her refuge, but not enough to keep her dark mood lifted. She was down in the dumps. It took all she could manage to keep food in the house but she didn't cook or do much housework. Keeping the bathroom clean and doing the laundry was as much as she could muster. All she could think about was how she might keep this miserable situation from ruining her life.

She hoped that seeing a movie with Henry would lift her spirits a little. So, when he knocked on the door at 6:30 on Saturday evening she did her best to be chipper. Her shiny dark brown hair was brushed to the top of her head in a mass of curls. She even had rouge on her cheekbones and bright red lipstick that she fashioned in a bow on her thin upper lip to make it seem bigger. The beige skirt and bright blue pullover with a white lace collar showed off her womanly figure.

"Hi, Catherine. Aren't you looking swell!" he said as he winked, smiled and rubbed his hand on her shoulder. He didn't know anything about what had transpired in the last couple of weeks. She was pretty sure she didn't want to tell him. She was ashamed. What she knew for sure was that she liked his hand on her shoulder.

"You don't look so bad yourself," she replied, leaning her body into his. "I think you have a new jacket. That dark green color matches your eyes." A warmth was replacing the cold anxiety and anger she had been feeling for weeks. As he helped her into her coat, Henry wrapped his arms around her and she responded in kind. After a long, romantic kiss, his hand moved down to her breast and she was on fire. He pulled her closer and she felt him pressing against her. The back door creaked open, and they pulled away quickly, trying to look composed.

"Dammit" Catherine heard Henry say under his breath. Mike limped into the living room just as Catherine was buttoning her coat.

"Hi, Papa," she said, fighting to sound as normal as possible.

"Hi, Henry. Where's your mother, Kiddo?" Mike asked. "Don't tell me she's still in that goddamn bedroom of hers. Jesus Christ! When the hell am I gonna get a goddamn meal in this house? A man is supposed ta get fed on a regular basis. This shit has gotta stop. Why aren't you cookin' for me? Yer a woman, ain't ya?"

She was not going to be trapped into cooking, not tonight. "Henry and I are going out to the movie, 'It Happened One Night.' You and mom can work this out yourselves." And with a casual wave, she opened the front door. "See you later."

When they were both settled in Henry's truck he asked her, "What the heck got into him?"

"It's a long story and I'd rather not talk about it. I want to forget about my insane parents for a couple hours. Let's go to the movie, eat some popcorn and hold hands."

The movie was a good distraction from home, but not from Henry. As soon as he got behind the wheel, he drove to their favorite place to park and make out. He couldn't drive all the way into the trees because it was still too wet and muddy. But the edge of the country road would work out fine. The moonless sky was as black as a Halloween cat. Hardly any cars drove out here. He had new tires, chains in the trunk, and a package of Trojan condoms in the glove compartment. He had thought about nothing else for the last two weeks and came well prepared.

After turning off the engine, Henry pulled Catherine over to him. Her lips were ripe for kissing, their tongues searched each other's mouths. Henry unbuttoned Catherine's coat and caressed her ample breasts. She responded with soft moans of pleasure, wild with passion. He fondled and kissed her. She was asking for more. She knew this was wrong, but she didn't want to stop. He touched her until she felt she was exploding. Pleasure flooded her body like an electric current. Never had her body responded than the way it did when she welcomed him inside her.

They lay in silence scrunched up in the truck holding each other tight. Henry put his hand on her head and told her he loved her.

"I love you, too, Henry," she whispered.

After they pulled themselves apart, Catherine's joy turned to guilt . . . and fear. What had they done? They made out and touched before but had never gone all the way. What if she got pregnant? She feared her mother might disown her, but, really, how could she after her own escapades? Reverend Knutson said it was a sin before marriage. Although she had sinned in many other ways, this seemed like the worst.

"What's wrong, Honey?" Henry said. "You're pretty quiet."

"What we did was wrong, Henry. We shouldn't be doing this until we're married. What if I get pregnant? I'm only seventeen."

"You were protected, and you'll be eighteen in a few weeks."

"How do you know all about this? Have you done it with another girl before me?"

"No. Never. But it seems so right. We're in love. We'll be married soon anyway, so it can't matter that much."

"Henry, you know all the stumbling blocks I have to overcome before I can even think of marriage. My parents are a huge problem." It all had to come out, she knew. "You wouldn't believe what happened the week before last. My mother and Gary Olson—remember him from high school?— were caught by a cop having sex in his car in City Park right after the big snowstorm. My mother always says sex is a dirty habit. It must not have seemed dirty to her that night. See, I'm just like my mother. They say apples don't fall far from the tree. Anyway, Papa found out and now it's a living hell at my house."

Henry took her hands, "Honey, this is not dirty. This was beautiful, and I love you!" Then, sternly, "It's time for you to get out of that insane house. You deserve a better life than that."

"I don't think you have the whole picture. It's not as easy as just moving out."

"If we get married, you'd have the perfect reason to get out. Let those two fight it out for themselves."

"But Henry, you know my mother is too unstable to take care of herself. Who knows when she'll have her next nervous breakdown? Or when she'll go wild like the past month or two? She doesn't stop moving. With my Mom it's either high as a kite or low as a bunker. My dad won't take care of her now, especially after that thing with Gary. My dad's a drunk. He's as unpredictable as the first snow in winter."

She paused, thinking she might tell Henry what had happened to Gary when his own parents found out, but she decided she wanted to get off the subject. "Besides, Henry, you know how much I like my job and the judge."

"Do you like the judge more than me?"

Catherine couldn't decide if Henry was joking or was serious. She chose the former. "You know that's a stupid question. Don't tell me you don't know my parents can't live without my paycheck. Papa's not fishing much these days. It's hard for him to hold a job. My mother has no way to make a living. Once we get married, I'd have to quit my job. Married women are looked down on if they work after they're married, especially now that so many men are still out of work. Can you afford to support my whole family?"

"Not right now, but I might if I get a job at the mill."

The mill? Really? And leave your father's new beer business? She decided he was just offering any fanciful argument in support of their marriage.

"I'm not finished," she said, impatiently. "The disaster with Mom and Gary brought back memories that I had forgotten about since I was a kid. I didn't understand what was going on then, but I think I do now. My mother cheated on my father before this. I don't think my father has been with other women, but I have a feeling that he knows and hates her for it. Maybe she's driven him to drink. I can't get married until I can figure some of these things out."

"What?" Henry exclaimed. "Are you kidding me? Your mother's been messing around before this?"

"Yup. I'm ashamed, I'm mad. But what can I do?"

"Why don't those brothers and sisters help you take care of your parents? Why is it all on your shoulders? You're the youngest. The others are settled in with jobs, probably earning more than you! It's not fair."

"That's a good point. It isn't fair, but that's the way it is. Stella sends money occasionally, but we can't count on it. The same with Charlie. I'm not sure if Steve or Clara have any extra money? I've never asked."

Henry was quiet for a while. "I don't know how to say this, Catherine, but I'm dumbfounded to hear that your mother has been cheating on your father. That's the worst thing a wife could do to a husband. Would you ever do that? Does it run in families?"

"Are you kidding me, Henry Goodman? How can you possibly think about that when I'm in such agony? I hate what my mother is doing. It's awful! I want you to understand what I'm going through right now, not whether I'm going to cheat on you twenty or thirty years from now!"

"Well, I'm sorry, but cheating is just plain wrong. I have lost all respect for your mother. I hope my mother doesn't hear about this. She'd have a fit."

Catherine fought for restraint. She was trying to find normal living in the wreck of her parents' marriage, and here was Henry, worrying what his mother might think. She could not keep acid from her tone. "Henry, I'm so sorry. I know your family is so much better than mine. It would be just terrible for you if they knew."

A lone car slid by on the dark road. She watched the taillights disappear. "Henry, I didn't choose this family. I wish to God I had a normal family, but I don't. I don't have a good idea what a normal family is. I know how your mother feels about my family, but I can't change it. Maybe you should find a girl with a better family. Your mother would like that."

Henry did not rise to the bait. "Come on, Cat. She'll see how swell you are after we're married."

"Your mother is a country schoolteacher. I admire her, but that doesn't give her license to judge everyone else. Your father isn't any classier than mine. He delivers beer and coal. Is that any better than fishing? Yes, you own a house and we rent. You're better off than we are. Well, whoop-de-do for you." The bitterness returned. "Passing judgment is not Christian. Your mother goes to church, but she sins like all of us. My mother cheats and my dad is a drunk. That's not Christian either. They'll all go to hell. And now we will too. There you have it."

Henry was exasperated. "What's Christianity got to do with it?" He spun away from her, gripped the steering wheel, turned the ignition key. "You obviously don't love me!" Gravel spit back from tires as he wrenched the truck onto the country lane. When they reached her house, Catherine slammed the door without saying goodbye.

Pepper was waiting for her when she walked into the dark living room. He jumped up on her lap as soon as she flopped on the couch. "What am I going to do about my life, Pepper?" Catherine was scared and angry with Henry. How could this evening begin so beautifully, the two of them embracing, awkwardly making love in the front seat of the old pickup, and then end with such anger? She had never been this angry at Henry. He had no idea what she was going through. It was easy for him to say she should move out and marry him. She didn't like his attitude toward Martha, that he had *lost all his respect* for her. What did he know about her life?

Catherine was especially furious that Henry had brought his uppity mother into the conversation. Well, bully for her! Catherine, now aware of her mother's dalliances, hated the thought. She couldn't bring herself to hate her mother, but she wanted those thoughts of her mother with another man banished from her memory. Of course, her father was no prize. They were both a mess. They probably didn't even like themselves. But they were her parents. She couldn't bring herself to abandon them, but being stuck with them only bred more resentment.

Her resentment was nothing, compared to her terror of being pregnant. Having sex before marriage was a sin against God. Could she ever go back to church again? Could she still sing in the choir? She was sure the church would reject her. So, would her friends and her family. She felt dirty and scared. As soon as the judge found out, her job would be over. Her work made her proud. The last thing she wanted was to lose her job.

What would she and her parents do without her income? The consequences were too ugly to think about. How could she have been that stupid when she turned herself over to Henry? She couldn't blame him. It was a woman's responsibility to fend off men—men couldn't help themselves. He would have stopped if she had told him to, but she had abandoned her own good judgment. It was her fault. As she vowed to herself that she would never have sex again until she was married, she remembered her mother's words: *Sex is a dirty habit*. She prayed for her period—her "friend," as Martha had taught her to say. Catherine was awash with shame.

Henry stopped over a few days after their argument. Catherine was still mad at him and gave him her famous cold shoulder—she could hold out for a long time. He didn't apologize but he was nice to her. When he asked Catherine to go for a ride with him, she refused and closed the door before he could respond. After the third time, he gave her an ultimatum. If she didn't talk to him, their relationship was over. He had never given her an ultimatum before, so she didn't know if he would hold his ground. She only had a short time to think.

Finally she said, "Okay, Henry. I'll go for a ride with you under the condition that we can talk about finding common ground. We can't talk in my house. My parents are both here, so we'll have to go somewhere else. I don't want to try to have a serious talk in your truck. Any suggestions?"

"Not off the top of my head."

They were both silent until Catherine finally said, "Let's drive over by the fishing boats. It's chilly, so no one's going to be there."

Catherine had no idea what Henry had on his mind. He looked distracted. She heard the waves lapping against the shore. The light breeze felt cool against her face, but it didn't relax her. She knew they could sit there all night and Henry wouldn't start the conversation, so it was up to her. She took a deep breath.

"Why did you come to see me three times?" she asked softly.

"You know I love you. I don't like it when we fight. I want to make up," he said as he reached for her hand. They were sitting on a log watching the water roll up on the sand and the undertow take it back.

"I don't like to fight either Henry, but we have several issues to confront."

She slid her hand from under Henry's as they watched the seagulls diving for fish. The boats in the harbor rocked gently as the water lapped against them. It was a nearly perfect evening in late April. Her father always came to mind when she was near the fishing docks.

Despite his evening drinking, despite his terrible treatment of her mother, she knew he worked his fingers to the bone on those boats, and that he always took a job if one was available. This evening she wondered how long he could keep working. He was slowing down. The bay had been his life and it had taken a toll on him. Beer and whiskey didn't help either. She loved him but she sure wouldn't want him for a husband. Did she even want a husband? At some time down the road, but not now . . .

"So, Henry, one of the things I need to talk to you is about marriage. I know you want to get married as soon as I turn eighteen, and that's in two weeks."

"Well, yeah, but we could wait 'til fall. That's a nice time to get married."

"Do you remember what I said about that, all the obstacles in my way? Did you listen?"

"Of course, I remember, but I don't think your parents should stop you. They made their bed. Now let them lay in it or get your sisters and brothers to carry the burden. It shouldn't all fall on you. It's not fair. I want this for your own good."

"How do you know what my own good is, Henry? Even though I have been working almost two years, I still feel young. I'm not ready to settle down! If we got married in the fall, I'd probably have a baby when I was nineteen. That's way too soon. I want to have some fun before I get married."

"Come on, Catherine. We could wait to have kids. And we can have fun even if we are married."

"Clara said she and Nels wouldn't have kids right away. But you know how long that lasted. I don't want to quit my job. I love it. Women are frowned upon if they work when they're married. I'm making good money. How much money are you making?"

"My dad pays me whatever he can. It depends on how much beer he sells. But I'd like to get a job at the mill. I'd make good money there. Plenty for us to live on."

"Do you like to go dancing? That's one of my favorite things to do. I could go dancing every night."

"Catherine, you know I don't like to dance, but I could go out and watch you dance."

"And who do think is going to ask me to dance if I'm with you? It's not just about dancing, Henry. You know that. I feel torn between you and my parents. It's gut-wrenching. I love you and I love my parents. How would you like to live with me and my parents—and support us? Think about *that*."

"That's not fair, Catherine. That's beyond my means right now. And, anyway, living with your parents wouldn't be any better than living with mine. Our own place! Just the two of us in a little cottage next to a river where I could catch big trout and you could cook them for me. What a life that would be—my dream!"

"Guess what, Henry. I don't want to live in the woods."

"Don't worry. You won't have to live in the woods. I'm a long way from being able to afford that. I'm just saying that's my dream."

"Then there's one more thing. What if I'm pregnant

right now? It's all I can think about. That would ruin both of our lives. I'm sick about it, Henry. I think of my mother who got married because she was pregnant. She was smart and ambitious and wanted to go to school, but she got pregnant. It ruined her life."

"Our situation is much different than hers," he shot back.

"Is it different, Henry? Is it really different?" Tears began cascading down her cheeks, her chin was quivering, her body heaving.

Henry tried to calm her. He rubbed her back. "Everything will be all right. You'll see."

"No, Henry. I *don't* see!" She choked out the words. "My life is complicated. I'm feeling overwhelmed. I need time—time without you, Henry."

She took his class ring off her finger and handed it to him gently. "I'm walking home. It's over."

Chapter 15. Save the Last Dance for Me (1940)

When Judge William Sullivan opened the door at Matty's Supper Club for the courthouse Christmas party, the place rang like a carnival midway. Above the blaring music barkers were yelling, "Go, girls, go!" and "Boogie till you drop!" He passed through the dimly lit barroom into the bright ballroom, the source of the commotion. All eyes were on Catherine and Betty dancing on a dining table to "Scrub Me Mama with a Boogie Beat." With arms swinging and legs kicking, they were quite a sight. The judge walked over to Otto, the county sheriff.

"Hey, Otto! They're damn good!" he shouted.

"Yeah, Bill, but I hope the hell they don't fall off! I need Betty on Monday morning," Otto shouted back.

Catherine and Betty twisted, twirled, hopped and slid under each other's arms until the music stopped. Catherine jumped off the table, almost into the judge's arms. Betty was close behind. The crowd was clapping and yelling for more.

"I really hope you two are having a good time tonight," the judge said, laughing at his own statement of the obvious.

"We're having the time of our *lives,* Judge!" Catherine said, as she began to catch her breath. "Wanna dance on the table with me? You could show your true colors!"

The judge smiled indulgently. He could tell that the two women had begun celebrating early. "You've got to be kidding, Miss Sabinsky. I'd kill myself."

"Aw, come on. Most of these people don't know you like I do. They think you're a stick-in-the-mud." Catherine said.

Betty chimed in. "Yeah, Catherine's right. Once you get on the table, or should I say if you can get on the table, we'll make sure you don't fall on that handsome face of yours, Judge. I promise."

Donny, the court photographer, started a chant, "You can dance and you can twirl—you can wiggle like a girl." Shouting and clapping reverberated throughout banquet room.

The judge laughed, pleased with the warmth and good humor that filled the ballroom. He had promoted this courthouse get-together for years and knew that the good will of the evening came back to work with everyone after the Christmas break. But it was time to settle in. He caught the sheriff's eye and pointed toward the bar.

"Otto, let's hit it. I need a drink before I can even think about dancing on the floor, let alone climbing on a table."

He had barely finished his sentence before a deputy handed him an old fashioned that the sheriff had ordered a minute before. Everyone knew it was the judge's favorite drink.

"I don't know if this one is as good as Jack makes 'em at Goodfellow's," Otto said, almost apologetically, "but at least it's got brandy in it."

"Thanks, Buddy." He took a big swallow. "Whew! Just what the doctor ordered. Come on, let's find a table so I can sit down and catch my breath. These guys are wild tonight."

They sought the quietest corner they could find. The judge took a moment to study the holiday decorations.

"Jim's work, right?"

The sheriff nodded. They both smiled at the notion that Jim Everson—a painfully shy and retiring accountant in the county office, a man so plain that he often passed unnoticed—would be at Matty's on a ladder hooking streamers of colored balls across the ballroom ceiling. The judge wondered if he even stayed for the party.

And party it truly was.

"Everyone was just milling around, nibbling and drinking, until your helper and her partner got things rolling," the sheriff said. "Yep, I watched them go to work. Catherine was the instigator, and Betty wasn't far behind. Before they got here, it was, ya know, small talk—How are the kids? Isn't it a cold one out there? Do you think it'll snow? Suddenly, our girls exploded into the room, ran to the jukebox with a purse full of nickels and started playing boogies. A couple beers later they were on the table. Thank God they took the tablecloth and the silverware off before they started."

"Yeah, Otto, it's hard to hold that twosome down. I don't know what Betty's husband thinks, but Catherine doesn't have to answer to anyone."

"Yeah," Otto agreed, "but they're both swell workers. They keep the morale of the courthouse high. They work hard and play hard."

The judge's thoughts drifted away from the holiday scene before him. "With our boys having to sign up for the draft now, it's not easy to stay on the bright side."

"Yeah, that's for damn sure. I'm glad we're still neutral, but Hitler and those Nazi sons-a-bitches are treacherous, plowing through Belgium, France, Norway—Christ, you name it!— killing, bombing. Frankly, Bill, it's scares the hell of me."

"Y'know, Otto, I've been watching that. My uncle Jack

was in the so-called 'war to end all wars,' got gassed in France. Now are we going to have to do it again?" The judge drained his glass. "I can't imagine that Great Britain can hold out against them for much longer. I'm telling you, Otto, we're going be in this war before we know it."

He looked over toward Catherine and Betty who were leading the others in the Lindy Hop. "It's good to have our girls keeping everyone's spirits up."

"Yeah, that's for sure," Otto chuckled. "Let's go buy them a drink."

Happy and spent, Catherine and Betty were the last ones to leave the party. Blisters on her feet, Catherine's shoes in her hands. Bare feet might be a problem in the snow but right now she couldn't stand her shoes for another second. They looked back at the tattered streamers hanging from the ceiling in the banquet room as they were leaving.

With a big grin Catherine said, "That room looks like the scene of a hell of a party. What a blast! I'll never forget this night. We must have danced to a hundred songs!"

"No one could keep up with us," Betty agreed, glassy-eyed. "The stodgy men wouldn't get out on the floor, except for the Lindy Hop and the couple of dances you had with the judge. Our dear William Sullivan is a *pret-ty good* sport."

"I'm gonna grab a few of those poor dilapidated streamers hanging from the ceiling. I'll put them in my room, so I can remember all the fun we had tonight. What would I do without you, Betty?"

Their arms around each other's shoulders with smiles on their faces, streamers dragging behind, they passed the bar, headed for the exit. Suddenly, Catherine stopped. She pulled Betty back with a jolt.

"What's going on?" Betty asked.

"Shhh! Stop right now," she said with a stern whisper, her index finger in front of her lips. "The bar! Look at the bar."

Betty had a hard time seeing in the dim light. Why did Catherine want to shush her and look at the bar? Betty craned her neck and walked a little closer. She recognized her friend Ruth sitting with a man at the bar. Did Catherine know Ruth, too? She ran over, tapped Ruth on the shoulder and gave her a big hug. Catherine stood alone behind them, not believing what Betty had just done.

Ruth pulled back, smiled at Betty. "I want you to meet my friend Henry. Betty, this is Henry Goodman. Henry, my long-lost friend, Betty. We went to church together years ago."

Somewhere in Betty's brain an alarm bell went off. *Henry Goodman,* she thought. *How do I know Henry Goodman?* Then it dawned on her—Catherine's old boyfriend! So, that's why Catherine acted so strangely. She didn't want to see Henry. Betty remembered how devastated Catherine was for months after they broke up a couple years ago. Henry's name had not come up much since then.

"Betty, your friend is standing over there alone. I'll go get her. We can all have a drink together. Is that okay with you, Henry?"

"Sure," he said without looking back.

Catherine saw Betty's friend coming toward her. Should she turn and run? The last person she wanted to meet was Henry's girlfriend. The joy of the evening was draining away quickly.

"Hi, I'm Ruth," she said, smiling and offering Catherine her hand. "Betty and I were fast friends. If you're a friend of Betty's, you're a friend of mine. Come on, I'll introduce you to Henry. Let's have a drink together. I need to catch up with Betty."

Catherine politely took the proffered hand, forced a smile, but shook her head. "It's nice to meet you, Ruth, but I'm really tired. I'm ready to go home. Could you drop Betty off at her house later? I need to go."

Ruth read Catherine's discomfort as shyness, and she took her arm and pulled her toward the bar. "I won't take no for an answer," she said, and called out, "Henry! This is—" and turning toward Catherine, "Oh, I didn't get your name."

"It's Catherine," Henry said softly. He made eye contact with Catherine and then looked down.

"Oh, you two already know each other!" Ruth played the ideal hostess. "That makes it even better! Here, let's move these bar stools around so we can all talk to each other. Betty, help me out."

After a quick round of drink orders, Betty and Ruth settled into serious catch-up, oblivious to the duo of Henry and Catherine standing awkwardly next to each other. Neither of the past lovers knew what to say.

Catherine felt weak and shaky. A thousand old emotions were stirring. Henry looked pale. What was going through his mind, she wondered?

Catherine timidly broke the silence. "How have you been, Henry? It's been a while— almost three years."

Henry moved his mouth to her ear and whispered, "Way too long . . . I'd like to kiss your beautiful lips right now."

Catherine was momentarily stunned by Henry's urgent tone, but the surprise was gone in a flash. He had tapped her own longing. His breath was hot on her cheek. The pulse of the evening's party throbbed in her chest. She let him take her hand and lead her into the darkened party room. Betty and Ruth paid no attention as the couple slipped quietly behind them. Once inside, he put his arms around her and kissed her long and gently as she melted into his arms.

He broke the kiss, whispered earnestly in her ear. "After you drop Betty off, wait for me on your porch. I'll be there before you can say 'sweet mama.'"

She held him for a moment. "What about your da—"

He cut her off. "Never mind about her. She's nobody, really. Come on. Let's make tracks . . ."

They gracefully returned. Henry looked at his watch, and Catherine yawned widely.

Unrehearsed, they played their parts perfectly, and Ruth and Betty, interrupted in their reminiscences, were calmly hustled out the door to separate vehicles.

Catherine pulled her coat around her while she sat on the top step waiting for Henry, ignoring her cold bare feet. When she saw the lights of Henry's truck coming toward her house, she jumped off the porch and ran to the street, hoping that the pain in her feet was not flesh being torn from her soles by the icy concrete. Before he could turn the engine off, she was in his truck and they were in each other's arms. Not a word needed to be said.

"Turn off the engine, Henry. Let's go inside. Mom and Papa are asleep, and my feet are freezing."

"You don't have any shoes on! What's the matter with you?"

"I know." She knew he was teasing. "I took my shoes off. I have blisters after dancing all night. I left everything, including my streamers, in my car. Let's go," she urged.

"No, we might wake them. Your mother and father are not the ones I want to talk to right now. How are the gruesome-twosome?"

"Henry, cut it out!"

"I know, Honey. I was kidding. I'm just happy, that's

all. I can't believe this is happening. Every day since you gave back my ring and walked away, I have been pining for you. I don't think a day goes by when I don't think what an idiot I was to let you go."

"Henry, I was the idiot." Her head rested on his shoulder. "I was in a bad place, feeling sorry for myself. I was torn between you and my crazy parents. It just took me down. When you told me you wanted to marry me, it was too much. I was so young . . ."

"We were both too young. I know that now. I'll always love you, Cat, no matter what."

An intense shiver ran through her. "Henry, I'm freezing. I think my feet might fall off. Come on. Let's go in the house. We can build a fire in the stove. We'll be cozy and warm. I'll make us some coffee."

Cuddled together on the couch the young lovebirds talked until daybreak. So much had happened to each of them in the three years since they parted. It was time to pick up where they had left off.

"Just before you broke up with me your mother had a serious nervous breakdown. You were scared she might die."

"Thank God she didn't die, but it's the same old stuff in my family. My mother is perplexing. She goes into the darkest places and then comes out of them like a whirling dervish. It's a good thing there are some normal spaces in between. Who knows why or how that happens, but it does . . . "

"My mother still tries to run my life," Henry said. "I have learned to ignore her, though, and that's the best way to deal with that woman."

"Does she still hate me?"

"Honey, she never hated you."

"Yeah, but she doesn't think I'm good enough for you."

"Let's cut the crap, Catherine. We're old enough now to do what we want. We can't let them run our lives anymore. I don't care what my mother thinks. Do you?"

"Well, Sweetheart, I don't care what my mother thinks, but I still care about what your mother thinks of me. I have a different situation than you. My mother is unstable. Sometimes she just loses it."

"I know that, Cat. We need to work together on that one. I'm ready to give some ground, but let's not talk about that now. There are more immediate things to consider—like the fucking war. I had to register for the draft last month."

"What?" Catherine sat bolt upright. "Are you going to be sent to war? That can't be true!" With both her hands on Henry's cheeks, she pulled his face to hers and looked directly into his eyes. "Please tell me you're joking."

"I wish I were. If we get into the war, I'm sure to be drafted."

They held each other tight. "I'm so scared, Henry. What are we going to do?"

"Well, I haven't been drafted yet, so we have some time. But the Nazis are on a rampage. England can't hold them alone for long."

Mike arose as dawn was breaking. Rubbing his eyes as he walked into the living room, he felt the warmth of the stove and smelled fresh coffee.

"What the hell is goin' on in here. Catherine, is that you? Did you make a fire?"

"Yup, and there's coffee on the stove."

"It feels damn good to get up to a warm house for once." As he looked around, he saw Henry curled up around Catherine on the couch. "Is there a goddamn ghost in here?"

"Good to see you, too, Mike. How've you been?"

"Well, if this ain't enough to shock an old man, I don' know what is. Jesus Christ, Goodman, what rock did you crawl out from under? I ain't seen you in years."

"You're going see more of me from now on. I hope you're ready."

"Well this ain't the worst thing, I guess. Yer not such a bad guy. Catherine could do worse. Hey, Kiddo, could you make yer old man a little breakfast?"

"Sure, Papa. Whoa, wait a minute, I didn't realize it was so late. I have to get ready for work. Why don't you just eat that left-over piece of butterscotch pie in the ice box?"

"Get yer mother up so she can pack my lunch pail. I might as well live alone for all the attention I get around this goddamn house."

Catherine invited Henry to supper that evening. They had no time to waste.

Catherine stopped at Stepniak's Market on her way home from work for a pound of hamburger and four potatoes. Meatloaf and baked potatoes would work along with Martha's canned green beans. She was yawning as she walked in the door. Martha, dressed in a faded gray housedress, was sweeping the wooden kitchen floor. *Better than a bathrobe*, Catherine thought.

"Hi Mom."

"What's in the bag, my dear?" Martha asked.

"Groceries. Henry's coming over for supper."

"Your father told me you and Henry looked pretty chummy on the couch this morning. I thought you were over him for good. How did that happen?" Martha appeared displeased that Catherine and Henry might again be an item.

"As Betty and I were leaving Matty's after the

Christmas party last night I ran into him. He was sitting at the bar with a date, but when we saw each other he ditched her. You know I never got over him, and he feels the same way. We stayed up all night talking."

"You better be sure you're not making a mistake. You're moving pretty fast, my dear girl," she admonished.

"I couldn't be surer. It is perfect. I am on top of the clouds and so is Henry. But, Mom, he had to sign up for the draft last week. He thinks he might have to go to war. How can I feel so happy and so scared at the same time?"

When Henry opened the door the aroma of the meatloaf filled his nostrils.

"Yum, Martha. I have missed your meatloaf and I brought my appetite. Nobody can make meatloaf like you."

"You're in for a surprise, Mr. Goodman," Martha said as she smiled and looked at Catherine. "Your girlfriend whipped it up. She's been doing a lot of cooking these days. I've been teaching her all my tricks."

"She couldn't have a better teacher, Mame. Can I call you Mame?"

"Well, that's what my family calls me. Clara's kids call me Mamie. You can call me whatever you like."

Henry was on his best behavior. Even though he and Catherine had been back together only a day and night, he knew they were going to spend their life together and he wanted to be on her mother's best side. There were a lot of complications that had to be sorted out before they could be married. He needed Mame as an ally.

Mike and Henry devoured their food. When Henry finally came up for air, he asked Catherine if she really made supper.

"I sure did, Henry Goodman. Every last bite of it,

except for the green beans. Mom canned them, so she gets some credit. Your plate looks like you licked it clean. You must have liked it," she said with a touch of pride.

"Now that I've tasted your cooking, Cat, I have a question for your father. Hey, Mike. Can I marry your daughter?"

"Marry my daughter? She's too damn young to get married to a whippersnapper like you. Who the hell is going to cook for me if you take her away?"

There was a long moment of silence, long enough for Henry and Catherine to look at each other, each thinking that her father was going to stand in their way. Then Mike spoke again.

"I'll make you a deal, Goodman, you son-of-a-bitch. If you can promise me a couple a' cases a Kingsbury a week, I'll gladly give ya my daughter," he said, slapping his knee and laughing out loud. "She's worth every goddamn bottle. I was hopin' somebody would take her off our hands pretty soon."

Then Martha spoke.

"*Ah, Gut*, how you talk, Mike. Hold *op. Ga vaid fra mig.*" Go away. You can't be serious, you old *dugris*. Take her away? Who's going to take her away? What about me?"

Oh, my God, Catherine thought. *When my mother starts talking Danish and calls my dad a pig, there's big trouble ahead.* She didn't know what to say next. She was over the moon about Henry's proposal, but his timing was wrong. He didn't know her parents like she did. She knew both of them were scared to death she would leave. She was worried her mother would go into a downward slide, another of those mental crashes that Dr. Koepp had called nervous breakdowns. Catherine knew it didn't take much. Her father, on the other hand, was putting on a good front.

He'd be drunk before the night was over. That didn't take much either. There was no more discussion of marriage. Mike took his beer into the living room and turned on the radio, and Martha silently rose to do the dishes. Catherine and Henry put on their coats, left the house and climbed into the truck. Henry drove off with no destination in mind.

"Well, Henry, there you have it. Are you ready for this?"

"Yup, you're worth it. We'll work it out."

"I'm ready to marry you now, Sweetheart. I've built so many friendships, have a wonderful job, and I want to settle down and have a lifetime with you, but . . ." Catherine paused, looked at the bright lights of anonymous homes passing by. What would their own home be like? "Henry, I don't even have the foggiest notion where to start."

Henry's own thoughts had wandered elsewhere, far from the idea of hearth and home. "Hitler—that son-of-a-bitch and his Nazis—I'm afraid he might mess up our plans, Cat. I don't want to go to war, but I don't want that hateful cretin taking over our country. He's getting closer all the time. I'm ready to fight for our country to the end."

"I know, Henry. I know how you feel about what's happening." Catherine had no sense of what combat or battle or fighting might be like. It all seemed like loss. "What would I do if something happens to you? I just found you again and now we have to worry about a war."

Henry looped back to Catherine's home and held her tight as tears rolled down her cheeks. Her words were plaintive, sad, bitter. "I hate Hitler," she whispered into his chest. "I hate the Germans. I'm so scared you'll get killed if you go to war."

Henry held her as she cried and told her how much he loved her.

"We're both tired. Neither of us slept a wink last night," Henry said. "I'm going home to get some sleep. You need some, too. We can figure this out when our heads are on straight."

Separated only by work or sleep, Catherine and Henry spent every minute together for the next several weeks. He became a fixture in the Sabinsky household. Marriage was paramount in their discussions about how to proceed with their lives. But before they could tie the knot, they had some tough decisions to make.

Where would they live? They wanted a place of their own, but that posed several problems. Could they afford to get their own place and still support Mike and Martha? Could Henry move in with Catherine, Mike, and Martha? That would be awkward, but much less awkward than Catherine's moving in with the Goodmans. Henry's mother, Louise, was not in favor of Henry marrying into the Sabinsky family. Catherine in her heart was convinced that Louise looked at her family as the ragged poor of Marinette. Henry's brother, Woody, and Henry's two sisters, Margie and Anna, were still living at home. Ken, the oldest, had recently married a woman named Mildred and lived down the road from their folks. Catherine was not interested in getting involved in the sibling rivalry that Henry occasionally mentioned.

Catherine knew she needed Clara's good advice. Getting advice from someone who wasn't Henry, Mike or Martha might help her ease her troubled mind. Her pockets hung heavy with candy to delight and bribe the kids. She needed alone time with her sister. When Catherine opened the door four pair of legs came barreling toward her followed by eight legs of the Boston Bulls. The kids and the dogs all jumped up on her at the same time. As usual, chaos reigned.

"Auntie Catherine, Auntie Catherine!"

"Come on and see our swell fort!"

"Here, look at my baby doll!"

"Lookit, lookit, I got a new truck!"

The dogs were barking and the kids were pulling her in different directions. The small living room floor was covered with trucks, dolls, building blocks, blankets, and couch cushions. It wasn't any different than any other time Catherine visited. No one was crying yet—a good sign! After clearing a space the size of her butt, she plunked herself down on the floor and enjoyed the wonderful mess. Neither softhearted Clara nor Nels had many rules for the tribe. As long as the children weren't hurting each other, they had free reign. Catherine pulled a handful of candy out of her pocket.

"Whoever sits down and zips their lips gets a piece of this yummy candy." She pulled her index finger and thumb across her closed lips to make her point. While the kids had the run of the house, they seldom got candy, so this stunt worked almost every time. Four quiet children sat down immediately. "You all sat down at the same time. You guys are aces," she said as she gave each one a candy. Even nine-year-old Glenny responded to sweet treats. She had their undivided attention.

As she reached into her pocket to pull out another handful of candy she said, "If you darlings play nicely while your mama and I are talking, you'll get to pick out another piece, whatever piece you want." Reaching into her other pocket she pulled out the pinnacle treat—four Peppermint Patties. "Whoever doesn't cry or fight when your mama and I are talking gets some of these, too." Four sets of eyes brightened, and four mouths curled up into a smile, but not one word was spoken.

Clara, wrapped in a worn and familiar bathrobe,

appeared breathlessly in the front room. "Catherine, this is a nice surprise. What did I do to deserve this?"

"I need you, Clare. I'm a mess. I don't know which way to turn, but first let me tell you the good news."

"I'm all ears. I could use some good news for a change." Clara shook her head in frustration. "These kids are driving me nuts and Nels is no help. In fact, when he's around, I feel like I have another kid. Moms says men are good for nothing, and every now and then I think she might be right . . . " She pasted on a bright smile. "So, what's your good news?"

"Henry and I are getting married."

"What? What are you talking about?" Catherine was stunned by the Clara's reaction. Was it just surprise, or was it disapproval? "You and Henry broke up a couple of years ago and now you're engaged? Have I missed something? How the heck did that happen?"

"Well, I feel like I'm the middle of a tornado. This is all happening so fast!" Catherine pulled herself up from her small island in a sea of toys and followed Clara to the kitchen table.

"Okay, here's what happened. I accidently ran into Henry at Matty's after our office Christmas party. I made dinner for Henry the next night, and after dinner he asked Papa if he could marry me. It happened that fast."

"So, you saw each other one day—at a party!—and he asked Papa for your hand the next day? Aren't you afraid you're moving a little too fast?"

"Mom asked me the same thing, but I don't think so. We never stopped loving each other. I never thought we couldn't work it out. I wasn't ready to settle down before. The issues are the same, but now I'm so ready I could burst. We've had a couple of weeks to talk about it and think about it, and I know I'm ready to get married."

Clara could see that her young sister would take this big step, no matter what she might advise.

"Have you set a date?"

"Not yet. We have so much to settle before we can set a date. I stopped over to see if you could help me sort this out. I don't think I can do this by myself. I'm losing my damn mind!"

The house was quiet. Catherine's bribes to the Johnson tribe were still working. The sisters sat silent for some seconds, but Catherine needed to blunt the edginess she felt. "Have you got a little rotgut or beer around here? I need something to calm me down. Coffee won't do it."

"Jeez, I don't know. Maybe Nels has a bottle around here. Let me go take a look in our bedroom. He might have something stashed in there."

Because Clara was the shortest of the brothers and sisters, she had to stand on her tiptoes on a chair to explore all the closet shelves, but after a few minutes she came back to the kitchen with a bottle of white liquid.

Catherine looked at the unlabeled bottle, then at Clara. "We sure as hell don't want to drink rubbing alcohol. That could make my bad situation even worse."

When the cap came off the bottle and the smell drifted into their nostrils, however, there was no doubt it was gin. The vapors alone could make them high. Clara felt like she was getting away with something—finding Nels' secret stash—and she loved it. She put a couple of jelly jars on the table and poured some gin into each one. Catherine rocked back, choking, after the first sip.

"Holy shit, Clare! We gotta find something to mix with this poison! It'll burn our guts out. Do you have any sour?"

Clara searched the icebox for something to mix with the gin. She dug past a bottle of syrup, a can of beans, soup from the prior evening's supper. She took out a dish of leftover mashed potatoes and placed them in front of Catherine. "Here. You want some potatoes in your gin?"

The potatoes struck a funny bone and they both started laughing. Clara crossed her legs and bent over. "I'm trying not to pee my pants!"

Catherine, bringing her hands to her face, said, "Me, too."

They rocked in their chairs, laughing until—as their mother always described such hilarity—'til they were 'blue in the face.'

It had been a long time since they laughed so hard together. When they were children it was Papa who sparked the laughter with his stories. Drunk or sober—and sometimes they didn't know the difference—he showed the greatest sense of humor in the Sabinsky family.

The children were restless, and Glenny, the oldest, walked quietly into the kitchen, witnessing his mother and aunt acting like children.

"You're not going to get any candy if you don't quiet down," he said, and his chance mockery of adult censure cause a new round of laughter.

"Oh, you are so right, Glenny," Catherine said, as she caught her breath. "I have lost any chance of getting a Peppermint Pattie. You and the other kids get mine. You are such a good boy for reminding us."

"Mama, you don't get any either," he said sternly. "Can I have your share?"

"You are all playing so well together, I'm going to give you an extra candy right now. Let me go get my coat." The kids were overjoyed, and they knew there was more to come if they minded their Ps and Qs until Mama and Aunt Cat were done.

Cutting the raw gin with water and a little maple syrup assured the sisters that they were protecting their stomach lining. It burned all the way down and tasted putrid, but it took the edge off—just what Catherine felt she needed. Sitting across from each other at the kitchen table, they finally got down to business.

"Can I push this table away from the wall? I'm squished back here. Your kitchen is small, and your table is big."

Clara ignored the comment. She was well aware of the size of her kitchen. Her bright yellow enameled table could barely fit their brood, but if it were any bigger, they couldn't get through to the bathroom in the back of the house. They had plenty of bedrooms, but they had outgrown their small living area.

"So, what's going on that causes you to need a drink so early in the day?"

"Where do I begin? First on my list is marrying Henry. That seems simple, right?" Clara looked at her and nodded. "Not so," Catherine continued. "Where we will live is question number one. Our house is too small for the four of us—and, anyway, can you imagine us living with Mom and Papa? I've been doing it alone ever since all of you left. It's awful, Clara. The tension is so thick you could cut it with a knife. I never know what to expect when I walk into that door after work. Will Mom be in our bedroom in her rocking chair with the door closed or will she be washing the walls? Occasionally she makes dinner and communicates. Sometimes she's sitting at the kitchen table with her head in her hands. Can you imagine starting a life together that way? I get a headache just thinking about it."

Catherine paused, took a deep breath and a haul of gin. "Is it really that bad, Cat?"

"No, it's worse. Then there's Papa. He gets home anytime between noon and midnight. He might come in whistling with a lunch pail full of fresh fish and a funny story about one of his co-partners in crime. On the other hand, he could come in late and drunk. If he's had a bad day, he takes it out on Mom and sometimes on me or Pepper, too. She sits at the table with her head in her hands or goes into our bedroom and shuts the door. He'll tell me to get that fucking dog out of his way or he'll kick the shit out of him. He might even do it, but he hasn't yet. There's no place for me to hide. Mom's in our shared bedroom and he's in the rest of the house ranting and raving . . . "

"Watch what you say, Cat. We have some big ears within hearing distance."

"Oh, yeah. Sorry. I want to go someplace where I can scream at the top of my lungs and say every curse word I know."

Clara got up from her chair and rubbed Catherine's back. "I knew it was bad, but not that bad. We're lucky you've done so much already."

"Take another sip, 'cuz I'm only getting started," Catherine said as she raised her glass. "To my screwed-up life. Money is another issue foremost on my mind. If I get married, I'll probably lose my job. If I get pregnant, my job is a goner for sure. So, we wouldn't be able to support Mom and Papa. Henry works for his father and doesn't have a regular income. I have no idea how we would support ourselves without my salary, let alone trying to support anyone else."

Catherine took the last swallow of her gin-maple syrup cocktail as her chin began to quiver. She couldn't hold the tears back any longer. Her head went into her hands. Clara was struck by her sister's pose, recognizing that Catherine was holding her head just as their mother sometimes did.

"And speaking of Henry, he might have to go to war," Catherine sobbed. "He had to sign up with the draft board a couple weeks ago. I'm so worried that he'll go away and never come back." She looked at Clara imploringly. "Clare, I don't know how to handle the uncertainty of everything in my life."

When the kids heard her crying, they tiptoed toward the kitchen. Glenny, the nine-year- old spokesman for the group, was worried about Aunt Cat and whether they would still get their extra candy.

"Auntie Cat is sad but she's okay," their mother reassured her brood, lined up in the doorway to the kitchen. "We all get sad and cry sometimes. Did that ever happen to any of you?"

"Well, sure, Mom," Glenny said. "It happens every day. But we're kids. We're supposed to act that way. You always tell us, 'get a grip.' Would it help Auntie Cat if I told her that?"

"Really, do I always say that?"

He looked back at his brothers and sister. They all started talking at once. "Yeah, every time, Ma. You don't rub our backs. We get yelled at all the time . . ."

Clara sensed this might be a good distraction for Catherine, so she chose to confront this mini-rebellion. "I'm not sure you're right. I remember earlier this morning when you were crying, Tommy, because Glenny threw his truck at you and it hit you on the cheek. You were wailing. What did I do then?"

"I don't know."

"I remember. I sat you on my lap, rubbed your back, kissed your cheek to make it better and said 'there, there.' Do you remember now?" Clara asked.

"Yeah, I guess."

"What do you think you all could do to make Auntie Cat feel better?"

With that Catherine lifted her head off her hands. Four sweet little faces were looking at her. Sandy patted Catherine's knee. "It's gonna be okay, Auntie. You'll see." Dickie, who was almost two, climbed up on Catherine's lap and gave her a sloppy kiss on the cheek. Glenny and Tommy were trying their best to say something nice, but they were big boys. Being manly was of the utmost importance to them. They managed a smile and an "I'm sorry."

Catherine wiped her tears on the handkerchief Clara handed to her and thanked the troops for their support. "I am going to be okay. I have a few more things to tell your mama, but I haven't forgotten about the Peppermint Patties." They smiled widely and clapped their hands. "I am so impressed with you. You have been such good kids."

"What does *impwest* mean?" Tommy asked.

"It means I'm proud of you."

When the two of them were alone again, Clara said, "You have too much on your plate, Little Sis."

"No kidding. And to put the proverbial frosting on the fallen cake, Henry's mother is a bitch." She said the word bitch very softly, so the little ears didn't hear it. "She's going to have a conniption fit when she finds out we're getting married."

"I see why you're a mess, Cat. It seems like money could help some. Too bad none of us are rich."

"Yeah, too bad. Well, thanks for listening to my sad-ass story. Henry and I have lots of thinking to do. We have each other. That's the best part. Maybe prayer would help." They looked at each other and smiled. "I gotta get going. Henry's waiting for me. First, I have to settle up with the gang."

"Just a minute, Catherine. I have some news for you, too."

"What, what? I spent the whole time talking and haven't asked you a thing about yourself. "

"I think I'm PG again. I missed 'my friend' last month."

"Wow, Clare! How do you feel about that? You said Dickie was the last one."

"Yeah. I thought so. That Nels. He doesn't take no for an answer." She clicked her tongue. "I don't know how I'll handle another one. Dickie is almost two." She shrugged, unsmiling. "Well, anyway, there's not a thing I can do about it, is there? Another mouth to feed. I'm kinda down, but what would I do without these kids?"

Chapter 16. The Lovebirds and Their Kin (1941)

All winter and spring Catherine and Henry talked of nothing but their wedding and future living arrangements, but they still hadn't come up with a plan. Driving home from work on a nice spring day Catherine felt sorry she wasn't going to see Henry that evening. Henry had practically lived at the Sabinskys' these days, and it would have been a wonderful evening to go for a walk, maybe down to the harbor as they so often did. Henry had told her that his father needed his help on a new beer storage cooler, so she was surprised when she spotted Henry's truck in the alley behind her house.

Oh, Jeez, she thought. *What's he doing here? I hope to God nothing is wrong.* Leaping to conclusions, she hoped even more that Henry was not trying to convince her mother she'd be fine living on her own. She didn't want to face having her mother back in that dreadful asylum. Henry should not be talking to Martha about this without Catherine at the table.

As she opened the back door, she was struck by the warmth of the kitchen and the wonderful, familiar smell of baking bread. Martha and Henry, chatting over coffee at the kitchen table, looked up with Catherine walked in.

"Hey, guys. Whatcha doin'?"

Maybe she misapprehended. Henry didn't look guilty of anything. In fact, he looked genuinely happy to see her. "Honey, where have you been? Mame and I have been waiting for you. I thought you might have skipped town." Henry gave Catherine a big smile, waved his arm. "Get over here, woman, and give your future husband a little kiss."

"In front of my mother?" Catherine joked. She walked over to Henry and gave him a peck on the cheek.

Martha rose. "Why don't you lovebirds go sit in the front room with your lovey-dovey stuff, so I can make supper?"

"I want a piece of hot bread before I leave the kitchen," Catherine demanded.

"If you want bread, you'll have to wait. If you want warm dough, you can have it now."

"You're a wiseacre, Mom. I guess I'll have to snuggle with my sweetheart on an empty stomach." She grabbed Henry's hand, pulled him into living room and plunked herself on the couch as close to him as possible.

"What were you and my mother talking about that you obviously didn't want me to hear," she whispered.

"Cat, there's nothing I don't want you to hear, but let me tell you what happened." He kept his voice low, too, although Martha's kitchen noises made clear she was focused on prepping the meal. "No sooner did I walk in the door than she was asking me if I was going to take you away. She's scared stiff to live alone or with your dad. I listened to her explain why it wouldn't work for you to move out and leave her with Mike. It's pretty much everything you've told me. When she ran out of steam, I asked her what she thought would work for her."

"Well, aren't you polite, Mr. Goodman! I'm impressed."

"Yes, so am I. She has never opened up to me before."

"So, what'd she say? I'm dying to hear it."

"First, she clearly ticked off the options. She knows exactly what she wants—to live with us, me and you—but not Mike. Obviously, she has put a lot of thought into this. Mike should stay in this house. He's close to the boats, his favorite watering holes and his drinking buddies. She wants us— meaning you, me and her—to find a nice little place away from Menekaunee, something that's bigger than this one so that she can have a room of her own. She doesn't think it's a good idea to share a room with you anymore. So, there you have it."

Catherine was stunned. Her mother, a planner and negotiator! "Are you kidding me? This is a woman who keeps her head down. The only decision she makes is what to cook. Are you sure she was clear-headed?"

"What do you think, Cat? I thought she was clear as a bell and has been thinking about this for a while. She has her ducks in a row. But she said even more. Wait 'til you hear this one! If I get drafted, she said, she'll be there to support you!"

"I didn't think she even knew about the war. I told them both you had to sign up for the draft, but neither she nor Papa acknowledged it. I've lived here my whole life and I have not yet figured out what goes on in that woman's head. I see her in those down times, and I forget how sharp she can be. She might be sharper than we think." Catherine paused, accepted that her mother might have hit on something that answered so many questions. "Okay, did the 'planner'"— Catherine making dramatic air quotes—"happen to have a way to pay for this nice bigger house, or how to take care of this one, for that matter?"

Henry and Catherine talked well into the evening, finally reaching the point where each found and shared what mattered most. Henry's top priority was to get married before he was drafted. Catherine argued that she did not want to get married until they figured out where they would live and how they would pay for it. They both agreed that Martha's plan was better than anything they had discussed before.

Maybe one of Catherine's siblings might invite Martha to live with them, leaving Catherine to watch over Mike, who might be easier to deal with than her mother. At least he had a sense of humor. So, maybe a place to start would be a letter to Catherine's brothers and sisters, explaining their plans and their situation. Catherine wasn't hopeful. Maybe the siblings might agree instead to send money on a regular basis to help the young lovebirds. She had nothing to lose. She had been the major provider for her mother and father since her brothers and sisters moved out.

By the time the night was over they agreed she would draft a letter to Stella, Charlie, Clara and Steve with a promise to Henry she wouldn't send it until he gave his approval.

After what seemed like a thousand drafts, she wrote:

Dear Stella, Charlie, Clara, and Steve,

I write you with swell news. Henry asked Papa for my hand in marriage and he said yes! This all happened fast! My head won't stop spinning. I'll write you the details of how we got back together in another post. We are madly in love and I am over the top! But, this does not come without challenges.

It's all about Mom, Papa and our living situations. Frankly, Henry and I can't begin a marriage living with the two of them. They are not easy, to say the least. My ideal would be if Henry and I could have a little cottage for two, but that's off the table in any event.

Mom came up with a suggestion that isn't bad. (Can you believe she's actually told me what she wants?) Papa would stay in the house and

Mom, Henry, and I would find a bigger place where we can all live comfortably. Henry agrees to this, bless his heart! Looks good on paper, right? Two big questions, though.

How can we break it to Papa that Mama is leaving him and how can we afford another place? My salary is barely supporting the three of us now. Henry works for his Dad, so his wages are inconsistent. Moreover, Henry is expecting to be drafted. He had to sign up a couple weeks ago. We want to get married before he goes to war.

Any suggestions will be welcome. I need a fairy godmother.
Love Always, Catherine

The letters went out the next day. By the end of March, after dozens of letters were posted back and forth, the siblings divined a plan to meet in Marinette in early May for a confab. Stella and Anthony hadn't visited since their move to Connecticut, so they were due for a visit, Charlie was able to arrange for time off the ore boats, and Steve and Helen would drive from Madison.

In the meantime, Catherine and Henry did more groundwork. One of the first items on their list was making peace with Henry's mother. Catherine dreaded the thought of it.

"Honey, we can't put this off any longer. We need to talk to my mother about our getting married, whether you like it or not. What would be the easiest way for you?"

"Does she even want to see me? Before we broke up, it was clear from what you told me that she didn't think I or my family were good enough for you. I've never even had a real conversation with her. Do you think anything has changed?"

"Cat, I'm not sure. She knows I spend every waking moment with you when I'm not working, but she doesn't ask any questions. I'm twenty-two. She can't tell me what to do."

"But she can make life a living hell for you."

"I haven't told her we're getting married."

"Henry Goodman, are you kidding? You haven't told your mother yet? It's been nearly two months since we've been engaged! Are you afraid of her?"

Henry hesitated. He didn't know what to say. His mother doted on her three sons but she tried to run their lives. Henry, like his father, kept as far away from conflict as he could. He knew his mother didn't want him to marry "that girl from Menekaunee." It didn't matter that Catherine was kind, smart, pretty, and had an impressive job. She came from a no-account family. Her father was a drunk, her mother had a reputation for being on shaky ground and the worst of it was they lived in the wrong part of town.

Louise wanted her boys to accomplish something more than she and V.R. had, which at this moment was running a small business selling a little beer and coal in the area. She had worked hard to get her County Normal Teaching Certificate and wished every day that she could be teaching in one of the Marinette County schools. Instead, she was spending all her time raising five children and helping her husband with his fledgling businesses. She felt he couldn't build the business on his own. She minced no words telling him if he would work a little harder and a little faster he'd be more successful. She ruled the roost. She made time to do the books and would go on some deliveries with him. Not only would she load and unload cases of beer and bring them into taverns, but she'd do a little sales work in the bars. Being a teetotaler didn't keep her from singing the praises of Rahrs and Kingsbury beer to the tavern owners. The couple sold beer to the taverns in Menekaunee, and they knew about all about Mike Sabinsky.

Louise sat front and center in a pew at the First United

Methodist Church every Sunday. She thought everyone else should be there, too. Neither V.R. nor his grown sons joined her—one of the biggest failings of her life, she felt—but her two daughters were faithful followers. Louise had no love for Catholics. Not under any circumstances would she allow one of her offspring to marry one. Hard workers—Lutherans, maybe some evangelicals—met her standards, so on that score Catherine was okay but little else about her was acceptable.

Henry promised to waste no time sharing their wedding plans with his mother, and Catherine wished him luck. They both agreed that they each had been blessed—or cursed—with difficult mothers.

"We have quite a pair, don't we?" Catherine mused.

"Yup, we do. And don't forget I have agreed to live with your mother, so the least you can do is get to know mine a little better."

Catherine begrudgingly agreed to visit his family, but only after Henry told his mother they were getting married.

Henry hated to confront anybody, let alone his judgmental mother, but he knew he owed it to Catherine—and himself—to cross this painful bridge. He soon found an opportunity, an afternoon when he was sitting at the round oak dining table piled with thawing clothes. He watched his mother iron, appreciating her system. She'd pick the clothes off the line, still frozen, and iron them exactingly, piece by piece. As she finished each of the men's work shirts, she'd put them on hangers and hang them on the top of the door frame. Henry watched as Louise admired each perfectly-ironed piece, noticing that if she saw even the smallest wrinkle, the shirt was off the hanger and back on the ironing board. Waiting for the right moment to speak, he was surprised to see how his mother even carefully pressed the men's snow-white tee shirts and folded just them, just so. He didn't remember ever watching his mother iron before. If he'd have thought about it more deeply, he might have grasped then that she wanted the same drive for perfection in her offspring.

How unusual for him to be alone with his mother, no sisters, brothers or father, no buffers around that afternoon. His body twitched as he thought of giving his mother the news. He was pretty sure what to expect—he'd heard some variation of it many times. *Wrong girl. Wrong for the family. Friends, neighbors, relatives will wonder what has happened to the Goodman family. Find a good girl from a good family.*

He sat and watched, trying to find the right way to open the conversation, finally just blurting out, "Mom, Catherine and I are getting married."

Louise hesitated and stared at Henry before she replied. She wasn't surprised. Henry was spending all his spare time away from home and she knew where he was. A few drive-arounds in Menekaunee after beer deliveries gave her all the evidence she needed, namely, Henry's truck always parked in front of the Sabinsky's run-down house—paint peeling off the siding, stairs and porch askew.

She didn't break stride. Grabbing a white shirt from the pile, slipping it over the end of the ironing board, she flicked a drop of water on the iron to check its heat. Louise pulled the shirt tight, pressed the iron along the line of buttons, and without raising her gaze from the shirt replied calmly, "Really. And just when did this come about, Mr. Henry Goodman?"

"Jeez, Mom . . ."

"Don't 'Jeez me,' Henry. You know how I feel about her and her good-for-nothing family. I suppose you think they're going to support you after you get married. You never think about how good you have it now."

"Stop!" Henry said, trying to fortify his resolve. "I don't want another lecture from you about how good I have it here. What do you want from me?"

Louise set the iron in its rest pad, folded her arms, shook her head in profound disappointment. Why could Henry not understand what was really important?

"You know full-well what I want, Henry. I want you to be happy, have a good life, marry into a good family that can help you become someone. Delivering beer with your father is not what I call a decent profession. Fishing and getting drunk with her father are not what I have in mind for you either. You're saying you want to live with a woman who's going to be just like her mother when she gets older? I should just say, go ahead and you'll be sorry. But I can't say that.

"Henry, the whole town knows Mrs. Sabinsky doesn't have all her marbles. You're smarter than this, I know you are. You can't really be serious."

"What about you, Mother. You went to County Normal for two years and have a teaching certificate. Why aren't you teaching school instead of hauling beer and coal around with Dad? You're a hypocrite, you know that? You don't drink or like it when others do, but your still push the beer sales. How does that work? You talk about everyone who doesn't meet your standards. You don't even meet your own standards."

"Watch that mouth, Henry Goodman . . ."

"You talk to me like I'm a little kid!"

"You don't know the half of it, my boy. If I didn't keep after your dad day and night, he wouldn't get anything accomplished."

"Now you're going a little bit too far, Mother. There's nothing wrong with him. He works hard. He never has a mean word to say about anyone. He's afraid to open his mouth around you, just like I am, okay, just like I've been . . ."

Just say it, man! Just say it to her! "Okay, Mom, here it is, straight up. I'm going to marry Catherine. I don't want to hear another word about it from you. End of story."

Louise did a quick calculation. There would always be time to derail this. *Just give in now and the moment will come.* "Well, Henry, let's wait and see. We have time to talk about this, and I know that one day you'll wish you listened to your mother."

Henry was becoming aware of how his mother had subtly controlled the lives of her husband and children. He felt himself finally in command of the moment. He walked to the back door. "We'll send you an invitation. If you don't come, I don't give a damn." He slammed the door behind him. Regret came and immediately evaporated. *I bet I'll be asked to pay for that and I don't care!*

Henry's father caught him on his way to his truck. "Hey, son, how about giving me a hand? I have to take a truck full a beer to Crivitz. I could use some help loading and unloading the truck, if you don't have anything better to do." The delivery was for Shaffer's Bar and Supper Club, which was having a big wedding on the weekend and needed a couple kegs of Kingsbury and twenty-five cases of Rahr's.

"Yeah, sure. I was about to feed and water Patches and Bessie, but Mom can take care of that. I rode Patches the other day to see how her leg was doing. She seems in pretty good shape. She scared the crap out of the chickens."

"Did you tell your mother about Patches?"

"I'm not talking to Mother. I'll tell you about it later. I'm sorry, but you'll have to tell her." Henry did not mention his planned marriage to his father. *Later,* he thought.

When Henry met up with Catherine after work, he told her his mother didn't approve of their marriage, but he saved her the humiliation of repeating the things his mother said about Catherine's family.

"What are we going to do now?" Catherine looked forlorn.

"We are going ahead with our plans. We can get married without her. I told her we'd send her an invitation. I don't even care if we do that. She's so goddamn stubborn and uppity. I'm pissed!"

In the meantime, Martha was riding high. Living with Catherine and Henry would be a dream. Life might be good if she didn't have to face Mike every day.

As the three of them sat around the kitchen table after supper, they set the date for the 20th of September, 1941. It was a wonderful feeling for Catherine and Henry. It was as though setting the date suddenly made their marriage real, something above and beyond all the family issues. They made a list of what needed to be done—talk to Reverend Sonnack, reserve the church, get the invitations, find a place for a reception, decide what Catherine would wear, find a place to live and the big one—find the money to pay for it all.

"Henry, what do your mother and father think of you two getting married?" Martha asked.

"They're happy to get me off their hands," Henry lied. He was embarrassed to tell Catherine's mother about his own over-bearing mother. What he was going to do about her he didn't know . . .

Just before Henry was leaving, he gavè Catherine a gift she would never forget. He told her he'd saved enough money over the last few years to have a wing-ding wedding celebration.

"You're not kidding me, are you? I mean, really! Don't tease me about this!"

"I'm not teasing, Honey. I've been putting a little bit

away every week. We're going to celebrate 'til the cows come home. Yes, Cat, we're going to have ourselves the party of our lives and a honeymoon, too, my little wife-to-be."

She threw her arms around him and kissed him until he was gasping for breath.

"I just wanted to let you know I told her. My dad asked me if I could help him with a big delivery this afternoon. I'm happy to help *him*, but not that mother of mine."

Later that day, Henry and V.R. rode along in a comfortable silence. Neither one of them were big talkers. After a while, Henry opened up.

"Hey, Dad, I got some good news for you."

"Yeah?"

"Catherine and I are getting married. We set the date, September twentieth."

"This September?"

"Yup. We're all set. We're going to have the celebration of a lifetime, plenty of Rahrs, plenty of food. She's a swell gal, Dad."

"Isn't this kinda quick. Didn't you two just get back together?"

Henry told V.R. the full story, including the impending possibility of being drafted.

"Where you gonna live? What about Mike and her mother?"

"We're working on that. Mame wants to live with us without Mike. That's going to take some doing, but we've got a little time. Her sisters and brothers are having a get-together in May to try to make some sense of it all. Her sister Stella is coming all the way from Connecticut.

"Are you okay livin' with Mame?"

Henry paused. *The diplomatic answer or the honest one?*

Diplomacy won. "Y'know, if that's what it takes to be with Catherine, I'll do it. Truth be known, I'd much rather have Catherine to myself. Anyway, we'll see what happens. I sure do want to marry that gal. She's the one for me—always was, always will be."

"Does your mother know?"

"Well, that's why you have to tell her about Patches' leg, not me. I told her we were getting married, she gave me a lecture, and I left. I'm pissed. I am goddamn pissed! She thinks we're better than they are. I don't know why she thinks we're so damn good. Frankly, Dad, I don't care what she thinks. I'm a grown man. She can't run my life anymore. I won't let her. Catherine is afraid of her. If Mother would accept Catherine, I'd be happy, but I've tried. I give up."

Cornstalks stood in rich, flat, snow-covered fields on both sides of the highway as the two men rode in silence for some miles. Henry's father then spoke, giving rare advice. "Your mother's a hard one. She might have a good heart, but you have to dig some to find it. You can't win a mouth fight with her. She's probably stronger than me. She could probably knock me over. I just try to stay out of the way."

"I told her I didn't care if she comes to the wedding, Dad. Honestly, I don't!"

"I'll be there, son. I'll get you all the beer you need. Hell, maybe I can even sell it to you at cost!" They both laughed, but V.R.'s tone was serious again. "You know how stubborn your mother is. I won't be able to do a thing about getting her to the wedding."

"When you don't see me around the house much, you'll know why. I'll sleep in my bed, and I'll come to work every morning, but otherwise I'm going to make myself scarce."

Later that day when Henry again saw Catherine, he told her she didn't have to worry about visiting his mother.

"That's a relief. Why not?"

"She doesn't think I'm ready to get married. She wants to keep me under her thumb forever," Henry said.

Catherine sighed, defeated. She knew the reason she would not be visiting was that she was not wanted in the Goodman household. Henry sensed her change of mood.

"Hey, let's not talk about my mother. Let's talk about us! We have wedding plans to make!" He took her in his arms to kiss away their troubles, at least for the moment.

March roared through northern Wisconsin, sometimes a lion and sometimes a lamb, but April promised early planting for onions, carrots, and radishes. As the end of the month drew near, Catherine and Martha knew it was five months to the wedding but only a couple of weeks before the Sabinsky gang descended upon them. They worked to get the house spotless. Every nook and cranny was scrubbed, dusted and polished. Catherine was brimming with excitement. She hadn't seen Stella since her visit before the move to Manchester, almost five years earlier. In that span a new niece, Margaret , had been born, and Catherine couldn't wait to meet her. Martha was ambivalent about the upcoming rendezvous. While she longed to see her offspring and their own offspring, these family get-togethers were hard on her. Whenever two or more Sabinskys were involved, booze flowed abundantly. Being a teetotaler herself, she hated the drinking, raucous laughter and foolishness, nor did she like all the attention Mike got on these tawdry occasions. He was the life of the party. She would have done just about anything to rid the house of alcohol and Mike.

Henry and Catherine had done some groundwork in preparation for the family meeting. They had tough decisions to make, especially those that dealt with the prospective living arrangements for Mike and Martha. This was the issue bringing the clan together, and this was where Catherine needed input from her siblings. It wouldn't be simple to get Mike to agree to live alone. Martha refused to live only with Mike, and Catherine couldn't bear the thought of she and Henry living with both her parents. What a way to start a life together! A crowded house, living on top of each other with little privacy. Worse, she couldn't predict when her mother might have one of her spells, when her father would come home drunk, or how her mother and father would relate to each other. Catherine's only hope was that her siblings could help take care of her parents. She'd had enough.

Chapter 17. Stella Drops a Bomb (1940)

Stella, Anthony and Margaret arrived first. Anthony had driven twenty-four hours straight from Manchester, Connecticut, to Marinette, Wisconsin. When Catherine saw an unfamiliar, big black sedan pull up in front of the house her heart started to pound, and she knew it was them.

Nobody else she knew would have a shiny black car like this beautiful Buick Century Sedan. The last time she saw Stella and Anthony, he was driving that swell red Ford Roadster.

Passengers were climbing out of three doors as Catherine ran down the porch steps with her arms open wide. She didn't know whom to hug first. Margaret, her three-year-old niece, looked up at her. Catherine picked up her niece and twirled her around.

"Who are you?" the little one asked shyly.

"I'm your Aunt Cat. Look at you. You're such a big girl already. Come on, let's go over and meet Mamie. I'll bet she has a treat for you. Look, she's out on the porch!"

"Who's Mamie?"

"Your gramma."

The prospect of something sweet banished shyness. "Yet's go get my teat!"

Stella had run up the stairs to throw her arms around

her mother. They were both crying and laughing alternatively.

"Mamie has a teat a me," Margaret said to her mother.

Martha looked at her beautiful grandchild for the first time. "Come to me, Margaret." She lifted the little one up, hugged her tight, tried to sneak a kiss, and walked in the house to the kitchen toward the cookie jar on the shelf near the warm cook stove. Margaret enjoyed the attention she was getting.

Martha lifted the cover. "You can pick whatever one you want, sweet little girl. Mamie loves you."

"I want a giant cookie this big," Margaret said stretching her arms out as far as she could reach.

Stella turned toward her daughter with a slight grin. "You mind your manners, Margaret. Watch out, Mom, she knows how to get her way. Her daddy spoils her."

"I'll spoil her, too, every chance I get. That's what grammas are for," Martha said.

Before they could get out of the kitchen, Clara—big pregnant belly preceding her—came in the back door with Nels, four Johnson kids, and Mike close behind. More hugging and kissing, a hubbub of voices, a kitchen overflowing with family. Sandy, Clara and Nels' only daughter, looked up at her grandmother hugging a strange child.

"Mamie, I want a cookie, too," she said as she pulled on Martha's dress.

Martha squatted down, still holding Margaret. "Sandy, this is your cousin who came to visit." She put Margaret down, picked up the cookie jar and made sure all the kids had one of her home-made frosted sugar cookies. Sandy took Margaret's hand and off they went. It wasn't long before the boys were wrestling and throwing each other on and off the couch.

Suddenly they heard a low, gravelly voice in the front room saying slowly, "What the hell are you little scallywags doing to each other on the couch?" It was Charlie, tall and handsome with curly black hair. Martha recognized his voice at once and came running out of the kitchen. She looked diminutive next to her drop-dead gorgeous son. He picked her up and twirled her around.

"Put me down, you crazy fool," Martha laughed with glee. Charlie smiled with half his mouth and shook his head.

"Charlie, my big brother, you are some kind of looker. I'll bet you can't keep the gals away," Catherine said as she took her mother's place in his arms.

"Well, I guess I have a couple of 'em in every port." Always a person of few words, he said no more.

"Hey, Anthony," Mike shouted across the kitchen. "How ya doin'? You're lookin' pretty goddamn good after all these years. Did ya bring any of that top-shelf whiskey with ya?"

Anthony pushed through the crowded kitchen over to Mike. "Good to see you, Mike. I was just about to open this bottle of Old Crow. How about a shot with a Miller chaser?"

"What did I hear about a Miller chaser?" Henry called as he came barreling through the back door with a case of Rahrs balanced on his shoulder, showing a bicep the size of a tennis ball. "Get rid of that Miller hogwash. I've got the real stuff here." He put the case on the floor, opened it up, pulled out a bottle, popped the cap, handed a bottle to Mike, and proceeded to open bottles until everyone had their own except Martha. She turned up her nose at the very thought of it.

Before long the party was in full swing. Food appeared from nowhere, and glasses with whiskey and beer were overflowing. The adults, except for Martha, were playing smear, Mike's favorite card game. The more they drank the louder and coarser they became. When Steve and Helen finally arrived, not one of them except Martha was sober. It didn't take the Madison couple long to catch up. Helen announced she was three months PG. Her provocative, red, low-cut dress was tight-fitting through the bodice and the hips. When Helen walked, her hips swung wide in both directions on top of her red satin spike heels. Her died red hair was piled high on her head, and her lipstick matched her dress.

Anthony called out to Helen. "Saunter over here, Baby, so I can tell if those big knockers are real."

"Why, sure, Tony Baby." She sashayed over to Anthony, leading with her breasts. "How you gonna tell?"

"Hey, Steve, can I give your wife's tits a squeeze to see if she's the real thing?"

"Ask her, but once you do, you'll never be satisfied again."

"Hey, Helen, how about a little squeeze?"

"Well, I'd be honored, Anthony," she said in a flirty little girl laugh.

Anthony walked over to Helen and fondled each breast. Helen led him on. Steve was enjoying the show his wife and brother-in-law were putting on. Stella, on the other hand, was over in a corner not paying attention to anything except keeping her whiskey glass full. Mike was staggering but still working to be the life of the party.

Martha, livid over the antics, gathered up the grandchildren and put them to bed with her. She lay sleepless, listening to the drunken soirée. She heard Mike telling story after story and the others egging him on.

"Hey, Mike, tell us that one about peeing in the bottle and giving it to your friend . . ."

"What about when the pony butted Big Louie into the hole in the ice . . ."

"Hey, I think you just cheated, you son-of-a-bitch—

where did that queen of hearts come from . . ?"

And then uproarious laughter. The louder it got the more Martha seethed. Finally, Clara came in to get her children, Henry kissed Catherine good night, and everyone bedded down somewhere—in bed, on the couch or the floor. They didn't notice where they crashed. Catherine was never sure whether Anthony and Stella had slept in his big sedan.

The next afternoon Catherine and Stella went to Clara's to talk about the wedding and Martha and Mike's living situation. Catherine pleaded for help.

"I've been taking care of Mom and Dad since you all left. I don't want to live with them after Henry and I get married. I can't stand it for another day. You've got to help me. I can't save a penny for a hope chest. It takes my whole paycheck every week to try to keep up with the bills. Papa can't fish as much as he used to." She started to cry. "The drinking is taking its toll."

Stella put her hand on Catherine's shoulder, rocked her gently. "Come on, Cat. Buck up. You're getting married! You should be the happiest girl in the world!"

"She's got her hands full, Stella, the poor kid," Clara said. "You can't believe what she goes through. Those two are a handful."

"It's not like I don't love them!" Catherine shook with sobs. "But, *dammit*, I want a life of my *own!* Out of that goddamn madhouse!" She looked pleadingly from one sister to the other. "I . . . just . . . feel like . . . just eloping! Moving away with Henry!" There would be no help on Henry's side of their new family. "His mother's a crab. She hates me because I'm not from"— her air quotes were like knives—"*a good family!*" She clenched her fists. "I . . . want . . . *out* of this mess!"

Catherine's outburst brought the kids running to the

kitchen. "What's a matter with Aunt Cat?" Glenny asked, his young face showing genuine concern.

"She's having a bad time, but she'll be okay," his mother assured him. "You kids know how you feel when you scream. But then you feel better in a little while. Just give her a little love."

They huddled around Catherine, and each found a wrist, an elbow, a little bit of their aunt to hold onto.

"Do you want some candy, Auntie?" Sandy asked. "Did someone hit you?"

"You kids are so sweet," Catherine said, wiping her eyes, regaining some sense of control. "No one hit me. I'm just having a bad day." Her face wet with tears, her nose running, she wiped it on her sleeve. "I'll be fine. Thanks for the hugs and kisses. What would I do without you?"

After the gang headed back to their forts in the front room, Stella glanced at her watch. "Well, we haven't solved anything yet, but we have to get back to Mom's. I promised Anthony I'd be home soon."

What for? Catherine wondered. Stella had promised her the afternoon. Maybe Catherine had just misunderstood.

As they parted, Clara and Stella agreed that much more talk, much more thought was needed to make this coming marriage a blessing for Catherine and Henry. Once in the car, Stella's smile disappeared.

"Catherine, where can we go to sit and talk? I need coffee, I need a drink—a drink would be better. Take me somewhere . . ."

Catherine sensed the earnestness in her sister's voice but didn't ask why. "There's a little place near the courthouse. Ye Olde Oake. You can get whatever you want there."

They settled into a booth. Catherine ordered coffee but

Stella asked for a whiskey on the rocks. "House brand, bar-run, whatever you got," she told the waitress." Her agitation was more apparent but she didn't speak until she had her drink in hand.

"Cat, I know you and Henry have problems, but I have problems of my own that I'm having trouble dealing with." Then she dropped the bomb. "Anthony is not Margaret's father."

"What?" Catherine was dumbfounded. She glanced around. No one was near—the place was almost empty. Her first thought, "Does Anthony know?"

"Yup. He knows. He was broken-hearted when he found out, but he's such a good man . . ." She reached across the table and took Catherine's hands. "He is *so* much better than I deserve. I feel worthless . . . guilty. I still have trouble looking him in the eye . . . But, Cat, promise me, *promise me!* Margaret can never know this. Anthony can't know that I told you. You must swear to never tell a soul about this, not Henry, certainly not Mom." She took half her drink in a single swallow.

"Oh, my God! What happened?" Catherine neglected her coffee, but her sister looked to finish her first drink before she continued. She waved for the bartender's attention, held up her empty glass.

"I'll tell you, but you must never talk to me again about it once you hear the story. I'm so stupid . . . and selfish." The waitress brought the second drink, and Stella began her story.

"When I was working in the lingerie department at Carson Pirie Scott I fell in love with a married man, who worked for the mayor of Chicago. I met him when he came to my department looking for a gift for his wife. It was love at first sight for both of us. He pledged his heart to me. He promised to divorce his wife and marry me, but we had to sneak around until then. He didn't want to damage his political career. We had a wild affair. I was totally consumed with him. Cat, honestly, I felt like the luckiest woman in the world. I wanted to spend the rest of my life with him. Every moment of every day. He swept me off my feet. He was the sexiest, most romantic, loving man I had ever met. He left poems and notes professing his love for me, brought me flowers, chocolates, left important meetings to make love to me when I was available . . . "

She gestured to her glass. "I'm going to need at least one more of these if I'm going to tell all this. Talking about this feels like I'm tearing my heart out of my body." Another big swallow.

"He began divorce proceedings, and we started planning for the future. One night when he was taking me back to my flat, we had a disagreement and he turned into a different person. Suddenly, he was screaming at me. I can't remember why, but I hadn't thought the argument was a big deal. Of course, I blamed myself. What did I do wrong? He blamed me, too. In the end, I was apologizing to him. I was terrified he would leave me, so I tried to shape up.

"The next day was back to normal, and I was so grateful. The romance was back, and the divorce was proceeding. I was set for life until"—a pause, her face stern, a deep breath—"until he got mad again. This time he tore my nightie and slammed my head against the wall. I apologized—I couldn't stand the thought of his leaving me.

"The abuse got more frequent and intense. I got more anxious, trying to be the best person I could be so that he would never get mad. Once, when he pulled a gun on me, I ran out into the street."

Catherine sat horror-stricken. She always thought of

Stella in Chicago, the brave one who left home young, the adventurer making a good living in the big city. Catherine always thought she alone in the family lived a nightmare. Stella took another drink and continued.

"It took a long time before I was strong enough to stand up to him. As wonderful as he was in the good times, that was how horrible he was when he raged. I knew I had to get out to save myself and I did, but I was still in love with the good guy in him. After his divorce was final, he begged me come back, but I stood my ground."

"What was his name?" Catherine asked.

"Nope," Stella said, "Can't, not gonna tell you that. Maybe I'm telling you too much already."

Her glass was in the air for another refill. Catherine frowned. "Stell, it's kinda early . . . "

Stella bristled, the booze showing its teeth. "Hey, you gonna listen to my story or not?"

Catherine acquiesced.

"Anyway, it wasn't too long after that that I met Anthony in a bar. He fell in love with me. I was smarter about men now, and I knew he was a kind, loving man. You know him. He wouldn't hurt a flea. I did not feel passion the way I had felt it, but I respected him. I knew he would take good care of me and he has taken wonderful care of me." Stella's face sagged in sadness, and Catherine sensed the drinks were catching up with her. "Such a fine man. And I hurt him so bad. I will never forgive myself." Her tone was self-pitying, maudlin.

Catherine sipped her cold coffee, Stella nursed the new drink. There were big missing pieces in Stella's story. "So, Stell, how did you get pregnant without Anthony? You were married and moved to Connecticut a couple years before Margaret was born."

"I'm getting to that. So, Anthony and I tried to get

pregnant from the beginning, but it didn't happen. I sat home every day with nothing to do. I missed my job, my friends. I was bored and down in the dumps. Poor Anthony. He tried everything to lift my spirits and I tried, too.

"Then one day, shortly after Anthony left for work, there was a knock on my door. I was puzzled. No one *ever* knocked at my door. When I opened it, there *he* was! I couldn't believe my eyes.

"We fell into each other's arms. He hung around for a couple of months. After Anthony left in the morning, he would sneak in, and . . . ah, Cat, I can't go on. I love my little sister, but I know you must think I'm horrible!"

Stella's chin was quivering, tears filled her eyes. Catherine was aware of the occasional glance in their direction by the bartender, who nonchalantly wiped a clean, dry bar. Lips compressed, Stella decided to go on.

"Well, I might as well tell you the whole ugly mess and get it over with. I realized I was pregnant shortly after he left. It was horrible. I didn't know what to do. Try to have an abortion? Leave Anthony and move back to Chicago? Pretend it was Anthony's baby? Maybe kill myself. I can't do this . . . talk about this . . . it's too painful. I need another drink."

Catherine was keeping track. This would be the fourth in less than half an hour. She knew she might have trouble getting Stella into the car.

Stella continued. "I decided to live a lie. I told Anthony we were having a baby and we celebrated our good fortune. We were both overjoyed. We had fun buying baby clothes, a crib, toys galore. The nursery was wonderful, colorful, filled with toys, books, clothes for babies. But I made one very big mistake. I wrote *him* to say I was pregnant and having an abortion. Talk about stupid!"

She stopped again. Catherine wasn't sure her sister could go on. Neither spoke for several minutes.

"This is the last thing I'm going to tell you and you must never mention a word to me or anyone else for the rest of your life. He came to Manchester while I was in the hospital having Margaret. How he figured out the timing, I'll never know. Using all his corrupt political skills he probably bribed a nurse or someone to let him know. Who knows?"

Catherine wasn't much of a reader, but the thought came, *this is the kind of wild story that you normally would find in a book. Not from my sister's own lips . . .*

"When Anthony walked into my room in the maternity ward with a big bouquet of roses, it thrilled me, but when I looked up at him to give him a kiss, his face was ashen. I knew something terrible had happened. I immediately thought it was the baby."

"Your boyfriend is sitting in his car in front of the hospital. There could be only one reason he would be there and I think I know what it is."

Catherine looked at her sister's face and saw varied emotions flash by. She must have been reliving that moment. Catherine didn't know if her sister was going to collapse on the table, stand up and scream, or simply stop talking. It was a critical juncture. Stella's face hardened.

"Anthony, Margaret, and I came home from the hospital, Anthony told me that if that son-of-a-bitch ever came near me or Margaret again, he would kill him. Ah, God, the wonderful man he is. Anthony said Margaret was his daughter, and we would never think or act any differently about it for the rest of our lives. Now, I can't face myself. I am consumed with guilt. How could I have done that to him?"

Stella had no more to say. She polished off her drink,

stood unsteadily, dug awkwardly in her purse, said numbly, "Ah, I'll pay," and handed Catherine a ten-spot to settle the bar bill. She leaned in the doorway while Catherine paid.

When they got home, Stella headed straight to the bedroom and didn't come out for the rest of the day.

Catherine stood in the kitchen for some minutes, almost overwhelmed by a flood of thoughts that had never crossed her mind before. She needed some place for peace and quiet. Every space in the small house was filled with Sabinskys. She'd had enough of them for a while.

She put her coat back on, grabbed the bottle of whiskey, a pack of Luckys and headed for the back porch. She hoped no one would find her back there.

Stella. Did Catherine want to hug her or slap her? What had Stella revealed to Catherine about their own family? How could Stella have cheated on Anthony? How could her mother have cheated on her father? Did it run in her family? Would she cheat on Henry? Henry had asked about that when he learned of Martha's escapades. She knew he must never know about Stella.

And what was Anthony doing with Helen? Would Henry touch another woman's breasts as Anthony had? Or was that simply what happened when everyone was drunk?

Why had Stella chosen her, Catherine, of all the family, of all the friends Stella might have, to reveal the truth about Margaret's father? It was just a reprise of her mother sharing the history of her father's first rape and her mother's first pregnancy. Why was *she, Catherine,* the chosen one to carry the load of family secrets? What was it about her that invited these confidences?

This weekend was supposed to be about my future. Why do I have the burden of knowing, with no one to whom I can speak? The whiskey, instead of settling her in for the late afternoon, seemed to send her plummeting down a rabbit hole. Is this how her mother felt when she had one of her spells? *Oh, my God! What if I have spells like my mother?* What's was the point of trying to get away, she wondered. She'd been trying to get out from under her obligation to her parents since she graduated six years earlier. After last night and today, Catherine thought it unlikely anything would ever change. *My family is not going to save me. It's all they can do to save themselves, and they're doing a piss-poor job of it!*

After a make-shift supper, Martha went to bed, Mike wasn't home yet, and Stella was still in the bedroom with the door closed. Anthony, Steve, Helen, Charlie and Catherine were sitting around in the front room drinking a sweet liquor from a fancy bottle that Anthony had brought. Among his other great qualities, Anthony kept the family well-supplied with booze.

"What are we drinking, Anthony?" Catherine blurted out. She was the only one to have the courage to ask, maybe courage from her time with the whiskey bottle on the back porch.

None of the others wanted to show their ignorance.

"Cream de menthe," Anthony said casually, as though he drank it every day.

"This is the best drink I've ever had in my life," Catherine said as she raised her glass to Anthony. *Could this be the medicine to clear my messed-up head?* she wondered. A couple of hours earlier she had felt her life was over, her family a wreck, life nothing but a burden, but she was feeling better now.

As the entire family except Mike, Martha and Stella sat in the front room making small talk, Catherine searched her brain for a way to turn the conversation to her and her parent's future. Wasn't this the reason everyone was here? She knew if she waited much longer, she'd be dealing with whiskey-infused wisdom. That wouldn't do. She wanted a serious discussion. *This is my opening,* she thought.

"Hey, guys," she started. "I need to have a serious discussion about Mom and Papa, and, of course, Henry and me."

"What is there to discuss? What are the issues?" Steve asked. Listening to his tone, Catherine was reminded of her mother saying, "He'd rather have a needle in his eye" than talk about this.

Anthony, the adult in the room, sought to shape the conversation. "I'm listening Catherine. I think, although I do not have your blood running through my veins, that you need some help with your parents. You've been holding them together, supporting them for many years now. The rest of us have a huge debt to repay."

"Yeah, Catherine. You've been a damn good daughter and sister," Charlie, the kind man of few words, added thoughtfully, nodding his head.

"Thanks, Charlie, Anthony. Don't get me wrong. I love Mom and Papa. But neither of them is easy. On any given day or week, Mom can move instantly from being down in the dumps to flying as high as a kite. She's not normal very often. I feel like I have to watch every word or deed, so I don't set her off. Papa can set her off with a glance."

Helen had seen very little of her in-laws, other than an occasional raucous holiday gathering. "Really? Mike seems so easy to get along with. He's a fun-lovin' guy!"

Her husband contradicted her. "You don't know the half of it, Helen," Steve said. "You haven't lived your life with him. He has a mean streak that's as evil as he is funny. You don't want to cross him."

"He's never hurt me physically," Catherine said, "but I've seen how he's treated Mom and you guys. Charlie, Steve, I remember the time he chased you around the house with a baseball bat. You both ran out the front door, jumped off the porch, and I threw your jackets down to you. Where did you go after you ran away?"

"Oh, yeah. I remember that. I thought he was going to kill us," Steve said. "I don't remember where we went. I don't even know what we did that made him so fucking pissed-off."

Charlie laughed. "Hell, I remember what we did. We stole his whiskey! That's the worst thing anybody could do to him."

Anthony, a good manager, moved the conversation from nostalgia back to the question they had to face. "What do *you* want, Cat?" he asked.

"I want out. I want to get married to Henry and move far, far away. I want you to have a turn with them—all of you! I've been spending every penny of my paycheck to keep the three of us afloat. I'll probably lose my job when we get married. Henry can't support all of us. He can't even come close."

"You deserve a medal for all you have done for Mom and Dad, Catherine," Steve said. "I didn't realize all you've been doing, but, Christ, you've been an angel. Helen and I can help you out."

Helen had reservations about any big commitment to these in-laws. "We have a baby coming in a few months," she reminded Steve. "We'll have another mouth to feed."

"I can handle this, Helen. We're fine. Why don't you go get us another drink?" he said dismissively.

"Hell," Charlie said in his slow, deep voice, "I'd be glad to throw in a few bucks a month to help out. I've been saving a little. I'd throw that in the kitty, too. How about a refill, Helen? This isn't funny what Catherine's going through. We gotta help her out."

"Thanks," Catherine said. "Money is a big deal—we need some—but living with Mom and Dad is a bigger deal. It's hell living with them. Who wants them? I'm happy to share."

"I can't imagine Dad living with us," Steve said. "He'd hate being cooped up in our house. He wouldn't have his buddies or the docks. He'd go nuts, and so would we, and there's the baby . . . Hey, I wonder if Clara would have an extra bed."

Catherine knew that was not an option. "Really? With all those kids and another one on the way?"

Anthony offered a new idea. "Stella and I could take the surly old goat. Him or Mom, but both of them might be too much. How you do it Catherine, I'll never know."

"What choice did I have? Everyone else left. This is not going to be easy. Now, if we were rich . . ."

Charlie laughed. "Well, *that* we ain't!"

They heard the back door open. Mike came limping into the front room in his mackinaw. "What the Christ are you all so glum about? I never seen a sorrier bunch of assholes in all my born days! Anthony, whacha servin' t'night?"

"Hey, Mike," Charlie said. "How are the boys at the Korn Krib? Looks like you got a little bun on already."

"Charlie, I told 'em you was here."

"Oh, yeah? Who?"

"Ears, for one. He bought me a drink when I told him. The word spread pretty damn fast. Pretty soon everyone was buyin' me drinks, tellin' me you better get yer ass down there."

"Hey, Mike," Anthony cut in. "We're talking about some pretty serious stuff here. Sit down and rest your weary bones. I want to tell you—"

Good God! Catherine thought. *He can't go there. He has no idea what he's in for with Papa.* She wanted out fast, and she stood up ready to run.

"Catherine, please sit down. You're a big part of this conversation. We'll never get anything settled if we don't talk about it."

Catherine surrendered. She sat. She knew how this would end and it wouldn't be pretty.

Anthony is so naïve, she thought. She knew he meant well, but he didn't know Papa.

"We're talking about living arrangements after Catherine and Henry are married," Anthony said.

"Hell, that ain't happenin' fer a long time. We don' hafta worry about that till the time comes. Let's have another drink and play a few hands a' smear. I need ta earn a few bucks t'night."

"How about we get this settled, then I'll whip your ass in smear, Dad," Steve said.

"Yeah, what's t'settle? By the Christ, a man can't even have a laugh in his own goddamn house."

Charlie knew better than to get into this discussion. He got up and went to the kitchen to get a beer. As he was walking back into the front room, he heard Anthony wrapping up calmly, "—would be hard to live with both of you—"

"You goddamn right it would be hard t'live with both of us! I don't want those newlyweds livin' with us. There ain't room for all of us in this house. They can find their own goddamn place t'live! We're not puttin' them up here. Give me another beer, Anthony."

Anthony got Mike the beer, sat back down and asked calmly, "How do you think you'll pay the bills without

Catherine's help, Mike?"

"What the hell makes you think I need any one to support me and my wife? *I'm* the one who pays the rent around here. Jesus fucking Christ! Let's play some cards."

He started getting up from the chair when his bad leg gave out. Charlie ran over to help him up. "Time for this party to break up. Let's call it a night," Charlie said. He walked Mike to his bedroom.

"Where do we go from here?" Catherine asked. "There's no way he's going to leave this house without a fight. I know him too well."

After a long and difficult discussion, no one came up with a good answer about the living situation. At Anthony's urging, however, each agree to send Catherine at least five dollars a month, more if they could afford it. That was the best they could come up with. They knew Mike would not budge.

Helen volunteered that she and Steve would try to visit more often to give Catherine and Henry a break. Anthony offered to go over the arrangement with Clara and Nels to urge them to try to relieve Catherine and to pitch in five bucks every month. Catherine knew in her heart that Steve and Helen or Clara would not be helping. Steve lived too far away, and Clara was swamped with her brood. She doubted they'd even send any money regularly. She had to face the ice-cold truth that she and Henry would be living with her mother and father.

Chapter 18. I Do? (Summer 1941)

The reality that Catherine and Henry would have to live with her parents after they were married was a hard pill to swallow. Neither Mike nor Martha could help each other or themselves. After a disappointing day of looking for a bigger flat that could accommodate the four of them, the couple stopped at Jimmy's Tavern for a beer. Cigarette smoke and the odor of stale beer met them as Henry pulled the door open. In a thin stream of sunlight coming in from a high window, dust mites danced. They plunked themselves down on the frayed seats of the barstools waiting for Jimmy to come over and serve them. He waved at them from the far end of the bar where he was in an earnest conversation with regulars.

"Boy, oh, boy, do you two ever look like you've been put through a ringer," Jimmy laughed as he wiped the bar in front of them. "Somebody get fired? Wreck your car?"

"Just a couple of beers, Jimmy." Henry offered a weak grin. "Give us whatever you got on tap, as long as it's Kingsbury or Rahrs."

"Hell, I don't carry that slop," Jimmy laughed and was back in a flash with two drafts of Kingsbury with small heads of foam, just the way Henry liked his beer.

"How about digging out one of those pickled eggs. Honey, you want one?" Henry asked Catherine.

"No, thanks," Catherine said. "My stomach feels a little queasy."

Keeping an eye on his other customers, Jimmy hung out at their end of the bar. "What the hell is wrong with you two? Mike told me you were getting married. I think that oughta' put a smile on your face."

"How would you feel if you had to move in with your in-laws right after you get hitched, especially those two?" Henry complained.

"Ahhhh. I get your drift. That'll be tough. Why don't you get a flat of your own?" Jimmy asked.

Catherine chimed in. "How could we afford two places, and—think about it—do you really believe those two could live together on their own?"

"Doesn't your dad bring in enough from fishing?" Jimmy asked.

"Sometimes he does, but then he spends it here or at the Korn Krib. He's not fishing much these days. And you don't know my mother. She could never stand up to him. He would drive her crazy!" Catherine said.

"If money's your biggest problem you both oughta try to get in at the paper mill. I'd bet they pay more than you're making now. I hear they're hiring men *and* women. Can you believe that? Girls working at the mill?"

"Yeah, what's your point?" Catherine asked. "You think girls can't measure up?"

Jimmy ignored her. "The draft is taking our boys from Marinette, the poor bastards, for at least a year. I'm glad I don't have to worry about the draft, but somebody's got to do something about that goddamn Hitler. If anyone can whip his ass, it's going to be us, I guess."

"Well, with wars all over the place, it's just a matter of time before we get involved, like we did with the last one, and then I'll get my draft notice for sure. Do you think the mill would still hire me if I'm in the draft?" Henry asked.

Catherine didn't wait for Jimmy's answer. "Henry, please don't talk about being drafted. I can't stand the thought of you going to war. That's way worse than living with Mom and Papa." Sorrow was visible on Catherine's face as she grabbed Henry's arm and put her head on his shoulder.

"Yeah, you kids got a lot to think about. I can see why you look like something the cat dragged in. Let me fill those empty glasses. One more beer can't hurt. Might even help. This one's on me," Jimmy said.

When they got back into Henry's truck, they decided they had nothing to lose by checking out the mill. Catherine abhorred even thinking about leaving her perfect job with the judge but making more money was the issue. Henry liked working with his father selling beer, but he wasn't making enough to support them. If Catherine's siblings came through with a little cash and they got jobs at the mill maybe they could afford a bigger flat, but they had to wait to see if the money materialized. Catherine knew they all meant well but didn't always follow through. She could depend on Anthony, but it was touch and go with the others.

When he heard the news, Judge Sullivan was as disappointed to lose Catherine as she was to leave her job, but she had to make the sacrifice. Henry and Catherine had both been hired at Southern Kraft Corporation, locally known as "the mill." Many of the male employees were being drafted and replaced with women. Catherine worked alongside men doing the same jobs and earning less than Henry or the other men. It didn't sit well with her, but she knew her place. Men ruled.

Whenever the lovebirds weren't working at the mill, they were planning their wedding and scoping out other possible living arrangements. Our Savior's Lutheran Church and Reverend Sonnack were available in September on the twentieth at 7 p.m., as was the Vasa Hall for the reception. The space was big enough for both the Sabinsky and Goodman families and their many friends. Of course, Catherine did most of the planning but Henry was paying. She had no complaints.

As they were cuddled up on the couch in the Sabinsky living room, listening to her favorite songs on the radio—"Stardust," "Chattanooga Choo Choo," "Daddy"—Catherine asked Henry to get a list of friends and relatives from his mother. "I want to order the invitations."

Henry just shrugged. "I haven't talked to her about the wedding, or much else, since our feud."

"Yeah, I know, but it would be nice if we could have at least a few of your family and friends there." She leaned over and playfully pinched his cheek.

Another shrug. This was a planning step he didn't want to think about. "I haven't talked to her much since she tried to talk me out of marrying you."

"Well, then can you come up with names and addresses?" She knew perfectly well he couldn't come up with a list.

"Hell, no. I know my aunts and uncles, but that's about it. She's got all that stuff. She's got the names of the beer customers, too. Okay, yeah, I guess I'll have to ask her, but I hate to give her the satisfaction. I can just hear her saying, 'Well, Henry, if you had listened to me in the first place.' Dad wouldn't have a clue. My sisters might have some of that stuff ... " Henry paused. "Maybe they could get a list from my mother. I'll ask Anna and Margie. If anyone could get some names together, they can."

"Good thinking, Honey. How about if I write Margie a letter?" Catherine asked. "Maybe she could ask your mother for names."

"Why not?" Henry said.

She was overjoyed that Henry had saved enough money to cover the costs of a real wing-ding reception—the buffet, food, beer, Vasa Hall, flowers, wedding attire, marriage license and honeymoon. She knew that Henry's savings could be used for more responsible things, but they'd only get married once. This was a time to celebrate.

One day in late May after her shift at the mill was over, Catherine stopped at The Smartshop to talk to her old mentor, Brownie, about a wedding outfit. As soon as Brownie saw her, she ran to Catherine with open arms.

"Catherine, I haven't seen you in ages. I'm so happy to see you."

"Me too, Brownie. I miss you."

"What brings you in here, my dear? Judge Sullivan told me you took another job. He's devastated by your leaving. He said he couldn't find anyone that even came close to doing what you did."

"I miss my job, too. It was swell—the judge and my friends, especially Betty. I wish I still had it."

"Then why in the world did you leave?"

"I'm getting married and we need the extra money."

"What? You're getting married! To whom?"

The words spilled out of Catherine's mouth as she revealed to Brownie the entire drama from the reunion with Henry at the Christmas party to the disappointment of having to live with her parents after they were married.

After Catherine finally took a breath, Brownie took her hand lovingly and looked into her eyes. "Let's sit down for a minute. I'll get you some coffee."

Catherine settled into the same chair she had sat in six years earlier when Brownie guided her from being a sixteen-year-old yearling to a classy young woman working for Judge Sullivan.

She wondered where she would be now if it weren't for Mrs. Johnson. Brownie set the coffee next to Catherine and took her own place at the desk.

"Remember the first time you sat in that chair? I think you were soaking wet from walking here in the rain. You were a scared little girl . . ." She paused, laughed, "You were actually kind of pathetic." Catherine laughed with her. "Now look at you—a young, confident woman who knows her way in the world."

"Oh, Brownie, you have no idea how pathetic I still feel. I am a young woman—you got that part right—but I have never felt less confident. I don't know what's going to happen. Henry is a wonderful man. I feel so lucky. But my mother and dad are a mess. I can't imagine Henry will want to stay married to me after he gets a taste of what it's like to live with them. He says I'm worth it. That scares me, too. I don't feel worth anything."

"Oh, my dear. I'm sorry you have your parents to contend with. You shouldn't have to bear all the burden of them. Your sisters and bro—"

Catherine cut her off. "We can't go there, Brownie. I've been down that road with them several times—they say they'll help, but I've found they don't or can't follow through. Anyway, thanks for listening. I didn't come in here to cry on your shoulder. I need an outfit for my wedding—you dressed me up right to get a job with Judge Sullivan. Now I need you to dress me for my wedding."

"Well," Brownie answered, "It's very generous of both of you to take care of your parents. I applaud you for that. Have you thought about finding a bigger place?"

"Yes, but first of all, there's not much available and the ones that are we can't afford."

"I so wish you and Henry had a place of your own. But I know you, Catherine. You'll work this out. You've come a long, long way in your short life. So, let's get to this wedding outfit. We want to knock Henry out when he sees you coming down that aisle."

"Here's the problem. I'm not a frilly, long white wedding dress kind of person. My sisters and brother didn't have weddings at all. I think Steve and Clara and Stella all got married by justices of the peace. I've only gone to a couple weddings—my mother isn't any help. So, I need you."

By the time the visit with Brownie was over, Catherine had what she believed was the absolute perfect attire.

The big day finally arrived. The lights were dimmed, and the pews were nearly filled in Our Savior's Lutheran Church as 7 p.m. rolled around. Lighted candles and potted palms placed around the altar created a sense of intimacy. The organist played "Nearer my God to Thee" as Catherine and sister Clara, the matron of honor, waited out of the view of the groom in a small vestibule at the back of the church. As readers of the *Marinette Eagle-Star* would soon learn, Catherine beheld her sister in "a lovely crepe wool dress with a Kelly green yoke topped by a brown felt hat swathed in veiling." Clara in turn thought Catherine was stunning in her "costume suit of coca brown tailored wool crepe trimmed with red fox fur." Fastened to her shoulder was "a corsage of yellow roses and gypsophila," and she sported "a stylish green hat on her wavy dark brown hair." They agreed they both looked fabulous.

When the organist began playing the wedding march, Clara had already begun her walk down the aisle. Mike was waiting for Catherine at the back of the church as the traditional "Bridal Chorus" resounded throughout the nave. Both father and daughter walked down the aisle nervously, but very different thoughts were coursing through their heads. Aware of all eyes on her, Catherine walked carefully, fighting the bride's nightmare of falling on her face on the way to the altar. Aware of all eyes on him, Mike, stone sober, twitched nervously in the "monkey suit" his daughter made him wear. This church was a long way from the Korn Krib.

When Catherine spotted Henry at the front of the church waiting for her, she smiled and felt a slight quiver in her lower lip. The sting of her own fingernails pressed into the palm of her hand reminded her that this wasn't a dream.

Standing face to face, Catherine's gaze fixed on Henry. She was only vaguely aware of the ritual words spoken by the cleric at her side. She was stunned into awareness when Henry, always a soft-spoken man and a man of few words, pronounced "I do!" in a voice that echoed through the church. This was his moment, a pledge he had hoped for the last five years to make.

Catherine, almost laughing in surprise, waited for her cue and said her own "I do" as fervently as she could, an arrow to Henry's heart. They slipped the matching thin gold bands on each other's fingers, vaguely heard Reverend Sonnack say, "I now pronounce you man and wife." What came through more clearly was, "Henry, you may kiss the bride." And kiss her he did, their first kiss as husband and wife.

As they walked out of Our Savior's Lutheran into the dark chilly night, they were pummeled with rice from the cheering crowd at the bottom of the wide concrete steps. The bride and groom ducked into the back seat of Nels' car. Clara was already in the passenger seat next to her husband.

"What a beautiful ceremony," Clara cooed. "The church was packed. I didn't realize you knew so many people. It was a hoot seeing Judge Sullivan sitting next to Papa's drinking buddies."

"I was a nervous wreck when I saw the packed church. I didn't think Papa and I were going to make it down the aisle. I was sure I was going to trip and drag Papa down with me! Could you tell how nervous I was?"

Henry reached around Catherine and pulled his new wife close. "I was a little nervous myself. I had tears in my eyes, Honey! You looked so beautiful."

"Did you see how the ring fell out of Ken's fingers as he was handing it to me," Henry said. "Lucky Sonnack caught it. My hand was shaking so much I couldn't have caught it. But I got it on your finger."

He gave Catherine a big kiss and told her he had been thinking of this day for so many years.

"Oh, Henry, I'm so in love with you." They held each other tight all the way to Vasa Hall. Nels and Clara kept their eyes on the road ahead.

By the time Mr. and Mrs. Henry Goodman walked through the door into the reception, the room was filled with a raucous crowd eager to get a glimpse of the bride and groom. Two hundred people had been invited and it seemed like they were all there. The three-piece band played its version of "Here Comes the Bride," and the guests held up their glasses and dah-da-da-dahed along with the melody as Catherine and Henry passed by, greeting everyone they knew.

The hall was decorated with crepe paper streamers and

garlands of silver wedding bells. One side of the hall was the dining area with round tables covered in white tablecloths and decorated with folded napkins, autumn flowers and leaves. Only a few folks sat at tables. Almost everyone else stood in the other half of the hall, a dance floor filled with knots of friends and relatives drinking mugs of Kingsbury, smoking cigarettes and cigars, all waiting for that moment when the wedding party would be seated at the head table.

Although Henry's mother had warmed a little toward Catherine, she had by obscure comment and occasional innuendo made it clear this would not be the kind of reception she would have preferred. Catherine got the sense that a different venue, maybe much more champagne, maybe toasts in crystal glasses, would have better suited Louise. It was obvious, though, that the final choice suited V.R., who appreciated the flowing kegs of Kingsbury beer and was happy with his own third beer in hand. He was having the time of his life with Henry's brothers, Ken and Woody, and their friends. Martha stayed close to her children and their spouses. Her two sisters and two brothers, whom she seldom saw, were nearby with their spouses and would sit at family tables. From the time he had arrived, Mike had been hanging around the bar with his fishing and drinking chums and a bartender from the Korn Krib.

Margie and Anna, Henry's sisters, were hanging close to the newlyweds. They loved their big brother and were eager to get to know their new sister-in-law. Margie had come up from Green Bay, where she was attending nursing school, and Anna was still in Marinette High. She was thrilled to learn that her brother was married to a woman who had not only graduated early but had been class valedictorian.

The buffet was generous with family-friendly fare—

fried chicken, potato salad, mashed potatoes, coleslaw, sliced ham, squash, corn, green beans and baskets of home-baked rolls. On a table near the buffet was a huge three-tiered wedding cake, decorated with white candied roses and loops of buttercream icing. A host of very young guests kept visiting the cake as they waited for their family to fill their plates.

Once the head table was seated and served, Ken gave a wedding toast.

"Congratulations   to   my   *little*   brother"—some smattering of laughter—"and my new sister, Catherine. Henry's the second of us to leave the nest and I hope they're as happy as Mildred and I are. Here, here!" he said as he raised his glass of champagne. Martha and Louise, the teetotalers, had grape juice in their flutes.

Henry thanked the crowd for coming and toasted his bride. "I'm the luckiest guy in the world to have Catherine as my wife. I thought this day would never come! She's the love of my life." That was as many words as he cared to say at one time. He took Catherine's hand, raised her from her chair, put his arms around her and gave her a big hug and kiss. A raucous cheer filled the hall.

Catherine had loved the Fred Astaire movie, "Swing Time," and she and Henry led off the first dance to "The Way You Look Tonight." She led him around the floor. No matter how hard it was for him to follow, she found it harder to lead. Henry pretended he was in charge and he did his best. He hated to dance, but he knew that dancing was his wife's passion. Before the song ended, at a whispered word from Catherine, the couple waved to waiting dancers and invited them on the floor. Henry waited patiently for Catherine to dance with her father, her brothers and her new brothers-in-law. What Henry had foremost on his mind was saying goodbye to everyone at this big party and getting on with the honeymoon.

When she finally walked off the dance floor, she put her arm through Henry's, and they walked arm in arm, making small talk with the guests and thanking them for coming. He eventually had enough and he pulled Catherine aside and whispered in her ear, "Okay, Sweetheart. I'm ready to have you all to myself."

After a wonderful three-day honeymoon at a lake resort in western Marinette County, they were more in love than ever—they were coasting on a cloud of passion. How could they not live happily ever after as long as they were together? Returning home late at night, they drove into the alley where Mike's truck and Catherine's car were parked. There was nowhere for Henry to park without blocking the others.

"Oh, Henry. Now what?" Catherine said.

"Well, I guess I'll have to park in front. We can work this out later. Grab your stuff."

Catherine walked into the kitchen with her arms full. Mike was sitting at the table paying tribute to a bottle of beer. "Where's yer husband? Did he leave ya already?"

"He had to move the car to the street—there was no room for his truck in the alley. Hi, Papa." She dropped her things and went over to give him a hug.

"Christ, now we got that to worry about. Where's he gonna keep that big fancy truck a' his?"

"I love you, too, Papa. Thanks for the nice greeting."

"We got a lot of stuff to work out now with the two a' you livin' here. I don't know how we're all gonna fit in this dump."

"We'll make it work somehow." Catherine looked around for her mother.

"Hey, Mike." Henry had overheard Mike's grumbling as he set the suitcases down. "I'm not any happier living with you than you are living with me, and I'm wide-open for ideas . . ."

Catherine sought to head off any angry words. "Come on, you two. Henry, help me get our things up there."

"Up there? You mean we have to sleep in that tiny attic room while they each get their own rooms down here?"

"Please, let's not fight over this tonight. We have some things to work out—"

"That's putting it mildly," Henry said as he climbed the rickety ladder to the attic. When he stood up, his head bumped the ceiling hard. "Jesus H. Christ!"

They got into bed together and Henry held her close, but she knew he wasn't happy. Why should he be? *This is all my fault,* she thought. She felt greater certainty that this was not going to work. She felt sick to her stomach as she tossed and turned, wondering how she could get through the next day. She had forgotten to check on her mother before they went up to bed. One more thing to worry about. She knew things were going to get more complicated as they tried to navigate their new living arrangement. She felt responsible to keep her mother, father and new husband happy. She couldn't see any way for that to happen.

She and Henry both had to be at work the next day at six—another short night. Mike was up dressed in his fishing clothes when she came down the stairs.

"Good morning, Papa," Catherine said.

Mike didn't answer. He was limping around the kitchen trying to make coffee, fill his lunch box and scrounge something for breakfast.

"What's going on with Mom?" Catherine said.

"I'm the wrong person t'ask about that woman. I ain't

seen her since you left on your honeymoon."

"Are you kidding me? She might be dead!" She ran to her mother's bedroom and threw the door open. Martha was sitting in her rocking chair in her nightgown staring into space. She didn't seem to notice Catherine. "Mom? Hi. How are you?"

"You'd think a daughter who'd been gone for three days would at least say hello to her mother when she came home," Martha said in a monotone.

"Oh, Mom. I'm sorry! I thought you were asleep. I didn't want to wake you. Papa said he hasn't seen you since we left our honeymoon."

"*Ja*, keep your 'sorrys' to yourself. That good-for-nothing man out there didn't come home till Sunday night, as drunk as a skunk. I keep to myself. It's easier that way."

"Have you eaten?" Catherine asked.

"*Ja*, I come out when he's gone. I listen for him to drive into the alley and then I make myself scarce."

"I suppose that's a good way to operate if you don't want to see him. Now that I'm back I'll try to take care of things. I'll stop at the store on the way home from work to buy some groceries. I have to go, or I'll be late." Catherine said.

When Catherine went back into the kitchen, both Henry and Mike were trying to avoid each other in that very small space.

"Catherine, get your coat on. We have to leave now so we can punch in on time," Henry said.

"Yes, I know, but we haven't made our lunches—"

That sparked Mike's complaint. "What the hell am I supposed t'do without a lunch—or breakfast either. We got two goddamn women in this house and not one of 'em raises a finger for me!"

"Hang on, Dad. I'm doing the best I can. We'll get organized, but it might take a few days."

As they walked out the door putting on their coats Henry said, "I guess the honeymoon's over." Catherine's heart skipped a beat.

Catherine asked Henry to stop at Stepniak's Market on the way home. She had plans to make a nice dinner to bring everyone together. Judging by what had happened last night and this morning, this would not be an easy task. What always seemed to work was chicken, mashed potatoes, and gravy. Henry waited in the truck while she shopped. When she got in, he eyed the bag of groceries. Frowning, he said, "I suppose we'll have to pay for groceries for the four of us now."

"Henry, honey, I know this is going to be hard on you for a while, but I will take care of things. Don't you worry your sweet little head about it."

"Christ, Cat. Spending all my time with you and them in that small house is going to be a nightmare. How can we afford to support all of us?"

"I don't have all the answers yet. I'm sure going to try to make it all work. Mike still fishes some, so that will help—"

"Yeah, when he doesn't drink it away—"

"I know, Henry, I know. Please give it some time. Give *me* some time."

When they came into the kitchen with their empty lunch pails and the groceries, Martha was sitting at the kitchen table in an all too familiar position—her head in her hands.

"Hi, Mom. I hope we didn't bother you too much this morning. We were pretty disorganized."

"You don't have to tell me. I heard the whole mess."

"Hi, Mame. Sorry about that," Henry said to his mother-in-law.

"Don't worry, Mom. It will take a little time—I'm already working on it. I bought a chicken for supper. I'll make sandwiches with the leftovers and pack our lunches tonight. We got home too late last night. If I get up at 4:30, I'll have time to make coffee and put together a little breakfast before we go. I'll leave food for you, too."

Martha shook her head. "It's all too much," she said as she headed for her bedroom.

"I'm going over to see if my dad needs any help unloading the truck. What time is supper?" Henry called back as he walked out the door.

Catherine sat at the table in her mother's position. She was exhausted. She didn't know how she could do it all before she had to go to bed, then get up at 4:30 and start all over. How could she possibly keep her mother, father and new husband happy? She knew it was her responsibility. She had to make it work. *Roll up your sleeves and get busy, girl,* she told herself.

By six o'clock she had put on the table a roast chicken, mashed potatoes, gravy and squash. She called to her mother just as Henry was walking in the back door.

"Cat, I didn't know you could make gravy! I got the right woman," Henry said.

"Of course, she can make gravy." Martha looked with pride at the one daughter she still had at home. "I taught her how to cook. Didn't I, Catherine?"

"You sure did, Mom. But you can still bake circles around me. I need some more lessons."

"Why do you need lessons, when I'm here to do it?" she said.

Just then Mike walked in the back door. "My truck is stickin' out in the alley, Henry. Yer gonna have to do a lot better next time. I don't want no goddamn cop givin' me a ticket when it ain't my fault."

"Maybe we should leave Catherine's car in the street so we can get both trucks in the alley," Henry said.

Mike looked at the dinner spread out on the table and held up the bucket in his hand. "What the hell! Yer eatin' chicken when I brought a nice mess a fish t'fry. Why the hell are you eatin' so damn early?" He paused, looking at three faces at the table. No one said a word. He shrugged, headed for the sink. "I'm hungry fer fish. I guess I'll have t'fry my own."

"Papa, give me the fish. I'll put them in the icebox until tomorrow night. Sit down and eat some chicken."

"Mike, the gravy is real good. So's the chicken. Sit down and eat with us," Henry said.

"We had a nice catch a'perch today. They won't be any damn good tomorrow. Who's in charge here anyway? It used to be me. Now we got two more bosses. I shoulda stayed at the Korn Krib." He turned and headed toward the back door.

"Papa! Give me those fish and sit down and eat with us!" Catherine ordered. "Let's start out on the right foot. Henry and I are going to be living here with you. I made this nice dinner for all of us and we paid for it! Four mouths to feed. How do we know if you're going to come with one fish, a bucket of fish, or nothing at all?"

She forced herself to let the anger drain away. "We are going to help buy the groceries and pay the bills. It will be easier with us here. You're going to have to try harder to work this out. If we can't, then Henry and I will move out and leave you and mom here to fend for yourselves. It's up to you and all of us. If we save some money, maybe we could rent a bigger place."

Without a word Mike sat down at the table and filled his plate. After a quiet supper, Henry and Mike sat in the front room listening to the radio while Martha helped Catherine with the dishes.

"I'm glad you're here, Catherine," Martha said quietly. "I couldn't live with Mike alone. I'll help as much as I can. But you know I get these spells—sometimes I can't pull myself out of bed."

"I know, Mom." She knew only too well.

Chapter 19. The Last Straw (1942)

Henry was just swinging his legs out of bed when Catherine's head popped up in the attic access. "Henry, I think I'm PG!"

"PG? What the heck does that mean?" He rubbed sleep from his eyes as Catherine quickly crossed the small room, plunked herself in his lap, and threw her arms around him.

"It means, Mr. Goodman, that we are going to have a baby!"

"Oh, Honey!" he said, suddenly wide awake. He put his arms around her and whispered into her neck. "How do you know? Are you sure?"

"I'm pretty sure. I'll have to make a doctor's appointment, but I haven't had my 'friend' for two months now. I'm not sure how all this works. I'll have to talk to Mom or Clara about it. My stomach's been a little queasy, too."

Suddenly serious, he said, "Well, that settles it. We sure as hell need to find a different place to live. We can't have a baby in this place."

"I know. I know. But I'll have to quit working as soon as I start to show. We'll have to live on your salary."

Even though money would be tight, Catherine was secretly happy that she could stop working at the mill. Taking care of her mom, dad and Henry was a strain. The physical work was enough, but nothing compared to the anxiety she felt trying to keep everybody in house happy.

Her mother and Henry depended on her to keep the trains running on time. Mike did whatever he pleased, which drove Martha and Henry crazy and forced Catherine to run interference. She saw this as her role, but she also saw that they found time for themselves while she had none.

Mike was drinking more and fishing less, which meant he was not bringing in much money. As per the plan they had made, Stella and Anthony sent money regularly, as did Charlie, but Catherine knew the household would be in bad shape if they had to count on Clara and Nels or Steve and Helen. Catherine knew in her heart they were all doing their best. With both she and Henry working, they had been able to put a little money aside every week for a bigger, better place. Henry still worked with his dad after his shifts at the mill and on weekends to earn a little extra money and to get away from the horrid environment in the house. He loved the beer business, so he was happy to be able to help his dad. He wasn't around much, and she missed him, but it was a blessing sometimes to have one less person in the house.

It had become normal now to wake up wondering what conflicts might arise. Mike and Henry continued to argue about how and where they parked their trucks. Mike and Martha never spoke civilly to each other. Each sparring partner came to Catherine with a complaint about the other. Complicating this, Henry's made it clear that he should have her undivided attention. How could she be a better wife? She was too tired when they went to bed to be loving. How could she be a better daughter? It seemed that every day someone was unhappy. Her responsibility, she determined, was to make them all happy and she tried her hardest.

Surprisingly, Martha hadn't had any sudden mood swings since the newlyweds moved in. She occasionally cooked and helped Catherine with the cleaning. Mike was the wild card. His daughter was the only one he would listen to. Every morning she got up at 4:30 a.m., made coffee, breakfast and lunches for Henry, Mike and herself, threw on some clothes, and raced off to work with Henry. After work Henry would drop Catherine at home so that she could go for groceries, run errands or start dinner. Henry went to help his dad. With occasional help from Martha, Catherine cooked dinner, did the dishes, and climbed the rickety ladder to bed in the attic. As she lay exhausted, she could hear the radio playing and pictured Henry sitting on the couch relaxing. Catherine wanted Henry in bed cuddling with her, but she wouldn't ask for fear it would make him feel bad. She didn't want anyone to feel bad. It was her job to keep them all happy. She thought she was happy when she made them happy.

On Thursday after work Catherine had an appointment with Dr. Zeratsky.

"Catherine Goodman, what brings you in?" he asked as she sat in a chair facing him in his tiny office. The desktop was full of jars and bottles with colored potions, a stethoscope, rubber gloves, pens and papers. She could almost hear his starched white lab coat crackle when he leaned forward to talk to her. His white hair matched his attire, and the only contrast was his black bow tie.

Catherine's legs were twitching as she tried to figure out how to talk to a man about her pregnancy. Just saying the word "pregnant" embarrassed her. Everyone she knew called her condition PG, avoiding the word. Her palms felt sticky as she wrung them in her lap.

Catherine gulped. "I think I'm going to have a baby." She could fell the blood rushing to her face.

"What makes you think so?"

"Well" she hesitated. "I haven't had"—she hesitated again—"my 'friend' for three months."

In a long medical career, the doctor had heard many euphemisms for menstrual cycles from the friendly "that time of the month" to the crude "on the rag," but Marinette's cute expression, "my friend," always made him smile. He said gently, "You mean you haven't menstruated for three months?"

She nodded.

"Your waistline—has it expanded?"

"Yes," she said as she bowed her head. "And, I'm pretty tired all the time."

"How about your appetite? Does any food turn your stomach?"

"Not really. My mother has always told me I had a cast-iron stomach. But sometimes I feel a little queasy."

"Well, let's get you up on the table to have a look, Missy."

Catherine winced when she heard 'Missy', but she got herself up on the edge of the table and followed his directives to lie down and put her feet in the stirrups while he covered her knees with a cotton sheet.

"I'm going to put a speculum into your genitalia so I can see and feel what's going on inside you. It might be a little uncomfortable, but it won't take too long."

Catherine wanted to jump off the table and run out the door. She had never experienced anything like this in her twenty-three years. Dr. Zeratsky was gentle, but it took everything she had to stay put. She put her hands over her face—it was hot. Knowing it was red made her even more embarrassed. When he finally asked her to sit up and drape the sheet over her knees, she was shaking.

The doctor handed her a glass of water and said, "By the time you have your fourth baby this will be like clockwork, but, yes, you are pregnant."

All she could think about was getting out of the office.

"I'm going to go out while you put yourself together. Please sit in this chair when you're ready. I'll be back in a few minutes so we can talk."

It felt like hours before he came back. "Well, young lady, everything looks good. I have calculated from the information you gave me and your pelvic exam that we'll see the wee one the first part of October."

Catherine smiled. She couldn't help herself. She and Henry were going to have a baby!

"It's important that you don't gain much weight, no more than fifteen pounds," the doctor said. "I'll give you some A and D vitamins to take daily. Do you smoke?"

"Yes," Catherine answered.

"That's fine. It will help you relax. Do you have any questions?"

"How long can I work?"

"That's up to your boss. I would say only a month or two more. Now that we're in the war, it depends on how much you're needed—but not too much lifting. You want to keep that baby safe."

Catherine left Dr. Zeratsky's office filled with joy and fear. She and Henry wanted a baby—there was no doubt about that. But how could they afford her not working? How could they possibly live with her parents and a baby in their tiny house? How could she take care of one more person?

Catherine drove straight to the Goodmans' home on

the west end of Carney Avenue. Henry worked in the small beer shed behind the house where kegs and cases were stored. She couldn't wait until he got home to give him the news. She hoped he was in the shed, because she didn't especially want to run into her mother-in-law. Things between them had gotten better since the wedding, but Louise still held Catherine at a distance. At least she was civil, maybe because Margie and Anna, Henry's sisters who enjoyed Catherine's company, had worked on their mother. As she drove into the big gravel driveway between the house and the shed she saw Henry standing on an old wooden platform holding two cases of beer. As soon as he saw Catherine's car, he set the cases down, swung himself to the ground and walked quickly to her car. He kissed her through the open window.

"What the heck are you doing here, Cat? Dad and I were just loading the truck for tomorrow's deliveries." He opened the car door for her to get out.

She looked into his eyes with a huge grin on her face. "Henry, I was right! You *are* going to be a daddy! I just came from Dr. Zeratsky's. He examined me—I can't tell you how embarrassing that was!—but he said everything looked good. The baby's due in early October. Can you believe it?"

"Yes . . . I mean, no . . . I mean, yes. I don't know what I believe." He was grinning from ear to ear. "This calls for a celebration. Let's tell Dad."

"Not yet. Okay? Let's keep this to ourselves for a little while?"

He wanted to share the news with the world, but he would respect her reluctance—for a while, at least. "Yeah, okay. I've got to get back to loading the truck anyway so I can get home for supper. What are we having?"

"Don't have a clue." She smiled and waved as she

turned her car around and joyfully sped all the way across town to their home on Lake Street in Menekaunee.

Shortly after Catherine got home Mike walked in with a mess of perch.

"Here ya go, Kiddo. You kin fry these up for supper. Those goddamn fish were runnin' like ol'-Billy-hell today!"

"Well, that sure makes my life easier. I couldn't figure out what we were going to eat tonight. What do you want with them?"

"Get your mother out here to make some waffles."

"I can make waffles, Papa. Let her rest."

"You can't make 'em like yer mother—git her out here. I ain't seen her in days."

Reluctantly, Catherine yelled from the kitchen, "Hey, Mom! We need you out here!"

Martha shuffled out slowly, and Catherine said gently, "Papa wants you to make some waffles to go with the perch. How about it?"

Without saying a word, Martha got out the flour, baking soda and powder, and mixed them together with an egg and milk. while Catherine fried the fish in lard. Dinner was soon on the table and Henry walked in just as they were sitting down.

Catherine breathed a sigh of relief. All four of them in one place and no one was unhappy yet.

"Now this is what I call a meal!" Mike said with a lopsided grin. As he shoveled in a bite of the waffle, warm maple syrup dripped down his chin and landed on his belly. He didn't seem to notice and no one else said a word about it.

"You look tired," Martha told Catherine after supper. "Go sit."

"You're right about that, Mom. Maybe Henry would take me for a ride. I don't feel like doing much tonight."

Henry was always happy to get out of the house. "Let's go, Cat," he said. "Damn good idea. Grab your coat."

"Do you know how to take care of a baby?" he asked as they drove through town. He put his hand on top of hers, giving it a squeeze.

"Jeez, I don't know. I've been around Clara's kids enough. I can't help but be a little nervous about it. I'm more excited than nervous, I guess. My mother sure knows how. She raised five."

Henry headed straight for Jimmy's. "Let's have a beer to celebrate. We have to start our son in the beer business early."

The bar was nearly full save for two stools at the far end, next to three guys engrossed in a game of smear.

"How can you be so cock-sure it's a boy, Mr. Goodman?" she said as she playfully hit him in the bicep.

"Because I want a boy, that's why." He put his hand on her shoulder. "You'll be a good mother, Cat. You know how to take care of everybody. I'm glad I won't be in charge. I wouldn't know how to start. That's what women are for."

Catherine pulled out a cigarette. Henry dug in his pocket for his lighter and lit it for her. "Dr. Zeratsky said that smoking will help me relax."

"Hey, Henry—Catherine. What's the occasion? Don't see you guys here very much anymore, except when I get a beer delivery."

"Life is a grind, Jimmy. I don't have to tell you that," Henry said. "Bring us a couple of taps—Rahr's with a light head."

Catherine and Henry clinked their classes and whispered, "To our baby!" Their eyes met. The air was heavy with the odor of smoke and beer at the dark end of the crowded bar. The noise level was increasing, and they were having a hard time hearing each other.

"Let's finish our beers and get out of here. I can't take the noise. It's a nice night to walk over to the harbor," Catherine said.

The sun had almost set when they reached the shore. They sat on a big log on the sandy beach. The remains of a fire lay in the sand in front of them with a few empty beer bottles scattered about. Waves lapped the shore. Seagulls flying low cawed and dove for fish. A light cool breeze compelled them to pull their warm jackets tight.

"I love it down here. The smell of the bay, the fish, the sound of the waves sloshing against the boats—this has been my life. Remember when we were in high school? We were here winter and summer—ice-skating, swimming, singing, fires, drinking beer, hooch. Those were the days. We were as poor as churchmice, but we didn't care." Catherine laughed softly. "Now we're still poor, but we care . . ."

"Yeah. It was great—until you broke up with me. I never thought I'd get over you. That was the worst time in my life. I didn't think we'd ever be together again."

"And look at us now, Honey! We're married. We're going to be parents! It's hard to believe, isn't it?"

Henry knew he had to bring up the housing question again. "Come down off your cloud for a minute. We have two serious things to talk about."

"I know what you're going to say, and I don't want to think about either of them."

"Nor me, but we can't just play this by ear. I will not raise my kids the way we're living now. The tension is killing us. Your dad is either jolly or mad and unpredictable. He seems to be hurtful, especially to your mother, more often than not these days. You're the only one who can relate to him, but I can see how hard it is for you. He's hardly civil to me. It must tear you apart to be in the middle of this mess all the time. You need to take care of yourself and the little one." He patted her stomach.

"You're right, Honey. I'm going nuts."

"I know you are. And I know you want to take care of your parents, but who's more important—them or the baby and me? I can't live like this anymore."

"What? Are you saying you'll leave me if we stay with my parents? Would you really do that to me?"

"No, I'm not going to leave you. I'm staying with you, but not with your parents—and that's final."

Catherine wiped her tears. "What's the second thing? You said there were two."

"I did and you know what it is, but you won't face that either. I'll be going to war. The situation on both fronts says that this is going to be a long war. I can't leave with you living in the situation we're in now."

"I don't know how to fix it, Henry. I'm a nervous wreck. I'm trying to make everyone happy, including you. I feel like giving up. Now I know why Mom stays in her room all the time. I'd like to sit in a room all by myself, too. This is an impossible situation." Catherine cried. "I can't do this anymore."

"Who exactly do you think will do it if you don't. We need a different place to live. I'll find one. You decide what to do with your parents." And he meant it.

Catherine spent a sleepless night as far away from Henry's side of the bed as she could be. She was scared and angry. She loved Henry with all her heart. They had a baby coming. She needed to keep this marriage together at all costs. Why couldn't Henry be more understanding of her obligation toward her parents? Why were her mother and father such a mess? How did she get stuck with them? Why couldn't her siblings help out?

She couldn't get out of bed the next day. She told Henry to tell the foreman she was sick.

"Awe, come on, Cat. Don't do this. You need to go to work."

"I can't, Henry." He could barely hear her.

"I don't think this is right, but I'll tell him. I hope you can get a grip on yourself." He walked down the stairs and out the door without his morning coffee or a lunch.

Mike was standing in the kitchen as Henry walked past. "Where the hell is my lunch? Where's the coffee? Catherine! Martha! Get out here, goddamn it!"

No one came. He yelled again—still no one came. He put on his jacket and stomped out the door.

Catherine lay in bed listening to the door slam twice. She pulled the covers over her head and tried to sleep. She dozed off but was awakened by noise from the kitchen. It sounded like her mother was making coffee. *Can I face her this morning? Not sure.* Dog-tired, she pushed herself to a sitting position. She wondered what was going on in her body. Her head was throbbing, and she felt confused. She slowly pulled herself up to a standing position and grabbed the bedpost to keep from falling. She felt dizzy, off balance. She finally found her robe and climbed down to the kitchen.

"What's going on, Mom? What are you making?"

"I'm making coffee and brown sugar muffins for us. Why aren't you at work?"

"How did you know I wasn't at work?"

"You think I don't know what's going on out here when I'm in my room with the door closed? I heard the whole thing. I felt a little sorry for Henry when he left without a lunch, but Mike—that bastard—I don't care if he ever eats." She pulled a chair out from the table. "Sit down. I'll pour you some coffee."

"Thanks."

Martha sat down across the table from Catherine. "How do you feel, my dear daughter?"

"What do you mean?"

"First of all, you look pale—like a ghost. Next, you haven't been yourself for a while. No open Kotex boxes around. Two-to-one, you're pregnant."

"What? You know I'm pregnant?"

"Yup. I've known for a while."

"Huh? I've wanted to talk to you about it this past week, but there was never a good time. You say you knew, so why didn't you say something?"

"I knew you'd tell me when you were ready. I've been around the block a few times—mothers know these things. Congratulations, Honey." She patted Catherine's hand on the table.

"I saw Dr. Zeratsky yesterday. He told me I was due at the beginning of October."

"So—" Martha counted on her fingers. "You have six months to go. How long are you going to work?"

"As long as they'll have me. We need to save up a little money."

"How does Henry feel about this?"

"Just like me—he's happy and scared. He's worried about going to war and leaving me alone with the baby. I don't want him to go to war."

"I don't blame you. It's a darn shame all these young men are being sent off to that terrible war, but you won't be alone if you stay here."

Catherine took a deep breath. *Is this the right time to break the news that we might be moving out?* They were both silent for a few minutes.

Catherine was stunned again by her mother prescience. "I know what you're thinking. You and Henry want to find your own place," Martha said numbly. She looked drained. "I don't blame you. I didn't want to raise my kids in this mess either. Always living hand-to-mouth, never knowing if Mike is going to be drunk or sober, if he'll be laughing or raging. I don't blame you for wanting to get out of this hell-hole. I knew you'd be leaving someday."

"Will you be able to live alone with Papa?"

"What choice do I have? I don't have a job. I can't do anything except keep house and cook."

"You haven't had a spell for quite a while—not since Henry moved in. You seem to be feeling pretty good."

"My dear girl, you just do what you have to. Don't worry about me. You need to have your own life."

Catherine thought her mother looked pathetic. She felt sick to her stomach, unable to bear the thought of leaving her mother alone with her father. How would they survive? Mike wasn't making enough money for the two of them to live on. She knew her very presence here was a buffer against the most extreme violence. What would happen to her mother if he got into a drunken rage when there were just the two of them in the house?

It was all suddenly too much. Without another word Catherine left the table and climbed the ladder to the attic bedroom. The world was closing in on her and there was no place to hide. She didn't want to see or talk to anyone or ever get out of bed. *Is this how my mother feels when she doesn't come out of her room for days at a time? I don't care if I ever talk to anyone again,* she thought.

Her dreams were terrifying as she dozed in and out of sleep—she was trapped in a dark, freezing room and not able to claw her way out, her baby became a monster inside her, Henry came home from the war in a body bag.

She must have cried out, because Martha was sitting beside the bed. Catherine was shaking and was drenched in sweat.

"Please, dear girl, I'm right beside you." Her mother put her hand on a tearful cheek. "I want to help you. What can I do?"

"I don't know. I'm so scared. There's no way out— nowhere to turn. Leave me alone," she pleaded.

Martha rubbed Catherine's cheek for a moment, then made her way down the ladder, knowing full well what her daughter was experiencing. *How many times have I felt this way?* she asked herself. She plunked herself down in a chair in the front room and did the only thing she could think of—she prayed.

"Dear God," she whispered. "I know I don't pray as often as I should. I don't go to church as often as I should either, but you're my only hope. Please help Catherine. I'm scared that she's having a nervous breakdown like I've had so many times in my life. I'll do anything you tell me to save her from this terrible affliction. Why does this happen? Are we too weak? We must be. I want to be strong for her. She's such a good girl. She's taken good care of us. Maybe she learned to be nervous from me. I hope not. Maybe I learned it from my father. Is that why he lost his land and money? He was so jolly one minute, then in his room alone the next. He worried about his business—about us. Please, please don't let her go to the hospital or the asylum. She's having a baby. Please help her keep that baby. Please, God. I'll try to be a better mother, a better wife. I'll go to church every Sunday. I'll give thanks every day. I promise."

She brought her hands to her face and breathed into her palms a soft "Amen."

Catherine was still in bed and Martha still in her chair when Henry came home from work.

"Where's Catherine," he asked.

"She's still in bed."

"You're kidding me, right?"

"See for yourself." Martha didn't look up.

Henry bounded up the ladder. "Cat, what's going on? Are you okay?"

"No."

"Is it the baby?"

"No."

"What the hell is it then?" Nothing in Henry's life prepared him for this strange moment, his wife skipping work, almost unresponsive, lying listlessly in bed. Anger and impatience warred with love and concern. "Do you have a cold? The flu?"

"I don't think so." Catherine's voice was so soft he could hardly hear her.

Frustration and impatience won. "It doesn't look like I can do anything here, so I'm going to my dad's." As he descended the ladder he called back into the attic, "I hope you can get out of bed to make supper." He left without stopping to say goodbye to Martha.

When Henry got home, Martha was in the kitchen cooking supper and Mike was nowhere to be seen. Henry went up the stairs to check on Catherine. She was still in bed, but awake.

"Have you eaten anything today?" Henry asked, genuine concern in his voice. Catherine didn't answer. He sat down on the bed next to her. "What's going on, Honey? I've never seen you like this before. I know you get nervous sometimes, but this seems worse than that. I hate to see you like this. Can I do anything?"

Catherine started to cry. "I don't know what's wrong. I don't have any energy to even get up to go to the bathroom and I don't care. I'm not hungry. I just want to be here by myself."

"Your mom's making supper. It smells like meatloaf. I'll bring some up for you." Catherine didn't respond.

Henry stood next to Martha at the stove. "Do you have any idea what's going on with Catherine?"

Martha sensed what her daughter was experiencing. Was Catherine on the edge of what Dr. Koepp so carefully called a nervous breakdown? Martha had traveled that path, knew the signs, but because she might be wrong she was not going burden Henry with that concern.

"Henry, she is dealing with a lot of stuff that women go through when they're pregnant, and she is worried about losing her job and about you going to war. Just be a little patient . . ."

Henry went into the front room and picked up the phone to call Dr. Zeratsky. It rang several times before the doctor answered. Waiting, Henry looked around the shabby living room—a frayed carpet, a threadbare couch, a bare bulb on a wire hanging from the ceiling. *We gotta get out of this place*, he thought. *Finally*.

"My nurse caught me just leaving the office, Mr. Goodman. What can I do for you?"

Henry explained Catherine's behavior—the listlessness, the lack of appetite—and the doctor acknowledged each symptom.

"As you know, I saw her a couple days ago. She seemed a little nervous, but I attributed that to her having a pelvic exam, which is a challenging experience for many new mothers. She's physically healthy. It could be hormones . . ."

Henry wanted something very specific. "What should I do? I don't know how to help her."

"Some of her symptoms sound like she could be experiencing some depression. Anything unusual going on in your lives?"

"Yeah, lots of stuff—besides the baby, I don't know when I might be called up, and we're trying to find a different place to live, to name a few."

The doctor gave his final thoughts. "Keep a watch on her for a couple days. See if you can get her to take a walk with you. Sometimes exercise works with depression. She must eat. That's most important for her stage of pregnancy. It's hard to know if it's situational or depression with a capital D. Your mother-in-law has the latter. Or she could merely be a little down in the dumps. Depression is nearly as hard on the family as it is on the patient. There's not much you can do—and that can be frustrating."

Henry got off the phone and paced. The doctor's comments gave rise to a whole new concern. What if she has what her mother has? And the baby! She needs to take care of that baby! He climbed the ladder to the bedroom.

Catherine was lying in bed with her eyes open but seemingly not focused. Henry's heart sank as he looked at his wife—the beautiful, vibrant woman he loved had metamorphosed into this emotionless stranger—pale, listless, unaware of his presence. He pictured the many times when she would jump into his arms with her legs around his waist, smothering him with kisses. He heard the echo of her infectious laugh, her wonderful sense of humor. But that's all it was right now, an echo.

He straightened the wrinkled sheets, sat down on the edge of the bed, touched her cheek with the back of his hand and stared at the empty face. Was she sleeping with her eyes open? She moved her head and blinked when he squeezed her hand and softly called out her name.

"Hey, Cat." He waited a minute—no response. "Honey, look at me. You need to wake up. Your mother's making supper. You have to eat."

"Henry." Her voice was so soft he could hardly hear her.

"Come on, I'll help you sit up." He tried to lift her shoulders and pull her up to rest her back on the pillows, but her body was limp.

"Let me sleep. I need to sleep. I'm so tired." Henry was frustrated.

"I'm going downstairs to eat. I'll bring you some food after supper. I want you to be ready to eat—I mean it, Cat. You can't lay here like this. Get over it."

Catherine heard everything he said. *I have to get up. I know I have to get up*—she thought—*but my legs and arms are too heavy to move. I can't face my family. I can't make them happy. What good am I? How can I take care of a baby, too? I'm good for nothing. I always knew it.* She lay there looking at the bare bulb hanging down from the ceiling and listening to the conversation downstairs.

"How is she?" Martha asked.

Henry felt helpless. "She's half dead. She can't just lie there and stare at the ceiling. She's got to get a grip on herself."

"Oh, my dear God. I'm a nervous wreck." Martha was wringing her hands as she sat down at the table across from Henry.

"Not you, too, Martha. I need your help. Please don't fall apart now. We need to get Catherine out of bed. Zeratsky said she needs to go for a walk—and she needs to eat."

"Leave her alone," Martha said.

"Are you crazy? I can't leave her up there to rot."

He grabbed his jacket from the coat rack and walked out the door to his truck. In a few minutes he was sitting at the bar in the Korn Krib. Lighting a cigarette, he took a deep drag and blew the smoke out through his nose. The ceiling was filled with cobwebs, and the last light from the setting sun filtered through the smoke in the room. He noticed Mike sitting at the bar, telling a story to a couple of his cronies, whose laughter suggested they had been at the bar for a while.

Mike didn't see Henry, who was keeping his head down and facing the opposite direction. The last person Henry wanted to talk to was Mike. Tommy came over with a beer and put it on the bar in front of Henry.

"You look like you need this," Tommy said. "Your old man's over there. Did you see him?"

"Yup." Henry was a man of few words and he shied away from conflict, but he knew if he talked to Mike right now it wouldn't be pretty. His father-in-law was a major source of Henry's problems.

"You ought to join 'em. It might put a smile on your face," Tommy said as he walked away.

"This town is too small for both of us," Henry mumbled.

On Mike's way to the toilet he noticed Henry sitting at the bar.

"Well, look who's here," Mike said as he grabbed Henry's shoulder. "I didn't plan on seein' you here tonight. Good fer you, buddy. Ya gotta git out away from them women once in a while. They're a sorry lot. Come on, sit with the boys, have a few laughs for a change." Henry didn't budge. "Come on! You look like you lost your best friend. I'll buy ya a beer."

Henry jumped off the stool. His face was crimson, his eyes were crazed. Mike was stunned when Henry grabbed his shoulder and glared into his foggy eyes.

"What the hell . . ?" Mike staggered backwards on his bad leg.

"Listen here, you bastard!" Henry had Mike by the front of his shirt. "You have a daughter at home who's pregnant and sick! You have a wife who is beside herself with worry!" Every bit of his anger and frustration suddenly focused on the birthmark-stained face in front of him. "We all work our asses off to keep you full of rotgut! You're here laughing, having a gay old time, while your family's falling apart—and you don't give a shit! You don't have the fucking guts to be ashamed of yourself!"

"You son-of-a-bitch!" Mike tried to pull back from the hand grasping the front of his shirt. "You move into my house, lock, stock and barrel and you think you're Mr. I-own-the-place!" Mike ripped free, but one button popped away. It could be heard hitting the floor in a bar that had gone silent. Mike raged on. "You can't even afford t'get a fuckin' place of your own, you young know-it-all piece of shit! We were doin' just fine 'til you moved in. Now I don't even have a goddamn parkin' place for my truck!"

Mike pulled his fist back as Henry lunged forward trying to get his hands around his father-in-law's neck. Mike's fist landed squarely in the middle of his son-in-law's face, and blood spurted from Henry's nose. Mike lost his balance as his bad leg gave out, and he fell backwards onto a table, sending beer glasses and an ashtray sliding to the floor. Henry pressed down, holding Mike's neck in a tight grip, as Mike tried to wrestle free, his feet slipping on the beer-soaked linoleum. Tommy came around from behind the bar and, joined by Ears and Don, worked to pull Henry off Mike.

Tommy handed Henry a bar rag for his nose. It wasn't the first fight he had had to break up.

Henry turned away from Mike, mumbled an apology to the bartender, said he would pay for the glasses, then turned back. "You'll pay for this, you fucking son-of-a bitch! I'm getting Catherine and me out of your dump. Then we'll see how you'll manage, you fucking deadbeat!"

Rag pressed to his nose, Henry drove around the Marinette-Menominee "loop" a few times before he went home. He hoped Catherine was still asleep. He didn't want her to see his throbbing swollen nose or his bloody clothes. It hurt like hell. He was sure it must be broken. He'd look like a mess at work in the morning. He could already hear the jokes and jeers. Enough of the guys in Menekaunee worked at the mill that the story would be told.

Martha was sitting on the couch in the front room listening to music on the radio when he walked in.

"*Ah, Gud!*" Martha's reversion to Danish reflected her surprise. "*Hold op. Ga.* Go—to the kitchen. You're covered with blood! *Ah, Gud!* What happened to you?"

"Got punched in the face by your good-for-nothing husband—that son-of-a-bitch." He held the blood-soaked rag to his face, but the front of his shirt suggested he had bled for most of his drive. A little blood still trickled from one nostril. "Catherine and I are getting the hell out of here as soon as we can find a place!" Henry spoke as though his nose was plugged. "He's out of fucking control!"

He stood at the sink, wondering what to do next, as

Martha came to his side. She gently turned him toward the light. "Bend over and let me get a good look." She put her fingers gently under Henry's chin moving it closer to her face.

"Hmmm . . . he packed you a good wallop. Hauling nets full of fish keeps that guy strong. Your nose is still bleeding. Lay down on the davenport with your head back. I'll get a cold washcloth. You're a mess. I didn't know he had that much strength left in him."

Martha came back with the compress. "Here, don't move," she said as the put the chilled cloth on his forehead.

"I need to check on Catherine. She hasn't come down yet," Martha said, but then added softly, "*Ah, Gud*, Henry. You can't leave me here with him. I'd rather be dead!" She tiptoed up the ladder, and saw that Catherine's eyes were open. "Dear girl, Henry's home."

"I know, I heard you talking. Where was he?"

"He went for a ride after he came down from checking on you. He ended up at the Korn Krib."

"Would you tell him to come up here," Catherine whispered. "I want him to lie down next to me."

"I wish he could do that, but he can't right now?"

"Is he drunk?"

"No, but he's not feeling well."

"Why? What's the matter with him?"

Martha was surprised and pleased Catherine was talking, but she was afraid if she told her daughter the truth she'd withdraw again. Martha knew full well how hard it was to get out from under the heaviness of depression.

"Henry was in a fight."

"What? Henry? He's not a fighter. Never have I even known him to raise his voice." She shook her head in disbelief.

"He's just a little banged up. Why don't you come

down and see him? I think he'd like that."

Catherine sat up slowly. She was dizzy and weak as she hung tight to the railing taking one rung at a time. She couldn't bear to think of Henry not being at the top of his game. When she walked into the front room and saw him lying on the couch with a bloody rag over half his face she gasped. She couldn't believe what she was seeing.

"Oh, Honey!" Gathering her robe around her legs, she sat on the floor next to the couch. "What happened to you, my darling? Can you talk?"

"Yeah, I can talk." He sounded as though he had a bad cold. "I'm happy you're out of bed. Are you feeling better? You're the most important one. You have to stay healthy. Just hold my hand and sit here for a minute." She could barely understand what he was saying.

"Can you tell me what happened, Honey?"

"Ask your mother."

Martha said without being asked, "All I know is your father punched him in the face at the Korn Krib. I don't know why."

Martha suggested to Catherine that they go into the kitchen to have a cup of coffee and let Henry rest. First, though, Martha brought Henry a clean cold compress. "Keep your head back," she said as she removed the first compress and took the bloody rag from his face. "You better lay low for a while, my boy."

Catherine had followed her mother into the living room. She needed to know what had happened. "Why did Papa hit you?" she asked.

"Because I got mouthy. I should have kept my big mouth shut," Henry said. "It hurts to talk."

"Well, don't talk then. We can hear about it later."

"No. I have to tell you—I'll go slow—I stopped at the Korn Krib to have a beer. I was down in the dumps because you were not feeling well. Mike was sitting there with his drinking buddies, having a gay old time. When he saw me, he came over and tried to get me to join them. He was half in the bag—all jolly, red in the face like he gets—and I wasn't in the mood. Ouch!"

Henry put his hand up to his face. "All I could think about was you lying in bed half dead and him spending our hard-earned money—*our* hard earned money!—laughing it up with his buddies like he didn't have a care in the world."

Henry looked up and waved his hand. "Hey, Mame, I need a glass of water. All I can taste is blood."

"That pig," Martha said, as she jumped up to get the water.

"Oh, my God." Catherine muttered.

"Let's face facts here, ladies. Mike is not going to change. He's a drunk—he'll drink himself to death. I don't want to be around to see that. I don't want my kid to grow up with a drunk—a mean drunk."

"Henry, he's not always mean," Catherine said.

"No, that's true, but he's unpredictable. Listen, Cat. It's him or me. I can't take this anymore. We are moving out."

They sat around the table in uncomfortable silence, not daring to look at one another.

Henry broke the silence.

"It's me or him. I'm not kidding. You can stay here with your mother and father or come with me. I'm moving out as soon as I can. I don't know if I can face your father. I might move back home until we get this straightened out."

Catherine looked stunned and even paler than she was before. "Henry, you can't do this."

"Yes, I can. I hate to be this way, but I need to protect my family—you and the baby. Someone has to have some sense around here. Martha, you've been living your life with this. No wonder you're so messed up."

"Henry—" Catherine said.

"No, I mean it. I mean every word I said. Either you get on board or I'm out of here— with or without you!"

Catherine looked at Henry with her eyes wide open now. "I've never seen you like this before. What has gotten into you?"

"You know what's gotten into me. It's a hellhole, this place. We have no privacy. I feel like I'm in jail when I'm here. I have to watch every word I say!" Henry tried to speak as emphatically as he could while lying on his back. "This doesn't feel like home. I tiptoe around trying to not make a wrong move for fear of setting someone off. This is no way to live—I want out!"

"That's just how I feel—every day—at least the part about tip-toeing around," Catherine confessed.

With that, he got up and walked to the ladder. His face was grim.

"Henry, get back here and sit down. You can't walk away from this—not after you opened up this can of worms." Catherine was getting her spark back. "What's your plan? Where are we supposed to go? We can't move tonight!"

"What about me?" Martha looked like she was going to collapse. "You can't live with him? How do you think I can live with him? For God's sake I've been tiptoeing around for thirty years!" She showed genuine defiance.

"Mame, I don't know what to tell you. I don't think you can live with him either. But we need a little time to sort this out—but this has to happen as fast as we can get it done,"

Henry said. "I'm determined to get the hell out of here."

Martha chose that moment to spring her little surprise on the struggling couple. "I have a little money stashed away that I've been saving up," she said.

Catherine's eyes widened. *Could this be true?* "How in the heck did you get money to save up? We can barely make it from week to week."

"Oh, I have my ways." Catherine saw a tiny gleam in her mother's eyes, a new set in her jaw. "Mike doesn't keep track of his money very well. I find some in his pockets when I wash his clothes and I always check the top of the dresser. Once in a while I take some from the grocery money. I never take so much that anyone would miss it. I have it in a very safe place and I'm not telling you where."

"How much you got, Mom?" Catherine said.

"To tell you the God's honest truth, I don't know. I haven't counted it for a while. I'm just telling you that—if you take me with you—I could help out a little . . ."

Chapter 20. Thirteen-Fourteen Elizabeth (1942)

Henry was relentless about moving out of his mother- and father-in-law's house. The fight with Mike in the Korn Krib was the turning point. As tired and worn out as Catherine was, she couldn't ignore his determination to find a new place. She agreed that they needed some privacy and that Mike was getting more erratic and difficult. Where Martha would live remained the stickler. It was obvious to everyone, including Henry, that she couldn't live alone with Mike.

Catherine needed to contact her siblings again.

Dear Family,

I have good news and bad news. The good news is that I'm having a baby in early October! Henry and I are excited to say the least! I'll probably have to quit work soon and that will be a relief. I've been pretty tired trying to take care of Mom, Dad and Henry, being PG and still working at the mill full time.

Now for the bad news. Henry and I have to find another place to live. The relationship between Mike and Henry is trying. Mom and Mike can't say a civil word to each other. It's a tense situation—hard on me. I feel like it's my job to keep everything running smoothly and I can't do it anymore. Sometimes I think I'm going to have a nervous breakdown just like Mom. Not to mention, with the baby coming we'll need more room.

What are we going to do with Dad? I love him so much, but he's intractable most of the time. He and Mom wouldn't do well living together without me, and I'm at my wit's end.

Henry already has begun looking for another house to rent. He won't stand still until we're out of here. Do any of you have any room for Mom? I worried about her the most. Dad has pretty much made his bed— if he has to stay here alone, he'll have to figure it out. But I have to say, I don't know how he'll support himself.

I need your help, guys. Please, please . . .

Love, Catherine

Stella was the first to reply, and she repeated the offer Anthony had made when the housing question had first arisen, before Henry and Catherine were married.

Dear Catherine,

Congratulations! You and Henry will be good parents. I still have some of my maternity clothes that I saved and it's obvious I won't be needing them. I'll send them to you. I wish I could see that little bump you have. So happy for you.

Anthony and I would love to have Mom live with us. We have plenty of room. It would be wonderful for Margaret to get to know her grandma. Just say the word. Do you think there's any chance Mom would move? I'm jealous of my friends who have family near them.

About Mike—first of all, I think the only way we could get him to move anywhere would be in a casket. He's a stubborn old bird and a problem to boot. I don't know what to say about him. I'd feel bad if he were alone, but I agree with you—he's made his bed.

You wouldn't believe how Margaret has grown. She's only seven and she's already up to my armpit. Her feet are huge. She's such a love. Anthony is spoiling her rotten.

Keep me posted. Send Mom out anytime—we could drive out in the summer and bring her home with us.
Love always, Your sister Stella

A reply from Madison trailed in a few days later.

Dear Catherine,

You're quite the girl, Little Sis. I could never do what you're doing. Helen would have no part of it. Taking care of our parents must be a hell of a job. We've talked about having Mom live with us. We really don't have the room. With the new baby we're exhausted. Kathy hasn't slept through the night once in her short life. We're both up most of the night. It's lucky Helen isn't nursing, so sometimes I can feed the little shit. Working long hours at the bank doesn't help much.

We could take Mom for a couple weeks at a time to give you a break, but it wouldn't work for us for us to have her move in. Helen doesn't have the patience. She doesn't take advice very well—I'm learning that. Ha ha.

I don't know what to say about Mike. He's a hoot at a party— a hell of a storyteller—but I know how mean he can be. I hope I can be a better father than he was. We were just talking about the time he chased Charlie and me around the table trying to catch us and beat the old-Billy-hell out of us. You didn't want to get between him and his liquor. He had a hell of a temper. I wouldn't want to live with him. Who would? I probably could spare a little money now and then to help him out if he had a place to live, but I don't feel like supporting his drinking habits.

Oh, and congrats on the baby. I hope you get more sleep than we're getting. Keep me posted.
Best, Steve

Charlie sent a postcard.

Hey, Catherine. I could send a little more money, but I can't quit my job. I'm not much help, I guess. I'll see if I can get home the next time the boat ties up in Chicago. Say hi to Mom and Dad. Yeah, you got it bad. Wish I could help. Charlie

Clara called.

"Jeez, Catherine. You don't have to send me a letter. You could have just called or stopped over."

"Are you kidding me, Clara? Tell me when I have time to call. I hardly have time to pee. I'm so tired and down in the dumps."

"Why don't you and Henry stop over? We could talk. I'm tired too. Not enough that I have these four kids but, you know I have another bun in the oven."

"Oh, my God—not another kid! Sally's just turned one! What's the matter with you?"

"Well, you know how that Nels is"—she chuckled. "I can't keep him away from me. Every time he hangs his pants on the bed post, I get pregnant"—another chuckle.

"Well, if I were you, I'd ask him to keep his pants on." Catherine was surprised to find herself smiling. That hadn't happened in a while. "You know what Mom always says—men are good for nothing."

"Yeah, I know. If he had to take care of these kids, I'll bet he'd keep his pants on."

"Stop it, Clara! I'm going to wet my pants. It's good to laugh. It's been pretty downbeat around here. I'll try to get Henry, when he's not looking for a house, to stop over with me. Maybe Saturday when Nels is around—and the two of you aren't in bed, for God's sake!" They both felt better after they talked.

Henry was late coming home from work that day.

"Hey, Henry. Where ya' been? Your supper's getting cold."

"I've been looking for a place for us. Jimmy's been asking the guys who hang out in the bar—he came up with a couple leads."

"Anything interesting?"

He sat down to a plate of cold meat loaf, mashed potatoes and Martha's canned string beans. Catherine was at the sink washing the supper dishes.

"Cat," he said looking around. "I don't see any ketchup on the table."

Catherine dried her hands, stepped over to the icebox to get the ketchup for Henry, and sat down in a chair across from him. "Tell me about the houses."

"I saw one on Pierce Avenue for twenty-seven dollars a month. It wasn't bad. It had two bedrooms, a nice front room. The kitchen had a gas stove."

"I want that stove. No more making a fire first thing in the morning."

"Yeah, but it's on a pretty busy street," Henry said. "It would need some work—painting the inside, replacing a couple of windows"—a mouthful of mashed potatoes—"that kind of stuff." A bite of meatloaf. Catherine waited as patiently as she could for more details. "It's, well, it's a little dumpy, but better than *this*," waving his fork around toward the corners of the kitchen. "It's available now. We could drive past it after I finish eating if you want."

Catherine agreed to go. Martha didn't make a peep.

"Jimmy told me about another one on Elizabeth Avenue, but I didn't have a chance to look at it. I think it's a little more expensive. Let's drive past that one, too."

Henry made quick work of the rest of his meal, and

they left immediately. As they were driving, Catherine told Henry she was feeling a little better and would probably go back to work the next day.

"I'm still really worried about what we're going to do with Mom and Papa. It would be nice to live in a better house—none of my siblings can help me much. Stella would take Mom, and that's great, but I know she'd never go. They all seem to think it's okay to leave Mike, so that's a little relief, but I am still going to worry about him living alone."

"Jeez, Honey. Give yourself a break. You can't feel responsible for taking care of your parents for the rest of your life. You have four brothers and sisters who don't seem very worried. Why should you be stuck with the job?" Henry paused for some seconds and then made his plea personal. "Think about *me*. I'm your husband. I want you to be a wife to me—and how can you if you're catering to your parents every minute?"

Catherine knew how it was supposed to happen—she should be taking care of Henry.

Privately she thought it was about time someone looked after her, but she couldn't see that happening in a million years. She had to admit she was a little resentful, but she knew her place. Were men really good for nothing, as she had heard her mother say over and over? Couldn't they take of themselves?

Henry interrupted her thoughts. "Cat, this is the house for twenty-seven dollars a month."

Catherine was not impressed. It looked like it sloped a little to the south and the outside needed paint. It looked small and dingy with a tiny yard. This was not a step up from where they were living now.

"Nope." she told Henry. "Same old, same old."

Henry agreed. "I want a house so bad—that's probably

why I thought it might do. Let's ride past the one on Elizabeth—1314, I think."

Malmstadt's grocery store was right in front of them as they turned onto Elizabeth Avenue. Lincoln Elementary School was across the street and thirteen-fourteen was only a half block away. *Nice,* Catherine thought, noting how mature trees lined both sides of the street.

"Henry, I love this neighborhood. It feels like home to me."

Henry pointed to a house with a "For Rent" sign in the front yard. "That's the place, Cat."

"Look at that porch! It stretches across the whole front of the house! I can see a swing at the end of the porch already."

"What swing?" Henry asked, studying the house closely.

"Oh, silly you, it's not there yet! We're going to put it up."

"Hold on, Honey. We haven't seen the inside yet, and we don't know what the rent is—Hey! I see some lights on. Do you think it's too late to knock on the door?"

The question was barely out of Henry's mouth before Catherine was out the door and headed up the sidewalk. Her knock was quickly answered by an older woman with a friendly smile. *It wasn't too late to knock!* Catherine saw above the smile a pair of bright eyes and a head of white curly hair.

Seeing Henry exiting the parked car, the woman said, "I'll bet you're here to look at the house."

"Yeah, and I hope it's not too late."

"It's *not* too late. When it's too late for us, we turn off the lights and lock the doors. I'm Alice, by the way."

Bing Crosby's version of "Deep in the Heart of Texas" was playing on a radio somewhere behind her.

Henry joined Catherine at the door, they introduced

themselves, and Alice invited them in. The small hall held a coat tree with three coats, and it opened to the right into a large front room where a man sat on the davenport, head cocked toward a console radio. Alice gestured toward the man. "That's my husband Leon, and he loves this song."

Catherine's first impression of the home was good. It smelled of lemon furniture polish, and everything seemed to be comfortably in place.

The quick tour reinforced that initial feeling of "rightness." A parlor between the front room and the porch faced the street through three double-hung windows. The two rooms were connected by an open archway. The tour turned left into a room the family used for dining that could also be used as a sitting room. In the back a bright white kitchen held a cook stove, an icebox, and plenty of room for a good-sized table. A window over the sink looked into the back yard, where Alice said she planted a big garden every spring. Across from the kitchen was a bathroom with a tub, sink and flush toilet with a bedroom on either side.

Catherine could barely temper her enthusiasm. Henry had forewarned her not to say anything about the house in case they needed to negotiate. She was nearly exploding, trying to hold back.

"Why are you moving, Alice?" Henry asked.

"Our son who lives in Marquette has been called up to serve our country. He's leaving behind a wife and three boys under the age of three. We're going to stay with Rose and help her with the kids while Tom is gone. We decided to rent out this house while we are there. Who knows how long this god-awful war will last?"

"I'm expecting to be called up soon," Henry confided. "I want Catherine to have a nice place to live while I'm gone.

We're going to have a baby in October."

"Congratulations! Do you have anyone to stay with you and the baby? It's hard to be alone, to be mother and father both."

"We haven't gotten there yet," Catherine said. "We're just now starting to make plans."

Henry decided to cut to the chase. "What's the rent?" he asked.

"Thirty-two dollars a month, furnished, and we'll be leaving in a month or so."

"How long has the 'For Rent' sign been out?" Catherine asked.

"Since yesterday, and we've already had two parties come through."

"Thanks, Alice. You have a nice place here. We'll talk it over and get back to you. Would you be willing to come down a dollar or two?" Henry asked as they were going out the door.

"I'd have to ask Leon about that."

As soon as they got into the truck, the words came bubbling out of Catherine's mouth like white water spilling over a dam.

"Henry, that house is perfect for us! Great neighborhood, two skips and a jump from a store—a parlor and a front room—even a dining room! I don't care if it doesn't have a gas stove or a refrigerator, I want that house! It's perfect! And Alice makes a good point—in that house Mom could stay with us while you're gone. We could make the parlor into a bedroom—we could put a curtain across the arch."

"Whoa! Settle down, Honey. We have some important things to consider—the rent is higher than we can afford, for one. We haven't even seen it in the daylight. I'm not sold on your mother living with us. You know that was not in my long-term plan when we got married. We don't even know if they'd rent to us."

When Catherine finally fell asleep, she dreamed she lived in a beautiful huge mansion, but she couldn't find the kitchen. Searching madly, she discovered bedroom after bedroom but no kitchen. How could she live in a house without a place to cook and eat? She heard a voice whispering that the kitchen was upstairs. When she found it, she was in heaven. A beautiful gas stove, refrigerator, a tiled floor. Everything was brand new and shiny—the kitchen of her dreams. Henry was sitting at a shiny glass-topped table. He asked her to sit down and told her they couldn't have this house—the neighbors didn't think they were good enough. She woke up sobbing.

In the morning as they were getting ready for work, Catherine made Henry promise that they would stop on the way home to look at the house in the daylight. He agreed. He liked the house, but she loved it. She couldn't get it out of her mind for a minute.

After their daylight visit, Catherine was even more obsessed. It was as beautiful on the outside as the inside. Alice told them Leon would rent the house for a dollar a month less, but that's as far as they could go. She also said there was another couple coming later that evening to look at the house. Catherine was beside herself. She wanted to close the deal right then and there.

"Tell me about your garden, Alice," Catherine said.

"Well, actually I have two—a big vegetable garden in the back that I'd be planting pretty soon if we weren't leaving, and a flower garden of perennials along the front of the porch."

"Really?" Catherine said, excited about space for a garden just for flowers. "What kind of flowers?"

"There are two big hydrangeas on either side of the steps and cone flowers and black-eyed Susans in the rest of the space."

"Oh, that seems dreamy," Catherine cooed.

Henry still wasn't convinced. They left without making a commitment.

"Come on, Henry!" Catherine said, as they sat at Jimmy's nursing their beers. "That house would be perfect for us."

"Not if we can't afford to buy groceries. I don't want to be worrying every month that we won't make the rent—and what about your mother? We can't decide on a house until we get that little detail figured out. You won't be working much longer. How's your dad going to pay the rent without us? We have a lot of shit to figure out."

"It'll all work out, Henry. Especially if we get the house."

"Cat, you're not thinking this through. We can't just jump into this thinking it will 'all work out.'"

There didn't seem to be any middle ground.

Sleep came hard for Catherine, but she finally dropped off. She woke up with a start when Mike came lumbering in. She heard the table creak, and something, maybe a chair, went crashing to the floor. *Papa must have fallen*, she thought, and she wondered if she should go help him. She held back, because she didn't want to awaken Henry, who remained soundly asleep next to her.

Shortly thereafter she heard her mother scream out. "Get out of my room, you monster! Get your filthy hands off me!" Martha shouted.

"Spread yer legs, ya goddamn whore!" Every word was slurred. "You let every Tom, Dick and Harry fuck you! Even

Catherine's chums! Now .. it's . . . *my* turn!'"

Catherine could hear the strain in his voice as he fought for breath. Her mother was clearly putting up a strong fight.

"Roll *over*, you bitch! I'm gonna . . . fuck you til yer blue in the *goddamn . . . face!*"

A blood-curdling scream tore into the attic, and Henry bolted upright. "*What in the Christ is going on here?*"

Catherine hugged Henry hard, pressed her face against his arm. "My father is about to force himself on my mother. It's so awful! I can't stand it! It's sure not the first time this happened. I never know what to do." Catherine was desperate, crying.

Then they heard a loud thump. "Holy shit! Catherine!" he said, leaping from the bed. "I think he's killing her!"

Henry scuttled down the ladder in his boxer shorts and T-shirt and charged into Martha's pitch-black bedroom. He couldn't see a thing, but he heard Mike's heavy breathing and Martha's whimpering. When he finally found the light, he saw Mike on top of Martha, one hand fumbling with his pants buttons and the other on Martha's neck, trying to hold her down. Her fists pounded futilely on his back.

"Get off of her, you asshole!" Henry cried. He seized Mike's shoulder and the waistband of his pants and pulled Mike off Martha. Stunned by the intrusion, Mike went limp and rolled face-up off the side of the bed. He fell backwards onto the floor, his head hitting first with an audible *thump!* before the rest of his body hit the raw wood. Martha scrambled to cover herself while Henry stood, gasping for air, looking at Mike's inert body. His first thought—had he just killed his father-in-law?

Catherine came into the room, glanced at Mike's half-dressed body lying next to the bed, looked wordlessly at her husband, and helped her mother step over Mike's silent form. Martha let Catherine lead her to a chair at the kitchen table. Catherine plugged in a small electric burner to heat water for coffee. They heard Mike groan, and Henry left his vigil over Mike, glanced once back into the bedroom, and joined them at the table.

Catherine felt a despairing humiliation. This was another of her father's assaults on her mother, as she had witnessed and fought so many times. She had told Henry that her father was abusive to her mother, but she had never told him in detail what sometimes happened when Mike came home drunk. What was Henry thinking now of them, of her?

Catherine was stunned at Henry's first words. There was no recrimination. "Where does Mike keep his stash?" he asked. "I think a shot of whiskey might calm all of us down."

"He keeps it locked up in his room so no one will steal it," Catherine said.

"Let's go look for it," Henry said. "Me or you, Cat?"

Martha, still deeply shaken, was about to caution the couple about Mike's anger if he caught someone in his bedroom and then realized the absurdity of her thought. Mike was still half-conscious on the floor of her bedroom and was not going to stop anyone from doing anything.

Cat volunteered. "I know his hiding places. I'll go."

She came out with a bottle in one hand, her other holding her nose. "His bedroom is gross. It stinks of dirty clothes, mold and booze—probably rotten food."

"I quit cleaning it." Martha said. "Why should I?"

Catherine put a glass with a shot of whiskey on the table in front of Martha.

"I'm not drinking any of that stuff. I hate it." She pushed it away.

"It'll relax you, Mame," Henry said, pushing the glass back toward Martha. "Tonight you need it. You'll feel better. You've been through a lot. Trust me."

Martha didn't have the strength to argue. She picked up the glass in front of her and took a sip. She shook her head and grimaced. "*Ah, Gud!*" She sputtered and coughed.

"Come on, Mame, you can do it."

"Get me a glass of water, for God's sake," she coughed. "Where am I supposed to sleep for the rest of the night? I'm not going in my bedroom with that pig on the floor. I can't even stand to say his name."

"After you finish your medicine"—Catherine smiled at Henry over her own little joke—"we'll tuck you in all cozy in our bed, Mom."

Catherine and Henry, covered by an old blanket leaking its stuffing at a dozen tiny rents, spent the rest of the night squeezed together on the couch. They were still awake when Mike, moaning softly and shuffling unsteadily, crossed back into his own bedroom and slammed the door.

Henry, spooned behind Catherine, said softly, "Your father is a goddamn monster."

Catherine had been waiting fearfully for Henry to angrily tell her she had not painted a clear picture of why she feared to leave her mother along with Mike, but her fears were quickly allayed as Henry went on.

"I understand, Cat, why you have said so many times you can't leave your mother with Mike." He held her tight. He had his own problems with his own mother, and he had not wanted to live with his mother-in-law. He knew they could never tell when she might sink into one of her dark states. Even though he wanted Catherine and his new baby all to himself, he now realized he would have to put up with Martha's unpredictable mood swings, because together they had to protect her from a sometimes-crazed husband.

They lay on the davenport for a while in silence. Catherine could feel his warm breath on her neck. Finally he said, "Against my better judgment, we'll have to take your mother with us. None of your family has stepped up to the plate. It's not fair that you have all the responsibility—but you do, so let's make plans."

"What about Mike?"

"I don't care about Mike. He can stay right here and rot as far as I'm concerned."

"This is so hard—but I know you're right. I'm so sorry you're burdened with my family, too. It's not fair to you."

"Well, it's not fair to you either. All we can do is try to make the best of it."

Catherine's head was spinning with the myriad of mountains she would have to climb to get through the next few days and weeks. But it was easier facing the future knowing they would be moving to a lovely house in a beautiful neighborhood.

Before finally drifting off to sleep, the couple decided they would talk to Martha after work the next day. They'd ask her if she'd like to live with them, leaving Mike behind, and asking, too, if she would be willing to help with expenses, using the money she had squirreled away. If there was enough to make up the difference in their present rent and the future rent at 1314 Elizabeth, they'd move.

"Oh, Henry, I love you so much. You're the best husband in the world," Catherine mumbled, yielding to sleep against the prospect of an early rise and a day of work.

As she packed boxes at the mill, Catherine could think only of her new home, her garden, the wonderful neighborhood where her child would grow up.

"I'm a nervous wreck, Henry," she said on their drive home from work. "I don't know what I'll do if we don't get that house." Her feet wiggled, her fingernails faced an onslaught of nervous teeth.

They found Martha on her hands and knees scrubbing the kitchen floor with Fels Naphtha and a scrub brush. She hollered to them to go around to the front door. Catherine came running up the porch steps and into the kitchen.

"Mom, Henry and I have to talk to you right now."

"You'll have to wait 'til I get this floor scrubbed. The water will get cold."

"Damn the water!" Catherine said. "We need you right now!"

Henry apologized for his wife, said he knew that Martha knew that Catherine, when she got something in her head, would not rest.

Martha, equally stubborn, *did* know. She took her own time, finished a little more of the floor, then wrung out her scrub rag, hung it over the edge of the pail, wiped her hands on her faded apron and walked into the front room.

Catherine pounced immediately. "Mom, how much money do you have stashed away?"

"What? What are you talking about?"

Henry intervened. "Hold on, Cat. Mame, let me explain. Catherine and I talked it over. We want to move out of this house before the baby is born or I get called up."

Martha gasped.

"Wait till I'm finished," Henry said. "While I'd like to live alone with Catherine and the baby, I realize after last night that we can't let you stay here alone with Mike. I see that now more clearly than anything your daughter has told me. So, when we move, we are taking you with us if you'd like to come."

"What about Mike," she asked. She wondered if she cared, but she knew he would have trouble on his own.

"I don't know, but what I do know is he won't be coming with us."

Martha looked at Henry in disbelief. Her hands started shaking, and her eyes filled with tears. "You're not kidding me, are you? I thought I'd have to live with him until they put me in my grave. I'd do *anything* to move out. Do you need money? Is that what you're talking about, Catherine?"

"Henry and I have been looking at houses. I think we've found the perfect one . . ."

"Yeah," Henry said. "The rent's over our budget, so we were hoping you could add a little something each month."

"I'll give you every penny I've saved if you get me away from that good-for-nothing bastard!" The promise of freedom from her husband lit her face. "I don't know how much I have, but I'll go get it right now."

"We don't need the money now. Keep it right where it is for the time being."

"Mom, wait till you see this house!" Catherine was already picturing where her mother would sleep. "You'll love it!"

As best she could, Catherine described every room in the house. "Henry and I are going over there right now to tell them we'll take it. Cross your fingers, Mommy!"

Martha couldn't believe what she heard. This was the best news since she was forced to marry Mike. She hoped she wasn't dreaming.

Catherine and Henry drove over to 1314 Elizabeth with a down payment in hand. When Alice opened the door, Catherine practically leaped into the entry hall.

"We're going to rent your house. I'm so excited!"

Alice shook her head, broke the news as best she could. "I'm so sorry to tell you, but the couple that looked at it last night took it on the spot. I was secretly hoping you would have gotten here first."

"You're kidding, right? This can't be true!"

It was true. When they got back in Henry's truck, she burst into tears. "What now? I can't bear this!" Her face was in her hands, her vision of their new life together dissolving.

Henry tried to soothe her, seeing her deep disappointment. "Honey, relax. We'll just keep looking. That's not the last nice house in Marinette."

Catherine was not to be consoled.

Henry sat at the kitchen table, explaining the situation to Martha, while Catherine sat in the front room, trying to cope with the loss of a dream. The thought kept coming, *Look at this dump. I want out. I want out . . ."*

"Does this mean I can't live with you?" Martha quietly asked Henry.

"No." Henry was disappointed, too, but he kept his feelings hidden. "We'll just keep looking."

Just then Mike walked in the back door. "Goddammit, Henry! You parked that fuckin' truck halfway in my space again. I'm sick and tired of not having enough room to park my truck in my own yard!"

Henry was stunned. It was as though the prior night had never happened. *How drunk was he?* Henry wondered briefly, but then the new thought came. *Soon it won't matter.*

"Mike, pretty soon you're not going to have to worry about where I park my truck. We're moving out. You'll have the goddamn back yard to yourself."

Mike raised his hand, one finger prominent. "Go ahead

and move! I don't give a shit! I'm tired of putting up with you anyway. The wife and I will have a little breathing room again."

As Mike walked toward his bedroom, Henry called out, "Martha is coming with us."

Mike halted, turned, sneered. "Don't be so goddamn stupid, you young punk. She's stayin' right here with me. I'm the boss around here. Don't think you can call the shots. Martha, git over here—tell 'em you'll be stayin' right where you are."

Martha didn't move or say a word. She sat on the davenport, her hands in her lap and head bent.

"Jesus fuckin' Christ! Look at me, woman! Tell 'em! Yer place is right here with me. Don't git any highfalutin ideas of leaving. You know what side yer bread is buttered on."

He started limping toward her, anger in his eyes, his fists clenched. Henry stood between the two of them and said, "Martha, get up and walk out the front door. Now! Catherine, you go with her."

Catherine and Martha moved swiftly out the door. Henry faced Mike, grabbed him by front of his jacket and pulled Mike's face close to his. "If you ever—if you ever!—go near Martha again, I will have you arrested or beat you bloody. Catherine and I are moving out."

Mike pulled back, seeking space to swing at Henry, but he was held tight and close. Henry's face was red, his teeth clenched, his words his own blows against a man he was coming to hate. His pronouncements came from the heart.

"When we leave, we are taking Martha with us! Got that? Until we find a place to live"—he gave Mike a little shake—"steer clear of Martha."

Mike pulled free, backed up, stood with clenched fists but did not try to swing. "You . . . snot!" His own face was red, brightening his massive birthmark. "Git yer fuckin' ass outa my house! This is my goddamn house!" Arms waving, his jacket pulled up and his navel exposed, Mike railed. "I bin in this house fer thirty years! I raised my kids in this house!"

Mike's voice sank to a bitter complaint. "Ya' been here for a few months and ya' think ya' own the place. All I can say is, git the fuck out! I'd like t'bust yer head open. I bet there ain't a goddamn brain in it."

Henry had seen immediately that, without the fuel of alcohol, all Mike's fire would be spent in words. "Mike, I'll say it again. If I go, Catherine and Martha come with me."

Mike turned, went out, slamming the back door, got into his truck and drove away. Martha, Catherine and Henry sat at the kitchen table trying to figure out what to do next.

Henry's words were bold, but there was nothing to back them up. Where could they go if they left the house? Clara's house was full of kids—no spare beds there. Henry was ruling out going to his parents' home. He knew that even a simple statement from Louise like "What would you like for breakfast?" would be a coded message to him saying, "I told you so."

"I think this is the worst day of my life," Catherine said. "I want to go to bed and never get up."

"Why don't you go to bed, Honey," Henry said. "You need the rest. I'll stay down here with Mame for a while."

"Catherine, you have to eat something." Her mother touched her arm. "We haven't even had supper yet. Let me make some Cream of Wheat. At least you'll have a little something in your belly," Martha said.

While Martha was standing by the stove, Catherine asked Henry, "How are we going to keep Mom safe tonight? Knowing him, he could do the same thing as he did before."

"How about we sleep in your Mom's bed and she can sleep in ours—or we could get a lock for her door."

Martha turned from the stove. "I don't want to feel like a prisoner in my own house. *Uh, Gud!* Okay, I'll sleep in your bed. You'll hear him if he tries coming up the ladder. Don't worry about that. I hear every sound you two make."

Henry and Catherine looked at each other wide-eyed.

"I know it's a blow not to have that house, but we did the best we could," Henry said. "I'll start looking again tomorrow."

"I've been looking almost every day, Henry. We'll never find another place as nice as that." She rose and walked to her mother's bedroom. "It doesn't matter anyway. I live in the middle of a mess. You do, too, Henry and it's my fault. Just when I think something nice is going to happen, it gets screwed up. What's the use?" She closed the door behind her.

Henry took a deep breath, opened the icebox and took out a beer. "Goddamn it," he muttered under his breath. He picked up a *Reader's Digest* from the end table next to the couch and sat down to read, but he couldn't focus. He knew this was going to be a hell of a problem to solve. Had he made a mistake? He did not want to admit his mother was right. He knew Catherine had a messed-up family, but he hadn't thought about the fact that it was now his family, too.

Both Catherine and her mother were down in the dumps. Martha thought she'd never get away from Mike. Catherine was heartbroken about losing the house, angry at and sorry for her father, and worried about bringing a baby into this mess. Henry was tired of living with a house full of sorrow and fear. Every night after work and while he was delivering beer, he tried to find a place for them to live. He'd drive up and down the streets of Marinette seeking "For Rent" signs, but he found nothing that measured up to the house on Elizabeth.

Mike was around very little during waking hours, and when he was around he usually had a buzz on. He would join them occasionally at the dinner table, silent. The bedroom arrangement was working pretty well. Martha didn't like having to climb the old ladder, especially in the dark, but she didn't grumble. She was spending more time in bed—not a good sign, Catherine thought.

One late afternoon Catherine was alone in the kitchen when Mike walked in the door. "Papa, what are you doing home so early?"

"I'm gettin' tired of hangin' around the taverns. I ain't had a good meal since I don' know when." Catherine thought he might be sober. He reached in his pocket, pulled out some crumpled bills and tossed them on the table. "Here's my wages fer today."

"Thanks, Papa. We can use it."

"It's a goddamn shame a man can't feel at home in his own house. What the hell's goin' on here?"

"You know what's going on." The notion that she might soon be out of here loosened her tongue, let her tell him straight. "You're a smart guy, but sometimes you are just plain mean—especially when you're drunk. You can be a nice guy, even a really funny guy, a great storyteller, but then the next thing I know you're in a fight or treating Mom like she's dirt. I know you won't hurt me, but whenever you hurt Mom it breaks my heart. It's not right, Papa."

"Yeah, I know. I'm good for nothin'." *He is sober*, she thought. Mike went on. "Your mother deserves better than me. So do all you kids." He hung his head and was silent.

Catherine pressed her advantage. *Might as well lay it out.* "You and Henry have your differences, too. You're always nagging him about something. It pisses him off and then I hear about it."

"Yeah, well, he just came in and took over my house. Who wouldn't nag? Son-of-a-bitch."

"Living in the house with all of you is hard on me," she confessed. "There's always tension. You and Henry, you and Mom, now even Henry and me. I try, but I can't take it anymore. If I don't get out of here, I think I'll end up in the Peshtigo nuthouse. You know I love you, Dad. You've been good to me. No matter where you live, I'll make sure you get taken care of."

"Hey Kiddo, can you make me somethin' t'eat?" Catherine sensed that her father might be resigned to the major life changes that were barreling toward him.

"How about some scrambled eggs and oatmeal? We're out of ration stamps this week and almost out of food."

Mike gobbled his eggs and oatmeal and limped off to his bedroom. Even the huge maroon birthmark on the left side of his face was pale. He looked pathetic. Catherine had tears in her eyes. She knew that, unless masked by booze, there was a good heart under all his bluster, and she knew he was ashamed of himself. How could she not feel sorry for this poor man who had a hard life, too? His brother was in prison for murder but that's about all she knew about his family and his past. Despite all the stories he told, he never spoke about his mother or father, and none of his kids ever asked.

She crawled into Martha's bed and pulled the covers over her head. When she heard Henry come in the back door, her whole body seized up. The last thing she wanted to do right now was talk to him. He had no understanding of her father. She mistakenly thought she understood how others felt, but her attempts to make everything rosy wasn't working. She deemed herself a failure. It was her curse. She felt she was responsible for everyone's happiness and put their needs before her own.

No matter what she did she couldn't make her family whole, and her resentment was growing—just like her mother's.

She heard Henry in the kitchen, trying to find something to eat. "Smoke Gets in Your Eyes" was playing on the radio. When he finally came to bed, he slept as far away from her as he could get, and that's just where she wanted him.

Henry and Catherine continued searching for a house. She reminded him every so often that if he had acted a little faster, they'd already have their perfect house. Henry fumed quietly and never replied.

When Catherine's pregnancy began to show, the head of the union informed her that she would have to leave her job. Being home every day was pleasant and productive. She and Martha were doing a lot of baking these days to fill up the time. The oven yielded bread, rolls, cakes, cookies.

But Catherine was restless. She had worked so many years, first for the judge and then at the mill. She filled some of her spare time looking for houses, but she found nothing that matched the dream home she had lost.

One afternoon when they ran out of flour, Catherine suggested to her mother that they go for a ride, stop at Clara's to see the kids, and check out the little grocery store on Elizabeth, kitty-corner from what had been her dream house. They parked the car in front of the store.

"I don't even want to look at the house," Catherine said.

"Well, why in the world would we come here then?" Martha asked. "Are you trying to make yourself sadder? Aren't you sad enough already?"

At checkout Catherine asked the clerk if he knew of any houses for rent in the neighborhood. She was so tired of asking and getting the same negative response, but she gave it a shot anyway.

"Funny you should ask. You know, there's a house across the street and down a couple of houses—it's the white one with the big porch— you know where I mean? The owner came in this morning with a sad story. The couple who was going to rent the house starting in May—well, the husband had a heart attack and died, so it's up for rent again. Their daughter is expecting Alice and Leon to be there in a couple weeks. They're all packed up—and now this happens. She's all worked up about it."

Catherine gasped. "Are you kidding? *Across the street?*" The clerk nodded and pointed to the house.

"Mom, wait here!" She went flying out the door, dashed across the street and high-tailed it up the front steps.

Martha scrambled to catch up with her daughter and yelled from behind, "Be careful! Don't be foolish! You'll lose the baby!" By the time Alice opened the door Martha had joined Catherine on the porch. Both were breathing hard.

Alice looked askance at the two women huffing and puffing. "How can I help you?"

"You don't remember me? I was here with my husband a couple months ago. We wanted to rent your house, but someone beat us by an hour."

"Oh, sure! That's why you look familiar."

"The clerk, the one at the store over there"—she pointed across the street—"said the house is for rent again." At least that's what she thought she said, but Catherine's brain was moving faster than her tongue and all Alice heard was something like "*houzisfrentagain!*

Martha put her hand on her daughter's shoulder. "Catherine! For God's sake, calm down!" She turned to Alice. "Catherine has been a nervous wreck, because they didn't move fast enough the last time. She wants to rent your house."

Catherine said, "I have a dollar in my pocketbook for groceries. I'll give it to you as a down payment right now." She looked around for her purse. "Mom, where's my purse? I need it right now! Where is it?"

"You left it on the counter of the store when you ran out like a wild woman."

Alice said, "Come in, my dear, and sit down. Ed will watch your purse. Don't worry—let me get you each a glass of water. Don't mind all the boxes. We're getting packed up to leave."

Catherine was showing signs of calming down and Martha was craning her neck to look around the house without being too obvious.

"So," Alice said, "It seems you want the house and we want a renter as soon as possible, so we probably have a deal. We want to be out of here in two weeks. Could you move in as soon as that?"

"Yes. At least I think so. We weren't planning to move so soon. We haven't even thought about packing."

"We don't want to leave the house empty. We'll give you a break on rent if you can get some of your stuff in by the time we leave. Maybe just one of you could move in."

The deal was closed. Catherine had her house.

Chapter 21. The Burma Road (1943-45)

The day after Henry left for the war, Martha wrote a postcard to her sister Mary in Chicago:

My dearest Sister,

Well, Henry has gone. He left yesterday at 10 a.m. and it was really tough to see him go. Poor Catherine. I feel so sorry for her. She cries and cries. I woke up in the night and heard her crying. The poor kid. I wasn't here when he said good-bye to Catherine and the baby. But it was plenty sad. I wanted to stay home but Catherine thought I better not. It's terrible. I do hope this war will soon be over. I cried so much this last week. Wish you were here to talk to Catherine. I got to work today and poor Catherine will be alone. I don't know how long I can keep this up. I'm afraid it's too much for me. I make thirty or forty pies to be out by noon every day. I got to have a job, but I got to think of myself. Maybe Catherine will go to work. I think it will be better for her. Henry's at Fort Sheridan for a while. Jeannie has a cough and still doesn't feel good. Will write more later.

Love, Martha

The baby's crying woke Martha from a sound sleep. She was waiting for Catherine to pick up Jeannie and nurse her, but that didn't happen. Martha took over. She picked the little one out of her crib and cradled her granddaughter in her arms.

"What's wrong, Little One? Do you miss your Daddy, too? It'll be a different place around here without him." She patted Jeannie's back and rocked the baby from side to side. "I'll bet you're hungry. Let's see if Mama's awake so she can feed you. There, there, Sweet One."

She knocked on Catherine's door and went in. Martha found her daughter sobbing underneath the pile of blankets and pillows. She hadn't stopped crying since Henry left the day before. Martha gently laid the crying baby on the bed while she attempted to uncover Catherine.

"Honey," she said as she gently rubbed her shoulder, "the baby needs to eat."

"I can't Mom, I just can't."

"But you must. Put the baby to your breast and let her suck."

Little Jeannie stopped crying as soon as she began to nurse, but Catherine didn't. "I'm glad you didn't go to work today," she said between sobs. "I thought I could manage, but you're right. I can't. I don't believe he's really gone."

"Yeah, Honey," Martha said. "This is a tough one. I feel sorry for you—and for Henry, too."

"What if he never comes back?" She put her free hand on her face as the tears cascaded down her cheeks.

"You're going to have stop your wailing or your milk will turn sour and we can't let that happen. I know it's tough."

"Tough isn't the word for it," Catherine sobbed.

"I already called the boss to tell her I wasn't coming in. She was a sour puss about it, but I don't care. That job is too much for me anyway. I need a break. Let her make all those damn pies for once."

Martha had responded positively to their move. Not

having to deal with Mike's unpredictable behavior put her at the top of her game. She felt free and a little sassy to boot. Because she loved to cook, having Malmstadt's Market across the street was a real bonus of the move. Once a day, sometimes twice, she ran over to pick up individual items she found she needed—maybe a can of beans or a tub of lard. Lard was still her choice for baking, despite growing fad of getting a package of margarine and squeezing the packet of yellow coloring into it. Ed, the clerk who had played his important role in the move to this house, let her run a tab when ration stamps ran out. They didn't have to worry about a bill until the end of the month, and these days they could almost always pay it in full.

But one month when things were tight, Ed happily gave her a little grace. In return, she brought him a homemade lemon meringue pie. When Ed returned the pie tin, he told her he had never eaten anything this delicious in his life. He gave a piece to his neighbor, Marion, who ran the Sanitary Bakery on Pierce Avenue. She ate two pieces and wanted another one, but he believed he had shared enough. Marion begged Ed to ask Martha if she would make pies for the bakery.

Martha appreciated the compliment and thanked Ed for relaying the offer, but she declined, saying she wasn't interested. She was sure it would make her a nervous wreck. The next time she stopped at Malmstadt's he asked if sixteen dollars a week would make a difference. It did indeed, and now Martha had been making pies for the Sanitary Bakery every day for almost a year. She told Catherine that this work was getting to be too much for her, but she confessed to herself that she didn't want to work because she wanted to spend more time with the baby.

Martha took Jeannie from Catherine's breast and lifted her to her shoulder for a burp. "Oh, how I love you," she whispered as she nuzzled her face into the baby's cheek and kissed her on the head. Jeannie responded with a smile that showed off her one and a half new tiny bottom teeth.

"Catherine, it's time to get up. You have to eat something."

"I know, Mom, but I can't." she said. She was listless.

"You have a daughter to think about. I know you're sad—I don't blame you. Now get up and I'll make you some nice Cream of Wheat."

Catherine's red puffy eyes and her distorted face gave her a pitiful look. Martha put the baby in Catherine's arms while she cooked breakfast.

"Your daddy's gone, Little One. He's going to be fighting in a war." Catherine kissed Jeannie on the head. "We don't know when he's coming back or if he'll ever come back." She started sobbing again.

When Catherine arrived at the breakfast table, Martha announced her decision. "I'm quitting my job, Catherine. You need my help around here. I've been making those damn pies long enough."

"But, Mom, we need the money! And why aren't you at work today?"

"I called in and told Carol what was going on. I knew you needed me."

Later that day Martha called the Sanitary Bakery again, this time to tell the owner she wouldn't be coming back. Carol begged her to stay, but Martha held firm. They finally agreed that Martha would work every Saturday.

May 7, 1943
Dear Henry,
Today is my twenty-fourth birthday. I feel like I'm fifty-four. Mom made me a sponge cake with butter cream frosting and four candles, and Clara and the kids came over. It was good to see them—as if anything

can be good these days. Clara likes the way I've arranged the furniture in the front room. I like it, too. The kids can't get enough of Jeannie. I had to watch them every minute. I was afraid one of the boys would poke her eyes out. Clara's belly is getting big and she still has a couple months to go.

I only cried half the day today. I'm making progress. I miss you so much. You've only been gone three weeks. It feels like three years! I can't believe you're not here on my birthday. I have to get used to your not being here, but it's the hardest thing I've ever done in my life. Not knowing when you'll come back really hurts. Oh, my darling, I hope you come back. Now I'm crying again. Will I ever get used to this? I can't get you out of my mind. Going to bed without you is the most lonesome time.

It's a good thing Mom is here to help me with Jeannie. You should see your baby girl, Honey. She laughs and coos and jabbers. I think she was saying "da-da-da-da," so I know she misses you, too. I tell her about you all the time. Yesterday when I was changing her, she took hold of her legs and put both feet in her mouth. It was the cutest thing. When I start crying Mom usually takes her. She says it's not good for a baby to have a sad mother. Jeannie changes so much every day—I can hardly believe it. Oh, how I wish you could see her!

Mike asks about you every time I go there. He's worried about me. He says I look like "holy fright." I'm glad he's finally getting used to living alone. He doesn't seem to mind it too much. It's a blessing he and Mom are separated. They both seem to be doing better without each other. He likes it when I bring Jeannie with me. He wants to give her candy already. What a guy. He's got a heart of gold. Too bad that damn drink has taken over his life.

Did I tell you Mom quit her job? Her boss was devastated. She agreed to work on Saturday, so she'll be bringing in a little money anyway.

Well, my sweetheart, I'm tired. Off I go to cry on your pillow. Do you know when they'll ship you out yet? Do you know where they're sending you?

I can't tell you how much I love you. There aren't enough words.

Love Always, Cat

Henry's reply came about a week later.

May 15, 1943
My Darling Cat,

I got your letter today. I'll bet I miss you more. We wake up to Reveille every morning at 4:30 and we don't stop until we go to bed. We're marching, running with packs, cleaning our weapons, doing pushups, eating slop. The only reason I'm not crying is I'm too tired. I flop on my cot and I'm asleep as soon as my head hits the pillow. They won't tell us when we're shipping out or where we're going. The guys are pretty nice, but we don't have much time to get acquainted. None of us want to be here, but we've got to stop Hitler and the Japs and win this war.

One funny story to surprise you. The last couple of Saturdays and Sundays we have gotten some hours to ourselves in the late afternoon after marching. I tried to get up some games of smear, and nobody in the place knows it—not even a few guys from Milwaukee! How did we learn this and they never did?

Okay, I can't keep my eyes open any longer. I want to hear more about our little girl. Boy, do I miss her, too.
Love Always, Henry

Catherine read the letter to Martha.

"Poor boy. What a life he has. I feel sorry for all the boys going to war—and their mothers," Martha said.

"Did I tell you Henry's brother Woody has been called up, too? He'll be leaving in a couple weeks. When I took Jeannie to see Louise the other day, she was really upset. She hates FDR—blames him for taking two of her sons. She called him a son-of-a-bitch—first time I ever heard her swear. I think she even had a tear in her eye, and here I thought she was too tough to cry." Catherine gave her mother half a smile.

"I don't blame her," Martha said. "I wonder if Charlie

will have to go. Lord help us if he does . . . What did Louise say about the baby?"

"She was fine in her own distant way. She was nicer to me than she usually is. She bounced Jeannie on her knee and told her to not let her mother and grandmother spoil her. That was meant for me. I'm sure I don't meet her standards as a mother. Her approach is 'Spare the rod and spoil the child.'"

"*Ja*, well, don't worry about her. You raise that baby your way. She doesn't bother to come over here and visit. It wouldn't hurt her."

"She bragged about her grandson Billy—how advanced he is. She sees him all the time—they live so close. I think Ken and Mildred take Billy over to visit pretty often," Catherine said. "I wonder if Ken will get drafted."

"He's probably too old," Martha said. "Louise might lose her marbles if all three sons were fighting and I wouldn't blame her. So many of the young men in Marinette are being called up." She looked at Catherine holding Jeannie and smiled. "How are our ration tickets holding up this week?"

"We're okay so far. We don't use much gas and we don't eat that much."

They sat quietly for a minute and then Catherine went on. "Louise asked if I had heard from Henry. I told her I've gotten a few letters and I write to him every day." She shook her head. "Henry's mother hasn't heard from him yet. I could tell her nose was a little out of joint about that."

As Catherine sat nursing, she tried to figure out how they would make ends meet without her mother's income, but a sharp little pain interrupted her thinking. "Ouch!" she cried. "You little stinker! It hurts when you use those two little bottom teeth to bite your Mommy's nipple."

"She's a little squirmer, isn't she?" Martha said as she

took the child from Catherine and put her on the floor. Jeannie was starting to crawl. "Pepper, leave the baby alone!" Although Pepper was jealous of all the attention Jeannie got, he welcomed every opportunity to lick her face.

"Maybe I should get a job," Catherine mused. "With so many men gone they're begging women to work at the mill now. I could make a little money. With you not working, things are going to be tight."

Martha rescued the infant from Pepper's ministrations. "I think you should go back to work. I'm here with the baby. I could take care of her—and you won't have so much time to feel sorry for yourself," Martha said. She cooed softly to Jeannie.

"Mom! Take that back! How am I supposed to feel? I love Henry and miss him so much!"

"*Ja, ja,* I know. You've got it tough, but so do a lot of other women these days. You might meet a few and you can cry on each other's shoulders. You should be proud of your husband for fighting for our country."

Catherine could see that her mother's patience was being stretched, and within two weeks Catherine had a job at the paper mill, the same one she had when she left the year before. The employees looked different now. She was surrounded by women in the packing department who had taken over for the men who had gone to war. Catherine had bristled at her mother's claim that all she did was mope around, but she acknowledged her mother was right about the work environment. She liked the camaraderie with the women who were in the same boat. She worked the three-to-eleven shift.

Relieved not to be working every day, taking care of Jeannie was Martha's cup of tea. Bedtime was their favorite time together. Catherine would put Jeannie down for a nap just before she left for work, and Mamie—the name all her grandkids called her—was ready when Jeannie woke up. Sometimes they'd get all bundled up and go for a walk. Mamie would rock Jeannie, read her stories, and play on the floor with Pepper.

When it was time for supper Jeannie's highchair tray looked like a smorgasbord piled high with fluffy mashed potatoes and mashed carrots, graham crackers and other food she could eat without choking. Catherine was still nursing her when she was home, but Martha was teaching Jeannie to drink milk out of a cup and eat from her tray at supper. Watching Jeannie stick her hands in the food and push the mash into her mouth was quite entertaining. That which missed the mouth was spread out on the child's face and the front of her bib, but quite a bit hit the target and Mamie called her a little chow hound because of the way she wolfed down her food.

The evening routine always ended with a bath in the generous kitchen sink. "Come to me, Sweetie," Martha would say, lifting the little one under her armpits from the highchair, setting her on the counter to strip off the food-encrusted bib and romper, and settling her into warm water.

As soon as Jeannie got in the water she splashed with her hands and laughed. The routine seldom varied. Jeannie would throw her rubber ducky on the floor, her grandmother would bend and pick it up, and the child, laughing and squealing, would throw it down again. Always there came a point when Jeannie struck a serious pose and raised her arms to be lifted out. Martha wrapped her in a towel, carried her into her bedroom and laid her on the changing table. Martha wouldn't have been able to tell anyone who was having more fun.

"Look at you, you little one. You are the apple of

Mamie's eye. Let me get that diaper and rubber pants on you before you pee on your table." Then she tickled Jeannie's belly, causing the child to laugh out loud—little baby belly laughs.

"You're getting bigger every day. Pretty soon you'll be wearing size ones. Let me see those little toofins. Smile for Mamie." Her first teeth had come in on the bottom, and the top three were peeking through. Sometimes Martha took Jeannie to bed with her, and before too long they were sleeping together every night.

During the day when Catherine was home, Martha did the housework, laundry and cooking so that mother and child could have time together. Jeannie was the center of both her mother's and grandmother's lives. Their routine didn't change much over the next two years while Henry was engaged in the Allied cause on the far side of the Pacific Ocean.

Henry's unit had been shipped to Burma, where American, British and Chinese allies sought to make inroads against the Empire of Japan. As well as being targets of the Japanese, Henry's unit endured monsoons, malaria and treacherous terrain to build the Ledo Road. Henry's letters downplayed the effort and danger, but one day Americans would learn that the death count building the 1,072-mile road led to the work being labeled "A Man, A Mile." Henry chose images—like the photo of him and his buddies holding a snake as long as they were tall—that made Henry's war effort seem like nothing more dangerous than one of Roosevelt's CCC projects. To his dying day, Henry would never describe in any detail what he had done and seen while building that road from India to China.

The redacted letters he sent home mentioned nothing about the war, but he took the time to illustrate them with crude drawings for his daughter. One included a sketch of a birthday cake, a chicken, a truck, a ship and a train.

Sat. Nov. 4 1944 Burma: Along the Ledo Road
My Dear Little Girl:

   Hello, my little Sweetheart. How are you? Mama has told me how much you enjoy getting a card or a letter so I will write you one tonight.

   Although I am so far away from you, I know just how you are and what you are doing every day. Mama writes and tells me all about you and I sure am proud of you.

   She told me about your birthday party and how excited you were and the nice cake you had with candles on. I'll bet it looked like this . . .

   How do you like Grandma and Grandpa's moo moo and chickens? Do they look like this . . ? Mama says you sure like to go there, and I am glad you do.

   Daddy is fine, but sure is lonesome and wants to see his little girl awfully bad. We sure will have lots of fun when we are together, and I will take you to Grandma's in this new truck I will get us . . .

   Someday I will be on a big boat—this big!—and then on a choo choo with this many cars, and then we will be together . . .

   Mama tells me what a good girl you are and how well you can say nursery rhymes, and how you say your prayers and how you like to read your books. She also says how much fun you have together and you and Pepper play and how you like to stay up late at night.

   Well, honey, I must close. Be a good girl and someday Daddy will be home. Goodnight, my Little One.
With all my Love from Your Daddy.

Five months later, Henry wrote:

Sun. Apr. 1945 Burma
Hi Honey,

   Here are a few little things I am sending you. There are two pillow tops. One for you and one for my mother. If you want another one let me know and I will get you another. I thought one is enough just as a souvenir, but whatever you think.

Also, the watch you sent me. All it needs is a balance staff so you can probably get it fixed. It may come in handy. Here's what those coins from India are worth from the littlest to the biggest: one-quarter anna is one-half a U.S. penny; the half-anna is a penny, and so forth for the one anna, the two anna, the four anna and the eight anna, which is 16 cents. One rupee is worth 30 cents.

There is also one French coin that one of the guys in my company said is from French Indochina. Here is also a smoke on me. I wish I could send you more. I wanted to get a few more souvenirs when I was on furlough, but I didn't have too many funds and you know how high souvenirs are. I looked for something for our Jeannie but didn't know what to get and couldn't find anything suitable. I will send her something someday though.

How do you feel about souvenirs, Honey? Do you want me to send you a few other things when I can? I don't care too much for them.

This is just a note to tell you what is in the package. And I will never tire of telling you how much I love you. Cause I really do. Bye for now my darlings.
Always your Loving Husband and Daddy.

Catherine tried to picture what Henry's life might be like. Nothing in the local news talked about Burma. She felt only a loss of his company but never a sense that he was in danger.

May 5, 1945 11:30 pm
Dearest Henry,

Will this war ever be over? I miss you more every day. I just got home from work after a long shift and I'm dead tired, but I wanted to write to you anyway. I know how much my letters mean to you—just like your letters mean the world to me. When I don't hear from you, I worry my head off. Please take care of yourself. Jean and I need you.

You should see your little girl! Do you believe she's almost three-years- old already? She runs through the house singing, "When's my daddy coming home, when's my daddy coming home?" She's getting in the habit of sleeping with me when she hears me come home from work. She crawls out of Mom's bed and snuggles in with me. It's so cute.

I'll stick this letter in a box on the way to the mill in the morning.

All my love always, Cat

When Catherine and Jeannie were having breakfast or playing, Jeannie would ask Catherine questions about this man she had learned to call "Daddy."

"Where is my Daddy, Mama?

"He's in the war, Honey, far, far away."

"Where is far, far away?"

"A place called Burma. He's building a road and protecting us from bad people—to keep us safe."

"How many more days before I get to see my Daddy?"

"Not many now, my darling. Let's hope it's not too many."

Martha taught Jeannie how to paste stamps in the ration book so they could buy groceries and gas, and she loved that job. She tried to get every stamp inside the lines. Martha praised her for being a "good girl" when she put the stamps in the book just right. Jeannie tried hard to be the best girl she possibly could. Behaving all the time was hard for her, but she didn't want to make her mother and grandmother sad. They were sad enough already. She knew for sure her mother was really lonesome for her Daddy.

Occasionally Catherine had gone out with Woody, Henry's brother, and her friend Alta. Woody had served in France after the Normandy invasion, but a leg wound from shrapnel led to his discharge. He limped when he walked, sometimes crying out in pain from the steel fragments that doctors had not been able to remove.

Martha felt nervous when Catherine would go out with her friends at night because she drank too much. Martha, a teetotaler through and through, hated drinking. Her parents didn't drink and her life with Mike had turned her against alcohol altogether. Catherine came home one night quite late and quite drunk. Martha heard her fumbling with the door and met her as staggered into the front hall.

"Look at you, Catherine! You've got puke all over the front of your coat." She helped her daughter struggle out of her coat and held it to be washed. She couldn't hold back her disgust. "You're no better than your drunken father! Drinking will kill you and you've got a daughter to think of. You're a holy fool mess."

Catherine protested weakly, slurring her words as she wriggled out of the coat. "Jeesh! get off my back . . . morning, noon, night . . . all I do is work . . ." She waved a disapproving finger in her mother's face. "I jus' go out 'n' have a little fun and you're after me."

Martha helped her daughter to a chair. "It's a good thing you don't have to go to work tomorrow. You won't be able to get your head off the pillow. You're lucky you have me to take care of the little one."

Catherine exploded when she heard Martha saying she was not a good mother. "Shut up! Leave me alone! You're jus' lucky I keep a roof over your head and have kept you alive my whole life! I work and work and work, and what do I get? Just some old stick-in-the-mud saying I can't have some fun!"

Jeannie came running from the bedroom crying. "Mama, what's a'matter?"

She ran over to Martha and hung on to her grandmother's legs. "Mamie, what's wrong with Mama? Is she sick, Mamie?"

"She's sick, all right, Jeannie! She's drunk. She's a drunken mess. You can sleep with me tonight. I don't want her to puke on you, too. Go jump in my bed."

"No, I want to sleep with Mama in my bed." She was sobbing and out of control. Her face was as red as a cherry sucker. Snot and tears covered her little face. Whenever her mother and Mamie argued, she got scared. She didn't know whose side to be on. Sometimes she'd dance around or do other silly things to try to make them happy. Catherine would go to her room and shut the door and Martha would tell Jeannie her side of the story. The little girl didn't know whose side to be on. She thought it was her job to keep everybody happy, unaware that she had taken the role her mother played for so many years. It didn't serve either of them well.

As they roused Catherine and led her off to bed, Jeannie confided in her grandmother. "I know everything is going to be better when Daddy gets home. We'll be happy every day," she said, her chin held high.

Finally, in the fall of 1945 Catherine got the letter from Henry that she had been waiting for since the day after he left. He would arrive in Marinette in two weeks on Chicago and North Western Railway's *Peninsula 400*.

Catherine and Martha hung rugs on the clothesline and beat them until every bit of dust was gone, washed the windows and the curtains. On their hands and knees they scrubbed the linoleum in the kitchen and bathroom and cleaned the wooden floorboards in other rooms with a scrub brush and Fels Naphtha soap. Catherine used her ration of stamps to buy brand new percale sheets for her and Henry's bed.

"What's that icky smell, Mamie?" Jeannie asked. "It's all over the place."

"Come over here and I'll show you." Martha put her hand into the scrub water and pulled out a big chunk of tan soap.

Jeannie's nose crinkled. She said, "Yucky, Mamie."

On the day of Henry's arrival Catherine and Martha baked bread, made soup, and pickled herring. The *coup de gras* for Henry's return would be Martha's butterscotch cream pie, Henry's favorite.

A heavy fog hung over the railroad station, and light from the tall posts lining the platform was dull and scattered. Families of the arriving soldiers dressed in heavy parkas and chooks waited impatiently. The cold misty air smelled of cigarettes and trains.

"My daddy's coming home! My daddy's coming home!" Jeannie shouted, waving a little American flag above her head. Catherine carried Jeannie on her hip as they joined the other families at trackside.

"If you don't stop wiggling, I might drop you," Catherine smiled. "You're hard to hold in your bulky snowsuit."

"Take off my dumb snowsuit! I want my daddy to see my new dress!" Pulling and tugging at buttons and twisting in her mother's arms, she fussed, "How can I get this snowsuit off?"

"Jeannie, you behave. Your daddy will see your dress when we get home."

They had gone shopping at Lauerman's to buy special outfits for the homecoming. Although the snowsuit hid Jeannie's new pink dress with white ruffles, puffy sleeves, and a swirly skirt, her new black patent leather shoes were visible and gleamed in the dim light outside the station. Catherine had chosen her best suit, one with big shoulder pads, but it too was hidden under the cold-weather clothing. She had put on "Tabac Blond" perfume, which Stella had given her years before. Martha was clad in the same green coat and brown hat with feathers she always wore in the fall.

Jeannie's determination to get her snowsuit off amazed her grandmother. "You're going to pull the buttons right off, and then what will we have?" Martha scolded.

"I want daddy to see my new dress! I don't care if I'm cold!" *I guess we spoiled this little girl*, Martha admitted to herself.

Jeannie wondered who this daddy of hers was going to be. She, her mother and Mamie had been a threesome for as long as she could remember. They talked about "daddy" all the time, but she never saw him. Catherine told Jeannie he left when she was a baby, but that he was always thinking of her when he wrote his letters. Now he was coming home on the choo-choo he had once drawn for her.

"Mama, when is that darn train coming? When is it coming, when is it coming?" Shivering relatives and friends of other returning soldiers smoked, paced, checked watches.

"I hope Daddy's the first one off the train," Jeannie said as she pulled on Martha's sleeve.

"Wait until you finally see your daddy," Catherine said. "He's the best daddy ever and he loves you to pieces. He'll be surprised when he sees your curly brown hair. You didn't have any hair the last time he saw you." Jeannie giggled, touched her head.

"Jeannie! Jeannie! Listen!" Catherine said urgently.

"What, Mama?" She didn't know whether to be frightened, and she looked around frantically.

"I heard a train whistle blow," her mother whispered,

holding her daughter closely. "If you listen hard, you'll hear the rumble of the train on the tracks. He'll be here any minute!"

The *400*, its headlight cutting a hole in the night fog, slipped into the station and halted in front of the crowd. People scanned down the length of the train, wondering what car would disgorge family members. When the first passengers began getting off the third car, the crowd moved hurriedly down the platform. Catherine was holding her breath scanning the face of each person. It seemed as though Henry was one of the last to disembark. Catherine spotted him, waved her hand above a family in front of her, and screamed, "Henry! Henry! We're over here!"

She handed her daughter to Martha and ran toward a tall man walking in the shadows of the dim lights. He was dressed in his army uniform and carried a huge duffle bag on his shoulder. When he saw his wife, he dropped the duffle bag, scooped her into his arms, and twirled her around and around. His garrison cap flew off his head. They kissed and held each other in a long embrace. Jeannie looked up at her grandmother and whispered, "What about me?"

Finally, Catherine broke loose and turned, beckoning Martha close. "Henry, take a look at your little girl. Jeannie, look. This is your daddy."

With a wide grin Henry stretched out his arms to the young girl. "Oh, Sweetheart, I have waited so long for this moment. Come to daddy."

He gathered her in his arms and kissed her cheek. Jeannie's whole body stiffened, and she turned and reached her arms out to her grandmother, who sought to reassure her.

"Give your daddy a big hug," Martha said. "He's so happy to see you!"

Henry assumed it was just the excitement of the

evening that prompted the child's reaction, and he bounced her in his arms. "If you give me a hug, I'll give you right back to Mamie," he said warmly. "Hey, I missed my little girl! I thought of you every night when I was going to sleep and prayed that you and mommy were safe."

His daughter would not turn to face him. She moaned and kept her arms outstretched toward Martha. She started to shiver. "I think she's cold. I'll bet she's tired," Henry said, and he handed the child back to his mother-in-law.

For Jeannie it had been a flash of terror. She had been waiting in a cold, dark, wet place with a huge loud engine hissing next to her and she was suddenly in the arms of a strange man who was holding her tight and kissing her. She wanted none of it.

"She doesn't know you yet, Henry," Catherine said, taking her daughter from her mother and pressing her close. "It might take her a little while. Don't feel bad, Honey. It's past her bedtime. She's exhausted. She's been running around all day saying her daddy's coming home. She's probably worn out. We'll put her to bed as soon as we get home. She'll be fine in the morning."

Catherine's voice was a soothing balm. Jeannie knew when she got home things would be normal again. She would be sleeping with her mother, and this evening would go away when her head hit the pillow. They walked to Catherine's old Ford, Jeannie's hand in her grandmother's. Catherine and Henry lingered behind, the couple and the duffle bag making a large dark silhouette against the light of the station lamps.

"Come on, Jeannie," Mamie said soon after they walked into the house. "You and I get to sleep together tonight."

"No. I'm sleeping with Mama," Jeannie said with a confident smile.

"Where do you think your daddy's going to sleep?" Mamie asked.

"He's going to sleep with you. You know how much Mama likes to sleep with me. She loves to cuddle up with me."

"Your dad and I aren't married. I can't sleep with a man I'm not married to. That's a sin."

"The davenport is a good place to sleep. You take naps there. He will be okay sleeping there."

Catherine and Henry went into their bedroom—the bedroom that Catherine and Jeannie had been sharing—and closed the door. Jeannie stomped to the doorway, opened the door, and found her parents, sitting on the edge of the bed, still kissing and hugging.

"Mama, I'm ready to go to sleep now. Tell Daddy he has to sleep on the couch."

Catherine thought this was just a minor misunderstanding. "Honey, I haven't seen Daddy for a long, long time. I have missed him so much. I want to sleep with him tonight. You'll be fine sleeping with Mamie."

"No. I won't be fine!" Pointing her index finger defiantly at her mother she declared, "I'm sleeping with *you!*"

Catherine picked her daughter up, told her she loved her and took her back to Martha's bedroom. As soon as she set the girl down, Jeannie screamed and grabbed mother's leg.

Catherine peeled her off, put her in bed with Martha and walked to her bedroom and closed the door.

Pulling away from Martha, Jeannie ran through the parlor and kitchen to the closed door and threw herself on the floor shrieking, kicking the door as hard as she could.

"Let me in! Let me in right now!" She cried and screamed and fought for breath, but the door refused to open. Martha came and gently picked her up, cradling her, patting her back, and brought her back to her own bed, where they spent the night. Unknown to both that night, they would share a bed well into Jeannie's teen years.

With Henry's return, things changed in the Goodman household. Catherine joined the many other women who had lost their jobs at the paper mill as soldiers were mustered out of service and returned to the community. She was now a full-time housewife—taking care of Jeannie, cooking the meals, packing Henry's lunch every day, doing the housekeeping, paying the bills, and taking care of Mike in his little bungalow on Parnell Street. At least three times a week she would go to Mike's to visit, clean, exchange clean laundry for dirty, and stock his refrigerator. While she missed work and her friends, she knew her place and didn't complain.

The family's biggest worry was Jeannie, who still would not let Henry come near her. Whenever he tried, she turned her head and screamed. Catherine knew Jeannie was scared and Henry was crushed, but she couldn't figure out a way to bring them together. She felt sorry for them both. It took a toll on her that the two people she loved most in the world didn't know how to come together. The vision of the happy family she had nursed during the war seemed to have vanished, like a dream at waking.

To help pay the bills, Martha went back to work as a pastry cook, this time at the Gateway Café in Marinette's twin city, Menominee, Michigan. This also gave Martha a little "pin" money for herself, and when Delores, her boss, told Martha she was selling her little black Ford with a rumble seat, Martha bought it on the spot. She had never driven a car before, but she was ready to spread her wings, take a risk. She found a new freedom. Frequently, on the way home from work she would visit Clara and the kids, a little midday coffee klatch. The dessert samples she brought from the Gateway were quickly devoured by her family. Work started at 5 a.m., making waffle and pancake batters and homemade cinnamon rolls for the breakfast crowd, followed by pies and cakes for lunch and supper customers. Without having to deal with Mike, she blossomed.

With Catherine's help, Mike was doing okay, too. Jeannie loved to go with Catherine when she cooked and cleaned for him. Jeannie would hop onto Papa's lap where he sat next to a cabinet filled with treats for her—usually a candy bar he had bought at the Korn Krib. He was fishing less and drinking more, but when they got there in the morning, he was usually as sober as he would be all day. Catherine's siblings were chipping in for his rent.

Henry worked day and night—with his dad during the day and the three o'clock shift at the mill at night. He wanted to help his dad build the business with the idea that he would own it one day, but the income was not enough yet to support the family. That gave him little time at home with Catherine and Jeannie. Catherine missed him, but she was happy that he was industrious. It was less stressful when Henry wasn't around because of the situation with Jeannie. After a few weeks she didn't scream anymore, but she still wouldn't go to him when he reached out to pick her up. There was an unspoken pall over the family.

It wasn't long after Henry got home that Catherine was pregnant again. Mike kept drinking, Martha kept baking, Henry kept working, Jeannie kept growing and Catherine tried to hold it all together. And so it went . . .

Chapter 22. More Babies (1951)

After dropping Jeannie off at school Catherine stopped at Clara's with younger daughters Lilly and Sally in tow.

"Hi, Clare," Catherine said as she stepped into the kitchen.

"Hey, Cat. What are you doing here? Didn't hear you come in. I was operating my new machine." She stepped back and proudly displayed a new, tall, white Sunbeam Mixmaster.

"Wow! Catherine said. "What have you used it for?"

"First time. I thought I'd better make something sweet. The boys were asking for cookies and I didn't have a one in the house."

"What did this thing set you back?"

"I know it's the top of the line but I don't know what Nels paid for it. He got it for me for my birthday."

"You must have been extra good to get a machine like that—if you know what I mean." Catherine gave a broad exaggerated wink, and Clara shot right back.

"Well," she chuckled and rolled her eyes. "Sometimes it pays off . . ."

Lilly stepped out from behind her mother to watch the process of cookie batter being spooned onto a cookie sheet. "Aunt Clara," she said with a smile on her face and her nose practically in the dough, "When will the cookies be done?"

Without stopping, Clara turned back and smiled to see her little niece. "Well, look at you, Lilly," Clara said. "You just had a birthday. How does it feel to be five?"

"It feels good! I had my favorite cake—chocolate with chocolate frosting and five red candles. I blew them all out at once!" Lilly looked proud. "Mommy told me that meant I didn't have any boyfriends. She's crazy, Aunt Clara," she smiled and added coyly, "I might have one boyfriend."

"You'll be in school next year, Lilly, just like Nelson." Clara said.

"Yup. I'm going to kindergarten next year. I can't wait. Then Sally will be the last one at home with Mommy. But Mamie's there, too, you know. She usually goes to work. She's home sick now. Mama gets kinda cranky when Mamie's sick."

"Lilly, where are your sisters?" Clara asked, tossing her spoon in the sink, sliding the cookie sheet into the oven, and grabbing the coffee pot off the stove.

"Sally's right behind Mama, sucking her thumb."

"What about your big sister?"

"Oh, you know where she is. She's in third grade already. She thinks she's smart, but I think she's a brat. I like it when she's in school. Then she can't boss me around."

Catherine looked at her sister and rolled her eyes toward the ceiling, giving Clara an immediate impression of what life must be like when Jeannie and Lilly were in the same room.

When they were apart, though, some kind of peace seemed to settle in the home. For a nine-year-old Jeannie did a pretty good job keeping the household in line when there were problems. When the three adults in the family were arguing with each other, Jeannie would race around madly, trying to make everyone happy. Her sisters didn't like her ordering them around. Lilly had a lighter touch, not quite as stern as Jeannie.

Clara poured two cups of coffee and joined Catherine at the table. Catherine now wanted her girls out of the room for at least a few minutes. "Clara, where are the boys?"

"They're doing something upstairs. I never know for sure what they're up to."

"Okay, girls—get up there. I need some time with Aunt Clara." Catherine tried to shoo her daughters toward the stairway, but Sally held back.

"Mom, I wanna stay by you," Sally whined, then stuck her thumb in her mouth and held her security blanket tightly over her shoulder.

"Listen! It's time for you to go find Nelson and Peter!" Catherine said. "I'm not kidding, you two!"

"I don't wanna piay with them. They too scawry. I wanna stay wight here," Sally said, hanging onto her mother's sleeve.

"Where are they, Clara?" Catherine asked again.

"Upstairs in one of their bedrooms. They were tearing apart an old radio last time I was up there."

"Is it plugged in?" Catherine asked.

"I hope not," Clara said.

"Go, you two! Find your cousins. Don't plug anything in. You could get electrocuted."

"I don't wanna play with them. They too scawy, Mommy," Sally said again.

"Get up there! It'll be fine. If they hit you, hit them back. Go! Now!" She pointed toward the stairs. "You have Blankie, Sally. It will keep you safe."

Clara knew from experience how well a bribe would work. "I'll tell you what," she said. "Go play nice with Peter and Nelson and when you get done you can have a cookie right out of the oven . . . with chocolate chips! That'll taste a lot better than that thumb, Sally!"

Clara watched the girls slowly walk up the stairs, then said, "What's going on with you, Cat? You look pretty down in the mouth,"

"That's for sure! I can't tell you one thing I'm happy about. Not *one!* It's not enough that Mom is depressed again, back in her bedroom—rocking all day, not eating. I think she's having another one of her spells. It drives me crazy. As you well know, nothing I do to try to help her works, Clara. I could just cry." She shook her head, and her quivering chin suggested she might actually weep.

"Not eating is bad," Clara agreed.

"Yup. It's the same-old, same-old. Today I put a spoon of Cream of Wheat up to her mouth and she just let it dribble down her chin. It's so damn frustrating!"

"Well, at least she's got that bedroom upstairs, so that she's not in the middle of things."

"Yeah, that's another thing. You and Nels moved into a house that was finished. It's been two years now and all Henry has time for is a little work here and a little work there. At the rate he's going, it may never be completed."

"Look on the bright side, Sis. Henry's folks offered you that acre of land next to their home and told Henry he could pay for it over time."

"It's not the land I'm worried about. Since V.R. died, Louise has continued that offer. It's space, Clare, it's bedrooms."

"You guys are doing okay, aren't you? Jeannie's with your Mom, as she has been for years, and the other girls share a room . . ."

Catherine cut her off. "Clare, I'm pregnant again." She stopped talking and looked down at her coffee cup, trying to force back her tears. "I was hoping when we got another bedroom that Jeannie could have her own, but it will have to be for the baby, and Jeannie and Mom will have to keep sharing a room. I hate to have that little kid be exposed to her grandmother's mood swings."

"What a surprise!" Clara quickly changed the subject away from living space, because Catherine had asked her several times if Clara and Nels could take Martha for a while and Clara always pled lack of space. She felt guilty, because she knew this was one way she could help her sister. "Another baby! Congrats, little sister. The more, the merrier I always say!" As an afterthought, to remind Catherine her family had been of service by taking care of Martha's father, she added, "Just remember I had Grandpa Beyer all those years. He died in an upstairs bedroom."

"Yes, I guess you did your share, too. I don't know how you do it with seven kids. I only wanted one, but as you once said about Nels, every time Henry hangs his pants on the bedpost, I get pregnant. I think Mom was right. Sex is a dirty habit. Henry can never have enough and I'm sick of it."

"Well," Clara confided, "I didn't want all these kids either, but I figure if he gets enough at home, he'll stay away from flirty women." She offered Catherine an enigmatic smile, suggesting that maybe she wasn't making such a great sacrifice.

"Well, good luck with that. Do you want another kid?" Catherine asked.

"No, I think I have enough, but"—again that smile— "you can never tell."

"Well, I sure as hell don't want another one!" Catherine shook her head, clenched her teeth. "I feel like sticking a damn coat hanger up my crotch."

"Catherine!" Clara was aghast. "You can't say things like that! You will go to hell *for sure*." She didn't know if her sister was serious. "That little baby wants to be *born*." She stabbed a finger at Catherine for emphasis. "You stop that kind of talk right now!"

Catherine slumped back in her chair. "Aw, Sis, I wouldn't do that, but that's how I feel." She looked imploringly at her older sister. "I gave all my maternity clothes away and I can't afford to buy new ones. And I want to work. I want to get out of the damn house once in a while. Besides, we need the money."

Clara went back to the stove and got the coffee pot. She refilled her sister's cup and gave the back of her neck a big squeeze as she returned to her chair.

Catherine went on. "We're stretched to the limit since V.R. keeled over. Henry hated to quit the mill, but you know how crazy he is for the beer business. That's all he's ever wanted to do, and now, since his dad died, he's working night and day, but we don't have much to show for it."

"Could you really get a job that would cover all the bills?" Clara furrowed her brow and shook her head. "I don't think so."

"Oh, Clara. It's so hard. He wants so badly to be a success. He's got a lot of work ahead of him to make that damn business show a profit and he's a wreck trying to make his payments to the brewery for the beer that comes in." Catherine took a drink of her coffee, put the cup down and rested her cheek on her hand on her bent elbow. "I need to work to keep us above water. I've been helping him with the books at the warehouse sometimes, too. Lilly is about to start school. Now I'll be tied down again with another squalling kid. I can't tell you how awful it feels."

"How you talk, Catherine! You should be ashamed of yourself."

"Well, I'm not. So *there*! How am I supposed to take care of Mike? You know how he is. He's drinking more than ever now. If I don't get over there every other day, he's up shit creek without a paddle. He doesn't buy groceries, but he makes sure he gets his alcohol. He has a kid down the street who gets it for him. Who's going to wash his clothes and clean his house and cook his food? He won't take care of himself—well, you know that. And Mom needs my constant care when she has her spells. It's too much. When she's down, I do all the housecleaning, all the dishes, all the laundry. Know what, Clara? If I could stick a broom up my ass, I could sweep the floor at the same time!"

Clara laughed. It was one of Catherine's favorite ways to describe having too many tasks at hand. "What does Henry say about you being pregnant?"

"I haven't told him yet. I'm so mad at him—he's getting the cold shoulder from me and he doesn't even know why. He's too busy with the business to even want to know how any of us are. When anyone asks him about the kids, he says, 'Oh, you'll have to ask Catherine about the girls. She gets all the credit for raising them.' I'd sure rather have help than credit!"

"That's a man for you," Clara said.

"Don't I *know* it! Speaking of men, have you heard from Charlie lately?"

"Nope. You hear from him more often than I do. Is he still sending money to help pay Papa's rent?"

"Yeah. He still sends money every month. I give him credit for that. And that's another thing I do every week. I try to get over to check on Irene and Florence. Have you seen them lately?"

Clara was tentative, finally said, "Yeah, I, uh, try to get over there but it's hard for me, and I feel guilty about that, too. They sit in that gloomy house day after day all so alone."

The family challenge of the sisters Irene and Florence was Charlie's own doing, and Clara and Catherine had asked each other many times what Charlie was thinking when he married Irene and brought her and her mentally retarded sister to Marinette.

Clara rose to check her cookies, took the sheet from the oven, and began lifting finished cookies onto a cooling rack. "Yeah, Charlie leaves them here alone and goes off on the boats for months at a time."

She sat back down and said quietly to Catherine as though the children upstairs might hear her. "That batch is warm and soft and we'll have one in just a minute." She looked toward the stairway. "We probably don't have more than a few minutes, because I know my boys at least will catch the smell of those cookies pretty soon."

"Poor Irene," Catherine said. "She just sits there. She doesn't know what to do with herself—and that pathetic sister Florence. She's the one I really feel sorry for. She acts almost like Sally except she doesn't suck her thumb. Can you believe she got all those problems from being struck by lightning?"

"I'm no doctor," Clara said, "but I think there's something fishy going on there. It doesn't seem right."

"I don't want to think about that. How about a cookie?" Catherine took a big bite. "These are delicious. I haven't made any cookies for so long . . ."

She shook her head and sighed deeply. "Florence sure as heck can't be alone. So, Irene and Florence sit there with each other every single day. Somebody's got to visit them. Mom used to stop by a couple times a week to see how they were doing, but she can't even take care of herself now." Catherine looked at Clara. "I just don't know how I'll keep up with all of this and another baby."

"Irene should have at least gotten her driver's license. She'd be so much better off. She can't even get her own groceries. I guess I shouldn't talk. But I couldn't get all these kids in a car with me anyway," Clara said.

"I guess Marinette isn't quite up to her standards," Clara went on. "Moving here from Chicago and her job at that big bookstore must have been quite a step down for her. I'll bet the days get pretty long, sitting all day with just her sister while Charlie's on the boats nine months of the year. It must get pretty lonely. Marinette is no Chicago."

The absurdity of the comparison made them both smile.

"Mom told me she thinks Irene hits the gin bottle regularly." Catherine confided.

"Yeah, and Charlie's quite the stud, but not much of a husband. He probably has a girl in every port. Poor thing, Irene. She didn't know what she was in for when she moved to Marinette," Catherine said.

"She keeps her long nails polished to the hilt, that's for sure," Clara said. "Her fancy red hair is turning gray, too. And didn't Mom tell you once Florence had black and blue bruises all over her arms? Do you think Irene pushes her around?"

"I don't know, Clara, but I feel sorry for her." Catherine wanted to put her head on Clara's shoulder and cry. She didn't want to feel sorry for anyone else right now. "Maybe she pushes Florence around when she drinks too much. Maybe . . . oh, I really don't know. What I do know is that she loves

Jeannie. Whenever we go over there, she always has a treat for her and the other girls, too, but Jeannie is her favorite."

Catherine smiled to herself and then shared her thought. "I get a kick out of Florence. Every time I tell her I have to go to the warehouse, she says, 'Don't wear it out,' and then she laughs. I think it's the only joke she knows in the world."

"Yeah, I know. She's pitiful and funny at the same time," Clara said.

The aroma of the fresh-baked cookies had its effect. There was a thunder of footsteps on the stairway, and Clara quickly interposed herself between the charging herd and the cooling cookies. She placed a cookie into each outstretched hand, making sure that Lilly and Sally weren't elbowed out of the queue.

"Well, that's the end of gossip time," Catherine said, rising. "I wanted you to feel sorry for me, but we both ended feeling sorry for Irene and Florence."

As she went out the front door she called back, "Let me know the next time you are making cookies!"

When she got home, she ticked off in her head all the things that she had to do—round up something for supper, start a load of wash, hang the wash on the line, pick up Jeannie at school, and, of course, at some point in the evening, tell Henry she was pregnant again!

Instead of tackling any of them, she went straight to the refrigerator, took out a beer, sat at the kitchen table and slammed it down in a few gulps. That felt so good, she drank another one—and then she cried. The load of wash went by the wayside, and she knew that Jeannie would walk home from school if she didn't see her mother's car. The refrigerator and canned goods would yield something for supper.

When Henry came home from work, he was exhausted and deeply concerned that there might not be enough money to pay for the beer that was coming by semi early the next morning. He wouldn't know until he had a good look at the books. Henry and Catherine, each in their own worlds, were irritable and scared.

Henry walked to the refrigerator, pulled out a beer, a raw egg and a glass from the kitchen cupboard. He held the glass up to the light and examined it carefully.

"Cat," he said, "You have to do a better job washing these glasses. Take a look at the smudges." She glared at him but held her tongue. Henry walked over to the sink, poured salt and a little water into the glass and gave it a good scrubbing.

"C'mere, Catherine." She silently got up and joined him. "Now take a look at this glass. D'ya see how clear it is?" He took another one out of the cupboard and held it up to the first glass. "Do you see the difference here? I can't get a good head on my beer with all this grease and scum." He brought the glasses down and continued his instruction. "Could you see to it that the kids or your mother don't get their hands on my beer glasses? I work hard all day and come home for a beer and I don't think it's too much to ask to have a decent glass."

Henry, confident that the lesson had been delivered, sat in his chair at the head of the table with his glass, the bottle of beer, and a raw egg. He poured his beer slowly into the salt-scrubbed glass, tilted it to get the perfect head of foam, cracked the shell on the edge of the glass, and watched the yellow eye float to the bottom.

He held up the glass to show Catherine the perfect presentation. She looked at him, speechless with anger and frustration, and turned to the stove to start making supper. She felt rage and resentment taking over. She was building up a good head of steam as he drank his mélange in one gulp. The pressure was too great, and the steam valve popped open.

"Give me a break, Henry Goodman!" She turned and shook a wooden spoon at him. "Your goddamn beer glass isn't clean? I'll tell you what I think you can do with that beer glass, and *it isn't pretty!*"

"What the hell is this all about?" Henry said. He was stung and truly puzzled. "I come home after working my ass off all day, and this is what I get?"

"Yeah, like I don't work my ass off?" She walked closer to Henry and looked him straight in the eyes. "Do you have any idea what I do every stinking day? No, you don't, do you?" She was still waving the stirring spoon, and for a fleeting second Henry wondered if Catherine was going to hit him with it. "Do you ever even ask me what my days are like? No! All you can talk about is 'the business.'" She was pointing the wooden spoon at him and screaming.

Henry stood up. "Take it easy, Catherine," he said, trying to find his most soothing voice. "Why don't you sit down and relax? Just . . . relax . . ."

His words had the opposite effect. "Don't . . . you . . . *ever* tell me to relax again! I can figure that out for myself!"

All three girls had come into the doorway and stood staring into the kitchen. Sally was sucking her thumb and holding her blanket with tears running down her cheeks. Jeannie tried to take a few tentative steps but was stopped by Lilly's tight grip on the back of her shirt.

"Mama, we're so scared. Please stop," Jeannie said.

"You girls get back in your bedroom. Go! Now!"

"Catherine," Henry said as he extended his arm toward her.

"Don't 'Catherine' me!" She looked at Henry with

disgust, then turned to the girls. "What did I tell you? Get back in your rooms!"

"I can't go in my room," Jeannie pleaded. "Mamie's in there and she's really sick, Mama!"

"Go into your sisters' room! Now!"

The girls raced down the hall into the bedroom and closed the door. "Catherine, just calm down," Henry said.

"Don't. I have no intention of calming down." She walked over to the refrigerator, pulled out a beer, opened the bottle and put it to her lips. After taking a long draw, she sat down and held the bottle up in the air.

"See this, Henry Goodman? I drink my beer right out of the bottle. I don't need a fancy-assed glass scrubbed with goddamn salt. You got that? I hope so. Now I want you to listen—and don't say a word until I'm finished!"

Henry was still trying to gauge the depth of Catherine's anger and wondering about its source. He didn't look her in the eye. He sat instead with his elbows on his knees, and he leaned over to put his face in his hands. He hated these confrontations with Catherine. All he wanted to do was run, but he knew she'd run right after him. Better to just wait and listen.

"What would be the worst thing that could happen to us right now? Huh? What?"

Henry had no idea what to say. He sensed that whatever he said would be wrong. He hesitated a little too long.

"Can't you even answer me? This is your fault, Henry!"

He stuttered a little. "I won't be able to pay for the truckload of beer that's being delivered tomorrow, and we'd lose the house?"

"You son-of-a-bitch. All you ever think about is that damn business! *No!* That is *not* the worst thing, Henry. The worst thing is that I'm pregnant again. I'm pregnant for the fourth time. All you can think about is your pecker. I told you to be careful—you promised—and here we are again."

She clenched her fist in frustration. "I don't want another kid! Don't you see I have my hands full already? You don't see anything! You leave the house every damn day, jump in your big-shot beer truck and have a beer at every stop along the way. Boy, that's some job! You have a gay old time with the bartenders. 'Come on, let's have a brewski!' In the meantime . . . "

"Okay Catherine, that's enough. Now you listen to me. You don't know the half of it. My job is a ball-breaker, lugging cases and barrels of beer in and out of the truck, up and down stairs, at every stop. That requires a lot of heavy lifting, but that's not the hardest part. Keeping the customers happy and getting them to pay their bills is like getting blood out of a turnip. We're living hand to mouth, Catherine. If I can't get them to pay me, then I can't pay for the beer. If I can't pay for the beer, I don't have anything to sell. I'm borrowed to the hilt at the Farmers and Merchants Bank. That's why I wake up with a sopping wet T-shirt every morning—I'm a nervous wreck."

"Don't even start on me, Mr. Bigshot. If we weren't having sex every fifteen minutes, I wouldn't be pregnant. I'd be able to go back to work."

"Do *not* give me that every fifteen-minute shit! I have to practically beg you to open your goddamn legs for me!"

And back and forth, until they reached grievances that went back to days before they were married. Catherine rose, stormed out of the kitchen and strode angrily down the hall to their bedroom, where she slammed the door behind her. When the girls heard the shouting diminish, they tiptoed into the kitchen. Henry was sitting at the table with an empty beer glass in front of him and his head resting on his hands.

Jeannie told her father they were hungry. Henry, who barely knew how to open a can of soup, was stumped. Catherine's place was in the kitchen and Henry's in the beer truck, but he was not going to the bedroom to get her and risk another tirade. He took a box of cornflakes out of the cupboard, a bottle of milk from the refrigerator, and he told Jeannie to help Lilly and Sally with their cereal. He kept a stash of Gold Brick candy bars in a safe place in the top cupboard. He reached up and pulled three out, gave them to Jeannie and told her when everyone finished their cereal they could have a candy bar. Then he headed for the door, waved goodbye and told them to wake their mother when they were ready for bed.

When Catherine heard Henry's truck pull out of the driveway, she got up. The girls heard her, ran to her, and wrapped all six arms around her, nearly pushing her over.

"Mama! Mama!" A mass of bodies seemed to float around her, and out of a mix of excited voices she heard one of her daughters say, "We're having breakfast for supper and daddy gave us candy bars!"

"Well, isn't this your lucky day," Catherine said, patting the nearest head. "Where did your daddy go?"

"Dunno," Jeannie answered. "He just told us to wake you up when we were ready for bed."

Goddamn him! Catherine thought. *Does he expect Jeannie to put on Sally's diaper? He probably doesn't even know she had a night diaper. And now he's a hero for giving them cornflakes and candy bars for supper. He can't even stay with the kids for a couple hours.*

Catherine knew she had to check on her mother. She could hear the creak of the rocking chair going slowly back and forth. She didn't know what to feed her. Maybe Martha would eat a little oatmeal tonight. Martha was going downhill fast.

So was Mike. Catherine brought Mike food every

couple of days, but most of it was still in the icebox when she came the next time. The garbage can held no food scraps, only a constant collection of empty beer and whiskey bottles. Catherine saw how this was likely to turn out: Mike would kill himself with alcohol poisoning and her mother would kill herself through starvation.

Catherine's brood followed her up the stairs and at the top Jeannie ran ahead to check on her bed partner. She put her hand on her grandmother's arm but got no response. Martha, stone-faced, continued to rock numbly, forward, backward, forward. Jeannie tried to climb on her grandmother's lap but, unaided, could not find a perch.

As the others watched from the doorway, Jeannie eagerly, desperately, sought to get a response from Martha. "I know how to make you happy, Mamie!" She rushed over to a small black RCA record player and slid a 45 rpm record onto the red and gold spindle. The Andrews Sisters and "Chattanooga Choo Choo" filled the room and Jeannie began dancing. Sally and Lilly joined in, but Mamie only rocked, unsmiling.

"Mamie, you love this song! Why won't you dance with me?"

Catherine came into the room, turned the music down, and touched her daughter's shoulder. "Jeannie, Mamie's sick today and can't dance with you."

"Mommy, she's been sick for a long time. She doesn't even say prayers with me before we go to sleep. She doesn't even talk to me anymore." She went back to her grandmother and tried to put her head in Martha's lap. Martha stopped rocking but made no other movement. "Please talk to me, Mamie! I love you!" Jeannie said, and she began softly sobbing.

It struck Catherine that Jeannie shouldn't be sharing a

room with Martha when Martha was deeply depressed and nearly catatonic. It also brought home the truth that Martha had over Jeannie's short lifetime been more a mother than Catherine. Catherine was working all the while that Henry was fighting the war in Burma, and Martha had raised the little girl. As soon as Henry got back from his deployment, Jeannie wanted nothing to do with her father. Martha again took over Jeannie's care. From the time of Henry's return, when they lived on Elizabeth, right through the move to the new home, Jeannie shared a bedroom with Martha. It terrified her now when her grandmother didn't acknowledge her.

Catherine didn't know what to do next. Everyone needed her and she had nothing to give.

Just like her daughter, she yearned to sit on Martha's lap and be rocked while her mother whispered to her, "There, there, my little one." She didn't want this baby inside her, she didn't know what to do for her mother or father, she didn't know how to help Henry while he tried to build a business and at the same time finish this house. Her family needed help and comforting. Who would comfort her?

She barely had the energy to put the kids to bed. *Where is Henry when I need him?* she thought, just as sleep overcame her. *Where are my sisters and brothers?*

Chapter 23. I Can't Live without Her (May 1951)

Visibly pregnant now, Catherine found herself numbly going through the motions of her roles as a mother, a wife, and a daughter. There were not enough hours in the day to meet the needs of her clinically-depressed mother, her chronically alcoholic father, her worried, nervous husband and the three daughters she loved with all her heart. She thought constantly, *What am I doing to these girls?* She felt they needed so much more than she could give them.

Lilly and Sally were acting out—probably the only way they could get her attention.

Jeannie was trying to take care of everybody—her grandmother, mother, father, and sisters. Her mother told her repeatedly, "You're such a good girl," and she surely did not want to let her mother down.

Henry was hanging on by the skin of his teeth, too. Besides delivering beer, keeping his customers happy and trying to make his interest payments to the bank on time, he was working every spare minute to finish building their house. With a new baby coming, they needed more bedroom space. Both Catherine and Henry were overworked and overwhelmed.

Martha rallied a little. She was eating at least, but she

wasn't interacting with the family. *Such a pathetic sight,* Catherine often thought, observing her mother shuffling around the house with her shoulders slumped and her chin on her chest. At least she was moving, but she still needed care and was no help to Catherine.

When Henry walked in the house one night after a long day of work and saw Jeannie, Lilly and Sally huddled together on the couch crying, he was shocked. Catherine always had the girls engaged in some activity or ready for bed, but she was nowhere to be seen.

"What's going on here?" he asked gently, kneeling in front of the girls.

"Mama's in bed and she won't get out," Sally cried.

"Mamie's upstairs rocking in her chair. No one will talk to us," Lilly said hurriedly.

"We're scared, Daddy! Who will take care of us?" Jeannie was desperate.

"Have you eaten yet?"

"No, there's nothing to eat," Jeannie said.

"I'm home now and won't leave until tomorrow morning when Mama is better. Everything will be fine." He patted their knees reassuringly. "I'll go check on your mother—you all just stay right here."

Henry opened the bedroom door quietly and tiptoed into the dark room over to the bed. Catherine's body was covered with blankets, her head covered with pillows, and she was not moving. He sat down on the bed next to her and gently removed the pillows. He was relieved to hear her breathing, but her breaths were fast and shallow. In the dim light he had a hard time seeing her face, but he had peeled back the covers enough to be struck by the fact that she appeared to be fully dressed. He put his hand on her cheek. It was very cool to the touch. She didn't move.

He called out her name softly. She didn't move. Suddenly he was as afraid as the girls.

How could she be sleeping so soundly? He wondered if she were drunk or had taken a drug. When he shook her shoulder, she was as limp as a damp sheet.

What to do? Nothing in the workaday world had prepared Henry for this. *She's cold,* he thought. *A warm towel on her forehead.* As he raced out of the bedroom he found Sally, sitting in front of the bedroom door with both her thumb and the edge of her blanket in her mouth. Jeannie and Lilly frantically followed him into the bathroom, crying "What's wrong, Daddy? What's wrong with Mama?"

He dug out a hand towel, turned on the hot water tap. *Sound calm,* he thought, although he felt his own panic building. *Just calm the girls down.* "Your mother is fine. She's just very tired and is having a hard time waking up. Big people get very tired sometimes. She'll be fine."

He forced reassurance into his voice. "Hey, you girls get ready for bed. I'll sit with your mother a bit and then come in to say goodnight."

He moved with forced deliberation into the bedroom, but he immediately closed the door behind him. He put the cloth on Catherine's forehead. He waited some seconds for a response, and when she didn't move he quickly rose, peered into the hall to make sure the girls were gone, and called Clara from the family's hallway phone. *Please pick up,* and he was relieved she came on after only a few rings.

"Clara, is Nels home?"

"Yes. He's standing right next to me."

"That's great! I need him to come and get the kids and Mame. I'll talk to you about this later." He had to keep has voice calm and the shared information at a minimum. No use broadcasting Catherine's condition to anyone who might be listening in on the party line. "Clara, please have him come—right now!"

"Tell me—" but he had hung up before she could ask anything else.

The girls had put on their pajamas, but he had them put shoes and socks back on. He walked back to the bedroom several times to check on Catherine, and this only made the girls more anxious as they waited for their uncle. All three were crying. Jeannie had dressed to leave but decided to make a stand. "Daddy, I'm not going," she said, trying to put on a brave front, fighting back her sobs. "I'm right staying here to help you make Mama better, and that's final! I know how to make her laugh."

Henry ignored the ten-year-old's pleas. "Jeannie, you can help me by running upstairs and telling Mamie she needs to go with you and she needs to get ready right now! Make sure she understands what you are telling her and that she gets ready."

When Nels arrived the girls and Martha were at the back door ready to go. Out of earshot of the kids he told Nels Catherine was extremely sick. They knew something was wrong, he said, but he didn't want them to know that it might be bad. He didn't know himself. He promised to call Clara as soon as he knew anything. Even as she was being directed into the car, Jeannie was still pleading to stay home, but the door closed on her pleas and Nels backed out of the driveway.

Henry went back into the house to check on Catherine. No change. Should he call Dr. Zeratsky? He'd be out of the office, probably eating his supper at this time. He tried to arouse Catherine again. No change. Maybe the ambulance?

How long could he wait before something terrible happened? He paced up and down the hall and back again checking Catherine at every loop, thinking, thinking.

Finally, he decided to call the doctor. His wife said he was eating his supper and might the doctor call him back later? After Henry explained the situation, Dr. Zeratsky came right to the phone. Henry was sweating profusely and could hardly get the words out of his mouth.

After hearing the symptoms, the doctor said it sounded like a drug or alcohol overdose.

"Was Catherine was taking any medication that you know of?" he asked Henry.

"No, not that I'm aware of. She's pregnant and has been down about that.

"Does she smell of alcohol?"

"Not that I could tell."

"I saw her last month, and she seemed somewhat depressed."

"I know that she's not happy about being pregnant," Henry confessed.

The doctor paused. "Hmm. Your mother-in-law has been taking imipramine for her depression. I'm pretty sure Catherine gives her the drug. Go right now to see if you can find Mrs. Sabinsky's pill bottle. I'll hold on."

Henry set the receiver and ran to the bathroom. After emptying everything in the medicine cabinet on to the floor, he found no pills. He searched Martha's upstairs room and unfinished bathroom. Nothing there, either. He was frantic. Where else might the pills be? Worrying the doctor would hang up, he ran back to the phone.

"No luck," he told the doctor.

"I don't know any other medicine she could have taken.

I haven't given her anything for her pregnancy. If it's an overdose, there's no time to lose. Get her in your car and drive her to the hospital! I'll meet you there."

Years of hoisting barrels of beer enabled Henry to lift the dead weight of his unconscious wife and carry her to the car. As he paused for breath at the back door he spotted a pill bottle standing prominently on the windowsill above the sink. He struggled to get the car door open, laid Catherine across the back seat, and raced back inside for the pill bottle. Sure enough, *imipramine!* The bottle held seven tablets.

Dr. Zeratsky and a nurse were standing next to a gurney at the hospital entrance waiting for Henry. Together the three of them got Catherine from the car and onto the cart. After giving the imipramine bottle to the doctor, Henry ran out to park the car. Winded, he met the nurse in the emergency waiting room.

The doctor had checked both Catherine's and Martha's files that he kept in his home office. The records confirmed his memory, that he had prescribed nothing for Henry's wife. He found, however, that two weeks earlier he had renewed a prescription for Mrs. Sabinsky for a month's supply of imipramine—one tablet each night at bedtime.

"There were seven left in the bottle you gave Dr. Zeratsky, so if your wife took the remaining pills she could be in trouble. Do you know if she was giving the pills to her mother?"

"Oh, I'm sure she was. My mother-in-law isn't in any shape to keep track of her pills herself," Henry said.

"Do you have any idea when she might have taken them?"

Henry was at a loss. "I was at work all day. My older daughter Jeannie was in school, and her sisters Sally and Lilly were home with Catherine and her mother. I didn't think to ask Jeannie when her mother went into the bedroom, but I still can't believe she would have taken the pills if she were home alone with the other girls."

"She's in the operating room to have her stomach pumped, and I'm sure the doctor has started already. He felt there was no time to lose." The nurse studied Henry for a moment, decided he would be okay if she left him. "I'm going to assist him now."

Henry tried to catch up with the nurse, calling out, "Are Catherine and the baby going to be all right?"

She kept her pace and called back over her shoulder "We have no way of knowing right now, Mr. Goodman. We'll have to wait and see. We'll keep you informed. Please stay back."

As he paced back and forth in the small waiting room, tears were running down his cheeks. Thoughts and self-recriminations raced through his mind, never stopping to wait for answers. *What can I do? What could I have done to prevent this? This is all my fault! We shouldn't have had sex. I should have listened more, been more supportive. How can I fix this now? I love her, but I don't tell her.* He was desperate. He was alone. He knew he couldn't raise his daughters without her. Tears turned to wracking sobs.

When the nurse came into the waiting room to make a report, she found Henry in desperate straits.

"Mr. Goodman," she said softly, taking his arm. "Listen to me. Sit down in this chair. You are not helping yourself or your wife by driving yourself crazy. You need to be the strong one right now."

He refused to sit. "What if she dies? I can't live without her! I know I can't! She takes care of everything, everybody! I love her!" He felt he needed to make the nurse see clearly how special Catherine was.

"Listen to me. Look at me." She was gentle but insistent. "We pumped her stomach. She's alive. You must be the strong one now. I know Catherine has a sister. Call her and see if she will come sit with you while you wait. She might give you some support and, besides, she needs to know."

Henry found a phone and explained the situation to Clara as concisely as he could, always aware of others who might be on the line.

"Oh, my God!" Clara wailed as Henry told her about Catherine. "Oh, my God! Sandy hasn't moved out yet. She can watch the kids while Nels drives me to the hospital. I'll be there as soon as possible!"

While he waited, he prayed. Henry wasn't the praying type, but it occurred to him that this might be the time to use what he had learned about prayer in Sunday school so many years before. He had long since stopped thinking that God was tuned into every appeal, but he found himself more calm when Clara arrived.

His head was bowed in thought when she sat down next to him. "I don't believe this!" were her first words. "What have you learned?"

"I've seen no one since I talked to you," Henry said. I'm hoping the doctor will come soon." He turned to Clara. "How are the kids? And Martha? I feel so bad about suddenly pushing all that on you and Nels . . ." He looked to be on the verge of tears.

"Henry! For God's sake! That's what we do for each other!" she touched his hand, tried to comfort him. "It's just took a little juggling and we found a space for everyone. I think your girls will sleep fine. They were exhausted from crying."

Clara said she had been thinking about Catherine so much since Henry's first call, trying to find any clue that things had gone so wrong. "I talked to her last week. I know she's not happy about being pregnant again, but I got the sense that this was simply just one more task she had to deal with, and she deals with so many so well . . ." Her voice trailed off. Here she sat, her sister just having had her stomach pumped of an overdose of a drug, and the past was as cloudy as the future.

"It's my fault, Clara. I know it's my fault! It's a bad time for us to be having another mouth to feed and a kid to take care of. And she has your mother and father to deal with. They're both in rough shape. Cat has so much on her plate right now. I wish you could help her a little more, but I know you have a lot going on and you were a great help tonight . . ."

Henry paused, once more seeing his wife in a new light. "Maybe she's got *too* much on her plate. Maybe she's giving up . . . " He paused, shocked at the thought he just expressed. It was his first intimation that Catherine hadn't just taken an overdose. Maybe she was actually trying to kill herself.

Clara missed Henry's statement, still framing an apology for not being able to help as much as they might have wished. "My houseful is a handful, and I don't drive. That makes it hard. Plus the fact that Nels is working night and day, leaving me with all these kids to take care of on my own. But I know Catherine does so much for Mom and Dad. I don't know how she does it. She's a wonder, Henry."

"She's not much of a wonder right now," Henry said numbly, rattled by his sudden new thoughts. He glanced down the hall again. "Dr. Zeratsky wouldn't give me anything specific. He just said we should know any time in the next couple of hours."

Henry's mouth started quivering. He sat back down. He

knew things were going to have to change and change greatly. "If she gets through this—" Clara patted him on the shoulder as the tears began to roll down his cheeks again. "If she makes it through this, I'll have to find someone to help her. She can't do it alone. She seems so strong and capable. She can do anything, Clara! She's a good person! She takes good care of the kids! She can be so funny, but sometimes she gets down in the dumps. She gets her sense of humor from Mike. But she gets down almost like Martha."

Clara thought for a while, then said, "Yeah, yeah, Henry, we have quite the family. Our mother has nervous breakdowns, and our father is a drunk. Whenever Stella comes to Marinette for a visit, Catherine says she finds liquor bottles hidden in the back of the toilet, the basement, in the garage. Stella hardly ever draws a sober breath anymore. Anthony loves her but his style is to celebrate everything with another drink. I don't know if he has any idea how much he's contributed to his wife's problem."

She went on. "I don't know about Charlie either. He brings Irene and her sister to Marinette and dumps them for nine months every year to work the boats. He drinks a lot, too, when he's around, and I think he drinks to ease his guilt. Irene's a mess. I don't think she ever draws a sober breath anymore either."

"I know all that, Clara, but my problem—our problem— is that Catherine seems to think she has to take care of everyone, to fix all these other problems. There's no way she can do that, but she tries and tries and tries." A lot was clicking into place for Henry. "Aw, Clara, it's going to be the death of her. I can see it now."

"I wonder if Steve could take Martha for a while," Clara wondered aloud. "Steve's okay, I guess. We don't see him very much. He and Helen are busy with their work—she opened a beauty shop in the back of their house, I heard. He's working for a collection agency. He could come a little more often to help out," Clara said.

The waiting room had long since held only Henry and Clara, which let them share their thoughts at something above a whisper, but the room itself did nothing to inspire calm patience. There were no windows to the outside, only the closed windows of a service desk long since abandoned for the night. A single lamp at a corner table contributed only a little more light for reading, beyond what the flickering fluorescent lights above them offered. Several long-out-of-date magazines sat on a scratched table—a *Life* magazine with photos from Korea, a *Look* magazine, a well-thumbed copy of *Popular Science*, featuring the art of buying and fixing antique vehicles. "They don't even have a *Reader's Digest*," Henry complained to himself, when he had first picked his way through the magazine offerings.

"This is hard, waiting here and not being told anything. You'd think they could tell us *something*." Henry looked at his watch, stood and started pacing. "I can't stand this!"

After that they sat silently, the smoke from Henry's cigarettes giving Clara a small headache. An hour later Dr. Zeratsky stepped into the room.

The doctor waved Henry back down as he stood to greet him. "Henry, you can stay seated. Hello, Clara," he nodded, and then delivered his observations. "We've pumped Catherine's stomach—she is going to live. Henry, you got her here in time." He paused to let this information sink in but then added in a grim tone. "We're not sure about the baby yet. Sometimes this procedure can result in miscarriage."

"Oh, my God!" Clara said.

"Does Catherine know this?" Henry asked.

"No. She's not been awake. We'll have to keep her here a couple days to make sure she's okay physically and mentally." The doctor looked at his watch. "Go home and get some rest. She's out of danger. She's going to need some help when she gets home. You'll have to find someone to stay with your family for a while until she gets stronger. Henry, consider that your wife may be depressed and overwhelmed, judging by her desperate measure."

Henry felt the doctor's comments only reinforced what had already occurred to him this long evening. "When can she come home?" Henry wondered. That knowledge would set the timetable for a lot of other actions before and after Catherine's return.

"Let's see how it goes," the doctor said. "She needs to rest and to know her children are being cared for. I know both her parents need care, too. See if you can rally some friends or family to step in for a while."

"Can we see her before we leave? I want to know she's alive," Clara said.

"Yes, you can peek in. She will be sleeping soundly. Don't try to wake her. She needs rest," the doctor said. "Call me tomorrow so I can give you the report."

As Henry drove Clara home, they admitted to each other they had never seriously thought about how much Catherine had on her plate.

"You know, Henry, when problems have popped up, Catherine has always had the ability to figure out how to fix them. When Steve and Helen and the kids came to visit, she, along with you, Henry, put them up. Anthony and Stella, the same. Martha has not been easy, and Cat takes care of Mike, who's going downhill. The thought of another baby was the straw that broke the camel's back," Clara said. "I've just taken her for granted."

"Yeah, I know. Me, too. She works hard. We both do, because I'm trying to make a living for the family, but Cat picks up all the slack," Henry said.

They tried to brainstorm a bit about how Catherine could get some help, but on the brief ride they came up with nothing concrete.

The fundamental reason that Catherine was in the hospital, had had her stomach pumped, was going to be in recovery for several days, was never discussed on that ride home. Henry's mind still recoiled from the notion that his wife would try to kill herself, and Clara was not going to raise the issue with him.

It was almost midnight when Henry loaded three half-asleep girls and his mother-in-law into the car. Martha sat in the front seat next to Henry, but they didn't say a word to each other.

He carried the girls to their beds, one-by-one, taking Jeannie last to the upstairs bedroom she shared with Martha.

Henry hadn't noticed the mess in the kitchen earlier. The spark of adrenaline still ran, and he took out a beer, prepped it with an egg, sat at the table. He could begin to take it in now.

Catherine never left dishes piled in the sink, but there they were. A pot of cold sticky oatmeal sat on the stove, a bottle of milk on the countertop, cold toast on a plate on the table. He tried to reconstruct her day. She must have fed the kids breakfast and sent Jeannie off to school. What did she do with Lilly and Sally all day? Did the little ones have lunch? Had they been alone all afternoon without lunch?

Martha came down the stairs into the quiet kitchen, sat

with Henry at the table. "Is Jeannie sleeping," he asked.

Martha nodded. "*Ja,*" she said.

Henry looked at his mother-in-law. Maybe it was the crisis of the evening, but something had snapped her into a full awareness of the moment. *She might remember,* he thought.

"Martha, do you know anything about what was going on with Catherine today?"

"I was in my room all day. She always comes up, but today she didn't." Martha looked around the kitchen as though trying to confirm where she was on this very strange day. "Where is Catherine? Is she okay?"

Martha's question made Henry realize that he had only bustled this family into the car, retrieved them from Clara and Nels, and had never really explained what had happened.

"No, Mame, she isn't okay, but she is going to be. She took several of your pills. She's in the hospital. Dr. Zeratsky doesn't know if she'll lose the baby."

"*Ah, Gud,*" Martha said. "*Hvad er det naeste. Gud Hjaelpe mig. Jeg kan lege sa godt dir.*"

"Jesus Christ, Mame! Speak English!"

"I think I'll die. She's the only one who understands me." Her whole body was shaking, and her face settled into the familiar repose in her hands.

"Yeah, that's it! English or goddamn Danish, she's the only one who understands everyone!" He cast an eye toward Martha. "I can tell you're not in shape to take care of the girls tomorrow."

"Oh, Henry, no! I'm too nervous. I can't do it." She was wringing her hands.

Henry told Martha go to bed. He sat in his place at the head of the table and surveyed a table full of dirty dishes and food scraps. It was as though he had been plopped into a different reality. When he put his head on his arms, cereal and toast crumbs crunched under the weight. What would make her do such a thing, leave this kitchen in such a mess?

He knew tonight how much he was in love with Catherine, and he was aware tonight that he hadn't given her much attention lately. He had left her to deal with the kids, the household, her mother and father all on her own. He had been focused totally on trying to make enough money to put food on the table and pay the interest on the business's many loans. Despite the new house, a new life here at the end of Carney Avenue, they were mortgaged to the hilt.

His mind raced from one problem to another, but he didn't have solutions for any of them. Jeannie needed to go to school, but Lilly and Sally were still at home. Martha was at home but couldn't take care of the kids. He needed to serve his customers. He had to find somebody to stay with Catherine and help with the kids when she got home from the hospital. What if she lost the baby?

First, though, he needed a plan to get through tomorrow. He'd take Lilly, Sally, and Martha to Clara's after he got Jeannie to school. He'd have to remember to pack her a lunch. Luckily it was his day to make deliveries in town, so he could get to the hospital, work his usual route, pick Jeannie up from school, drop her at Clara's, finish his deliveries, go back to the hospital.

Henry had the presence of mind to wind the unused alarm clock. Catherine always was up ahead, prepping coffee, making lunches. He climbed into the couple's empty bed. He was learning how to deal with business problems, but all this family uproar was out of his league. Final thoughts before a bit of sleep finally came. What the hell was he going to do with Mame? She was barely hanging on. Mike, too.

The alarm barely gave him enough time to get Jeannie's lunch and make his own coffee. He would leave the kitchen a mess, hoping that Martha had the presence of mind to clean up. When he dropped the girls at Clara's in the morning, she told him she had called Steve last night and he was on his way to Marinette.

"Really?" Henry said. He breathed a small sigh of relief. He didn't know what Steve could do, but another person to help couldn't hurt.

"Bring Jeannie here after school and I'll make supper for all of us," Clara said. "Maybe we can figure out a way forward for the next couple months."

"Thanks, Clara. I appreciate it. I'm off to the hospital. I'll see you around three-thirty. Then I'll ask my brother to finish my deliveries so we all can put our heads together. I sure appreciate your help."

When Henry opened the door to Catherine's hospital room, he was struck by the strong smell of bleach and antiseptic. The shades were drawn. The only light came from small bulb in the corner of the ceiling. He heard someone moaning, and he hesitated. *Was that Catherine?* he wondered. As his eyes adjusted to the dim light, he saw that there were two beds in the room, separated by a curtain. The inert body in the nearest bed was clearly Catherine, he saw, and the moaning was coming from whomever lay in the second bed.

Catherine lay silently, her chest rising and falling with slow breaths. A small plastic tube ran from her right arm to a large bag of clear liquid hanging from a something like a hat rack at her bedside. She was oblivious to the light, to the restlessness and moaning of the person in the next bed, to Henry's presence. He touched her cheek and it felt cold and clammy. He didn't know if that was good or bad. He stood looking at her for a long time.

Henry knew he had to move on. He put his head next to her ear and whispered, "If you make it through this, I'll be a better husband. I know now how much I love you."

By the time he got to Clara's after picking Jeannie up from school, Steve and Martha were sitting at her kitchen table with a bottle of Kingsbury in front of Steve and a cup of coffee in front of Martha. Clara was at the stove stirring a kettle of something that smelled good. Henry walked over to Steve, put his hand on Steve's shoulder and said, "By God, it's good to see you. Thanks for driving all this way. Life's a bitch sometimes, Buddy."

"I'm glad to see you, Henry," Steve said as he stood up. He reached out to shake hands but opted instead for a full hug. "What a hell of a mess! I'm so sorry for you and Catherine. Jesus Christ! We never know what life is going to throw at us, do we?"

"Hey, Clara, you got another one of those?" Henry said pointing at Steve's beer. Beer in hand, he sat at the table, feeling energy drain away. There was much that needed to be said, but at his moment he had no wish to say anything more to anyone.

Campbell's Mushroom Soup was the basis for a pork and veal casserole with egg noodles, and the aroma filled the downstairs. The smell carried Henry back to his own kitchen, where Catherine often made this dish—one of her favorites. The connection made him shiver.

Steve, as was his style, was dressed to the nines—shirt and tie, brown wingtips. "Damn, Henry! I'm just sick about Catherine. What a gal she is, my sister! There's nobody like her."

Henry, his brow furrowed and his chin on his chest, did not connect with his brother-in-law's celebration of Catherine.

He only saw the image of her inert body in the hospital. He was dead-tired and felt defeated.

"How was Catherine when you stopped there today?" Clara asked.

He shook his head. "She's out cold, but at least she's still living . . ."

Clara fussed with the dinner prep, waited for her next question and finally asked, "Did you talk to Dr. Zeratsky?"

"He wasn't there. Nurse Jenkins, who apparently runs that floor—now there's a perfect crab for you!—says Catherine's stable and thinks she'd be off the sedative tomorrow." It had taken Henry some minutes to find out who to ask about his wife' condition, and the exchange left him resentful. He was the husband, for chrissakes! "Getting information from her was like getting blood out of a turnip!"

Steve decided this was the right moment to engage Henry. "Clara and I had a long talk this afternoon. We have a few ideas to run past you."

"Clara, get me another beer, will you?" Henry asked. "I'll need another one before I'm ready to think about ideas."

"This is the last one I have, Henry," and she opened a bottle of Fox Head 400 and set it on the table in front of him.

"The last one? What the hell?"

"Well, my family doesn't drink much."

"I can see by what you buy and what you have that I need to put you on my route." It was the closest he had come to humor in the past twenty-four hours. "How about whiskey?"

"Nels has some on the top shelf of the bedroom closet, I think. Do you want me to get it?"

She poured a shot for Henry and Steve. The bottle was near empty. Henry slammed the shot, screwed up his face and washed it down with the last beer.

"We need to get you stocked up for sure! That cheap whiskey could rip your guts out."

Steve decided the time had come to begin his pitch. "Henry, listen to me. Clara and I think I should bring Martha back to our house in Madison and take care of her until Catherine gets better. She's not going to be able to take care of her mother after all of this. Helen won't be crazy about the idea, but she'll have to grin and bear it."

Henry immediately saw problems with that plan but the benefits were more important. "It sure would be a load off Catherine's mind—and mine, too," he conceded. "She's a big drag on us when she has her spells." Privately he knew that Steve's offer would be received like Stella's offer. His mother-in-law was never going to agree to leave Marinette.

"On another note," Steve went on, "I went over to Parnell Street to see Mike this afternoon, too. He's a mess! He can't live on his own anymore. You should see his house. It's a pigsty! It smells like shit—real shit!—and moldy food. He can hardly get out of bed to get to the john. I think his mind is a little screwed up, too. It took him a long time to recognize me."

Clara, like Henry, was struggling to find the signs they had missed that led to this crisis. She turned from the stove, stood at the end of the table. "Catherine has been going to see Papa every few days, but maybe she didn't make it this week."

To Clara it was a puzzle without all the pieces. "We talked on the phone almost every day, but she never mentioned she was desperate. She's always been so strong. Maybe I just didn't pay attention to what she was saying about this pregnancy."

"Mike's got to go to a nursing home. That's all there is to it." Steve had a clear view of his father's condition. "That, or he's going to die in that house."

"How the hell can we afford that?" Henry said. "Everything we come up with creates a new problem. Life is too goddamned hard! And we don't even know if Cat's going to pull—"

Steve interrupted. "Henry, I know this is really hard on you at many levels. Let Clara and me take care of the practical problems. You take care of Catherine and yourself."

"Easy for you to say," Henry retorted. "You don't have a business to run."

"Clara, give Henry another shot of that rotgut," Steve ordered. "Listen to me! I came here to help, goddamn it! Catherine is still in the hospital, and they're not going to let her out until they think she's ready to go home—that could be a week or two. Visit her in the hospital and run your business."

"I'll take care of the girls," Clara said. "They'll be fine here until we figure something else out."

"I'm taking Mame home with me, but not before I get Mike into some kind of care facility," Steve said. "That will be a start. I'll stay at your house—you'll have empty beds—and I'll see to Mame until we leave. Now you and I are going to the hospital to see how Catherine is doing and come back to Clara's to eat the delicious dinner she's making for us. By the way, Clara, what's for dessert?"

Dessert, and dinner itself, were a long way from Henry's mind at the moment. It was a bit of light at the end of a long emotional tunnel to feel that someone in his wife's family was finally going to really, really help them with Martha and Mike.

Henry visited Catherine twice every day during her recovery. The first couple of days were like the first day, Catherine lying asleep with the needle in her arm leading to the bag of mysterious fluid. It was hospital mumbo-jumbo to

Henry, but when he finally asked, he was told these bags delivered medicines and nourishment to his wife.

She slept in a mostly-darkened room, separated from her mumbling, snoring roommate by a canvas curtain. Henry, sitting in an uncomfortable armchair next to the bed, held her hand and rubbed her legs in the way he knew she liked. His visits weren't long. He hated being in the hospital, but he made sure she knew he cared.

On the third afternoon something magical happened. Henry had brought Catherine a gardenia plant, her favorite, to brighten the dumpy room. She must have smelled the flowers before he even set them on the bedside table. Her eyes popped open.

"Oh, Henry, I love gardenias. I'm so happy you remembered."

Henry was thrilled beyond anything he might have expected! It was so much like Catherine's waking in the morning, or waking from a nap, or waking from dozing in the car on a long drive. It was not like waking from the edge of whatever dark place she had been. He reached over and cradled her head and kissed her lips. He almost confessed that Clara had given him the idea to get Catherine some flowers and had reminded him to look for gardenias.

"Henry, ring the bell for the nurse. I want her to raise my bed so we can talk a little. I feel better today, especially since my room smells so good."

Henry stayed much longer—his deliveries could wait today—and he felt unbelievable relief that she was talking and smiling. He was suddenly aware how long it had been since he had seen her smile. By the end of the visit she asked Henry to lower the bed so she could take a nap.

When Henry went back to Clara's, everyone was

waiting impatiently at the kitchen table for the daily report. They all struggled through a mini-crisis that arose when Sally discovered her Blankie was missing and Martha confessed that she had hidden it, believing her granddaughter was too old for such a prop. They settled around the table, Sally with her ragged comfort blanket in hand and her thumb in her mouth.

A huge smile on his face, Henry described as best he could the joy at seeing Catherine's smile as she awoke. He made a point of thanking Clara for the great suggestion to bring gardenias.

The good news about his sister delivered, Steve took the floor. "Now that Catherine is out of the woods, I think I'll leave as soon as I get Mike situated in Eklund's Nursing Home. Mom, how would you like to come to Madison with me for a while until Catherine is feeling better?"

"What?" Martha was taken completely by surprise.

"Kathy and Jill haven't seen you for a long time. They need to spend some time with their grandmother. You'll be surprised to see how much they've grown."

"Where am I going to sleep? I can't imagine . . ." Martha was flummoxed. "No, I don't think that will work. I can't leave Catherine. She needs me." She looked down at the table and started wringing her hands. Her head wagged back and forth and remained down. "I can't do it. I just can't."

Clara, preparing to serve the big family meal, wiped her hands on a towel and sat down next to her mother. "Mom, we talked this over and we think it would be better for both you and Catherine if you stayed with Steve and Helen until Catherine has recovered fully."

"You can't make me do this. Catherine needs me." Martha pleaded.

"Catherine can't take care of you, Mom," Steve said.

"You haven't been doing well lately. You don't get out of bed sometimes. Catherine brings you food. She's going to need someone to take care of *her,* and she's not going to be able to take care of *you.* I hate to be the hard-ass, but you don't have a choice. I'm going to take you back home tomorrow so you can pack a few things. We'll leave the day after tomorrow."

"Clara, can't I stay with you?" Martha sought any option.

"Every bed in my house is full, including the davenport. There's just no room. You can have your own room at Steve and Helen's. Helen can give you a new hairdo in her beauty shop. It'll be good for you to have a change of scenery," Clara said.

"We're moving Mike into Eklund's, probably tomorrow," Steve said, looking directly at Martha.

This was news to Martha. "What? Do you mean the nursing home?"

"Yup. You got it. He can't take care of himself anymore and Catherine can't take care of him either. Like I said before, she has to take care of herself and the baby growing inside her."

"The baby's okay then?" Martha asked, relieved. Henry had not included that information in his family report this night.

"Yes," he said. "The doctor said he thinks the baby will be fine."

Martha felt a twinge of sadness come over her. "When is Mike going to the nursing home?" she asked Steve. Even though Mike was a poor excuse for a husband, she had been married to him for nearly her whole life. They raised five kids together. She knew that he would spend the rest of his life there. She wondered if she should say goodbye to him before she went off to Madison. Who knows when they'll ever let her come home again?

Steve had completed all the arrangements. "The director at Eklund's said they'd have a bed open in a couple days. He'll be much better off there."

"Clara, I know it must be hard on you to have three more kids underfoot. Are you sure you can do this?" Henry asked.

"Yes, Henry. It's working out fine. It's the least I can do for you guys. All the kids who are old enough to pitch in, do. Three more little mouths to feed is not going to hurt me . . . "

Steve got Mike settled in at the nursing home and he and Martha set off for Madison three days later. Martha had hurriedly packed some clothes, was not sure of what she had and what she might need. For her, it was a trip into the unknown.

As Catherine continued to regain her strength during her convalescence in the hospital, she and Henry talked about what happened before she took the pills and what would happen after she got home. Catherine was adamant in her denial that she had tried to kill herself that day. Her nerves were so on edge, she said, that she couldn't function.

"I felt myself getting woozy, dizzy, like I couldn't quite figure out what was going on. I lay on the couch, but my legs were restless no matter where I put them, so I had to stand. When I got up, I thought I'd fall over. I tried to take care of the girls, but I couldn't. Sally asked for a glass of milk. I got to the kitchen and I didn't know why I was there. My brain was going a hundred miles an hour, but I couldn't focus on any one thing. In the back of my mind, I knew I hadn't checked on my mother but, on my way upstairs, I realized I hadn't fed the kids breakfast . . ." She took a deep breath.

Henry could tell Catherine was getting worked up again. *What can I do to calm her down?* he wondered. Maybe he should call a nurse? He felt himself getting tense.

Henry took her hand and rubbed her arm. "You're in a good place, Honey." He got up from his chair and put his hand on her forehead and rubbed her temples. She seemed to relax a bit. "Maybe you should try to rest. Maybe a nap."

She took another deep breath. *Henry needs to hear the whole story,* she said to herself. *I don't want him to leave until I get this off my chest, but I don't know how I can go on.* She closed her eyes for a moment.

Henry continued to lightly touch her face and gently massage her scalp until he thought she must be asleep, but as soon as he stopped touching, her eyes opened wide. "Don't go, Honey. I need you to stay a little longer."

Henry assured her he would stay until she got to sleep. With her eyes closed, she took up where she left off.

"I need to tell you the whole story. I didn't know what to do or where to go. I tried to wash the breakfast dishes, but I couldn't even do that. I got distracted after I washed the first dish and I was on to something else. Then I'd pace. The girls wanted me to play with them. It's hard to describe how devastated I felt. I thought I was having a nervous breakdown. It was so scary."

"I'm sorry, Cat. I never realized you were in such a—"

"Henry, please! Just listen!"

Chastised, he sat back to listen.

"I thought that if I could make it to the girl's nap time, maybe I could take one of Mame's pills to calm me down and so I could get a nap, too. I'd never taken any of her pills before, but I was at wit's end. I put the kids down for a nap. Lilly didn't want a nap, but I made her have one anyway. I knew Jeannie was walking home from school. So I got Mame's pill bottle off the windowsill, tried to shake out one but I got more than one. I just took them all. At that point I hardly knew what I was doing. I know now it was terrible, I thought I was going crazy. I didn't care about anything—not *anything*—except to get rid of the awful weight of my nerves."

She reached over to take his hand. "I'm so sorry, Henry."

Henry gave his hand limply, trying to digest what his wife had just confessed. Catherine's thoughts and feeling were so unlike anything he had ever experienced. "Jeez, Cat. Did you really have to take the pills? I don't get it."

Catherine's anger flashed. "Of course, you don't get it! If you've never had to deal with it, you wouldn't get it. You know how you feel when you wake up with a wet T-shirt, because you're worried about how you're make the next payment at the bank? Well, my dear husband, multiply that by a million! At the moment I took those pills, I really didn't care if I died."

"Oh, Cat! You can't say that! What about the girls? What about me? How could we get along without you?" His hand was still in hers, and he reached out and grabbed her wrist to bind her to him. "I love you so much, Cat! I'm scared you'll do it again!"

"I'm scared, too, Henry. I don't ever want to feel like that again. It's the worst I've ever felt."

Catherine's recovery was long and difficult. She stayed in the hospital for ten days, waiting for the doctor's okay that she was in his opinion emotionally and physically stable enough to come home. He was also waiting for word from Henry that he had found help for Catherine. This assistance was in the form of Henry's Aunt Hazel, unmarried and living in California, who had agreed to come to Wisconsin to stay with Henry and Catherine to give them both moral support and help with the girls. Hazel didn't do housework or cooking, but she was good for Catherine's and Henry's spirits.

When Jeannie wasn't in school she wouldn't let Catherine out of her sight for five minutes. She buzzed around like a little mother making sure Catherine ate, didn't drink too much, went to bed early, and that Lilly and Sally didn't make any noise. She gave Aunt Hazel instructions before she left for school every morning. Catherine told Jeannie repeatedly what a good girl she was, which only prompted her daughter to do more mothering.

Henry arranged for his Aunt Elsie to move in to help Catherine and the baby after Hazel returned to California. They were delighted to have Catherine home.

In January, Catherine gave birth to a healthy little girl. She named her Violet.

Chapter 24. Time Flies (1964-66)

Catherine sat in an overstuffed chair with her arm around Violet. They were settled comfortably under a cozy warm blanket. Outside, spurred by a strong swirling wind, snow was piling up on the big picture-window ledge. This was a blizzard unlike anything the community had seen in years. As often happens in any good Midwestern storm, schools were cancelled but a variety of businesses struggled to stay open. Henry was one of those folks who said, "Hey, you don't stop for a little snow!" and he was out on his delivery route. Catherine was a little nervous about Henry's outing in this storm, but she knew enough of driving to know that his loaded truck had an edge in maintaining traction on the snow-covered roads. Warm, comfortable, and contented, Catherine smiled to herself and squeezed Violet even tighter.

"Can you imagine when you were born ten years ago that I didn't want to have you? You, sweetie pie, are the best mistake Dad and I ever made. Now I don't know what I would do without you."

Violet tried to make sense of this confession. Was there some long-ago decision that parents made that she didn't understand? "Why didn't you want me?"

Catherine felt wonderfully warm under the blanket she

shared with her youngest daughter. Her revelations flowed so comfortably as the pair sat, insulated from the cold wind raging outside.

"Well, Sweetie, it was a bad time for our family. Mamie and Papa were both sick, so I was taking care of them. I was running over to Papa's every day to cook and clean for him, and I had Mamie, Jeannie, Lilly and Sally at home. Daddy was working hard to keep his business going, so he was gone most of the time. Everything was a big mess. I didn't know how I could take care of another kid. Then you came along." She gave her daughter a big squeeze. "You were such a good baby. It seemed you knew you needed to be good."

Violet, cuddled closely, looked up into her mother's eyes with a big smile on her face. "I'm glad I was a good baby," she said.

The intimacy of the moment, lying wrapped up in a blanket with her mother, the warm colors of the living room a vivid contrast to the gray storm swirling outside the window, would stay with Violet forever. She would always picture this scene and recall her mother's judgment that she was her mother's best mistake.

They sat in silence for some minutes, listening to the wind. Then Violet said, "I don't remember Papa very much. Was he a good dad to you?"

"Sweetie, he was pretty sick and in a nursing home by the time you were born. I guess he was as good as he could be. He was a fisherman. He brought fresh fish home for us to eat all the time. He was the best storyteller ever—so funny! He would make everybody laugh. When I was a teenager, I would make Papa's lunch. Sometimes, when I opened his lunch pail, I'd find a frog—once even a snake. He was quite the trickster."

"A snake in the lunch pail? That's creepy!" Violet said.

She tried to picture the scene. "What would you do?"

"I'd scream and yell. Papa and Uncle Charlie would laugh their heads off." The fleeting memory of her father's jokes and tricks gave Catherine a silent thrill that she knew she could never really explain to her daughters. If she tried, she felt she would have to explain Mike's meanness and anger at his wife, the girls' beloved Mamie.

A blast of wind shook the house and snow swirled past the big window. They huddled a little closer.

"Papa was in a nursing home when you were a baby," Catherine explained.

"What's a nursing home?"

"It's sort of like a big hospital where people go when they're sick and can't take care of themselves. Papa drank too much and hurt his brain."

"That's scary, Mama." Violet paused. "Jeannie says sometimes you drink too much. I don't want you to hurt your brain. Jeannie says you don't take care of yourself very well. She gets upset when you drink too much. I don't want you to die."

Catherine sensed that Violet was near tears, that Jeannie's comments had been troubling the girl for a while. "Jeannie is a worry wart," Catherine said dismissively. "I know how to take care of myself. I am just fine."

"I miss Jeannie so much," Violet said.

Away from home and living in an adult world, Jeannie in her new realm was now Jean. She had just graduated from college and was living in Madison with her husband Dan. What a miracle that was for her! Four years earlier she had begged her father to let her go to college, but Henry couldn't understand why any young woman needed a college degree to get married and have kids. Almost as important, Henry's youngest sister had gone off to college and had become a Democrat. That was the last thing on earth he wanted to have happen to one of his offspring.

Now that Jean had graduated, Catherine and Henry were proud of her but still a little skeptical of her motives. She was working when she should have been home taking care of her husband and starting a family. There was always a little tension when she came home to visit.

Jean's parents felt now that she acted as though she knew more than all the rest and she seemed to like to throw her weight around.

"When is she coming home again?" Violet asked. Her older sister, who appeared to be at home in a much larger world than Violet understood, was a kind of hero.

"I know she wants to visit Mamie, so probably pretty soon."

Martha was dying. Her children knew it, but they never actually said the words, "Mom is dying." She had been diagnosed with throat cancer nine years earlier, which had triggered another nervous breakdown. This episode sent her this time to the Winnebago State Hospital, where she had undergone another series of shock treatments and radiation. The radiation treatments, while they burned black the skin on her throat, had kept the cancer at bay for a while. The shock treatments had erased the cancer diagnosis from her memories, but the cancer was silently killing her. Catherine was nursing her mother at home.

"I wish Mamie would get better," Violet said.

"Me, too, Honey. She's been sick a long time," Catherine said.

They both saw Henry's big beer truck pull into the driveway. The white vehicle might have been lost in the swirling snow but for the bright red "BUDWEISER" in large capital letters emblazoned on the side. Catherine and Violet ran to the back door to greet him.

"Oh, Honey, I'm so relieved you're home. Is it as bad as it looks out there?" Catherine kissed him on the cheek while he was brushing the snow off his jacket and kicking it off his boots.

Henry patted her shoulder. "It's a son-of-a-bitch. If I hadn't had the truck, I wouldn't have made it home. The snow is building up on the roads and there's a layer of ice under it. It's treacherous driving. The plows have only hit the main streets. Everything else is a mess." He continued to peel off layers of clothing. "I didn't even try to get to the warehouse. I'm in for the day. Hey, how you doin', Squirt?" he said, spotting Violet hovering at her mother's side.

"I'm okay. I just hope my pony's okay out in the storm. Should we check on him?"

"Patches is okay. I put her in Gramma's barn this morning when it started to snow."

"I wonder if I should go sit with her. I'll bet she's lonesome in the barn all alone."

"She's not alone. Bessie is in the barn too and so are the chickens. They'll keep each other company."

"Who's going to milk Bessie?"

"Probably Gramma. The animals are all fine. Don't be such a worrywart." Henry pulled an envelope out of his jacket pocket and handed it to Catherine.

"What's this?" she said as she examined the elegant envelope. It was addressed to Mr. and Mrs. Henry Goodman in beautifully embellished lettering. The return address, Anheuser-Busch Companies, was written in red ink. On the back of the envelope across the top were the words "Remember Every Soldier in Every War Died under Battle."

"What does this mean, Henry?"

"It's how old Adolphus Busch named the beer, they say. Each word in the sentence starts with a letter in the word Budweiser from back to front."

"That's too complicated for me," Catherine said.

She pulled the card from the envelope and read it out loud: "Mr. and Mrs. August Busch request the honor of your presence at a gala event to honor our top performing Budweiser dealers in the Midwest. Saturday, March 15, 1964, in the ballroom of the Grand Hotel, St. Louis, Missouri."

Henry saw the puzzled look on his wife's face. "We made it, Cat! We finally made it big time!" He pointed earnestly at the invitation in her hand. "We're going to be honored! Who'd have thought we could have done this? Ten years ago, I was wringing my hands and having night sweats because I didn't know how we could pay for the next delivery of beer. Our debts are paid off and our sales are better than ever. We're going to celebrate, by God! I wish V.R. was here to see this."

"I was born ten years ago, Daddy," Violet offered.

"Yes, you were. You were our lucky star, Violet." He picked her up and twirled her around.

Catherine felt none of Henry's excitement. "We're not going to St. Louis, are we, Henry?" she asked tentatively.

"We sure are, Cat! We have worked it and we have *earned* it!"

Catherine felt her heart pounding and her head spinning. She was nervous just thinking about going. "I'm not sure that's such a good idea. It's a long way."

"It's not as far as Connecticut. Stella and Anthony drive farther than that almost every year."

It wasn't really about the long drive, although that was a worry. Catherine was sure she wouldn't know how to act at fancy gatherings. What would she wear? The nicest place she ever went was Marinette's Elks Club. She couldn't pull off an event in a—what did the invitation say? —a "*grand ballroom!*" If Henry now fancied himself a big shot, she thought, *he can just go by himself!* Besides, they'd have to find someone to stay with the kids and take care of Martha.

She'd wait to tell Henry she wasn't going. She didn't want to burst his bubble yet. The party was two months away.

Henry was ready to begin celebrating that moment. "If it weren't still storming, I'd take you to Red and Ed's for a nice juicy T-bone and a few drinks."

She didn't think she had ever seen Henry this happy— not even when they were married or when any of the girls were born. She wished she felt as good about their accomplishments as he did.

"Have you told your mother yet?" Catherine asked Henry.

"No, not yet, but I can't wait. She thought you and I wouldn't amount to anything—but look at us now!"

"She still doesn't like the way I'm raising the kids. She called Jeannie a spoiled brat," Catherine said.

"Well, that 'spoiled brat' graduated from college. You must have done something right, Cat. I sure wasn't any help. I'm proud of her, but . . ."

"But what?"

"I'm sure she's a Democrat. That doesn't make me happy. She voted for Kennedy, for God's sake! Hard to believe one of my kids voted for Kennedy, a Democrat *and* a Catholic!"

"Yeah, so? I don't care about politics. What good does it do me?"

Henry put his hand on Catherine's shoulder and smiled. "As long as you vote for who I tell you, I don't care either," he said, laughing.

The next morning, as soon as Henry left for work and the kids were back in school, Catherine picked up the phone from its cradle and stretched the cord across the hall to the stairs going up to the second floor.

"I am a nervous wreck, Clare."

"What now?"

"Well, you're not going to believe this. Henry got a letter from the Budweiser mucky-mucks. We're invited to some highfalutin' dinner honoring the Budweiser distributors in the Midwest. It's in St. Louis and Henry wants us to go."

"Oh, my God!" Clara said. "Cat, that sounds like a great honor, but isn't that a long way away? Are you going to go?"

"Well, I sure as hell don't want to. I guess the top brass didn't know my nickname when I was a kid was 'Fishguts.' You can take the girl out of Menekaunee, but you can't take Menekaunee out of the girl."

"You know you'd hurt Henry's feelings if you didn't go." Clara, like Catherine, was always worried about everybody's feelings.

"I'll be like a fish out of water. You know what Papa used to say when he talked about big shots—remember?"

"Yeah, he'd say that they think their shit doesn't stink," Clara laughed.

"Yeah, and I agree with him. I hate those pretentious people who think they're better than anybody who doesn't belong to a country club. They make me sick."

"You never know, Cat. You might meet a bunch of folks just like you and Henry."

After the call was over, Catherine sat down at the kitchen table near tears. Nothing in her conversation with Clara helped her decide whether she could or should go. She wanted to celebrate with Henry but the thought of traveling and being with people who she thought might believe they were better than her brought her to her knees. When she was a teen— before she became a stay-at-home housewife—even when she worked for the judge and thought nothing of dancing on a table, she was happiest being with Betty, with the sheriff's deputies and other courthouse staff. Now, her self-confidence was okay when she was with her own kind of folks, people who were down-to-earth, like bartenders, garbage collectors, cooks and waitresses, gas station attendants and mechanics, butchers, and grocery clerks. She was out of her element, a shrinking violet, with anyone who seemed to eye her as someone inferior, people like doctors, schoolteachers, bankers, lawyers, ministers, and pretty much anyone who felt they had to be part of a country club to be recognized in the community.

She was so absorbed in these thoughts she could barely hear Martha calling from the living room. The throat cancer and radiation treatments had taken a toll on her mother's voice and strength. She could get herself to the bathroom and up the stairs to her bedroom with help, but she was declining. Her voice was weak.

"Open these curtains, Honey? It's too dark in here." Martha pointed to the curtains on the window above the couch where she lay, and Catherine opened them wide, letting in the brilliant light from the snow-covered world outside.

"Could you get me a little bit of Cream of Wheat with just cream, no sugar? That sugar burns my throat."

When Catherine brought the warm cereal Martha thanked her, adding, "You do too much for me. I hate to be so good-for-nothing. I can't even take care of the kids."

Catherine set the bowl on a TV tray next to the couch. "Do you want me to feed you or would you rather try to eat it yourself?"

Martha propped herself up in the corner of the couch, leaned forward to take a bite, and watched cream dribble onto her robe from the shaking spoon. She tried again and implored her daughter, "Please help me."

"Listen, Mom," Catherine said, settling on the couch beside her mother and carefully lifting each spoon to her mother's lips. "I am so happy to help you, and the kids don't need care anymore. Lilly is seventeen already, and Sally is not far behind. Jeannie is a college graduate—grown up and married. Violet will be around for a few more years, but she's easy. She's growing up fast under her big sisters' influence." She looked at her mother tenderly. "You always took care of me and the kids whenever you could, and that's something I will always remember and thank you for."

Martha was lucid but she was deep in the belief that she was now nothing but a burden. "I'll bet Henry is getting tired of me lying around here day and night. But, y'know, I won't be around much longer."

"Stop it, Mom! If you keep eating and walking a little bit every day, you'll get stronger." Catherine was more comfortable with the fiction that her mother would recover. "Getting stronger will help when you're done with those terrible treatments. They take a big toll."

When the bowl was two-thirds empty Martha lay her head back, signaling she was done eating. "I heard you talking to Clara on the phone," she whispered. "I wouldn't want to go to a fancy shindig either. Those damn hoity-toity rich people are a pain in the backside. They don't know what it means to work for a living."

"I don't know, Mom. It's so confusing. Clara said that maybe it was a party of a bunch of people like us, but I don't see 'us' in some kind of grand ballroom." She lightly massaged her mother's right arm. "I don't want to hurt Henry's feelings. Here's a guy who's worked hard for every penny he has. He's not thinking about who's going to be there, except he's thinking he should be, you know?" Catherine felt herself falling into an agreement that they would go. "He deserves the honor. I'd rather stay right here with you and the kids, and, besides, what the heck will I wear?"

"You've got some nice dresses, Catherine."

"My house dresses won't do, and neither will my 'farmer' shoes. Remember Jeannie and her friends called my nice brown oxfords with the crepe soles 'farmer shoes?'"

"I don't remember that, but that's no surprise. I don't remember a darn thing," Martha said.

"I wish Stella lived closer. She goes to Anthony's bigwig parties. Remember when she and Anthony visited us when they were first married, and she gave me all those sophisticated clothes for my first job with the judge? That's when I figured I had some class."

"Yeah, I remember that, although how I can remember what happened more than twenty years ago, when I can hardly remember my own name . . ." Martha shook her head, ". . . but I remember how I had to alter most of those dresses and suits to fit you. You never know . . ."

If she *did* go, she'd need *something.* "I think maybe I'll write Stella," Catherine said. She couldn't get the trip to St. Louis out of her mind. She had never been out of Wisconsin. She and the family had visited Steve and Helen in Madison a few times. Once they went to Milwaukee to the Wisconsin State Fair, but as far as travel goes that was about it.

Dear Stella,

How are you? I haven't heard from you in a while.

I hope everything is okay.

I have a favor to ask you. Henry and I are invited to a Budweiser event in St. Louis. It's for all the big wheels who have sold a lot of beer. The invitation looked like it had been sent by royalty. So, what the heck should I wear? You're the only one I know who could tell me.

Mom is hanging in there. She's trying hard, but I think she's losing ground. You might think about coming home. I don't know if she'll last until summer.

Say hi to Margaret and Anthony. Is Margaret pregnant yet? Jeannie isn't. I don't think she's ready. She's taking birth control pills. Can you believe it? Clara thinks it's terrible. She says Jeannie might never be able to get pregnant if she takes those pills. I don't know what to think.

Things are changing too fast for me.

Love, Your baby sister,

Catherine

The invitation to the St. Louis event was a disruption for Catherine, whose family life had finally seemed to settle into a routine that suited her just fine. The past few years had been good for Catherine and Henry. They were able to pay their debts and finish the house.

Until her recent decline, Martha had done well after her last series of electroshock therapy and Mike's death.

When she went out to church or to coffee klatch with her sisters, she'd pick her best clothes—getting "all dolled up," as she'd admit—in matching hat, gloves and purse. She was back at her job at the Gateway Cafe, and every day the family would find on the kitchen counter delicious pieces of pie, cake or rolls that Martha brought home from the Menominee restaurant. When Jeannie was fourteen, she and Martha finally had rooms of their own, and Martha bought her granddaughter a new bedroom set for her new room. They had shared a room and a bed since Henry had come home from the war when Jeannie was three.

After Violet was born, Aunt Elsie, another of V.R.'s sisters, stayed with the Goodmans until Catherine was on her feet again. For several years after that there were no crises in the household. The girls were growing up and doing well. Jeannie, a college graduate with her own job, lived in Madison. Lilly, Sally and Violet were in school, and Lilly would be graduating from high school this spring. Martha's cancer was the only difficulty the family was facing, and, sadly, her recovery now seemed much less likely.

Although her concern about her mother dominated her thoughts, the March trip to St. Louis still nagged at Catherine. She had never actually told Henry that he ought to go alone. She promised herself to bring it up but postponed that conversation from day to day. One day she heard a knock on the door. Who would that be? She wasn't expecting anyone.

When she opened the door, the mailman handed her a box and a letter. She saw the box was from Stella. She thought she knew what was in the box. When she ripped it open, she found a baby blue linen dress with a matching jacket. She was thrilled. As she was crumpling up the packing paper, an earring fell to the floor. It was beautiful—it looked like a sapphire stone on a silver base. Where was the other one? Just as she was beginning to panic, she found the other one in the crumpled paper and breathed a sigh of relief. Stella had come through again! All Catherine needed was shoes. She should be able to handle that, but she'd quiz Stella before she'd decided.

The letter was from Jean. She had earlier let her mother know after she got her first job that she was no longer Jeannie. Catherine rolled her eyes at the announcement, but she would respect her daughter's wishes. She concluded that her daughter must be going through a know-it-all stage—after all, she had a college degree. The real news of the letter was that Jean and Dan would be coming to visit the following weekend. Even though she sometimes felt that her oldest daughter could be a real pill, she was thrilled to hear the news.

"What should we eat this weekend?" Catherine asked the girls.

"Jean loves it when Dad grills steak for Sunday noon dinner," Lilly reminded them, "and you could make twice-baked potatoes, Mom."

"Can he grill in all the snow?" Violet sounded skeptical.

Sally piped up, "What would you know about it, you little twerp!"

"Sally—watch it!" Catherine wanted to tamp down any friction among her daughters before the weekend arrived. This was going to be a special family gathering. "Good ideas, Lilly. He likes to grill year-round and will be overjoyed to use the new grill. It's his pride and joy. He'll probably want potatoes in foil, too."

"Aw, come on, Mom. We always have those. We never have twice-baked anymore," Lilly whined.

Catherine ignored her and asked if they had any other suggestions for other meals.

Catherine cooked with great pride. She, Martha and Clara loved talking about new recipes. They competed with each other over whose cooking was best. After eating at Clara's, Catherine would say to Henry or the girls that she didn't think Clara's meatloaf was as good as her own. She was not happy if any of them disagreed. She decided to call Clara to see what she would recommend for lunch and supper on Saturday. On Friday they'd all go the Elks Club for a fish fry. That was standard fare. Now that Danny was in the picture, Catherine tried a little harder to be proper. He was from a family that belonged to Riverside Country Club, so she was a little uncomfortable when he was around. As usual, she thought she didn't measure up. Henry enjoyed going to the Elks to show off his family. Now that he was the Exalted Ruler, they treated him with respect. Catherine felt more comfortable there, the same way she felt at the Silver Dome Bowling Alley.

When Jean and Danny turned into the driveway at 5:30 p.m. on Friday the whole troupe ran out to the car. Violet jumped up on Jean with her arms around her neck and legs clutching her waist. Catherine was worming her way toward Jean to give her a hug, but Danny was in the way. She gave him a tap on the shoulder and a big smile.

"Violet, where are your shoes, you little stinker. You can't be walking around in the snow in your socks," Jean said.

"Oh, I don't need shoes. My feet are tough." She wanted Jean to know how grown up and independent she was, but mostly she wanted her to laugh.

They all stumbled into the kitchen where Henry was sitting in his place at the end of the table, chair turned sideways to the table, holding a glass of beer with a nice head and a raw egg floating to the bottom.

"Skoll," he said as he lifted his glass to his mouth. Jean yelled, "Hi, Dad!" but rushed past him into the living room to see her grandmother. Martha was lying on the couch, her eyes closed, her face the same color as the gray cushions. Jean could not believe what she saw. Her beloved grandmother—the woman who had raised her as her own child—was deathly ill.

Catherine had warned Jean that Martha wasn't doing well, but to see her lying there so helpless and weak broke Jean's heart. She tried to put on a happy face, but she couldn't. She bent over give Mamie a hug and kiss and she felt her tears start to flow.

"Thanks for coming, my little Jeannie," Martha said in a voice so weak that Jean could hardly hear her.

Catherine set a bowl of broth and rice on the metal TV table next to the couch. "Mom," she said, "maybe Jean can help you with your supper."

"I'm tired of everybody taking care of me," Martha said.

"I want to take care of you, Mamie," Jean implored. "You took care of me all my life. I will never forget that. Remember when you bought the record player for our room? You bought my favorite records and we would put a stack on before we hopped into bed and we'd listen to them while we'd fall asleep. Sometimes you'd tickle my back. I loved that."

"Yes, I remember," Martha said softly. "I'd get up and turn off the music after you went to—" She started to cough and couldn't finish. Jeannie put her ear near her grandmother's mouth to try to hear her words. She rubbed Martha's swollen arm as the woman continued to cough, and Jean's heart hurt as she watched Mamie struggle. She would do anything to help her. In the background Jean could hear the commotion in the kitchen as Catherine was coaching Jean's sisters to get ready for the Elks Club's Friday-night fish fry. Jean couldn't bear the thought of leaving Mamie alone.

"Mamie, I'm going to stay with you while the others go to the Elks. I want to be with you."

"You go," Martha said. "I need to rest—you go right now."

Catherine turned and saw her eldest daughter whispering quietly to Martha and she strode directly to the couch. "Jean, you need to come with us. Your dad and sisters would be extremely disappointed if you stayed here. Mamie will be fine alone and will be right here when we get back. Try to feed her a little more broth before we go—she needs to eat. I made some custard this afternoon. That goes down easy. She can have some before she goes to bed."

They all piled into Catherine and Henry's station wagon—dark green with wood-paneled sides—three in the front and four in the back, all looking their Sunday best.

"Violet, get your leg off me," Sally complained.

"Where am I supposed to put it?" was the quick response.

"On the floor!"

"There's no room on the floor."

"Don't put it on me—sister germs! Yuk!"

And so it went for the rest of the ride. Luckily, the club was only ten minutes away. Danny didn't say a word.

"Danny, I suppose this kind of behavior doesn't happen at your house." Catherine was hoping he wouldn't go home and tell his own parents how unsophisticated and ill-mannered the Goodmans were.

"No, it's never like this, but we're all grown up now," Danny said.

"Was it ever like this?" Catherine probed.

"No. My dad wouldn't have put up with it," Danny said. Catherine opted to press no further.

Before Henry could even order a beer, Al, the bartender, had set two full glasses in front of him. He waved in the direction of two men at the far end of the bar, who raised their glasses when Henry looked their way. "Roger and Jim bought you a beer, Henry. They're offering you a drink, too, Catherine. What'll you have?"

"An old fashioned." she replied. The kids and Jean each ordered a coke. Danny also opted for an old fashioned.

He knew that Jean didn't order a drink, because she wanted to keep an eye on her mother's drinking. He knew, too, that Jean had earlier thought if she didn't drink, maybe her mother wouldn't either, but that hadn't worked.

Henry, normally a man of few words, opened up after a couple of drinks. He made the rounds of the bar and stopped to chat at every table. None of the family was charged for a single drink all night. Elks members kept telling Henry what a nice family he had, but he kept giving Catherine all the credit. He spoke with sincerity, because he believed that raising the girls was a woman's job—nothing he was expected to get involved with—and he felt she had earned any praise.

Jean checked her watch throughout the evening. She neither drank nor socialized. She just wanted to get back to Martha, feed her some custard and put her to bed. When the family finally got home, not only did Jean put her grandmother to bed, but she slept with her, as she had for so many years. It felt right to cuddle with her ailing Mamie.

The weekend passed quickly. Saturday night after dinner, Catherine washed the dishes as Jean and Sally dried, Lilly put them away and Violet stayed as close to Jean as possible. As they worked together Catherine started singing Lutheran hymns, and all the girls joined in. She had gone to church mainly to sing, and she had passed along her love of hymns. She would start a song, and as her daughters picked up the melody, she would sing harmony. The task of washing and drying the dishes and cookware of a big family meal passed quickly as "Rock of Ages," "I Come to the Garden Alone," and "What a Friend We Have in Jesus," resonated through the kitchen into the front room. Danny sat at the kitchen table, marveling at the spontaneous concert. Henry sat contently in his living room chair, paging through a *Reader's Digest*. Martha lay on the couch, a calm look on her face and happiness in her heart, feeling the family's love for one another.

Much to Catherine's delight, the girls and Danny agreed to go to church with her on Sunday morning. She felt proud parading down the aisle with her beautiful daughters to their usual pew in the second row. Henry didn't go to church, because the Lutheran church, aware of his beer sales business, had denied his membership, but Catherine made sure the girls had made it to Sunday school.

Catherine and her sister Clara had often sat next to each other in church and despite the presumed seriousness of the service they seemed to find delight in giggling to one another. Their laughter might arise from something as simple as turning to the wrong page in the hymnal. The Sunday routine often included a short walk to Clara's after church, where a chicken and homemade dinner rolls might be in the oven. The girls always delighted in a quick taste of a stuffing sandwich on a warm roll.

The family drove directly home this Sunday, and when they arrived, they could smell the charcoal grill was already at work. Henry had shoveled a path from the back door to his grill, and there he stood, the proud chef. He was a sight that made them laugh. He was dressed in a heavy jacket and a hat with the earflaps down. He posed with a long cooking fork in his gloved hand, and he had placed a bottle of Budweiser within easy reach in an adjacent snowbank. No sooner was the table set than Henry walked into the kitchen with a large white platter holding a stack of steaming T-bone steaks and packages of potatoes wrapped in foil.

Everyone was seated and starting to dig in except Catherine. She seldom sat until she was certain everyone had what he or she needed. First, she set a large steaming bowl of yellow kernels in the center of the table. "This is the last jar of sweet corn I canned in September," she said. Then she waited for the requests she knew would come.

"Hey, Mom, could you please bring the pepper?"

"Catherine, do I see any butter on the table?"

"Mom, could I please have milk instead of water?"

At that moment they were one happy family.

"Remember when we used to have food fights?" Sally asked. "They were so much fun!"

"Yes, and remember what I did when that happened?" her father asked.

"Yeah—I remember," Sally said. "You never yelled at us. You would get that look on your face like, *how did I get a family like this?* I know you thought it was disgusting. You'd just leave the table quietly with a sad face and go to your chair in the front room and turn on the TV."

"Yeah, Henry, you really hated it when I got involved," Catherine laughed. "You wouldn't talk to me for a while, but in the end, *I* was the one who had to pick up all the peas and mashed potatoes that everyone had flipped on their forks at each other."

"But you'd do it too, Mom," Sally reminded her mother. "One time you laughed so hard you peed your pants!" They were all laughing now—even Henry smiled a little. Danny was having trouble picturing it. This was something that would never have happened in his home—at any meal at any time.

This Sunday dinner was something special, and they all felt joy in being together. They knew they loved each other and always would.

Jean, who had fed Mamie her Cream of Wheat before the family feast, knew it was time to say goodbye. She suspected she would never see her grandmother again, and it broke her heart. They clung to each other silently and cried. Jean wept for most of the drive back to Madison.

Six months later Martha died in her bed. After a tumult of physical and mental challenges, it was a peaceful ending. Catherine found her mother cold in her bed, and she and Henry sat in the morning to plan Martha's final days. Word would go out immediately to Stella and Anthony, Steve and Helen, and Charlie, wherever his shipping line might find him.

Catherine had lived with her mother her entire life. It would be a dramatic change for her, Henry, and their girls. This would be the first time since Henry and Catherine were married that they hadn't had both or one of her parents living with or caring for them.

All of Martha's children and grandchildren were at the funeral. They said their goodbyes and exchanged stories about her and the family. They agreed that her bouts of serious depression and anxiety had affected her life negatively. Some thought she ought to have been stronger in avoiding or dealing with her spells. Those who had lived most closely to their mother's travails—Catherine and Clara—believed she had tried as hard as she could to hold her depression at bay. The whole family agreed that her life with Mike had been hard and had taken a heavy toll on her. The siblings were all loyal to their mother and loved her in spite of her emotional problems. She was a good woman.

The siblings were in different stages of their lives. Steve and Helen had a good life and two grown daughters making their own way. Steve enjoyed his job in banking and the prospect of promotion, and Helen' beauty shop in the back of their home was a special resource into what was really happening in Madison.

Clara and Nels had lived in Marinette all their lives and

Nels' insurance sales provided a good income, while Clara, who had always been a homemaker, watched their seven children grow and leave the nest, one by one.

The lives of the other children were more troubled, and alcohol—and maybe a hint of depression—played an important role in their lives.

Charlie's wife Irene, beached in Marinette as he cruised the Great Lakes, drank to still her loneliness as she waited for her husband to come home at the end of each shipping season. They had no children.

Stella had never gotten over leaving Chicago and her management job at a giant department store in the city, but she fondly embraced her husband Anthony, an executive at General Electric in Connecticut. They watched their daughter grow and marry and leave home. Stella drowned her own fits of depression with alcohol.

Even though she had a supportive husband and a more prosperous life, Catherine shared with her brothers and sisters her bouts of anxiety and depression that she had experienced during her life. One daughter was out the door, ready to begin her own family. Three girls remained at home. She could only pray that they might be spared the emotional challenges she and her late mother had faced.

After the funeral, they all gathered at Catherine and Henry's where the booze, beer, and left-over funeral food were plentiful. They laughed and cried about happy times and horrible times during their lives with their parents. Now they were truly orphans. It was the beginning of a new era.

Chapter 25. Henry (1971-73)

Six years after Martha died and four years after Violet left for college, Catherine and Henry were living the good life. Their house was paid for, Henry's business was thriving, and two of their daughters and three grandchildren lived close by in Marinette. Their other two daughters lived in Madison. These last four years were the first time since they were married that Catherine and Henry had lived by themselves.

While Catherine rattled around the house, trying to fill her time, Henry was busier than ever. He was bound and determined to keep building the business, and his goal was less work for himself and a comfortable life for them both. He wanted to buy another truck, hire two more deliverymen, and get a bookkeeper. He was getting close to his goal and wasn't going to stop until he reached it. Catherine was all for the expansion. The trip to the St. Louis fete had changed her mind about the business, and she had taken pride in Henry's success, reflected in the praise from folks that turned out to be just working folks like Henry and Catherine.

One quiet evening Henry was sitting at the table having a beer in his usual fashion, an egg on the bottom of a sparkling glass. Catherine came into the kitchen, grabbed a bottle of beer for herself—Henry always preferred to stock the home with bottles rather than cans—and joined Henry at the table.

"Honey, I don't know what to do with all my spare time. You're so busy and I don't feel useful." Then she said the words that had run through her head for days. "Maybe I should get a job," she said calmly, as though the thought had just occurred to her.

"A *job!*" Henry looked at her in surprise. "What kind of job? You've *got* a job! What's wrong with being a housewife?" He took her comment as a whim and sought to reassure her. "Relax, Cat. You've almost killed yourself taking care of everybody else your whole life. How about taking care of yourself for a change?"

Catherine saw that this conversation was going to go on a bit. How could Henry even suggest she should lounge around the house when he was on the move all week? He had no idea what he was recommending, because he didn't know what the empty house was like all day. She rose and went to the pantry and came back with a bag of potato chips. "Lay's," she said. "My favorite chips," and she offered the opened bag to Henry.

"No thanks," he said, waving them away. "They'll just fatten me up." He knew Catherine was always trying to lose a few pounds and he like to tease her about it.

"That's a smart-ass remark, Mr. Goodman. You're going to get it!"

"I hope so," he smiled. Catherine smiled back but was immediately serious again.

"Enough foolishness. Let's get back to my potential job. It's not my nature to be sitting around coffee-klatching with the neighbors—or my sister, for that matter."

This would have to play out, he realized. "What do you want to do?"

She shifted around in her chair, took a swallow of beer, shrugged her shoulders. "I don't know." She confessed. "Maybe a secretary. Y'know, Henry, I can still type sixty-four words a minute. Or, I'd be a good waitress, too. I'll bet I'd make lots of tips," she teased.

"Come on, Cat. I don't want you to be waiting on tables." He patted her knee. "We're finally making a good living. You don't need to work. But, hey, on the other hand, I could use you to deliver beer."

"That's real funny, Henry Goodman, although I could ride with you in your big new truck and keep you company." She waited for his reaction to that idea, but she had instead directed his thinking back to his couple of weeks of work.

"I'm busier than ever, a blessing and a curse. I'm working my balls off from morning to night. I wish I had someone to take care of the emergencies that come up after I go to bed."

"That's true, Henry. Someone else could take those calls you get at midnight from the bartenders who run out of beer."

"Yeah, I hate that." He knew that Catherine was always disturbed for his sake when he had to make one of those late deliveries. "I tell those idiots—even some of your old Menekaunee buddies—to keep an extra keg in their coolers, but 'Naw,' they say. 'We're all set. We've got enough to last us.' Then they call at midnight. Such a pain in the ass."

"What would happen if you didn't answer the phone, or if you said, 'This is what I've been telling your guys. It's your problem until I get there in the morning.' Why not?" Cat asked.

"What would happen? I'll tell you what would happen. I'd lose a paying customer. That's what would happen. They push Budweiser because I keep them happy, and I keep them happy by keeping them in beer." He paused in thought, then, "Hey! What's for supper? It smells good."

"Meatloaf, baked potatoes and squash. An oven supper, but it won't be ready for half an hour yet. You came home earlier than usual tonight."

"Yeah, I'm tired tonight. I guess I might as well have another beer. Can I get you one, too?"

"You might as well. It's nice to just sit here and talk for a change." As she watched Henry rise slowly she added, "You seem to be more tired lately."

"I think it's because I have so much on my mind. I don't have time to do the books the way they should be done. I've got a pile of stuff on the desk a mile high. I look at it and groan. I can't stay on top of everything and it drives me crazy."

"I'm sorry,. Honey. You've got your hands full. Is Woody doing any better?" Henry's brother was a whole separate problem within the company.

"Not really. He's not drunk *every* night he brings the truck in. No, I'd say *only* half the time."

"My God, Henry, that's not good!" She hadn't known how badly things were going with Woody. "If he gets picked up for drunken driving or gets in an accident, it ends up on you!"

"Yeah, no shit! But what am I supposed to do? He's still mad that I got the business, even though he wasn't ready for it. How the hell can I fire my brother?" He sighed as he delivered the two beers. "Come on over here and sit on my lap. You haven't done that in a long time."

Catherine smiled and moved onto Henry's lap. They weren't exactly comfortable, but it was nice to be close—to be touching.

"Cat, get up for a minute."

"I just sat down."

"I know," Henry said as he gently pushed her off his lap. He took her hand and let her toward the bedroom. "What are you doing?" she asked, half resisting. "It's the middle of the day, and dinner's almost ready"

"Shhhh," he said as he began unbuttoning her dress. "Lie down on your stomach." He gently rubbed her back and back of her legs. "Just relax."

They relaxed together.

Catherine gave the job notion considerable thought, and a few days later—after Henry had settled at the table with his beer and egg concoction after a hard day's work—she pounced.

"Honey, I have a great idea. I'll be your bookkeeper. I can help you out and it will keep me busy. It might take me a little time to learn your system, but I'm sure I can do it."

Hit with a new idea, Henry immediately thought of objections. "I don't know, Cat. It might make you nervous. I know you're smart enough—I just don't want to rock your boat. You've been pretty stable lately."

Catherine was sure it was a good idea for both of them. "Come on, Henry. You can at least give me a chance. If it gets too much for me, I'll quit. I promise."

After a few of his other arguments were knocked away, Henry had to agree it might be just the thing for both of them, and they were both pleased that it was. Catherine was a quick study. She had the payroll and office work organized in no time. She liked knowing about the business, and Henry was greatly relieved to have that side of the operation off his plate.

These were good times for Catherine and Henry. Working together suited them. But while their relationship took on a new intimacy, they were fiercely competitive in their extra-curricular activities. Both were good athletes, and after Henry returned from the war they had become avid bowlers and golfers—their main sources of entertainment.

Henry bowled on Wednesday nights in a men's league with his best friends. Jack was the owner of the Silver Dome Supper Club, Butch was a pharmacist, and Kenny managed a local business. The four men had been friends for years.

Catherine bowled Tuesday nights in a woman's league with her old high school friend Alta, with June, who was Jack's wife and a housewife like Catherine, and with Marion, a local caterer married to Kenny. The women's friendships, too, went back many years.

Henry and Catherine bowled league doubles on Sunday nights during the fall, winter and spring. In the summer they both golfed similar schedules with mostly the same people. Charlie's friend, Ears, would join them occasionally at the small, affordable course just south of town.

One evening, just as they sat down to supper at their big empty kitchen table the phone rang. Henry heard Catherine say, "June, how the heck are you? I haven't seen you for three days." After a long pause she said, "I'll talk to Henry and see how he feels."

"How do I feel about what?" Henry asked as she hung up the phone.

"June ran into Marion and Kenny having supper at the Dome. They're going to Jack and June's when they finish to play some cards and they want us to come."

"Jeez, Cat. It's a workday tomorrow. I was hoping to watch a little TV and go to bed."

"Come on, Honey. We don't have to stay long. We don't even have to play cards. We could have a couple beers and come home."

"Yeah, okay. But I'm not going to rush. I want to eat

my supper in peace." Henry had a big plate of meatloaf, baked potatoes, and fresh corn from their garden.

"I'm going to miss this corn," he said as he chewed down a row of kernels slathered in butter and salt. The butter was dripping down his chin. "Hand me a napkin, would you? The only thing I don't like about corn on the cob is that it's messy."

Henry did not like to have food on his fingers or raspberries seeds in his teeth.

"This will be the last corn from the garden," Catherine announced. "I picked all that was ripe today. I'll can it tomorrow after I get back from the warehouse."

"Yeah. We don't want to waste this stuff. It'll be just as good in November when there's snow on the ground. How about the tomatoes?"

"I canned a bunch of them already. I'll get the rest this week before it freezes. We'll have about twenty quarts by then. Take a look in the fruit cellar. I've put up peaches, pickles, green beans. I still want to make sauerkraut—we have quite a few cabbages out there. The beets can wait."

Catherine cleaned up the dishes and off they went. Finding a parking place at Jack and June's was always a problem, because their home was attached to the Dome. In addition to being a popular place to eat, the facility also housed a dance hall and operated a bowling alley. When they came here for dinner, Catherine always favored the restaurant's crispy fried chicken. As far as she was concerned, the Dome had the best. In addition to being good friends with Jack, Henry favored the Dome because it was one of his best customers.

"It's about time you let loose, you old goat," Jack said as he put his hand on Henry's shoulder. "Kenny and I are kicking the girls' asses. Take your jacket off and get yourself a beer."

"I'd love to get out more, but, Jesus Christ, I'm working all the time. Catherine won't let me slow down. She's a regular slave driver," Henry said with a grin. "Since when are we playing cards in the middle of the week?"

"We're not going to live forever. It's time for us to have some fun. Our kids are gone. Time to party," Jack said.

Henry walked around the table and stood behind Kenny. "How you doing, Mr. Reinke?"

"I'm great. I love to take money from my wife."

"Oh, shut up, mister. Now that Catsy's here, you're going to change your tune. She's always on the winning side." Marion said.

"Let's not get into bullshit about winning," Henry said. "How would you like it, Jack, if your wife bowled a three-hundred game and shot a hole-in-one. She's a ball-breaker."

Henry was only half-joking. When Catherine beat him in golf or bowling, it took some edge off the fun. It happened frequently and caused more than a little friction in the Goodman household. It didn't seem right that a woman should beat a man in these sports, and it made him wonder if he was lacking something. He was a fine athlete, but so was Catherine.

"Get yourself another beer. We'll deal you guys in," Jack said.

"No, go ahead. We're just going to have a couple beers and leave. It's been a long week already and it's not done yet," Henry said.

"Henry, just plant your ass on the nice chair with the soft pillow! You'll feel so contented you'll never want to leave," Jack said.

They all laughed, including Henry. He and Catherine joined the game. They drank beer and played pinochle joyfully until midnight when Henry stood up and invited the whole gang over for breakfast.

"Great idea!" Kenny said. "Let's go! Why the hell not?" They all agreed it was a great idea. For most, the evening of drinking had soaked away some ordinary common sense.

Only Marion was hesitant. "We better be careful driving," she said. "I haven't had a drink, so I could drive everybody."

"What kind of wimps do you think we are? I can drive better drunk than you can sober," Jack said.

They all piled in their cars and followed the leader. Before they sat down at the kitchen table, Henry had a frying pan in each hand. As he raised one over his head and pointed the other at the group, he laughed and proclaimed, "I'm a two-pan man!" This struck everyone as very, very funny.

"Catherine, get over here and help me."

"Are you kidding, Henry Goodman? You made your bed, and now you lie in it." More laughter.

Dry scrambled eggs and overdone bacon arrived at the table and was scarfed down in no time. Six friends who loved each other had another night to remember. Getting up the next morning was not nearly as joyous as the night before.

"Holy shit!" Henry sat slumped at the same kitchen table they had left in a mess only four hours earlier. "This is going to be a rough day," he mumbled as he held his head in his hands. It was.

In February Lilly came home from Madison to celebrate her 24th birthday. Henry grilled his famous T-bone steaks, and Catherine made Lilly's favorite, lemon cake with buttercream frosting. Violet couldn't make it home that weekend, but the rest of the family, including the granddaughters, were there to celebrate. The usual chaos reigned. After the festivities were over, Catherine washed the dishes and Jean, Lilly and Sally dried them and put them away. They all sang hymns while they worked. Sally left briefly to check on the kids playing in the front room and noticed her father was asleep in his chair. When she came back to the kitchen she asked, "Mom, how can Dad sleep through all this chaos?"

"I don't know, Honey. I thought you might find him playing with the kids. Normally he'd be out cleaning up the grill—even shoveling. He's working too hard, I think," Catherine said. "He's just getting a little lazy."

"He doesn't look good to me," Lilly said. "I was surprised when I saw him yesterday. He looks like he's sick. Does he have a cold or something?"

"You really think he looks different than he did at Christmas?" Catherine asked. "I see him every day and I haven't noticed, really. But now that you mention it, he seems more tired. I've been thinking he's working too hard. But then I think he's getting lazy. Remember, we're both getting old."

"Mom, you're only fifty-three, for God's sake," Jean said.

On Sunday night after the girls left, Catherine looked at Henry asleep in his chair, undisturbed by the "The Ed Sullivan Show" blasting out of the TV. She touched his shoulder and his eyes blinked open. He looked up at Catherine almost sheepishly.

"Oh," he shook his head, "I didn't realize I was asleep. I guess I'll go to bed. I'm tired for some reason."

"It's early, Honey—only 7:15."

'It was a busy weekend with all the celebrating. It wore me out."

"Are you feeling okay, Henry? I'm a little worried about you. So are the girls."

"I've been having a little pain in my lower stomach. I've asked Butch about it. He gave me some pills. Maybe I should try taking a couple."

"I'm not sure your pharmacist should be doctoring you. I know he's a good buddy and golfing partner, but he's not a doctor."

"Ah, he knows what he's talking about. He probably knows more." Off he went to bed.

The next morning, as soon as Butch's pharmacy opened, Catherine walked straight to the back of the drugstore where Butch crafted his potions.

"Butch, I'm worried about Henry. The kids were over this weekend and they said Henry looked peaked. I've noticed lately that he doesn't have much pep. Last night he went to bed at 7:30. He said he talked to you about a pain he had in his stomach. You gave him some pills?"

"Boy, I'm glad you're here Catherine. I'm worried, too. Yes, I gave him some pills to ease the pain and begged him to go to the doctor. He's either stubborn or scared, but he has refused to go. He asked me not to tell you," the pharmacist confessed. "He didn't want you to worry. I know he has blood in his urine. I saw it for myself when he peed in the woods when we were golfing. I told him to go see Zeratsky, but he said he didn't need a doctor. He says he's working too hard. I was about to go against his wishes and call you."

"Oh, my God, Butch! I've been thinking all along that he's been working too hard, too. I've even been a little irritated about how much he sits in his chair and doesn't do his regular chores around the house. What's wrong with him?" Catherine's heart was thumping in her chest. It was all sounding like a lot more than just working too hard.

"I don't know. I'm not a doctor, but I do think he's a

sick man. I'm worried about him. He's not taking care of himself."

Catherine knew Butch was right. She had been afraid something was going on, but she didn't want to face it either. She left the drug store and went directly to the doctor's office to make an appointment. She knew Henry's route was in town today. The doctor's secretary said she could squeeze Henry in later that afternoon, and Catherine booked an appointment for 4:30.

Catherine went to the warehouse to do her bookwork hoping she'd get there while Henry was still loading the truck. The huge garage door was open, and Henry's truck was in the garage. She parked and walked in.

"Hi, Cat. I didn't know you were working here today. I'm just about to leave."

"I'm glad I caught you. Like it or not, you have an appointment with Dr. Zeratsky at 4:30 and I insist that you go. You are not yourself and I want to know why."

"Jeeze, Catherine. What did you do that for?"

"Henry, we're not going to debate this. You're going. I will meet you here at four. We're going together."

"Holy shit! You're a ball breaker."

"Yup. Someone's got to knock some sense into your head."

Catherine was playing the tough guy, but she was scared to death. She knew she couldn't live without Henry. She prayed the doctor could fix him.

Henry was waiting for her in the office at the warehouse at four. He looked uncomfortable. He didn't like doctors, but he was worried, too. He was finally admitting to himself that something was wrong.

Catherine stayed in the waiting room while Henry was

being examined. After what seemed like hours Dr. Zeratsky called her in.

"I've examined Henry. I can feel what I think is a tumor in the area of his bladder. We don't have the equipment in the office or the hospital here to do the kind of exam he needs. He has blood in his urine, and his red count is low. I am referring him to Dr. Renes, a proctologist in Green Bay. I've already called his office and set up an appointment for Friday."

"Friday? I can't get away that soon," Henry said.

"Yes, you can, Henry," Catherine said. "I can change your routes around and get Kevin to help Woody. That's why we hired Kevin."

They made the trip to Green Bay in silence. Henry fretted a bit about the business being operated without him, and Catherine could only pray that the specialist would not have much more to say than what Dr. Zeratsky had told them. A tumor. Take it out. Rest a bit, and life would go on.

Catherine went through another long wait. Finally, after a series of tests and examinations were completed, Dr. Renes told Catherine what he had just told her husband. Henry had advanced bladder cancer and it had spread to other parts of his body.

Life at home became solemn. No one in the family, including Henry, ever spoke the word cancer aloud. It's was always, "Dad's condition" or "Henry's medical problem." Radiation treatments were prescribed, and they all clung to the wish and hope that this would cure him. No one was willing to accept the fact that this vigorous, ambitious, fifty-three-year-old man would die. They fought with all their resolve against the common wisdom that cancer was a death sentence.

For the next four weeks Henry insisted on driving himself to Green Bay for the treatments. Whoever accompanied him would then drive home. Back home, Henry would doze off in his chair. His friends—he had many—would visit and sit and talk with him even when he dozed. Catherine hoped and prayed it was the treatments that made him so tired.

Two weeks after the radiation treatments were finished, Henry was very weak. Catherine went with him to Green Bay to see if the doctor might prescribe another kind of medicine or a miracle. Henry insisted on driving. Jean was at the house with her two little girls to see them off. She gave him a big hug and as he climbed behind the wheel she told him she loved him. It was the first time in her life she had ever said those words to her father. He returned her love for the first time in his life. It was the last hug she would ever be able to give him.

After a short examination, Dr. Renes sent Henry to Bellin Hospital. Here, he would spend the last week of his life.

Six weeks after the initial cancer diagnosis Henry Goodman took his last breath. Jean and Violet had spent the night in the hospital with him, holding his hands, putting water on his lips and into his mouth with a moistened Q-tip.

"Violet and Jean are here with you Dad. We love you so much," Jean said. Her father offered no response.

Dad," Violet said, "You're the best dad in the whole world. We love all you do for us."

The nurse told them Henry could hear what they were saying. They didn't know if it was true, but they hoped it was. They sat tearfully with their father, trying to show their love every way they could—touching, kissing, hugging, whispering . . .

Catherine, Lilly and Sally were asleep in a small hotel across the street from the hospital.

When Violet called to tell them that Henry's breathing was getter softer and shallower, they dressed immediately and were in the room in minutes.

Henry's wife and four daughters were at his bedside as he drew his last breath. They sat in silence as nurses placed Henry's inert body on a gurney and covered him completely with a white sheet. They followed the gurney to the hallway and watched as it was wheeled down the hall away from them, making a left turn and disappearing from sight.

With Lilly at the wheel, Catherine and her daughters made the drive from the Green Bay hospital back to Marinette in shocked silence. Only a few words were mumbled.

"He seemed to be at peace," one said.

"I don't think he was in pain," another said.

Each was trying to accept the reality of Henry's death, because it had only been a few weeks earlier that they had convinced themselves that the radiation treatments would save him. His death came too quickly for anyone to mentally prepare for it.

Catherine was numb. Henry was gone. He was her rock, her stability, her alter ego. Tonight would be terrible and tomorrow did not bear thinking about. She didn't think she could put one foot in front of the other without Henry. She quietly shared the front seat with Lilly, occasional sobs shaking her body on the hour-long drive.

As they reached the outskirts of Marinette, Lilly asked gently if her mother felt like stopping at the funeral home to start making arrangements for the funeral. "It's Tuesday already—do we want to go into the weekend?"

Catherine bolted upright. "Did you say it was Tuesday? Oh my God! I'm supposed to be working at the polls today. I wonder if they got someone to take my place. We can't go to the funeral home! We have to stop at Park School so I can vote at least! I never even told them I wouldn't be there to work!"

Has my mother lost her mind? Lilly wondered. Only moments before, Catherine was sitting as though catatonic, and now seemed to be charged with an irrational energy. Lilly's private thoughts had been focused on the challenge of getting her mother into the house, and now the grieving woman was insisting on voting! Did she even know who was running?

Jean chimed in. "Mom, you don't need to vote today. It won't hurt to miss voting once. I think it's only a primary anyway."

Catherine's grief changed into a snarling anger. "Oh, little miss who thinks she knows everything! I am going to vote!" She turned and looked at her three daughters in the back seat. "And, just for your information, I am going to take over the business, too! I want you all to know, I am not a weakling! I'll show you just how strong your mother is!"

She turned back to Lilly. "Drive this car to Park School! I'm voting! And anyone who doesn't agree with me, just put that in your pipe and smoke it!"

At the school Sally got out of the car to assist her mother in case she needed help, but Catherine shrugged her off and marched into the school as if she were one of the candidates casting a key vote for herself.

As they waited in the car, Catherine's daughters tried to find words to make sense of her sudden change. "Wow," Jean muttered. "She must be in some serious shock. She needs to go home. Maybe we can get some food into her. Maybe we can fix her a whiskey chaser or two so she can calm down . . ."

Lilly, who had the second most years with her mother, admitted that her mother had an intense stubborn streak, one that had gotten her through many challenges. "I think we'd maybe better to let her do what she wants. She'll win anyway and just resent anyone who gets in her way."

On the drive home no one said a word about the sudden detour to the school.

Catherine was true to her word, and she dutifully went to Henry's office at the warehouse every day for next couple of years. In the prior twenty years Henry had turned a fledgling beer business operating out of his father's backyard beer shed into a profitable enterprise. That growth included a huge warehouse next to the Chicago & North Western depot, because Henry's beer deliveries now came by train. Along with their personal debts, all company debts were paid, and the distribution business was turning a good profit. Catherine was determined, for Henry's sake, to keep the business thriving.

She had learned to do the bookwork quickly, and she was confident that she would be able to run all sides of the business. Sadly, however, little by little she and the business started collapsing together. One fateful day, a Budweiser management team from St. Louis paid the Marinette business a visit. Their stern message was that her sales were slipping, while at the same time Budweiser sales around the country were hitting new peaks. The company had always respected Henry's success, but if the local distributorship was going to carry the Budweiser product, it had to be turned around—and fast.

It did not end well . . .

Chapter 26. Nonny (1973-1994)

Catherine's daughters and her growing family of grandchildren, despite frequent and joyful visits to the familiar home at the west end of Carney Avenue, failed to see the signs leading to her breakdown. It would be one of their most difficult crises.

Catherine was fifty-three years old when Henry died. Even though she had a full arc of life left, she couldn't think about the future. It was hard enough getting by hour to hour, day to day. She yearned to be strong, but yearning was not enough. The Goodman Beer Distributing Company that Henry had built from the ground up was hers now. Catherine Goodman, the girl from Menekaunee, was the sole owner of a thriving business. She didn't want her daughters to know that her head was spinning, her heart was broken, and getting up in the morning to face another day took enormous effort.

She took over with the assumption that, having done the bookwork for the business for the last couple years, she could just round that out with any extra tasks that needed to be done. She soon found out how very wrong that assumption was. Paying the bills, managing Woody and the other drivers, keeping customers happy, communicating with Budweiser headquarters, maintaining vehicles and the warehouse, and many other tasks made for a heavy load. Henry had done so much that she, sitting at a desk, opening mail and logging receipts and bills, had never seen or thought about. Until the last two weeks of his life he was still running the business.

Catherine told herself she just needed time—she would give herself time—to learn the ropes. She was determined to do this for Henry and the family.

Her grandchildren were her refuge. Jean and Sally now both lived in Marinette with their husbands and four daughters between them. The little girls loved their Nonny, and Jean and Sally made sure they brought them over often. Jean's daughter Jenny was the oldest of the four, and it was she who gave Catherine her name when she couldn't say grandma. It stuck.

One evening after a grueling day at the warehouse, Catherine was sitting in the living room in Henry's old swivel chair when she spotted Jean's car pulling into the driveway. Before she could even get up a four-year-old towhead was jumping into her lap.

"Nonny! Nonny!" Jenny threw her arms around her grandmother and gave her a big kiss. "Look what Mommy let me buy at Ingy's!" She pulled a red Blow Pop out of her pocket.

"Oh, my word!" Nonny said. "That looks so good and I'm so hungry! Are you going to share that with me?"

This was an old joke. The first time Catherine had done this, the little girl guessed that her grandmother had misunderstood the offer. With a frown she pulled the lollipop back to her chest and covered it with her free hand. Jenny had made it clear this was for showing, not sharing.

This time Catherine was offered the candy. "Yes, but just one lick," Jenny said. Catherine laughed.

At the same time, two-year-old Angie stood on Nonny's feet, arms outstretched, looking for assistance to join her sister in her grandmother's lap. She might not have been sure of her words, but she let it be known in no uncertain turns she wanted up. Nonny always had room for more than one on her lap at a time. Angie made a grab for Jenny's Blow Pop, Jenny pushed her away, Angie started crying, it was a lap-full of free-for-all. But their grandmother just smiled and in no time had all three of them laughing.

Jean sat for a few minutes, absorbing the way her mother settled the rowdy pair of girls, then asked. "How's everything at the warehouse?" Despite her mother's smile, she looked pale and tired.

"It's the same. Hard. But we're still in business." She waved her daughter off. "I don't want to talk about that place. I just—" as she bounced the girls up and down on her knees— "want . . . to . . . enjoy . . . these . . . *kids!*"

Jean bided her time. She was concerned. She knew as she had watched her mother over the past year that Catherine was not enjoying her position as CEO of the Goodman business. She broke in on the Nonny games again. "Are you sure you want to keep doing it?"

Catherine was aware of her daughter's concern, but she saw no alternative. "Who else is going to run it? I can't just let it go. Do you and your sisters want to take over? I'd be *thrilled* to turn it over to you. You know as well as I do that your father would want us to keep it going."

Jean frowned. She was not relishing living back in Marinette after some wonderful years in Madison. *The last thing I would want is to be stuck here running a beer business*, she thought. To her mother she said, "It's not something for me. I want to teach. But maybe Lilly, Sally or Violet would want it."

"Maybe I should ask them," her mother said. Jean could see that this was all talk, that Catherine really believed this was her own responsibility. More conversation was not going to go anywhere.

"Danny's golfing tonight, so I thought you might like company for dinner," Jean said. "The girls always love to come over here, and it's no fun for me to cook for just the three of us."

"Hey, tell me about it," Catherine replied with fervor. "I have no gumption after I get done with a full day's work to cook a meal, especially just for myself. But Jeannie—Jean—to tell you the truth, I don't have a damn thing to feed you. I'm old Mother Hubbard, and the cupboards are bare."

"Well, this is your lucky day then, Mother dear! I stopped at Ingy's and bought a chicken. I was thinking we could cut it up and deep-fry it."

"Yeah, I'd like that, and it just so happens I have fresh Crisco in the Fry Baby."

The granddaughters were unloaded from Catherine's lap to find the toys and dolls that Catherine kept in a trunk, and the women shifted to the kitchen. As she settled into a chair, Catherine studied her daughter. "Do you know what you're doing?" She got up and took a cast iron kettle out of her pantry. She handed the kettle to Jean, saying, "You know you can't throw the chicken right into the fryer, right? You have to parboil it first."

Jean bristled a little. *I know how to fry a chicken.* Did her mother think she never cooked, had not helped prepare meals her whole life? *She treats me like a kid.* "Oh, thanks for the kettle, Mom." She would coddle her mother, not argue her case.

Continuing to dig out the utensils that she knew Jean would need, Catherine added, "I still have some potatoes from the garden. We could mash them. Angie could eat those."

After Henry died, Catherine had given up her social life.

The couples she and Henry had hung out with often asked her to join them when they got together, but she always refused. She felt like a fifth wheel. Eventually they stopped calling and she was glad. She got called for a few dates, but she always refused. Her life consisted of her family, the business, and her garden.

So it was especially wonderful for her when her daughters and granddaughters were around. She could put any problems from the warehouse or with Budweiser out of her mind. This was most important. There was something so real and solid about family, and she felt her best when she could be with those babies.

Over the next two years Catherine plodded along as CEO and CFO of Goodman Beer Distributing Company. She knew in her heart she was not doing right by the business. Every week seemed to bring some sudden problem she had not encountered before, often needing immediate response. A proper solution called for all the experience Henry had acquired as he built this business, and the staff was of limited help. Catherine felt overwhelmed and very alone in making the decisions that would resolve this never-ending onslaught of little crises. A particular problem in-house, Henry's brother Woody was still drinking on the job, and she wasn't strong enough to stand up to him.

At the other end of the business chain, the Budweiser mucky-mucks were asking why sales weren't increasing in her distributorship when Budweiser was becoming the best-selling beer in the country. They were skeptical of her abilities and she knew it. Being a woman didn't help either. Catherine had lived so many years with a spouse who had thrown himself day and night, seven days a week, into making this business successful, and it was her mission to save it. She often sat at her desk, having no idea which way to turn, whom to speak with, how to fix this or that, how to respond to this customer or that one. And always, a key thought that underlay every decision was that she was not going to tell her daughters how desperate she was.

They soon found out.

Violet had recently graduated from UW Madison with a bachelor's degree in nursing and had moved back to Marinette with her fiancé. Her phone rang at 8 a.m. one Tuesday morning. "Hello," she said in her normal greeting voice. All she could hear was a weak voice speaking incoherently.

"Hello!" she said again, a little more urgently. Was this some kind of crank call? "Who is this?" The voice on the other end was gasping for breath, sobbing. The voice said, "Come!" and she suddenly recognized her mother's voice. She hung up the phone and raced to her car.

When Violet got to her mother's house, she found the woman lying naked in a pool of blood in the hallway, right below the phone cubby-hole. Violet quickly made tourniquets out of cotton dishcloths, wrapped her mother's wrists, checked for vital signs, and called for an ambulance. While she waited for the ambulance to arrive, she got a pillow for her mother's head and, struggling as best she could with her mother's inert body, she got a sheet partly wrapped around her. She followed the trail of blood back to a bathtub filled with bloody water. She drained the tub, rinsed it as best she could, wiped up blood on the floor, and lay down next to her mother to keep her warm.

Violet rode with her mother in the ambulance to Marinette General Hospital, holding her mother's hand and praying she would live. She wasn't sure how much blood her mother had lost, but it seemed to have been considerable. Catherine remained unconscious for the entire trip.

As soon as Catherine was wheeled away from the emergency entrance, Violet called her sisters to give them the dreadful news. Lilly, who lived in Madison, said she'd leave for Marinette immediately. Sally dropped her kids with a friend and rushed to the hospital. Jean immediately left the local school where she was teaching. They sat in the waiting room for what felt like an eternity before the nurse came out.

"Your mother is going to live." They breathed a collective sigh of relief.

"Can we take her home?" Sally asked.

"The doctor will be out with a full report as soon as he can get to you. In the meantime, you might want to go to the cafeteria for coffee or breakfast. It could take a while."

They walked to the cafeteria. Jean was impatient. "I can't figure out why this has to take so long. I want to see her. Violet, you're a nurse here. Don't you have some pull?"

"Jean, I started my job three weeks ago. No, I have no pull. The doctor might be taking care of other patients. If she's not critical they might be having her rest—I don't know. Maybe they have her sedated. You're the one who makes things happen. Why don't you find out?" The crisis was putting them all on edge.

"I'm sorry, you two," Sally confessed. "Maybe I'll feel better if I walk around. I'm so scared."

They were together back in the waiting room an hour later when the doctor came in. He grabbed a chair near the door and plopped it down so that he could face the three daughters. He looked straight at Violet. "You look familiar to me. Why is that?"

"I'm a nurse here, but I just started. Violet Goodman," she said somewhat self- consciously.

"I'm Dr. Boren. Nice to meet you." He extended his

hand. "Who's your family doctor?"

"My mother sees Dr. Koepp."

"Well, I won't make a final decision before I talk to Dr. Koepp. But here's what I think. Someone who wants to take her own life must be very sick—depressed, desolate. One of you found her, correct?"

Violet acknowledged that she had found her mother.

"It was very important that she was found in time," the doctor said to Violet. "Do you live with your mother?"

"No, but she called, and her voice was garbled. I flew over there, found her lying in the hallway, wrapped her wrists and called."

"You did a professional job of first aid, young lady, and you saved your mother's life. You will be a good nurse." Then, to the three daughters, "She must have changed her mind about dying, and that's why she called. Do any of you know why she might want to die?"

The women shook their heads.

"Has she ever tried anything like this before?"

Jean quickly looked at Sally but got no answering look. *She must have been too young,* Jean thought. Jean knew that Lilly— on her way from Madison—would certainly remember that night, so many years ago, when they had huddled together fearfully and then were shipped off to their aunt and uncle's home. But the message then had been that this was just an accident. No way to say for certain she had tried to kill herself. Best not to mention that event with the pills.

"Nothing that we know of," Jean said.

The doctor continued, trying to soothe the family. "I know this is a painful experience you're all going through, but your mother needs professional help right now. I'm going to recommend that she be taken to Bellin Hospital in Green Bay to spend some time in the psychiatric ward. The staff is great. The nurses and doctors there will be able to help her. If Dr. Koepp agrees, we'll see if they have a spot for her. She's medicated and resting comfortably. You all go home and wait until Dr. Koepp contacts you. Whom should he call?"

Violet nodded and raised her hand, said she would be at her mother's home, and then asked, "How long will she have to stay there?"

The doctor paused. "That's not my area of expertise." He could sense the daughters' uncertainty about their mother's future, but he would not have known that they all were recalling the tales of their grandmother's confinement in "the asylum." He offered his best reassurance.

"Violet, ladies, the team there is extremely professional, and they will first make sure she has the physical strength to leave. They will also have regular sessions with her to see how willing she may be to share what was in her mind when she took this act. They are not going to keep her against her will. They will just try to help."

Shaken and distraught but somewhat reassured, the three daughters went back to Catherine's to finish the cleanup and to wait for Dr. Koepp's call. It came just as Lilly arrived. Yes, there was a bed available for Catherine in the psychiatric ward at Bellin. She was awake, but groggy, the doctor said. He asked if they wanted to drive her to Green Bay or send her in an ambulance. After a brief conference, it was agreed that Jean and Sally had kids and jobs to tend to, and that Lilly would drive with Violet, following an ambulance to Bellin. The doctor said that Catherine was to have no visitors for at least a week. He gave them a number they could call once a day to check on her progress.

When Dr. Keopp agreed Catherine was ready to be

moved, the caravan of ambulance and two daughters set out in the morning. When Lilly and Violet returned from Green Bay in the late afternoon, they said they had had a chance to accompany their mother to her room. She seemed to be calm but was heavily medicated, Violet said.

The nurse had informed them Catherine would have individual therapy with a social worker every day, a psychiatrist once a week, and group therapy daily. Crafts were available around the clock, but, as per Dr. Koepp's directive, there would be no visitors for at least a week. They were asked to call ahead to see if their mother was ready for visitors during any regular visitor hours. The doctors would determine her course of medication, and it was important that someone in the family keep Catherine to her schedule.

A week later—as the doctor had predicted—she was not ready for visitors, but by the end of the second week she welcomed their visits, if only for a short time. She knew she needed to keep calm, and the medication helped. Catherine confessed to attending nurses that she regretted trying to kill herself. When she thought of her grandchildren, she realized what a grave mistake she had made.

Catherine spent six weeks in the psychiatric unit at Bellin. By the time she got home she was—with the help of an open prescription for Ativan—her own best self. The hospital stay was pivotal in helping Catherine to realize that she either must get help running the business or she must sell it. The details of the sale were hard to set in place, and then it was done. Henry's business was someone else's business, not hers. She would to her last days be nagged by the thought that she might have done more, but at this moment her days were filled with loving family. Regrets, later—relief, now.

Christmas Eve 1979 turned out to be a jolly time for

the family. While Henry's absence was still profound, Catherine was in her glory. The house was resplendent with Christmas trimmings. The artificial tree placed in the middle of the bay window was adorned with a multitude of colored lights, homemade ornaments from the grandchildren, favorite ornaments she had collected over the years, and finished off with many strands of tinsel on every branch. A sprig of mistletoe hung in the doorway between the kitchen and living room, and electric candles glowed in every window.

From Henry's swivel chair Catherine could survey every corner of the long narrow living room without turning her head. It thrilled her that all her daughters, spouses of the married daughters and her seven grandchildren were all there. Her brother Charlie had retired from the lake carriers and was living back in Marinette full time. He had sold his home after his wife and sister-in-law had died and rented a house close to Catherine. Relatives were delighted when he showed up for the holidays.

There were bodies everywhere—in the chairs, on the couch and covering the floor.

Opening shared presents offered a chaos of ripping papers, shouts of excitement, and a growing collection of debris. Not a single bit of beige carpet could be seen under the piles of red and green torn and crinkled wrapping, new toys, clothes, and people.

On the end table next to Catherine's chair was her traditional glass of crème de menthe on chipped ice. With the weight of the business off her shoulders and the extra time to prepare a Christmas feast, she felt she was the author of this celebration of daughters and granddaughters. Jean, while keeping a celebratory eye on her own daughters' excitement, kept another eye across the room on her mother's drinking.

After all the presents were opened and as the mothers worked to sort packaging and paper from the actual gifts that had been opened, Catherine raised her glass. "I hope to hell you all had a great Christmas," she yelled.

She started to rise from her chair, but Violet quickly came over to her. "Mom, settle down. We're not done."

Not done? There was nothing under the tree that had not been opened, but she nodded, sipped her drink, and settled back, wondering what was in the works.

Violet left the room, went to the garage, and came back with what turned out to be the finest present of all—a yellow Labrador Retriever.

Catherine didn't know what to think. A puppy? Why would she want a puppy? She accepted the soft, warm gift on her lap and then—suddenly!—she flew back forty-two years to the memory of Nels, her brother-in-law, bringing Pepper into her life just when she needed that quiet and loving companionship most dearly.

She began to cry, and her daughters suddenly felt they had made a terrible mistake. Why would they think their mom wanted a dog? They watched as the squirming little dog looked at Catherine, stretched his neck, and licked her face. What kind of bonding goes through a dog and his loving owner? It was instantaneous, and her kisses returned his.

"Thank you! Thank you! Thank you!" Catherine said as she cuddled the puppy to her breast.

The daughters were relieved and thrilled to the sight of their mother with the puppy.

Sally asked, "Mom, what are you going to name your buddy all curled up in your lap?"

"Sally, you just named him," Catherine said." He was "Buddy" from that moment on.

By the end of the week the company had left, and reality was setting in. It was good to have Buddy in the house, and Catherine was attentive to his training, but she was starting to feel a little anxious. Fortunately, she had her Ativan, the prescribed drug that lessened her anxiety. It had gotten her through the last couple years. She had recently upped her dosage with the doctor's permission. He had given her a wink-wink for an open prescription.

One February weekend in 1979 Jean came up from Madison—as she now did every weekend—to be with her two daughters. She had gone back to the University of Wisconsin to work on her doctorate, and the children were living with their father, Dan, who had stayed in Marinette. As per her weekend visit routine, Jean had picked up Jenny and Angie and brought them to stay with her at Catherine's.

After the girls were settled in with the toys and dolls that Catherine kept in the house, mother and daughter sat down in the living room. Jean asked Catherine about an Ann Landers column, titled "Take Care of Your Mothers," that she had seen taped inside a cupboard door.

"I was surprised to see that column. What's that all about? Are you feeling that way?" Jean was worried that her mother might be slipping into depression again. She stood up, walked behind Catherine, and rubbed her shoulders.

Catherine took a big breath and sighed. "Oh, it's nothing," she said.

"It's something, Mom. What's going on?"

"Well, the days get pretty long when I'm here alone all the time. I get kind of blue."

This puzzled Jean. "Aren't you still going out with Mary on Friday nights?"

Mary was a companion, a retired high school gym

teacher, whom Catherine had met years before on the Little River golf course. They had played together a few times, but Catherine had pretty much given up the game. Their connection continued through fish fry outings and shared notes on their respective gardens.

"Well, yeah, we still go out, but I see her for only a couple of hours. She's getting on my nerves anyway. She's so damn cheap," Catherine said.

"How does her being cheap affect you?" Jean asked.

"Okay, here's an example. Last summer she weighed everything she picked from her garden. She lets all her vegetables get so big you can hardly chew them. They're tough. What's wrong with a nice young tender carrot? I don't get it." She looked at Jean and shook her head.

"And here's another thing." She went on. "Every Friday we order the same damn fish fry at Dory's and our check is always the same. Fifteen-ninety-seven. When we split the bill, she insists that one week she pays the extra penny and the next week I do. It drives me nuts! How can anyone be that damn cheap?"

Catherine sat back in her swivel chair and glanced out the window. "I'm tired of her, anyway. The only thing that keeps me going is Buddy." He was cuddled on her lap as she gently stroked the underside of his chin.

"Maybe you need to go on another trip," Jean suggested. "You and Sally had a blast when you went to Hawaii. We were all so surprised when you went. We didn't think you liked to travel, but we were wrong."

"No, you were right. I hate to travel. I just went for Sally's sake. She was having a hard time trying to raise those kids by herself after Tom died in that terrible fire. Those poor kids are going to grow up without a father."

Hmmm. She doesn't seem to remember that she was the one that urged Sally to go on the trip. While she was still in town, Jean had tried to track her mother's ups and downs. The idea for that trip must have popped up in one of the manic phases, Jean thought.

"Well, I know you had a good time. You couldn't stop talking about how much fun the two of you had. It was nice you could do it for Sally, but you had fun, too."

Catherine didn't want to talk about her trip. She had something else on her mind. "I'm not exactly happy that you're divorcing that wonderful husband of yours, you know. How do you think that makes me feel?" She wagged her index finger at her daughter. "You'll never find a man like him again. It breaks my heart that you are going off to get some kind of a hoity-toity education and leaving your kids."

"I know that's hard for you to understand and I'm sorry it's painful for you, but I will be with them every weekend, summers and holidays and they will be back with me in two years. In fact, I hope you'll let us stay with you when I come to Marinette." Jean looked at her mother for approval. None came. She was a little shaken herself, because she felt terrible leaving the kids behind.

"Mom, Danny and I have it worked out so the kids will be fine. It hurts me, too, but I'm trying to take care of myself and the kids. I have wanted to be a college professor all my life and this is the only way I can do it."

"You are so *selfish!* What about those poor kids without their mother? Do you know how this hurts me? I would never, *ever* have done anything like that to you or your sisters. I still don't know how to explain this to Clara and Stella. I wish the kids could live with me. I hate being alone."

Wait till she finds out that Lilly is getting a divorce, too, Jean thought.

It wasn't long after Jean's visit that Catherine went into another deep depression. She stopped eating and sleeping. She sat in her swivel chair in the living room rocking all day and sometimes through the night. In her own dark world, the image never came to her that her behavior mirrored that of her mother so many years before.

Catherine's doctor admitted her again to the psych ward in Bellin hospital where she was treated for four weeks.

When Jean picked up Catherine, an attending nurse warned her that her mother was "riding high" on the manic side of her mood swings. The net effect on Jean of her mother's racing thoughts and buoyant mood was that the trip back to Marinette—normally a one-hour drive—would take the entire day.

As they pulled away from Bellin, Catherine's first request was to go to a swimming pool dealer. "Where's a good place to buy a swimming pool, Jean?"

Jean wasn't sure she had heard her mother correctly. "What? Did you say swimming pool?"

"Oh, yes, I certainly did!" Catherine said gleefully. "I have a whole back yard that's practically empty. I can take down the clothes lines and have a perfect place for a pool."

Jean was trying to gauge how serious her mother was being. "Are you planning on doing a lot of swimming?"

"Yup. It will be good exercise. My hip is giving me some problems. The doc said swimming would be good for me. He suggested I go to the Y, but that's silly if I can swim in my own back yard."

"Pools are expensive, Mom." *I wonder how she thinks she's going to pay for it.*

"Hey! Loosen up! What the hell—I can't take it with me. Let's live a little, for God's sake! Jean, you've always been a wet blanket. Get over it!" She poked her daughter in the ribs and hooted in laughter.

Jean reeled a bit from the "wet blanket" accusation. *Okay, if that's what she wants.* "Let's do it! But I don't know where to buy a pool." She glanced around as she drove, as though they might be passing a pool shop at that moment.

"Stop at that gas station right there!" Catherine pointed to a Shell station across the street.

Jean looked down at the gas gauge. "Mom, we don't need gas. The tank is almost full."

"I know that, you goofball! We can ask there where we can buy a pool." In her mind's eye she already saw her grandchildren jumping and splashing. "You might like it, too, if you loosen up a little." She was having a grand time hectoring her daughter.

"You're in rare form, Mother" Jean said. She might be the butt of her mother's teasing today, but she had to admit her mother's gleeful behavior was almost contagious. *This is going to be quite the ride home,* she thought. Little did she know what was to come next.

The store to which they were directed turned out to be one of the best in the area.

Catherine didn't simply buy a pool. She bought a large in-the-ground pool with a slide. Jim, the salesman assigned to her, seemed to pick up on her exuberance, and he nodded agreeably when she said the wanted the best pool they had. He laughed with her a little bit when she said that her husband, if he were still alive, would hate this idea. His smile was more forced when she confided, with a genuine grin, "He can't do much about it now, can he? He's six feet under."

The sale complete, the installation schedule set, Catherine turned to Jim at the door. "Where would you go to buy luggage? I plan on doing some traveling and my suitcase is in bad shape."

Uh-oh, Jean thought. *Where is this going?* She wondered if she ought to ask for a phone to call one of her sisters, but Catherine was already headed for the car. Jim had claimed no expertise in luggage sales but thought that H.C. Prange's would probably have what the woman wanted.

Jean didn't want to be the day's "wet blanket," and she dutifully drove her mother downtown to Prange's. Catherine's choices were made quickly, and they were ready to leave with a full set of luggage, which included a special case for Catherine's cosmetics.

"Where do you plan to go, Mom?" Jean asked, as they rolled their selections to a freight elevator. She recalled a conversation some months earlier when her mother had stated adamantly that she really didn't like to travel.

"Maybe I'll go back to Hawaii. I liked it there. You wanna go with me?"

Jean didn't answer. She was wondering if she was letting too much happen too fast.

Catherine halted. "Say, as long as we're here," she said, passing the linens' department, "I need some new sheets. Buddy has pretty much ruined mine. Did you know he likes jellybeans in the middle of the night? I keep a dish of them on my bed stand so when he asks, I have them right there."

How does he ask? Jean wondered. "Does he bark?"

"No, silly! He puts his paw on my arm and wakes me up."

In addition to the luggage they left Prange's with three sets of sheets and pillowcases. In the car on the way back to Marinette she told Jean she needed a new car and today was the day to buy one.

"I'm too tired to look for a car today, Mom. Could we save that for another day? I need to get home to the kids. Sally's had them all day."

"See, there you go again, being a wet blanket!" Catherine settled back in the passenger seat. "I think I'd like a baby blue Chevy."

They didn't buy a car that day, but they did stop at Sequin's House of Cheese, where Catherine bought moccasins for all the grandchildren and a huge bag of assorted cheeses.

Catherine's bout of mania went on for several weeks. One night when Jean and Lilly were visiting with their kids, Catherine took the whole family to the Elks Club. Holding high above her head her favorite brandy old fashioned glass that she had brought from home, she led the charge through the back door into the bar. "Fill 'er up!" she shouted. Everyone, including the bartenders, laughed. They loved her.

Jean, still the "wet blanket," cringed.

As crazy as the idea had seemed to Catherine's daughters when she bought the pool, it turned out to be a godsend. The grandkids loved it. From Memorial Day to Labor Day the pool had swimmers, and Nonny had company. Violet's sons Adam and Barry would ride their bikes to the pool, or Violet would bring them herself and stay and visit with Catherine.

Occasionally Catherine would swim, but most of the time she sat in a lawn chair and watched the kids. When they had enough swimming, they'd come inside, where there were no rules for grandchildren. They'd eat snacks that were forbidden at home, watch TV any time of day, run through the house dripping wet to go to the bathroom, or just hang out with their grandmother. All eight of her grandchildren knew she loved them unconditionally. They could do no wrong in

Catherine's eyes. When they were little, they'd love to cuddle with her as they sat on her lap and used her "booby" as a pillow.

Catherine made it crystal clear to Jean, Lilly, Sally and Violet that she made the rules for the kids when they were at her house, which meant they had *no* rules. Nothing was off-limits as long as it was safe.

Thanksgiving was approaching and Catherine was getting anxious. Anxiety had been her constant nemesis. Ativan helped, but anxiety, like an unseen predator, still lurked. When it got bad enough, she knew that depression could be close behind. Thinking of having the whole family at her house was giving her more pause than usual this year.

The phone rang during a Packers game. Catherine considered not answering it, but she thought it might be one of her daughters. She didn't want to miss a call from one of them.

"Hi, Lilly," she said. "I'm watching the Packers right now. They're behind 14-7. I'm a nervous wreck." When Lilly asked if she should call later, she said, "Yeah, I want to talk to you, but Lynn Dickey is having trouble and I need to keep an eye on him."

When Lilly called back Catherine immediately asked, "Are you and the kids coming for Thanksgiving?"

"Yes, the kids are chomping at the bit. Every day they ask me, 'How many days now 'til we go to Nonny's?'"

"Is John coming too?"

"Mom, you know we're getting a divorce. No, he's not coming."

"How about Jean? Did she say Danny was coming?"

"I don't know about Jean. She's so busy with school and work that I hardly ever see her. You know she and Danny aren't living together. Call her."

"I see Danny a few times a week. He's down in the mouth. He comes over at noon and watches the soaps with me. Y'know, Lilly? He's a wonderful man. He takes care of those kids all on his own. I don't know what she's thinking. Those poor kids living without their mother . . ."

"She sees them every weekend, Mom. She'll have them at Thanksgiving and Christmas," Lilly said. "We'll all be at your house for Thanksgiving. What can I bring?"

"Your husband!" Catherine snapped.

Lilly with her two girls and Jean with her two girls arrived at Catherine's about the same time. It wasn't long before Sally and Violet marched in with their kids. Catherine was surrounded by the people she cared most about in the whole world. For supper she had made a huge pot of vegetable-beet soup and homemade Parker House rolls for supper. She made her delicious apple slices for dessert.

"Nonny, you made my favorite soup for supper. I love it," Angie said. "You're a good cooker." Others echoed the girl's praise.

There weren't any leftovers. When she put a pan of apple slices in the middle of the table, everyone except Catherine dug in with their forks. Henry would not have approved, Catherine thought. As she got the vanilla ice cream out of the freezer, Buddy was tight on her heels. He was used to getting ice cream for dessert. Buddy and Catherine ate supper together every night— a forkful for Catherine, a forkful for Buddy from the same fork. He'd sit on the floor next to her place at the table waiting for his turn. When they were done, he walked over to the refrigerator to wait for Catherine to get the ice cream out. He weighed 117 now. She passed plates of ice cream around. Only a few crumbs were left in the pan after they were all finished.

Thanksgiving morning was chaotic. Catherine was anxious. Dinner was at noon and it was ten o'clock when she realized she had forgotten to buy whipped cream.

"I'm running out to get whipped cream. Come on, Buddy," Catherine yelled. This was a good excuse to get out of the house and away from the commotion.

Lilly and her oldest daughter announced they wanted to come along. Catherine wasn't happy about it. She wanted to get away, but she held her tongue. Buddy was in the passenger seat as usual. Lilly opened the passenger door to get in and tried to chase Buddy into the back seat.

"Oh, no, you don't!" Catherine cautioned her daughter. "That's Buddy's place. Get in back."

Really? Lilly thought, but dutifully complied.

Buddy sat tall in the passenger seat, scanning the road for other vehicles. Spotting one, he would bark ferociously.

"Mom, please get him to stop," Lilly begged.

"If you don't like Buddy's barking, don't get in my car. He's protecting me."

Lilly was stunned. "Really, Mom? You put Buddy ahead of me?"

"Why wouldn't I?" Catherine said casually. "*He* is with me all the time. *You* are only here once in a while." She enjoyed getting in that little dig on a daughter who had left town.

As they walked into the house, the wonderful smells of roasting turkey filled their nostrils. Lilly had realized how easy it was to wind up on thin ice with their mother, and she warned her sisters to handle Catherine delicately. The rest of meal preparation and presentation continued without incident, however, and at twelve sharp platters and bowls heaped with sliced turkey, mashed potatoes, thick brown gravy, homemade dinner rolls, cranberries, and squash filled the table.

The adults sat at the kitchen table with the white tablecloth and cloth napkins they used on special occasions. The eight grandchildren sat in the living room at two card tables covered with festive plastic cloths. Their mothers had fixed their plates and arranged their places to minimize any possible damage.

The adults passed the food around the table in no particular order.

"Hey, Jean, pass the turkey down here."

"Wait, don't pass it yet. I didn't get any."

"Don't hog the gravy on your end of the table."

Catherine, in her usual manner, didn't sit down until she was sure everyone had what they needed.

"Mom, this is the most delicious turkey you're ever made," Violet said. Catherine, exhausted after making this luscious dinner, basked in the praise. As they had for many years, Catherine and the girls did the dishes together while singing hymns in harmony. At that moment they were a happy family.

After dinner Jean and Lilly sat in the recreation room in front of the fireplace that Henry had built not too long before he died. It wasn't used much anymore. Lilly had built a roaring fire and she invited Jean and Catherine to have a glass of crème d' menthe in front of the fire. The sisters tried to catch up on how their kids were doing, how Jean felt about going off to school again, leaving the girls home with Danny during the week, how Lilly liked her new job with Xerox. Finally, Catherine couldn't stand listening to her daughters talk about their new lives.

"What am I supposed to tell my sisters and friends about you two? It's humiliating. Especially you, Jean. Going off and leaving your kids. Why do you need to get any smarter? I'm disgusted with both of you."

Jean immediately got defensive. "Listen, Mom. I'm doing what is good for me for a change. Maybe you should have tried that. I don't want to lead a life full of regrets. If you don't let up on me, I'm not staying with you when I come home on weekends. I can stay at the Holiday Inn with my kids."

Then Lilly spoke up. "I agree with you, Jean. Men do what you're doing all the time. I'll bet that doesn't bother you, Mother. Yeah, and here's another thing. Do you think I should be staying with my creep of a husband who was screwing his girlfriend at the very moment I was giving birth to his baby?" There was venom in her voice, and she sought to nail her point for her mother. "The times are changing, Mom, and women ought to have the same rights as men. You might try to be more open-minded."

"I'll show *you* how open minded I am." Catherine coaxed Buddy off her lap and rose abruptly. "Good night. Come on, Buddy. You and I don't have to listen to this."

Catherine walked out of the room without another word and went to bed. Although tension hung palpably throughout the house for the rest of the weekend, Catherine, ever the expert on giving her foes the cold shoulder, tried to be civil for the sake of her grandchildren.

Chapter 27. The Last Hurrah (1994-1997)

Jean, Lilly, Sally and Violet sat around a table in the psychiatric ward at Bellin with their mother. Catherine, although at that moment a patient in the ward, was holding court.

"See that woman over there with the ugly hair and red shirt?" The daughters' heads were bent toward their mother as she held her fingers at her waist and carefully pointed across the room at a woman sitting on a chair in the corner, softly mumbling to herself. "She's wacko,"

Catherine whispered. "She had me put my head on her stomach so I could hear the voice of Jesus Christ." She did a quick spiral of her finger around her ear.

"What did Jesus tell you?" Lilly asked.

"To get the hell out of this place as fast as I can!" They all laughed.

Catherine had been admitted to the hospital a month before when she experienced another deep depression. With a nod toward the woman in the corner, she confided to her daughters, "I'm not that crazy, girls."

"Well, then, we'd better get you home," Violet said. "Let me try to find out if they think you're ready."

Violet walked over to the nurses' station, where three nurses in their white uniforms were busy reading files. Violet had earned a reputation for professionalism at Marinette General and she generally had an "in" with the other nurses, even in Green Bay. She went right to the head nurse. "Dawn, do you think my mother is ready to go home?"

The nurse pondered this question for some seconds and then looked up at Violet. "You know, I think she is." She nodded her head as if she were still thinking. "Catherine seems to be doing quite well and her doctor thinks so, too. She's in good spirits and she isn't manic, which is a blessing. I think with some medication she will do fine at home."

Dawn promised Violet she would immediately talk to the doctor. Violet walked back to the visitor's room with a smile on her face. She could feel the warmth of the sun that shone brightly through the big windows. Spring was on its way.

"The head nurse says she thinks you can go home, and she's confirming that with the doctor. She says you're pretty stable—not too high and not too low."

Several other families were visiting with their loved ones, while other patients watched *The Days of Our Lives* on a small TV in the corner of the room.

Away from Catherine for a moment, Jean confided, "She's not as manic as last time, when she bought a pool and fancy luggage on the way home."

Sally laughed. "That pool turned out to be the best thing she ever did. She has her grandkids around her all summer long."

The doctor's okay came quickly, and as the daughters packed up her things Catherine voiced a concern. "Boy, I hope they send me home with enough pills. I can't get through a day without a few. I don't want to end up here again with all these nutcases."

Back in Marinette the girls stopped at Violet's to pick

up Buddy, where he had stayed while his mistress was in the hospital. Catherine sat with the passenger door opened. The dog burst from the front door and bounded down the steps, and Catherine suddenly had a hundred-plus pounds of a loving animal sitting in her lap and licking her face until it was dripping wet.

Catherine was delighted to be home. She took off her coat, settled into her living room chair, and turned on the TV. Buddy sat beside her with his head in her lap. They looked into each other's eyes with true love. Her daughters divided up the tasks of settling their mother back home—unpacking her suitcase, doing laundry, changing sheets on the bed, grocery shopping.

They sat and chatted a bit before the daughters left to be with their own families. Catherine's heart sank. She was alone again. She was thrilled to be with Buddy, but she wanted a human companion. Even Bellin, despite the circumstances, at least provided a buzz of human activity.

A couple weeks after Catherine had come home, Charlie popped in early in the morning, just as she was starting her breakfast. He lived nearby and visited often.

"Hey . . . Catherine," he said in his deep slow voice, as he settled in across the table. "Well . . . I need a shot 'a whiskey . . . I'm kinda shaky this morning . . . I had a rough night. My hip's giving me terrible pain."

She eyed her older brother. "You're drinking kind of early in the day, aren't you?"

"Well . . . yeah. Hell, you might have to give me two, as long as you're up. I don't know what else to do."

Catherine set a shot of Jack Daniels in front of her brother. "I can't see why you don't get your hip replaced. You complain about it all the time."

"Hell," he said, downing the shot. "I'm too damn old for an operation."

"Yeah, I know that's what you think, but the doctor said you're healthy enough."

"Your back operation didn't do you much good." Charlie countered.

"You're right about that—neither one of them did. But my hip surgery was good. I don't have pain in there anymore. It's a miracle."

The kitchen door opened and in came Jean. "Surprise!"

"Jean, what are you doing here? Why are you in Marinette?"

"I have a meeting at the Marinette UW campus, and I thought I'd surprise you. I have a couple of hours. Uncle Charlie, too! I hit the jackpot."

"Hi . . . Jean," he said, low and slow. "How's your car runnin'?"

"Good, Charlie."

"You still got that Volvo?"

"Yup."

"Say, how are your bowels?"

Uncle Charlie asked the same questions every time he saw her. Jean wasn't sure why he wanted to know about her bowels. She thought maybe he was worried about his own bowels. She was struck by how old he had become. Jean loved him and his wonderful stories. She always asked him to tell her a story every time she saw him.

"How are you feeling these days, Uncle Charlie?"

"His hips are killing him. The pain keeps him awake at night." Catherine answered for him.

"That's too bad. I'm sorry. Can you still tell stories?"

"Oh, I told you all my stories already."

"What about the one where you were on the ship in the Pacific?"

He thought for a while. "You mean the one where the Japs were bombing us?"

Sometimes, Jean thought, *it's as though every word is a struggle, except when he's telling a story, and the words seem to flow.*

"Yes. That's the one."

"Well . . ." He thought for a while. "The Nips were bombing the piss out of the American and British ships one after another. Ships all around us were going up in flames. Folks on deck said they couldn't see a foot in front of them for all the damn smoke. We were all scared shitless waiting for the next bomb to hit us. My knees were knocking, I'll tell you."

He held out his shot glass to Catherine, who got up and refilled it.

"I was a fireman on the ship, down in the hull gettin' ready to die. The only thing that would take my mind to a different place was to cut a notch in a wooden pole for every woman I had screwed in my life. Hell, what I realized was that when you turned 'em upside down they all looked the same—pink and juicy."

"Charlie," Catherine said. "You add a little more to that story every time you tell it."

"Well, hell, I might as well tell the truth," he said with a cat-that-got-the-canary smile on his face. Charlie seldom showed a full smile—but he emanated acceptance and goodness.

"Why are you drinking so early in the morning?" Jean said.

"Hell, I can't walk, I can't sleep, so I might as well drink."

Jean looked back and forth at her mother and her uncle facing each other across the table. "You two should live together," she said. "You could keep each other company and help each other out."

Charlie moved in a month later. With few belongings. the move was easy. The girls were thrilled their mother had a companion. They liked visiting him as much as visiting her.

Catherine and Charlie quickly established a Sunday ritual—church followed by lunch at the local Kentucky Fried Chicken. They seldom missed a Sunday.

On one memorable Sunday Catherine had gone to the bathroom and on her return was picking up their plasticware and napkins when she thought she heard Charlie calling to her.

"Catherine, your whole ass is hanging out!"

"What are you talking about?" she called back.

He said it louder. "Your whole ass is hanging out." Diners were turning their heads to see what was going on. Some were laughing.

She reached around and immediately realized she had tucked her pleated skirt into her girdle as she was leaving the stall. She fled back into the bathroom in embarrassment. When she came back to their table, she cursed her brother in a harsh whisper. "What the hell were you doing, yelling across the dining room about my ass hanging out?"

"Jesus, Catherine. I thought I was doing you a favor. What was I supposed to do?"

"Well, not that!"

As soon as they got home Catherine called her sister Clara and each of her daughters. She laughed so hard when she told them the story that she her wet her pants.

But when Catherine found out that Charlie had a girlfriend, her laughter turned to anger and disgust with a little snarky jealousy thrown in. Sally's good friend Karen often came with Sally when she visited her mother. Karen and Charlie became good friends. In fact, they became such good friends that Karen started visiting without Sally, and soon after that she started going right upstairs to Charlie's room without even saying hello to Catherine.

Catherine could wait only so long during these visits before she planted herself at the foot of the stairs yelling, "Charlie what's going on up there?"

One day she asked him point-blank. "What exactly do you do up there with a woman who's the same age as my daughter?"

Charlie put on his favored sly smile and said not word.

One morning he came downstairs wearing clean pants and a freshly ironed shirt. A still handsome man at 84, he might have been described as quite dapper, however dated his wardrobe might be.

"Well, where in the hell do you think you're going, Mr. Dressed-to-the-Nines?" she mocked.

"Karen's picking me up. We're going for a ride."

"Well, you can make your own lunch, Mr. Cradle Robber. I'm going for a ride, too!" Catherine did, indeed, go for a ride, and Charlie didn't hear the last of it for a long time.

When Charlie came home, she met him at the door with her hands on her hips and a sour look on her face. "I hope you and Karen had a nice time in the parking lot at Little River."

"What the hell are you talking about?"

"Don't think I don't know! I took a ride, too. I saw your head from the back window of Karen's truck, but Karen's head was nowhere to be seen. You're nothing but a dirty pig!"

That was the last time Charlie saw Karen.

Months later, Charlie came in from feeding the birds, sat on a kitchen chair, mumbled a few unintelligible words, and slowly toppled onto the floor. Charlie's death at the ripe old age of eighty-five was a personal loss for Catherine but also a setback for her. She was alone again.

Over the next few years Catherine's health deteriorated. She suffered two coronary artery spasms caused by blockages. During one of those stays in the hospital due to her heart attacks, she contracted spinal meningitis. Violet was the only daughter who lived in Marinette during those years and was still working as a nurse at Marinette General. The others came to visit and spend some weekends with their mother, but Violet was on constant call.

One weekend when Lilly came to visit her mother, Violet confided in her. "I'm so relieved you're here, Lilly. I need a break. I'm running back and forth to take care of Mom all the time."

"I can only imagine. I frankly don't know how you do it with your boys at home, a full-time job, a husband to take care of and a house to keep up. I couldn't do it. I know that."

"My house is a mess. I don't even know what the kids are eating half the time. I only hope they still have some clean underwear. Mom's getting worse. She doesn't want to be alone, but even more she doesn't want to be in a nursing home. She asked me to promise that she would never have to go to one. I think she's too frail to be alone."

After Catherine went to bed, Lilly and Violet began brainstorming. Who was available to help with Catherine's care? Lilly was working for IBM in Madison, Jean was a professor at UW-Stevens Point, and Sally still had her cosmetology business in Green Bay. None of them could leave their jobs and families to move in with their mother, and Catherine did not want to leave her house.

"I'm trying to convince Sally to move back to Marinette

to live with Mom," Violet confided. "Sally told me last week that Susan needs to come back to Marinette to finish a half credit to graduate from high school. I wonder if Susan could live with Mom. She would love to have one of her grandchildren living with her."

"That would be a little respite for me," Violet added. "That only covers one semester, but it gives us some time to try to figure something out."

"Susan would be a big help to Mom, and it would lighten your load," Lilly agreed. "I can see that she's losing ground fast."

The next morning at breakfast, Lilly asked Catherine, "Mom, do you ever go for a walk?"

"Once in a while. I know I should, but my back hurts so much when I walk—I don't like to be in that much pain. I'm worn out just walking to the neighbors and back. And what if I fall?"

"Do you have any pain pills?" Lilly pushed on.

"The doctor won't give me any because I take Ativan."

"How much Ativan do you take?"

"As much as I need. Usually four a day. I have an open prescription."

"Huh?—That sounds like a lot."

"That's how much I need to keep going."

Lilly knew that sometimes her mother slurred her words and would doze in her chair. Could it be from the Ativan?

"Sally told me Susan has to come back to Marinette to finish her degree. Would you like it if she moved in with you?" Lilly asked.

"Well, I sure would. I'd love to have my granddaughter live with me. I don't like to be alone. I don't want to drive any more, but I have to get groceries."

It occurred to Lilly that her mother probably shouldn't be driving—period—with the amount of Ativan she was taking.

The deal was done. Susan moved in with her grandmother for six months and they had a wonderful time together. Susan took great care of Nonny but eventually she had to get back to her job in Green Bay. Fortunately, she was there the day—as she quickly reported to her mother and her aunts—when her Nonny put a chicken in the oven at three hundred fifty degrees with the grocery plastic and price tag still on. Susan rescued the chicken and the oven, but everyone knew something had to be done. Catherine couldn't be left alone.

At this point, Sally's life had taken another turn. She thought this might be a good time to sell her Green Bay hair salon and move in with her mother. A huge responsibility was lifted off all their shoulders. Jean, Lilly and Violet would spell Sally on the weekends, and Violet would be a backup for Sally in case of an emergency. Violet thought Catherine was in the early stages of Alzheimer's. Her doctor confirmed Violet's suspicions. Sally moved in when Susan moved out.

Sally made regular reports to her sisters. Mom was sometimes "a little mixed up," Sally told them. She might put her glasses in the refrigerator or get ready for church on Tuesday— small things at first. Sally had the knack of making jokes about the small stuff and she and her mother could both laugh about it. She never put her mother down for losing or not remembering things.

One weekend when Jean was spelling Sally she made one of her mother's favorite suppers—roast chicken, gravy, and mashed potatoes. Catherine sat at the head of the table where Henry used to sit. Buddy sat on the floor to her right. Jean watched her mother take a bite of chicken, then put another bite on her fork for Buddy. That went on for the entire meal. Buddy even ate iceberg lettuce with Thousand Island dressing.

When Jean was clearing the table to do the dishes, she noticed Buddy was sitting quietly in front of the refrigerator.

"Mom, I think Buddy has to go out. He might need to pee."

Catherine laughed till her eyes were wet with tears.

Jean did not see anything especially funny in a dog's needing to go outside for a minute. "What are you laughing at?"

Catherine managed to get out the words, "He's just waiting for his ice cream."

Jean remembered now the Thanksgiving when she had first seen her mother feed ice cream to her dog from her own spoon, but the ritual had expanded. The two scoops shared between Catherine and Buddy now included a generous dollop of Hershey's chocolate topping.

Jean had many wonderful stories to tell her girls. It had been a good visit, and it was clear how much Buddy had become a real and essential companion to her mother.

Meanwhile, Sally continued to deal in her own supportive way with her mother's unpredictable behavior.

"This morning I looked at Mom, and she looked so pretty and normal and happy that I thought everything would be fine today," she told Lilly in a late phone call, after Catherine had gone to bed. "The next thing I knew, she wanted me to go out in the yard and give ice cream cones to the four little Black girls she saw there. I just told her, 'Yup, I'll get right on that,' and she thanked me. Lilly, sometimes I don't know if I should laugh or cry. Maybe both . . ."

Catherine became more isolated in her thinking as time

went on. Her last family event was the wedding of Jean's daughter Angie.

"Mom, Angie's getting married on Saturday," Sally announced. "We're going to Madison for the wedding. Hey, she'll be your second granddaughter to get married!"

"We just went to her wedding. I can't keep up with these kids. What happened to her husband?"

"No, Mom, that was Jenny's wedding in January. Now it's September."

Catherine still didn't catch on. "She wasn't married very long," she mused aloud. "I don't get that. Your dad and I were married a lot longer than that."

Sally coached her mother about their schedule. "I have to go to church tonight. I have laid out our wedding clothes on your bed and I'll pack them when I get home. We're leaving early tomorrow morning so we can get settled in before the rehearsal dinner. You're going to see all your grandkids."

"Oh, my God, really? Where will they be?"

"At the wedding. I'll be back by eight."

The door was locked when Sally got home from church.

"Mom! Mom! Let me in!"

Nothing from inside.

She called again. Still her mother didn't open the door. "I'm calling the police if you don't let me in!" Sally shouted.

Catherine must have been hovering behind the door. She answered immediately. "Why should I let you in? You're late. You know I hate it when you're late."

"Yes, I know that. The service lasted five minutes longer that it was supposed to."

"I know damn well church doesn't last two hours. Where were you?" Catherine was very angry.

"Goddamn it! If you don't let me in, I'm going to kick the door down—and I mean it!" She started kicking the door and pounding on it, and finally she heard the latch click.

"Don't you ever do that again, Sally Costello!" Catherine turned from the open door and stormed into her bedroom with Buddy close behind.

The next morning, Catherine was up at four. She remembered she had to go to Angie's wedding today. She found the clothes that Sally had ready for packing and took pride in herself for being ready to go before even Sally got out of bed. When Sally came into the kitchen, she saw Catherine standing at the sink all dressed for the wedding in Sally's clothes. They were two sizes too big for her, but she didn't notice. *Should I laugh or cry?* Sally asked herself.

She did both.

Dressed for the ceremony, Catherine looked beautiful in her silk flowing lavender top and matching pants, but her eyes were vacant.

The wedding was held in the Assembly Chambers in the Wisconsin State Capitol.

Catherine, looking around, asked Violet, "Where am I?"

"You're at Angie's wedding, Mom."

Just then Angie and Hugh, her husband-to-be, walked over to Catherine, who was sitting on a bench waiting to be seated in front of the gathering. Angie, dressed in her beautiful white wedding dress, threw her arms around Catherine. "Oh, Nonny, I'm so happy you're here. Mom told me you might not make it. This means the world to me. I didn't know what I'd do if you couldn't come. I love you so much!"

"Angie, didn't you just get married. I was at your first wedding. It's a lot warmer now than it was then, that's for sure."

"Oh, Nonny, you're so sweet, but that was Jenny's wedding. When she got married in January, it was cold. You remember Hugh. We came over in the summer to see you and take a swim in your pool. You made us my favorite beef vegetable soup. You'll have to tell me how you make it."

"I'll see if I can find the recipe."

"You don't make that with a recipe. You make it by heart."

"I do?"

Being in a strange place with a hundred people at the wedding and reception confused Catherine even more. She made no eye contact with anyone and only talked when someone asked her a direct question. Danny, Jean's ex-husband, got her out of her chair to dance slowly to "The Girl That I Married."

Walking into her house after a long difficult weekend, Buddy ran to her. Her eyes lit up. She bent down as far as she could to let him lick her face. He could have knocked her down easily with the 117 pounds he carried, but he treated her gently. Happy to be back in familiar territory, she breathed a sigh of relief.

"Come on, Mom, let's go for a walk," Sally said on a beautiful fall day at the end of October. The sun shone bright, the red and gold leaves danced around the yard—

"My legs hurt too much. I can't walk."

"I know you can make it to the pool."

"Sally, it hurts when I go down the stairs."

"I'll help you down the stairs, get you into your pool chair and I'll bring you coffee. There won't be another day like this for a long time."

"Well, then, why don't you go sit by the pool with your coffee, if you like it so much. Leave me alone."

"Let's make a deal, then. You stay in now, but you have to promise you'll go to the store with me later."

"We'll see." Catherine was using a walker now.

The visiting nurse had told Sally to keep her mother moving around with short walks during the day, but that was much easier said than done. Catherine had always been stubborn, but now she was even worse. Sally tried so hard to do everything the doctor ordered, but Catherine only cooperated when she felt like it.

"Okay, young lady," Sally said in a chipper voice. "It's time for us to go to the store. Here's your walker. I'll help you down the steps."

"I won't go unless Buddy can come with us."

"Deal." Sally said. Buddy barked constantly in the car. She hated to take him, but she complied in order to get her mother out of the house. "You know Buddy can't come into Quentmeyer's."

"What do you think I am? Dumb?"

Catherine put the things she wanted in the basket, including three boxes of microwave popcorn and two twelve-count packages of toilet paper.

"It looks like you plan on eating a lot of popcorn," Sally said, trying hard not to laugh.

"Damn right," Catherine retorted. "It's better than the crap you feed me."

"Okay, Miss Sassy Pants, bring on the popcorn. Thank God. Now I won't have to cook so much."

As they were getting back in the car, Buddy was wagging his tail and licking Catherine's face.

"What do you have in your mouth, Honey Boy? You smell like laundry detergent."

"That's because it is laundry detergent," Sally said.

"Buddy, what did you do? You are a bad boy."

"Don't talk to my dog like that."

"Mom, the whole back seat is full of liquid detergent. Buddy chewed up the plastic bottle of Tide. Buddy. Damn you." Sally was angry. "It will take me hours to clean this up."

"Sally, for God's sake. It's just a little soap. Let's get home in a hurry so I can wash Buddy's mouth out. Poor thing. It must taste terrible. How'd he get into the soap in the first place?"

"I don't know. Maybe I left it in the car the last time I ran to the store."

"See, it was your fault. If you had brought it down the basement like you should have, that never would have happened. Poor Buddy."

Sally knew there was no sense in trying to defend herself. Her mother took Buddy's side every time. It took five trips through the car wash to get all the soap out of the back seat. Buddy did get sick and Sally had to clean that up, too. She was so happy that Jean was coming to take over for the weekend.

"Oh, Jean, I can't tell you how happy I am you're here. It's been a tough week."

Catherine slowly limped into the kitchen using her walker. It looked like she didn't quite know how to move her feet. "Jean, I'm glad you're here. Your sister needs a lot of help."

"I sure do," Sally laughed. "She's a trip and a half. If I drank, I'd be half in the bag right now."

"Did she tell you, Jean, that damn sister of yours left a full bottle of Tide in the car?" Catherine asked.

Jean took it as a good sign that Catherine and Sally could laugh about these incidents.

Sally was an angel. She could find humor in most every situation, even during the bad times and even when it hurt her heart. When Catherine told her a parade was marching past the house, Sally said, "Yeah. Take a look at the majorette. She just dropped her baton."

"Well, that was clumsy," Catherine replied.

One day Catherine screamed, "There's a man outside the door with a knife! I'm so scared."

"Don't worry, Mom. I'll call the police right away. They'll be here in a minute." Sally let her mother have her dreams and her visions. She never tried to say, "Oh, you're just imagining that," which might have made Catherine feel ashamed or hurt.

It wasn't long before a hospital bed was installed in the front room right alongside the bay window. Catherine forgot how to move her legs to walk. For a while, Sally could lower the bed and help her mother get into a wheelchair so she could go to the bathroom, but that didn't last long. Sally learned from a visiting nurse how to use a Hoyer lift to get her mother out of bed and into the tub or onto the toilet.

One weekend when Jean was spelling Sally, Catherine didn't recognize her. "Mom, my heart just skipped a beat. I'm your daughter. I'm Jean. Jeannie."

"Who? You must be kidding," Catherine said. "I don't have a daughter named Jean."

Jean handed Catherine a card she had sent her mother early in the week. Catherine looked at the envelope and said, "Oh, look! My daughter Jean sent this to me. I can tell by her writing."

Jean was stunned. Her mother didn't recognize her, but she recognized her handwriting. *Oh, Mom,* she thought. *I would dearly love to know how your brain is working.* She knew Alzheimer's was a mystery. She could only wish her mother didn't have it.

When Sally got back on Sunday afternoon, Jean was in the middle of a crisis.

"I can't find Mom's teeth! She had them this morning when I was cleaning her up. Somehow since then they disappeared. You know how she feels about her teeth. She won't let anyone, including us, look at her without her teeth. She's had her mouth covered with a washcloth all day."

When Catherine saw Sally, she mumbled through the cloth, "I need teeth."

After Jean left Sally continued the search for her mother's dentures. They were nowhere to be found.

"Did you swallow your teeth, Mom?"

"Are you crazy?" Catherine mumbled through the washcloth.

Just before they were turning in, Buddy walked slowly into the living room and sat next to the hospital bed.

"Buddy, what are you chewing on?" Sally walked over and discovered Catherine's teeth in Buddy's mouth. "Mom, Buddy's got your teeth. I can't get them away from him. How did he get your teeth?"

"Oh, Buddy," Catherine said. "I knew you would find my teeth. How could I live without you?"

Catherine stopped eating in early August and slept most of the time. A nurse came regularly now to help Sally bathe and care for Catherine's other needs. She hadn't been out of bed in months. Sally would play her favorite hymns on the organ. Catherine twitched when she heard "Nearer My God to Thee" and "He Walks in the Garden Alone." Playing brought Sally peace and she hoped it gave her mother the same.

In the last week of August, Sally called her sisters to tell them the end was near. An ambulance had been ordered to take

Catherine to the hospital. Her daughters spent the last days of their mother's life with her in her hospital room. Grandchildren and other relatives came and went. Her daughters held her hands, rubbed her head and feet, put their hands on her cheeks and forehead, and gave her sips of water with a spoon. They told wonderful and sometimes funny stories to her and thanked her for all she had given them.

Then, one fateful day she lay quiet, comatose. Her daughters and grandchildren stayed by her bedside, afraid to leave the room. Shortly after noon, she stirred, coughed, opened her eyes wide and raised her head. She settled back on the pillow and quietly died, surrounded by the family she had loved so dearly and who loved her with all their hearts.

She had come a long way from the Menekaunee girl called "Fishguts," who lived on the wrong side of the tracks, to Catherine Goodman, an upstanding member of the Marinette community. She had spent her energy taking good care of dysfunctional parents, four daughters who had their ups and downs, a husband, and her eight grandchildren. Unfortunately, she had never learned to take care of herself. Her offspring would now carry on the legacy of this caring and complicated woman. She brought them—as best she could—into a new era. Her work was done.

THE END

Cast of Characters

The Sabinsky Clan

Catherine	The Girl from Menekaunee
Martha, aka Mame, Mamie	Catherine's mother
Ivy & Myrtle	Martha's sisters
Mike	Catherine's father
Big Louie	Mike's brother
Clara	Catherine's sister
Nels	Clara's husband
Tommy, Glenny, Sandy, Dickie, Nelson, Peter, Sally	Clara and Nels' children
Steve	Catherine's brother
Helen	Steve's wife
Kathy & Jill	Steve & Helen's Children
Stella	Catherine's sister
Anthony	Stella's husband
Margaret	Stella & Anthony's daughter
Charlie	Catherine's brother
Irene	Charlie's wife
Florence	Irene's sister
Grandpa Beyer	Catherine's grandfather
Pepper	Catherine's Boston Bull

The Goodman Clan

Henry Goodman	Husband of Catherine
Louise	Henry's mother
V.R.	Henry's father
Hazel & Elsie	V.R.'s sisters
Woody	Henry's brother
Ken	Henry's brother

Mildred	Ken's wife
Billy	Ken & Mildred's son
Margie & Anna	Henry's sisters

The Goodman-Sabinsky Clan

Jean Goodman	Catherine & Henry's oldest daughter
Dan	Jean's husband
Jenny & Angie	Jean & Dan's daughters
Lilly Goodman	Catherine & Henry's second daughter
Bella & Laurie	Lilly's daughters
Sally Goodman	Catherine & Henry's third daughter
Susan & Michelle	Sally's daughters
Violet Goodman	Catherine & Henry's last daughter
Adam & Barry	Violet's sons
Nonny	Catherine's nickname to granddaughters
Buddy	Catherine's Golden Labrador Retriever

Minor Characters in Order of Appearance

Bud	Bartender at the Korn Krib
Franky, John, Corny	Fishermen and Mike's drinking buddies
Jibo	Young Catherine's dance partner
Tommy	Bartender at the Silver Dome
Alta	Catherine's high school friend
Principal Harbort	Marinette High School principal
Mr. Bromund	MHS algebra teacher
Miss Newell	MHS English teacher
Miss Frothingham	MHS typing teacher and advisor
Mr. Bates	MHS shop teacher
Mr. Blackman	MHS history teacher
Miss Green	MHS Latin teacher
Mr. Forber	MHS teacher
Miss Brooks	MHS teacher

Miss Libal	Principal Harbort's secretary
Miss Austin	MHS music teacher
Judge William Sullivan	Catherine boss
Freddy	Bartender at Jimmy's
Jimmy	Bar owner, bartender
Ears	Henry's golfing companion
The Ingersons	Young Martha's employers
Brownie Johnson	Owner of The Smartshop and Catherine's mentor
Betty	Catherine's courthouse friend and co-worker
Dr. Koepp	Martha's doctor
Babe	Henry's banjo-playing friend
Rev. Knudson	Lutheran minister who welcomes Catherine back
Mr. Mack	Ice cream shop owner
Donny Metzger	Courthouse photographer
Ruth	Henry's date and Betty's friend
Rev. Sonnack	Lutheran minister who marries Catherine and Henry
Dr. Zeratsky	Catherine's pediatric physician
Alice & Leon	Owners of 1314 Elizabeth
Ed	Clerk at Malmstadt's Market
Jack & June	Catherine & Henry's sports and card partners
Butch	Henry's pharmacist
Marion and Kenny	Friends of Catherine and Henry
Dr. Renes	Henry's Green Bay doctor
Dr. Boren	Catherine's emergency doctor
Mary	Catherine's senior companion
Karen	Elderly Charlie's young girlfriend

Afterword

I wrote this book primarily to follow the trail of mental illnesses, including clinical depression, anxiety disorder and bipolar disorder, that have afflicted my family over several generations. The symptoms have ranged in various individuals from overwhelming worries that aren't temporary, distractibility that interferes with normal life, a constant sense of hopelessness and despair, an abnormally elevated mood, and even attempted suicide. These disorders have been severe enough to require treatment that has included different degrees of psychotherapy, medication or hospitalizations in medical or psychiatric wards.

The question has always raged: Is this learned or is it inherited? There is still a stigma associated with mental illness. Did my mother and grandmother suffer so deeply because they were weaklings who couldn't pull themselves up by their bootstraps? Or were they born with a condition that predisposed them to mental illness like others are predisposed to cancer or heart attacks?

I observed firsthand the pain and suffering of my mother and grandmother and my alcoholic grandfather. I vowed I would be stronger than they had been. I was determined not to go through the anxiety or depression that plagued my family. I wouldn't need pills, alcohol or hospitalizations to get me through life. I thought I knew more, was stronger, and could manage my life better than they had. After all, I had gone to college and had married a man whose parents belonged to a country club. All would be A-OK with me. I believed I didn't need medication or therapy to live a happy well-rounded life.

I lived in denial for years. Even though I *tried* to be happy every day, it didn't work. By the time I was thirty with two wonderful little daughters, a loving husband, and a job I liked, I still lacked self-confidence and inner happiness and I couldn't figure out why. I reluctantly started psychotherapy, but I didn't want anyone to know. I was ashamed that I couldn't find contentment on my own. I got a divorce. I moved to a different city. I got a PhD. But, I still felt weak and defeated. When I was in my early forties, I started taking medication prescribed by a psychiatrist. I tried to hide that even more than the therapy. I was ashamed. I started and stopped medication many times over the years, thinking each time I was ready to do it without that support.

Now, gratefully, I know what I need. I cannot be mentally and physically healthy without my medication. It's not a matter of where I live or how many degrees I have or to whom I am married. It's how I feel inside. I no longer feel shame.

I am proud I have spent countless hours in therapy and that I take Cymbalta, my anxiety drug, every day along with the other medications I need for my physical health. I accept myself for who I am.

Attitudes regarding mental health have changed since my ancestors experienced mental illnesses. I celebrate the progress that has been made.

Acknowledgements

In my wildest dreams I never thought I would write a novel. Over time I had written some thoughts on paper that I called poetry. I happened to share it with my dear friend, Marsha Rossiter once when we were chatting. She, in turn, shared her lovely poetry with me. The two of us, together with Patricia Nevers, made a plan to submit our writing to each other on the third Thursday of every month. We called ourselves the Sweet Little Writing Group (SLWG). It was a wonderful experience that helped me gain enough confidence to even consider writing a book.

If it weren't for Barry Fulton, this book would not have been written. Barry encouraged me to start writing and invited me to attend numerous valuable writers' workshops and classes for which I am extremely grateful. His tireless support continued as I went through the final steps to publication.

My deepest gratitude goes out to Bob Meissner, my partner and fabulous editor and writer, who lovingly edited and reedited every word in *The Girl from Menekaunee*.

Many thanks to Dr. Jennifer Presley, a retired education policy expert, Mary Lynn Hall, herself a writer, and Torrey Robeck, a vociferous reader, for the countless hours they spent reviewing, editing, and offering valuable suggestions and selfless oversite of the near-final manuscript. I am beholden to them for their helpful insights and sharp eyes to make this book much better.

My appreciation also goes out to my dear friend Jody Olsen who offered her unwavering support in so many ways. Over the last two years, she cheered me on when I was going through the ups and downs of my writing project in ways that only Jody can. Her gentle, tough-love approach encouraged me to take my book to the end. I am so grateful.

Many thanks to Davor Dramikanin for his lovely artistry, imagination and patience designing the front and back covers of my book. It looks fabulous.

And finally, I want to acknowledge Dr. John Daken, my former psychiatrist, and Sue Berman, my acupuncturist. They used their professional magic to help me discover the person I really am and want to be. They still metaphorically sit on my shoulder to help me through a tough situation or enjoy a moment of pride for a problem well-handled.

About the Author

Nancy J. Kaufman earned her master's degree in Behavioral Disabilities and her doctorate degree in Learning Disabilities from the University of Wisconsin-Madison. After completing her master's degree, she taught students with emotional disturbances and learning disabilities in elementary and high schools. After completing her PhD, she became a professor in special education, a department head, a dean, and an assistant vice chancellor in the University of Wisconsin System for the remainder of her career. She was a pioneer in starting programs in public schools in the 1970s for students with behavioral and learning disabilities, and she is the co-author of a book for teachers and parents, *Asperger Syndrome: Strategies for Solving the Social Puzzle*, as well as numerous other academic publications.

Nancy is a Wisconsin native, now living in Silver Spring, Maryland. She is a world adventurer with a lifetime interest in outdoor activities including sailing, downhill skiing, and SCUBA diving. In her retirement she became a yoga instructor. She pursues a variety of interests, including collage art and weaving Navajo rugs. Her most important role is as a devoted mother and grandmother.

Made in the USA
Middletown, DE
14 May 2021

39700185R00314